FATHOMING THE ι

¶ For Jon and Jack, both inspirations in very different ways.

Fathoming
the
Universe

SUE BODDINGTON

Best Wishes
Sue Boddington.

Privately printed for
    Sue Boddington
    Dacia, 99 Poulshot Road, Poulshot, Devizes, Wilts SN10 1RX
    sue.boddington@virgin.net

by The Hobnob Press
    30c, Deverill Road Trading Estate,
    Sutton Veny, Warminster, Wiltshire, BA12 7BZ

Design and typesetting by John Chandler. The text is set in 12 point Doves Type, leaded 2 points. Doves Type is a digital facsimile, created by Robert Green, of the celebrated face made by Edward Prince in 1899 for the Doves Press, based on Jenson's 15th-century Venetian type.

ISBN 978-1-906978-36-5

Born and bred in Wiltshire, SUE BODDINGTON graduated from Bristol University in History, English, Theology and Philosophy. After flirting with teaching, acting and singing, she joined Wiltshire Library Service, holding the posts of Senior Librarian Adult Learning for the county and Community Librarian for the Calne area. Now retired, she still lives in Wiltshire and is the voluntary curator of Calne Heritage Centre.

Chapter One

THE HORSES GREW NERVOUS as they rode deeper into the forest. The patches of sunlight breaking through the thick canopy of oak and beech became rare. It was the silence that was unnerving, so profound that the sudden call of a jay or woodpecker and the rustle of a forest creature in the undergrowth were magnified to a degree that startled the travellers and echoed in their ears. They were enveloped in a cool, dark greenness that seemed to be drawing closer around them.

Elizabeth stole a glance at her brother. She could feel his agitation. He sensed her looking at him and made an attempt to appear confident.

"We shall find the right path Lizzie," he said with what little confidence he could muster.

She shook her head. "I fear we are lost James. It must be late afternoon already. I would not wish us to be in the depths of this forest when it gets dark."

She turned to the eldest of the four men who rode with them.

"What shall we do Jacob?"

The man stroked his greying beard in perplexity.

"I am sorry Mistress Elizabeth. I was certain sure the path we took would lead us around the edge of the forest and back on to the road, but it is some years since I used it. I should never have encouraged you to take it. The fault is mine. Your father will be so angry with me."

She touched his arm reassuringly. "No, you are not to blame. Perhaps if we retraced our steps-"

Before Jacob could reply another of the four servants charged with the duty of escorting Elizabeth and James Norrington to Frome cut in- "Listen, did you hear that?"

Jacob gave Mark Wheeler a withering look. He was the senior steward in the Norrington household and did not take kindly to being interrupted by an underling. Undaunted, Mark, a skinny lad with a pock- marked face, continued, "Chopping, it sounds like chopping. There may be foresters nearby."

They all listened. He was right. The distinctive sound of an axe striking wood rang through the trees. Even allowing for the heightened sound in the contrasting silence, it must have been near.

Relief flooded the faces of every member of the party. Jacob adjudged the sound to be coming from the right of them; to follow it they must leave the path and push through the trees, but it seemed to be their best course. Giles and Peter Smith, the twin brothers who looked after Sir Neville Norrington's horses were both burly fellows. They were the bodyguards, young men proud of their strength and eager to be seen wearing a sword. Jacob Whyte ordered them to go on ahead and force a way through the trees to make the passage easier for Elizabeth and James. They swore colourful oaths as branches snapped back in their faces with stinging force.

"Mind your tongues in front of Mistress Elizabeth," Jacob called out sharply and they mumbled reluctant apologies.

The location of the sound was farther away than they had calculated. It was ten minutes before they broke through the trees to find themselves on the edge of a clearing. Several trees trunks lay on the ground, broken branches scattered around them and at the far end of the clearing three men were working. One was hewing at a tree trunk while the other two were loading lengths of wood into a cart. A sturdy cob, harnessed to the cart, grazed patiently.

The two wood stackers wore the dull, brown, hemp jerkins common to country labourers. The man with the axe however was dressed in a white cambric shirt with full sleeves, worn loose over his hose. Elizabeth had never seen a man attired with such casual freedom out of doors. The late afternoon sun penetrating into the clearing shone on his dark brown hair, which glistened with perspiration.

Jacob proposed that he should ride across and ask directions, but James urged his horse forward.

"No Jacob, I am leader of this party. Father expressly charged me with the duty of getting my sister safe to Frome. I will ask."

The steward glanced across at Elizabeth, who inclined her head in assent. James Norrington was almost thirteen, but he was small for his age, underdeveloped physically. He was aware that he could be mistaken for a ten year old and it pained him. How he hated the nickname sparrow legs bestowed on him by his more robust cousins. He feared no one would take his authority seriously because of his size. His father always adopted a sharp, haughty tone with anyone beneath his station in life and James hoped that if he did the same he would be respected. His sister saw things differently. She was inclined to believe that the way to get respect was to give respect to others, no matter what their degree. She followed him across the clearing.

She understood and sympathised with his sensitivity over his lack of inches and did not want him to lose face in front of the servants, but neither did she wish him to give offence to strangers.

As they crossed the clearing she took a longer look at the man in the white shirt. He had spotted them now and put down his axe, leaning casually against the cart. He was around thirty, approaching six feet in height and well-made, with wide shoulders and a deep chest. Although he was slim hipped, his legs were strong and muscular. Caught in the sunlight, the details of his person seemed unusually defined to her. His shirt was unlaced at the neck and she saw that he wore at his throat a large lump of veined turquoise on a leather string. His left ear was pierced with a golden hoop earring. It was the current fashion for men to cut their hair short and styled with artifice, but his was past his collar, thick and unruly. She was aware that country folk had little time to care about fashion, but they always dressed with simple respectability. There was an air of defiant disregard for propriety about this man that was compelling. She chided herself for being so aware of his physicality. She was not silly child any more, to be stirred by a handsome man. She was seventeen now and on her way to the house of her future father-in-law where she would be married.

James reined in his horse a yard or so from the foresters and demanded in his haughtiest tone of the man in the white shirt, "You, forester, can you tell us the way out of this forest?"

He tried to make his voice sound as deep as possible. The man looked at him with amusement.

"Depends where you want to go."

"Don't you be bold with me churl," James snapped, his face flushing, "I am the son of Sir Neville Norrington, escorting my sister to Frome and you will address us with respect."

To his astonishment, the man laughed, showing strong white teeth. James was used to those of lower status hanging their heads and muttering apologies when they were rebuked by their betters. There was mockery in this man's dark green eyes. He was not sure what to do next, but he was rescued by Elizabeth, who put her hand out to restrain the Smith twins from attempting to intimidate the forester, saying, "You must understand that my brother is anxious for my safety. We sought to pass through the edge of the forest on a path my father's steward knew in the past, but we must have taken the wrong one and have lost our way."

"I beg your pardon Mistress Norrington if I sounded too bold to your brother's ear. I meant no disrespect."He gave a half bow to acknowledge his fault, but the corners of his mouth still curled with traces of amusement. James felt like hitting him with his riding whip.

"If Frome is your destination you are still some way from the road and Frome itself is nigh thirty miles away."

He spoke with the soft local burr of the area, but not in a heavy dialect that they could not interpret.

"You would do well not to travel in these woods after night fall-swarming with robbers and brigands."

He emphasised the last two words, directing them at James, knowing the boy was scared underneath his bravado, which pricked his indignation even further.

"What would you advise we do?" Elizabeth asked.

"The house of Sir Thomas Mountfield is but two miles away. You had best ask for shelter overnight and someone will guide you out of the forest in the morning. Just follow that narrow track over there." He gestured to a path way on his left. "It will take you straight to the house. Sir Thomas is out in the forest at present, but he will be home soon. Ask for the housekeeper, Joan Bushy. She will receive you hospitably."

Elizabeth thanked him and Jacob ordered Giles and Peter to lead the way once again. As they moved forward they purposely rode so close to the forester that he was forced to step back to avoid being jostled by the horses. James smirked with satisfaction, thinking that it served him right for his insolent manner and attempted to stare the man down as he rode past, but he regretted it for he was defeated by the direct, challenging gaze that met his own and looked away.

The man continued to watch the party as it moved away along the track. He was thinking how gracefully the girl sat in her side-saddle, her body moving in harmony with the rhythm of the horse. The men who had been loading the cart earlier came up to join their companion, grinning broadly.

"That was a naughty trick to play on them Master," one of them said with evident pleasure, "I liked the bit about robbers and brigands."

"Well," the man replied, picking up his axe, "You know the vein my humour runs in. I could not resist it."

All trace of the local lilt had disappeared from his voice to be replaced by the educated accent of the gentry.

"That silly little popinjay in his velvet bonnet trying so hard to sound like his father. Sir Neville was always pompous and arrogant. The boy has some hard lessons to learn and I think his sister would be the better teacher."The track that the Norrington party followed was so narrow the horses were obliged to pick their way with care and it seemed to go on for ever.

"Surely this is more than two miles," James complained. "What if he has made fools of us and sent us in the wrong direction out of spite."

"Why should he do that?" his sister asked.

"Well, he may be one of those jealous, rebellious fellows who would do anything to spite their betters. He looked to me like the sort to foment rebellion. I mean, what honest man would show no shame to be seen with his shirt flapping loose outside his hose in front of a gentlewoman?"

"Oh James, you are only saying that because you failed to impress him."

Elizabeth could not help thinking that the forester was justified in his amusement as she looked at James sitting in his saddle with his hands on his hips, a picture of indignation.

"If he did put us on the wrong track," Peter Smith said belligerently, nursing his fist, "Giles and I will go back and mash his head to a pulp."

"You will do no such thing." Jacob's voice was stern. "Violence is your answer to every situation. I know your wit is limited, but you and your brother must learn that there are other ways to solve problems besides brawling."

At that moment the house came into view.

"I knew he spoke the truth. You two wouldn't recognise the truth if it bit you on your fat noses," Mark Wheeler sneered at the Smith brothers.

Mark was London born and bred. He had come into Sir Neville's service when the knight was lodging in London and needed extra servants. He was not happy in the country. The crowded, noisy streets of the city were his territory. He took every opportunity to mock the Smith twins, whom he considered thick headed bumpkins.

"Shut your mouth you poxy little piss pot," Giles Smith growled back at him.

Jacob had grown very weary of their carping at each other on this journey.

"If you three continue in this way throughout the rest of this journey, I will have you all turned out of Sir Neville's service when we return home," he warned.

They knew it was no idle threat. Jacob Whyte was a fair man, but he would not tolerate indiscipline and was always mindful of Sir Neville's good name.

James backed up the steward's admonition. He was well aware that his father would not approve of the servants brawling, but he secretly felt some satisfaction at the thought of the Smiths roughing up that forester.

Elizabeth was paying no attention to the conversation. She was eager to approach the house.

Riding side saddle might look elegant and ladylike, but over long distances the position cramped her legs. She envied men's ability to sit astride a horse, the freedom of movement it afforded. An image strayed into her mind of the man in the white shirt. How fine he would look unencumbered by layers of garments, riding fast on a powerful horse, the wind blowing through that towselled hair. She pushed the picture away from her thoughts and concentrated on the house instead. She was struck by the quiet beauty of what she saw.

A wide circle of forest had been cleared and the house sat in the centre. The path widened as it led up to the house and either side of it were beds of heather and deep purple lavender, which gave off a sweet, fragrant perfume. To one side of the house was a small apple orchard, the trees still in blossom as it was late May, adding to the general fragrance. Eglantine and honeysuckle climbed in profusion over the porch of the front entrance.

The house itself was a medium sized, two storey, timber framed structure, the panels between the box style framing filled in with plaster daubed over wickerwork wattle and whitewashed. The framework of vertical and horizontal timbers was fitted with diagonal braces at the corners to keep the grid upright. The timbers had been treated with pitch to protect them from the weather, which gave them a dark, treacle-like hue.

Double terracotta coloured chimney pots stood at both ends of the roof and another was set lower down at the back on the right side. In the front were four mullioned windows, large for the size of the house, set with panes of diamond shaped glass. There were windows each side of the building too and an unusual feature, a window set right in the middle of the roof at the top of the frame, touching the central ridge. A visitor to the back of the house would find four more windows. Clearly light was important to the builder of this house to balance the darkness of the surrounding forest. A long timber barn stood several yards from the house, at right angles to it.

To Elizabeth's eyes the house seemed to fit its setting perfectly.

"It's beautiful," she said, more to herself than to any of her companions.

"It's not very big," James commented irritably. "It's like a yeoman's house. Who is Sir Thomas Mountfield? He can't be very important if he lives here."

"I have heard father speak of Sir Robert Mountfield," his sister replied. "He is a Justice of the Peace and Member of Parliament like father. I believe he lives in Salisbury. Perhaps Sir Thomas is related to him."

Elizabeth wished that James was not so concerned with status. During the past year his awareness of it had become so acute that it seemed to be the only thing that mattered to him. He accepted his father's values without question. She tried to soften his attitude without criticising Sir Neville, but she had made little progress of late. She was sorry that he could not see the beauty of this setting and could only feel that it was inferior to Norrington Hall.

As they drew near the front entrance, two enormous wolfhounds bounded out of the orchard barking with loud, deep throated voices. The horses were startled and James was hard pressed to keep his gelding from rearing up on its hind legs, which did not improve his ruffled temper. Peter Smith reached for his sword, fearing one of the dogs was about to attack his leg, but from the depths of the orchard came a long, sharp whistle and both creatures, ears pricked, ran back into the trees without hesitation.

"Well trained animals," Jacob approved, "That is a good sign."

He peered into the shadows of the orchard hoping to see who had called the dogs back. He caught a movement, but it could have been a bird or a squirrel. Dismounting he approached the front door. It was a solid oak door of double thickness with metal strap hinges and the frame set flush into the wall. A wooden porch with benches either side protected it from the weather. The scent of the eglantine that twined over the roof of the porch floated down to them on the light breeze. Elizabeth thought how pleasant it would be to sit in that porch to read or contemplate.

Jacob lifted his hand to knock on the door, but before he could do so, it swung open and a plump, middle-aged woman dressed in a dark blue kirtle, the skirts protected by a linen apron, stood there. The apron had seen much use for the colour had faded, but the garment was crisp and clean. So was the white coif she wore on her head. She looked the very picture of respectability. She introduced herself as Joan Bushy and listened attentively as he explained their situation and how they had been advised to seek hospitality at Sir Thomas Mountfield's house. She asked him who had directed them there. Jacob admitted that he had not inquired after his name, but when he gave the housekeeper a description of the forester, she nodded and smiled to herself.

She suggested that the men take the horses to the barn and then come to the kitchen by the side door where mugs of small beer would be waiting for them. Then she stood back to let Elizabeth and James proceed her into the house.

They found themselves at the head of a long passage, about twelve feet wide that ran down the width of the house with a back door at the far end. Along both sides of the passage, set around four feet from the walls of the rooms on either side were thick oak pillars, decorated all over with carvings. They were the supports for an open gallery, railed along the edge. It curved across the back door so there was access to the upper rooms on both sides of the house. The purpose of the window in the roof was clear now for it let daylight into the passage. In fact there was another window the other side of the roof ridge, making a double skylight in the middle of the passage where the rays of the sun and reflection of blue sky filled the bubbles in the greyish glass. Half way down the right side of the passage was a curious stair case, closed in at the bottom with cupboard doors, but twisting up in an elegant spiral to reach the gallery above, so that the climber stepped up through a square opening on to the floor of the gallery.

The housekeeper had opened the door to the first room on the right and the Norringtons were about to follow her when the door at the far end of the passage was pushed open. The two wolfhounds they had encountered earlier ran in. They ignored the visitors and headed through the open door nearest to them, which judging from the savoury aroma emanating from it must have been the kitchen. It was what they saw next that made their mouths drop open simultaneously. A woman came through the back door dressed only in a garment that looked like a white under-smock with no sleeves. It reached only to her knees so that the whole of her lower legs were exposed and she was bare-footed. Her black hair hung straight and heavy to her waist and her skin had a russet brown hue. She stared at them for a moment with almond shaped eyes that were as black as her hair, then followed the dogs into the kitchen.

Elizabeth and James exchanged glances. The boy's eyes were wide with astonishment and something akin to fear. He opened his mouth to speak, but his sister held up a finger to silence him. The placid expression on Joan Bushy's face had not changed as she ushered them into the parlour, where she bid them take off their outdoor garments. Elizabeth was pleased to shed her loose outer gown with its fur trimmed sleeves and collar. The air was fresh when they first set out, but now the atmosphere was warm and sticky as if a thunder storm was brewing. The housekeeper helped her untie the gown and laid it carefully across a coffer in the corner of the room.

"Shall I take your cloak Master Norrington?"

James shook his head. "No, I will keep it on thank you."

He was clutching the strings of the cloak as if he expected her to pull it off his shoulders and make away with it. Joan Bushy had a gentle manner. Her hazel eyes were warm and sympathetic.

"Now you both sit down and make yourselves comfortable. I will fetch you some small beer. Perhaps you might care to try a restorative drink of my own invention, made from fruit juice and herbs. It quenches the thirst well."

Elizabeth thought she would like to try it, but James opted for the beer. The moment the housekeeper left the room James said, "What sort of place is this Lizzie? Did you see that woman, in a smock with her legs bare? Shameless as a Southwark whore."

"Don't be coarse James. How would you know what such a woman looked like?"

"Perhaps she is a mad woman," her brother continued, his imagination in full spate, "Who lives in the woods and runs about with the wild creatures. You saw how dirty she was."

"No, that was not dirt. She is clearly from a different race, a race with browner skin than ours. Our ships sail to many parts of the world now and often bring foreigners back with them. Other races may have different customs regarding dress. I expect she is a servant here."

She had to admit to herself that the sight of the woman had startled her as well. She did not want to contemplate James' mad woman theory. Her brother refused to be mollified.

"Well she should be made to behave like a respectable English woman now she is here. Perhaps if she is mad they are afraid to cross her in case she flies into a rage and stabs people."

He pulled out the short dagger he wore at his belt and stabbed furiously at thin air to illustrate his point.

"Oh James, put that away."

They heard footsteps coming down the passage and he hastily shoved the dagger back into its sheath as Joan reappeared carrying a tray on which were a tankard of beer, a glass of restorative and a large plate of almond marchpane decorated with coloured comfits. James had always loved marchpane. It was his favourite sweetmeat, but he was suspicious of everything in this house now. He watched anxiously as Elizabeth took a long drink of the fruit and herb mixture. She commented on how refreshing it was and took a piece of marchpane. James waited a few moments until he was satisfied that his sister was not about to fall to the floor clutching her throat, poisoned by something the mad woman had added to the food or the drink. Then his desire for the marchpane got the better of him. He took a big bite and found it to be some of the best he had ever tasted, rich in almond flavour with a hint of ginger. He felt foolish to have been so suspicious and took another bite. Joan stood there smiling and Elizabeth said,

"This is a well- appointed parlour."

The walls were oak panelled, but brightened with a large Flemish tapestry woven with gold and silver threads and several rugs with oriental designs in pure colours. The table, chairs and stools were all good quality. The only other pieces of furniture in the room besides the coffer were a corner cupboard fixed to the wall and a bench beneath the window. Pewter candlesticks stood on the table and the bench. The wooden floor was covered in rush mats that had been sprinkled with lavender petals. Elizabeth was impressed by the stone fireplace with a timber lintel across the top, beautifully carved like the pillars in the passage.

"There is a fireplace in every room of the house," Joan announced with some pride, "Except the pantry of course. It gets very cold here in winter. We had four foot snow drifts to deal with last winter. That door over there leads into the dining room and beyond that is the library, Master Tom's- Sir Thomas' study." She corrected herself as if she was worried that the visitors might disapprove of her talking of her master with such familiarity.

Elizabeth though was pleased with the affection in Joan's voice when she said Master Tom. She had probably known him from his boyhood. Lizzie's mother had died when she was seven and James only three. He hardly remembered her, but Lizzie kept in her mind a clear picture of her mother's face. She had been supported in her loss by Kate, her nurse, who looked after the children devotedly, although she would stand no nonsense. Joan's round, friendly face reminded her of Kate, who had died of a chill two years past. Elizabeth missed her calm, practical presence.

"Sir Thomas will be here soon. If you will excuse me, I must begin to prepare dinner."

As she closed the parlour door behind her, Joan decided that she liked the girl. Her eyes were honest, her manner courteous. The boy however seemed ill at ease and sulky. She had just gone into the kitchen, when Tom Mountfield strolled in through the back door, followed by the men who were working with him in the forest.

"Something smells good," he said, walking into the kitchen to find Joan's daughter Sarah stirring a pot of stew with a ladle and his housekeeper cutting big chunks of bread. Ned Carter and Toby Aycliffe were cousins.

They lived in the village on the edge of the forest about six miles away and came over most days to help Sir Thomas with the forestry and any other job that needed doing. He paid fair wages and Joan Bushy fed them well. They went straight to the kitchen table and sat down. Sarah began to ladle the steaming stew into bowls already set out for them. The wolfhounds were lying on the floor gnawing at bones, but when Thomas came in they stood up and ambled over to him. He leaned over and squeezed both their heads under his arms as they pushed into him eager for his affection. Joan Bushy tapped him on the shoulder with the wooden spoon she was holding.

"Shame on you Master Tom, playing tricks on poor lost travellers," she scolded, not very seriously.

He laughed. "Well you know what a wicked man I am Joan. I wouldn't have done it if the boy had not been so peremptory. It takes little effort to speak to a labouring man with courtesy."

Ned and Toby nodded their agreement, their mouths full of stew.

"Twas hard not to burst out laughing when he called you a churl," Ned said, coughing in an effort to talk and eat at the same time.

"Yes, you found it funny because you imagined his embarrassment when he discovers that I am Sir Thomas Mountfield, but if he had been speaking to either of you in that manner you would have been less amused. Young Master Norrington's manners need mending. Where are all our visitors Joan?"

"Mistress and Master Norrington are in the parlour eating marchpane. Their servants came into the kitchen for beer and I served them ham and cheese with a loaf. Lord preserve us how those two great brothers stuff themselves. No wonder they are such a size. Hector and Ajax do not like them one bit, keep growling at them. One of those brothers, Peter I think is his name, reckoned that the dogs tried to bite his legs when the party rode up to the house. He boasted that he would have chopped their heads off with his sword if they had. I don't trust them Master Tom- rough, resentful men."

"I agree. They have a bullying manner about them. Where are they now?"

"The steward took them all back to the barn. I told him they could sleep in the kitchen or my own little parlour tonight, but he said the straw in the barn would be comfortable enough. I feel happier with them out of the house. I did not care for the way the skinny one with the pockmarked face kept eying Sarah. But we can't let Sir Neville Norrington's steward sleep in the barn. He seems a dignified, respectable man."

"You are right- as always. What shall we do about it?"

"He can have Sarah's room and she can sleep with me."

"Are you sure you will be able to control yourself Joan Bushy with such a handsome, well-set, dignified man in the chamber next to you?" Thomas asked wryly. Sarah giggled and Joan hit him on the arm with the spoon.

"Where is Dawn Light?" Tom queried, suddenly becoming aware of her absence. She was always the first to greet him when he returned to the house.

"She had no wish to be in the kitchen when the servants came in to eat and she would not go into the parlour because the Norringtons are in there, so she has taken refuge in the library."

There was a thoughtful expression on Thomas' face as he crossed the passage and walked into the library, the wolfhounds padding after him. His wife was always wary of strangers and how they would react to her. Their regular visitors were few in number and she had grown easy with them, but she resented the intrusion of strangers, as if she feared they might tempt Tom away from the free life they lived together back into more sophisticated society.

She was sitting at his desk, near the window which afforded a view of the gardens at the back of the house and was busy sharpening his quills with a pearl-handled penknife. She jumped up when he entered, ran over to him and put her arms around his neck. He kissed her and she stood looking up at him intently, her arms still around his neck.

"Has Joan explained to you about our visitors?

She nodded, disengaging herself from him and running her hand along the back of the tallest of the wolfhounds.

"Those men are bad. One of them try to stab Ajax with sword."

She spoke her words with a staccato rhythm, the sound of a language more guttural than the English tongue in her voice.

"Did they see you?"

"No. I whistle the dogs back from the trees. The girl, the boy, they see me."

"Indeed. What did they do?"

"Stand like this." She opened her mouth wide in imitation of a dropping jaw.

"Like fish without water."

Thomas laughed at her impersonation. "Well they have had a very sheltered upbringing. They have never seen anyone quite like you before. They have not had my good fortune. You must meet them at dinner Waaseyaaban. They are our guests."

She wrinkled her nose in discontent.

"Don't worry. They are only staying the night. They will leave in the morning."

He lifted his arm, looking at the sweat stain on his shirt.

"I suppose we had better don some finery in their honour and I need to bathe after all that logging and coppicing we did today. I must not appear before the Norrington children smelling of toil. It might offend their delicate sensibilities."

"I wash your back my Makwa."

"That sounds like an excellent plan. Come-"

They left the library and Thomas stuck his head around the kitchen door calling, "Joan, I need a bath. Is the bath tub still hanging on the wall in the brew house?"

The housekeeper confirmed it and added, "Shall I warm some water for you?"

"No, tis a warm enough day. Cold water will do. We will get some from the pump."

He reached behind the door and picked up two large wooden buckets. Joan handed him a flannel cloth and a knobbly piece of soap that she took from a cupboard on the wall.

"Dusk will be on us soon. Ask Sarah to light the candles in the parlour and the dining room in readiness and take bowls of water into our guests so they can refresh themselves before dinner. Dawn intends to strew my bath with rose petals so I will be exceptionally fragrant at the dinner table."

So saying he took hold of his wife's hand and they went out of the back door, running across to the brew house, the buckets banging together and the wolfhounds in close pursuit.

Five minutes later, Ned and Toby, having filled their bellies well, decided to set off for home. Joan stuffed a pannier full of fresh vegetables and a slice of beef cut from the roast she had prepared for dinner. Beef was a rare treat for poor folk. They could not afford such a luxury. The cousins were well rewarded for their services to Sir Thomas and were aware that their standard of living was higher in consequence than many of their village neighbours. They were willing enough to share any surplus with them to allay petty jealousies.

Passing the brew house on their way to fetch their horse, they heard laughter and splashing noises coming from the building and grinned at each other knowingly. The cousins did not have the means to keep a horse each, so they bought one between them, a powerful shire horse, which they named Samson because of his great strength.

They rode double on his back to and from Sir Thomas' house and he was useful to pull loads too heavy for Tom's cob. They also loaned him out to local farmers for hauling which earned them a few extra pennies. He was grazing inside the fenced area at the side of the orchard with a small flock of sheep and goats for company. When he heard Ned and Toby's voices he ambled over and put his great head with the white blaze down the nose, over the fence rails. Toby slipped his halter on and threw a blanket over his back, then stood on the lower rail and mounted him. Ned opened the gate and Toby gave him a hand up to sit behind him. Riding away they heard a guffaw of laughter. Looking over his shoulder Ned saw Giles Smith leaning against the side of the barn, clearly amused by the sight of them both astride the shire, without saddle or stirrups, drumming their heels against the horse's belly.

"Ignore the oaf," Toby advised. "That lot think they are so high and mighty because their master is a member of parliament and a justice. I know who I would rather work for."

His cousin agreed wholeheartedly.

The rain began gently at first, and then increased in intensity. Now it was drumming against the window panes and the sky had grown dark. Elizabeth was grateful that the servant girl had lit the candles earlier. Besides the candlesticks, there were fat beeswax candles in sconces on the walls. Tallow candles always smelt greasy, redolent of the animal fat from which they were made. They coated the tongue and created an acrid taste in the mouth. Beeswax candles had a pleasant, less intrusive fragrance.

Lizzie and James had washed their hands and faces with water brought to them by the housekeeper in bowls made of smooth, polished wood. The owner of the house had not yet appeared and James was growing impatient.

"I hope this rain has stopped by the morning," he said, "I want to get away from this place."

Thunder was reverberating somewhere in the distance and he hoped it was not moving their way. He did not like thunder storms. When he was six, he had seen a lurid zigzag of lightning strike a church steeple. There was an explosion and chunks of masonry tumbled down close to where he and his father were sheltering. He could not get the image out of his mind for weeks and could not understand why God would allow the elements to harm a church.

Sir Neville told him it may have been because some of the congregation practised Catholicism in secret. He had never forgotten that and believed Catholics to be very dangerous ever since. He had confessed to no one, not even Lizzie, how afraid he had felt when the great Spanish war fleet came to attack England the previous summer. It was exciting too because his father helped the Lord Lieutenant raise the militia and James rode around the county with them, but beneath all the busy preparations for war and the defiant, patriotic stances taken by his father's friends, there was an atmosphere of dread. James had read parts of John Foxe's book which told the story of how the present queen's sister, the Catholic Queen Mary, had married Philip of Spain and sought to bring England back to the Church of Rome. Foxe painted vivid pictures from eyewitness accounts of Protestant martyrs who were burned at the stake for their faith. James was appalled and fascinated by these stories. There was one tale that impressed him in particular about a young girl called Elizabeth Folkes, who was instructed to strip for the fire. She tried to give her petticoat to her mother and was not allowed to do so. She defiantly threw it away, shouting, "Farewell all the world. Farewell faith, farewell hope. Welcome love."

He could only imagine himself trembling with fear in those circumstances. Last summer he wondered what would happen if the Spaniards were victorious and England became Catholic again. His family were staunch upholders of the Church of England and his imagination conjured up pictures of them all being dragged away to a horrible death. When he heard the news that the Spanish fleet was vanquished, he ran to the very farthest part of the gardens where no one could see him and danced around cheering and singing at the top of his voice.

He was recalling that wonderful feeling of elation when the door opened and a man entered. He was dressed elegantly, but not extravagantly in a burgundy coloured doublet, silver grey breeches and hose, with garter bands at the knees that matched the colour of his doublet. He bowed to them and said, "I am sorry to have kept you waiting for so long. I am Sir Thomas Mountfield. You are most welcome in my house."

They looked at each other in astonishment. It was the man in the white shirt that they had met in the forest. Elizabeth could not help saying, "You made sport of us earlier today Sir Thomas," but there was no anger in her voice and he fancied that her eyes betrayed amusement. It pleased him for he had formed a good opinion of her at first sight and her reaction confirmed it.

"I apologise. I often have a perverse desire to amuse myself at the expense of others, but there was no malice intended I assure you. I have been roundly scolded for it by my housekeeper already. I hope you will forgive me."

She inclined her head, smiling, but James was mortified.

"You put me in a false position Sir," he complained, his tone hot. "I must now beg your pardon for calling you a churl."

Sir Thomas shook his head. "You owe me no apology Master Norrington. The apology is due to the man you thought I was. But let us forget this morning and start afresh. It gives me great pleasure to offer you both hospitality and I will set you on the right way myself in the morning."

James was still smarting, wondering what kind of man would play such a trick on gentlefolk, go around improperly dressed and keep mad women in his house. Granted he looked and spoke the part of a gentleman now, but the boy could not be sure what might happen next.

"I hope you have suitable accommodation for us," he said sulkily.

Elizabeth gave him a reproving glance, but Thomas only smiled.

"Well, unexpected guests are few here, but Joan always keeps the beds well aired."

"I must have a bed chamber of my own," James burst out, suddenly fearing that the man would judge him to be much younger than his years, "I will not share a room with my sister."

"I did not expect you would Master Norrington. You are much too old for that."

His tone was not mocking and James was somewhat mollified by the comment, even though he was determined to dislike Sir Thomas. Elizabeth looked at Mountfield, grateful that he had divined her brother's sensitivity concerning his size. Although he found it hard to resist teasing James, she was certain that he was a compassionate man at heart.

"We can offer a bed to your steward also. Your other servants will do well enough in the barn. Hay can be a sweet and comfortable bed. Dinner will be served soon. Perhaps your steward would care to join us."

James bristled at that.

"At Norrington Hall we never eat with servants."

Tom was struck again by the boy's similarity to his father, Sir Neville. He had an urge to laugh, but smothered it not wishing to antagonise James further and explained, "We are a much less formal establishment here than Norrington Hall. I have two servants only, Joan Bushy and her daughter Sarah. They are part of the family. We work beside each other, so it is natural that we eat together too. But I have no wish to make you uncomfortable. I am sure Joan and Sarah will be happy to entertain Jacob in their own parlour this evening."

Tom could see that the girl was distressed by her brother's rudeness. He judged her to be sixteen or seventeen. She was very beautiful. Her face was a perfect oval with a firm chin, her skin flawless. The large eyes were the colour of a clear blue summer sky. He saw intelligence and integrity in her gaze. He fancied he detected admiration also but decided that he was flattering himself and dismissed the thought.

The contrasting elements in Tom's nature had always made him attractive to women. His character was strong; he was physically bold and he possessed a quick wit that was sometimes acerbic, but he was also scholarly, with a passion for literature, the arts and learning in general. He had travelled to the New World, fought in the Low Countries, darkened his sword with the blood of other men and knew it was necessary to be tough to survive. Yet there was an innate gentleness in him, a sympathy with the less fortunate in life and for all parts of God's creation. He exuded a natural sexuality that drew women to him and he had to admit that when he was younger he took advantage of it. He refused to be pressurized by his father into marrying, not certain what he wanted in a wife. Never having much respect for the norms of society, he wished to marry for love and felt justified in searching for it.

Now he was thirty one, disillusioned by many of his experiences in life, but he had found what he was looking for in a wife. Unfortunately his father did not agree with his choice and there was little he could do about it.

"The approach to your house is so charming," Lizzie was saying, eager to balance James' ill manners. "I love the lavender beside the path and the apple blossom. The house sits so well in its surroundings. The design is unlike many others I have seen."

"Perhaps that is because I planned it myself Mistress Norrington."

"That explains it," James muttered. Elizabeth frowned at him, but once again Mountfield only smiled.

"Indeed you may be right. I am no master craftsman, but the house is designed to suit our purposes, not to follow present fashion or impress others."

"I am sure it must suit your purposes admirably," Elizabeth said quickly before James could make another remark. "Do you have gardens at the back of the house?"

"Yes for vegetables and herbs mainly. We try to be as self-sufficient as we can. I would show you, but the rain is too heavy now and the light is fading-perhaps tomorrow before you leave." Elizabeth expressed a desire to look more closely at the curiously carved pillars that supported the gallery. He acquiesced at once, motioning her to proceed him into the passage way. James followed with a sulky demeanour, not wishing to appear interested in wooden pillars.

The carving was remarkable. A variety of animals, both wild and domestic twined themselves around the pillars, so skilfully wrought they were alive with movement. They were all bound together by foliage and flowers carved with equal realism. As Lizzie reached out to feel the texture of the wood, she drew back her hand sharply, startled by the sight of a serpent twisting out towards her. She could have sworn the creature's tongue was flicking with a snake's silky speed. Looking up she noticed an angel or two peering down at her.

"Some of the work is my doing," Thomas explained, "But I hired the best wood carver in Winchester to improve my skill and help me complete the work. He is a good Christian and always adds at least one angel to his handiwork. He believes it benefits his soul. They fit in well I think, sitting there looking after the wonders of creation."

Every pillar was different and while Lizzie continued to look at them, Tom stepped into the kitchen to make Joan aware of the altered arrangements. She had taken food out to the men in the barn and the steward was sitting in her parlour. She was not in the least put out by the changes.

Thomas opened the back door. The rain was sheeting down, bouncing as it hit the ground.

"Look," he said to Lizzie, "You can just about see how it is arranged."

Peering through the rain and the descending gloom, she could make out neat squares of garden in rows either side of a flagstone path with different plants in each patch. James, standing beside her looked also.

"It is very ordered," he acceded grudgingly, "But it is a husbandman's garden. At Norrington Hall we have a geometric knot garden with parterres and a mound with a spiral path leading up to a bench where we can view the garden. There is a maze too and two summer houses."

Elizabeth felt like kicking his ankle but restrained herself in front of Sir Thomas.

"My wife is the true gardener here," Mountfield said.

"Your wife?" Elizabeth was taken by surprise. As the housekeeper had met them rather than the mistress of the house, she had assumed that Sir Thomas was a bachelor or a widower.

"Yes. I am sorry that she was unable to greet you earlier. You will meet her at dinner in a few moments. She plants and tends everything. I just do the digging, with the help of Toby and Ned, the two men you saw with me in the forest. Every plant my wife touches is eager to grow. She has magic in her fingers."

"What is the building at the end of that lovely arbour?"

Elizabeth pointed to an arbour roofed over with wickerwork, making a tunnel that supported an abundance of wisteria. She could just make out a small building at the end of the tunnel.

"Ah – the end of the tunnel is less fragrant than the beginning I fear. That is the privy, with a cesspit behind it. At least the arbour protects you from inclement weather when you have need to visit it."

"We have garde robes inside the house," James piped up, deliberately using the grander word and confident that at last an insult had struck home. He was disappointed because it bounced off Thomas like the rain off the ground.

"Oh don't worry Master Norrington. There are close stools in every bedchamber so you won't have to go outside in this dark, wild place during the night and guests are not expected to empty them personally."

Joan popped her head around the kitchen door to announce that she would be serving dinner in a few minutes. Thomas pulled the back door shut and led his guests to the dining room, where a sturdy oak table was already laid with pewter plates and tankards, the metal glowing softly in the light of the candles in the candelabra standing in the centre of the table. There were knives, forks and spoons too. It was customary for travellers to carry their own cutlery with them when they dined with others, for not every host possessed more than was needed for his immediate family. The Norringtons had not packed theirs because their father assured them Sir Bartholomew Hanham always provided his guests with solid silver cutlery. Besides Elizabeth was more than a guest, she was a prospective member of Hanham's family. She was pleased that this omission did not cause any embarrassment to Sir Thomas, who seemed well supplied with utensils, even though they were not made of silver.

He was about to motion them to sit down, when he heard soft footsteps in the passage way and murmured, "Ah, here she is."

His wife was just outside the door and taking her by the hand he drew her into the room.

"Let me introduce you to my wife, Waaseyaaban."

Standing before them was a woman dressed in a loose fitting broadcloth kirtle which reached just below her knees. It was the shade of a green apple. The wide sleeves were elbow length. Along their edges and the edge of the scooped neckline were strips of embroidery, geometric designs picked out in glass beads and pearls. Similar panels of embroidery decorated the shoulders. The garment was cut all in one piece without a fitted bodice so there was no need for lacings. It could be slipped over the head. Around her neck on a silver chain was a lump of turquoise, identical to the one Thomas wore. Hers was enhanced by a string of baroque pearls and another of coloured beads. Silver and bead bracelets adorned her smooth brown arms and in her ears were silver hoops hung with pearls, coral and turquoise. Her black hair reached her waist in two thick plaits with green ribbons interwoven into them.

There was an awkward silence. Elizabeth, though astonished was struck by the woman's exotic beauty. Ever mindful of her manners she said, "I am very pleased to meet you Lady Mountfield."

James however was thunderstruck. He just stood there with his mouth open. Tom was reminded of his wife's comment about the fish out of water and had to purse his lips close together to prevent himself from laughing aloud at the expression on the boy's face.

This was even worse than the embarrassing discovery that the forester he had called a churl was Sir Thomas. This was the wild woman in the under-smock. She was more modestly dressed now but she still looked outlandish to James. How could this be Sir Thomas' wife? She was a savage. A Christian man could not call a savage his wife. She was staring at him with a grave intensity. Her eyes troubled him. Their blackness had a liquidity; they glittered like obsidian. Surely a witch's eyes would look like this.

Elizabeth nudged him and he muttered a greeting that was barely audible.

"Waaseyaaban is from the Croatan people of Roanoke Island on the coast of the Americas," Tom explained. "We find that English folk find it hard to get their tongues around her name. It translates roughly as Dawn Light. In classical times she would be called Aurora. She is happy for you to call her

Dawn Light. Lady Mountfield is not a title to which she is accustomed, though I thank you Mistress for your courtesy."

He seemed genuinely pleased by her words and Lizzie felt a warm glow in her chest and hoped there was no blush reddening her neck and cheeks.

"Does she understand our language?"

"Yes. She speaks English and understands it even better. She knows more English than I do Croatan. You can address her directly. You don't need me as an intermediary- although I must tell you that the Croatan people do not chatter as much as we do. They consider conversation for its own sake alone a waste of energy."

At that moment Joan and Sarah bustled in carrying between them two dishes of sliced beef in rich gravy, a platter of roasted nut cakes, two bowls of steaming hot vegetables and slices of bread. They were deposited on the sideboard and Thomas invited his guests to sit at the table. James sat there thinking how unbearable this meal was going to be. Lizzie would be disappointed if she expected him to make conversation he told himself. Joan was ready to serve the meal but Tom prevented her.

"No, Dawn Light will serve our guests tonight. You go and charm that steward."

She gave him an old-fashioned look, but there was affection in her eyes and Elizabeth wondered once again if she had known him from his childhood.

"Has Joan been with you a long time?" she asked.

"She was my mother's servant, but she came here to help make our lives easier just after we built the house and she chose to stay, which is our good fortune."

"Then she knew you as a boy Sir Thomas?"

Lizzie felt some satisfaction that she had divined correctly.

"Oh yes- always rapping me over the knuckles with her wooden spoon when I couldn't keep my fingers out of her sweetmeat jars. But she saved me from plenty of beatings by my father by providing me with an alibi or covering up some of my more hare-brained antics."

Elizabeth could imagine that he had been a very adventurous child.

Dawn Light had served them with meat and gravy and was now holding out the first bowl of mixed vegetables. She served Elizabeth, but when she reached James he held up his hand.

"No, we do not eat vegetables at home. Father says vegetables are food for peasants and they gripe your stomach."

In the second bowl were buttered parsnips and without speaking Dawn Light offered that to him, but he refused. Thomas took the bowl from his wife and helped himself to a goodly portion. That little quirk of amusement was playing at the corners of his mouth.

"Is a nut roast more to your taste?" he queried, pushing the platter of nut cakes in James' direction.

The boy nodded without looking at him and took some off the platter. There was silence for a while as the four of them ate their meal, James stealing a glance now and then at the Croatan woman. He wondered how he could be expected to enjoy his food when he was sitting opposite a witch. He was certain he would suffer from dreadful indigestion all night.

Thomas broke the silence. He sat playing with the golden hoop in his ear, looking thoughtfully at Elizabeth before he said,

"May I inquire why you are on your way to Frome Mistress Norrington?"

She told him that they were going to the manor house of Bartholomew Hanham where she was to be married in mid-June.

"I am affianced to his nephew Anthony. As I have no mother to arrange the wedding details, Sir Bartholomew's wife, Lady Agnes has kindly offered to act in her stead. My father will join us a few days before the wedding."

"Sir Bartholomew's mother was the daughter of an earl," James informed them. "He has a huge estate and a house in town. It is an excellent marriage for Lizzie because he has no children and has adopted Anthony as his heir."

Tom raised his eyebrows but did not comment. Elizabeth wished James would not harp on things that clearly did not impress their host one iota.

"Do you know the family Sir Thomas?" she asked.

"Yes I do."

"Anthony Hanham also?"

"We have met in the past, but he was only a lad then. He is almost ten years younger than I."

Elizabeth knew Anthony to be twenty one. She had reckoned Thomas to be around thirty and had guessed correctly again. He was looking at her very directly.

"How many times have you met him?"

"Only twice, but that is often the case is it not?"

He nodded. "Do you approve of your father's choice?"

"It is not my place to question my father's choice. I hope Anthony and I may live comfortably together."

James was bridling. How dare this irritating fellow quiz his sister so.

"Indeed," Tom reflected, "An arranged marriage often turns out well and if living comfortably together is all you seek then it probably will."

Elizabeth had found Anthony distant and affected at both meetings, but had put it down to shyness. She was nervous and assumed that he was too. He was a handsome young man and she hoped their relationship would grow into love.

"I will certainly try my very best to be a good wife."Her sincerity touched Thomas and he smiled at her.

"I am sure you will. It's just that there is much to be said for marrying for love, although I realise that women do not have the same freedom of choice as men. Mind you, it can also be a dangerous course to take. Not everyone is as fortunate as I have been."

He reached out and stroked Dawn Light's forearm with his fingers, a sensuous, loving caress. James looked down at his plate, embarrassed. He did not consider it gentlemanly to show physical affection in the company of others. His father would not approve of it he was sure. Perhaps this witch had enslaved Sir Thomas with a spell or a potion. He was relieved when Joan Bushy came in with the sweet course, a plum and almond tart in creamy custard.

When the meal was over and Sir Thomas had filled glass goblets with a fine red wine, Elizabeth would have been happy to sit there for the rest of the evening talking to their host. She felt her cheeks glow warm with the effect of the wine and she was eager to ask Tom about his life; how he had met Dawn Light. When he suggested they go into the parlour she was about to agree when James stood up and said with determination,

"My sister and I are tired. We must go to bed now and be off early in the morning."

Lizzie knew how uncomfortable he had been all evening and let him have his way with a sigh. Her reluctance did not escape Dawn Light however, who was watching her keenly. Thomas went across to Joan's parlour to ask her to show the Norrington's to their bedchambers. Jacob Whyte was still there, his feet resting on a foot stool, a tankard of beer in his hand. He scrambled to his feet when Thomas entered and bowed.

"I trust you have been well looked after."

"I have indeed Sir. Your housekeeper is most hospitable."

"Good, but I must take her from you now to attend your young charges."

In the passage way Tom murmured, "Most hospitable," in Joan's ear.

"Away with you and your teasing," she responded, laughing.

James was happy that it was Joan who showed them to their bedchambers and lit the candles rather than the foreign witch. He did not fancy the thought of her padding beside him with her soft footsteps along the shadowy gallery. Lizzie stopped to look up at the windows in the roof above them. The night was so dark and stormy with rain streaming across the panes that she could see nothing of the sky, but she imagined how pleasant it would be on a clear night to stand in the gallery and study the firmament. The more she saw of this house, the more she liked it.Looking down she saw Sir Thomas and his wife go into the parlour. His arm was around her waist and she was leaning into his shoulder. He kissed the top of her head and their bodies seemed in perfect harmony. Elizabeth could recall few displays of affection between her parents, although as she was so young when her mother died, she assumed that she lacked the understanding to interpret the signs. She was sure her father had grieved over the loss of his wife, but he was not a man to show tender feelings. He called that womanly. He had conceived a fancy to marry again, three years after Mary had died. He paid court to a widow of independent means for some months, but eventually she chose a younger, more dashing husband. Sir Neville swallowed his disappointment and had not been disposed to consider remarrying after that.

Kate, Lizzie's nurse, had told her what happened between a man and a woman in the bedchamber and warned her that intercourse was not always a pleasure, but a good wife should be obedient to her husband's desires and always try to please him. The thought of this nagged at her mind if she allowed herself to contemplate it and she tried to convince herself that if you loved and respected your husband, all would be well. Observing the intimacy between Thomas Mountfield and Waaseyaaban encouraged her in that hope.

In the cosy bedchamber she stripped to her under- smock. She felt safe in this house and despite the noise of the rain, the rumbling of the thunder and the heavy atmosphere, she soon fell asleep.

Her brother's feelings were the exact opposite. James was nervous. Every creak of the floor boards set him on edge. Despite the heat, he feared to undress and lay on top of the bed cover. He would have felt more at ease if there had been a key in the lock or a bolt on the door. His chamber was next to Sir Thomas 'own and after he had lain there sweating for about an hour, though it seemed longer, he heard the door of the next room open and the sound of voices. He could not make out the words, so he got up and pressed his ear to the adjoining wall, but it was no clearer.

James had heard many stories about witches, how their bodies were often strangely shaped, how some of them had three breasts. A curiosity gripped him so strong that it overcame his fear. He crept out of his room into the gallery. Mountfield's bedchamber door was slightly ajar, the soft light of candles showing within. He saw Sir Thomas, dressed only in his breeches, walk across the room into the shadows and out of his line of vision. The woman was in the four- poster bed, partly covered by the counterpane, but her breasts were exposed.

He leaned closer to the door, his heart pounding, wondering what he would do if he could prove she was a witch. He could not see Thomas Mountfield and had no idea that the man had sensed a presence outside the door. Tom thought he had heard footsteps in the gallery. He put a finger on his lips to warn his wife not to comment and pointed at the door. Then he approached the door from the side that was not visible to anyone peeping through the opening. Suddenly he whipped the door wide open and a startled James fell at his feet in a heap.

"Master Norrington-have you lost your way again?"

James' face flushed a vivid pink. There was no valid excuse he could make and felt he must tell the truth.

"I- I believe she is a witch sir and she holds you in thrall with spells and charms," he stammered. "I wished to see- well witches are deformed creatures-"

His voice tailed off. Tom's face was impassive.

"Did you hear that Waaseyaaban?" he said to his wife, "The boy fears you are a hideous witch. Shall we allay his fears?"

To James' horror the woman threw off the bedclothes and stood naked in the centre of the room.

"Well, take a good look boy," Thomas demanded. "Satisfy yourself."

James lifted his gaze. She was lithe and well-formed, everything about her body normal, the brown skin shining in the candle glow. His pulse was racing.

"You see- no horrible deformities. No horns, no lumps or pustules, no tail- a body as normal as any English woman, though finer shaped than many I have seen. You have seen a woman naked before?"

James nodded, unable to take his eyes off Dawn Light.

"Yes sir," he mumbled, "Last summer my cousins and I hid in the bushes and watched some village girls bathing in the pond."

"Did you like what you saw?"

"Yes sir."

"Good- and do you still believe my wife to be a witch?"

"No sir."

James was struggling hard not to cry which would have shamed him more than ever.

"Then go back to your bed before your sister wakes and finds out what you are up to. You wouldn't care for that I fancy."

"No sir."

Thomas took hold of his hand, pulling him to his feet and he fled back to his bedchamber, his confusion made worse by the explosion of laughter that came from the room behind him. Dawn Light lay back down on the bed, laughing with her husband.

"I wonder who has filled his head with such arrant nonsense," Thomas said. He had never believed in witchcraft, but he knew that many did, even educated folk. "Poor boy, I have some sympathy for him. He is at that stage in life when he is keenly aware that he is no longer a child, but is not yet a man. It's a difficult time. You struggle to understand who you are. Although there are so many new things to discover and the prospect of the future is exciting, it also makes you fearful. I would not go back to that time for anything."

He sat down on the edge of the bed and pulled off his breeches, adding,

"In truth, even now there are times when I am not sure who I am or what is the purpose of life."

Dawn Light stroked his back. She loved the feel of his big shoulder bones under her fingers.

"I know who you are. You are my Thomas, my brave Makwa."

Her confidence in him always soothed his doubts. He rolled over on to the bed and drew her into his arms.

Elizabeth Norrington had woken early, just after dawn. She imagined that this household would breakfast early and wanted to be ready. She poured water from a ewer into the bowl on the table by the window and washed her face and hands. Then she dressed and went out into the gallery. She looked into James' room. Her brother was sprawled on the bed fully clothed but sound asleep. She assumed that he had spent a restless night and only recently fallen asleep, so she left him to sleep a little longer. The door of the large chamber was wide open and the room was empty. She walked around the curve of the gallery above the back door and realised that there was another staircase that must lead down into the kitchen. It was closed in and straight like a step ladder, not an elegant spiral like the one next to the parlour. She could hear voices and the clanking of pans.

She went back to her room and opened the casement pane in the window. This bedchamber was at the back of the house and the window faced the vegetable plots she had glimpsed briefly the previous evening.

It was still raining, but less heavily now and the atmosphere much fresher, the threat of thunder gone. A gang of rowdy sparrows sat on the wisteria arbour squabbling with great energy, flapping their wings and pecking at each other. As she watched them, a robin landed on the casement ledge and perched there regarding her intently with bright, dark eyes. She made tweeting noises at the bird and it tilted its head to one side, then flew away.

Something else caught her eye, Sir Thomas Mountfield running down from one side of the gardens. He must have been out in the rain for some time for his shirt, worn loose as it had been when she saw him first, was soaked through and clinging to him. The wolfhounds ran beside him with long, loping strides, their grey coats darkened several shades by the wet. All three, man and dogs, seemed to be enjoying the rain. They disappeared from her view through the back door into the house.

Lizzie continued to gaze out of the window for a while as the rain gradually ceased and the sky began to lighten. She was pleased that the rain had stopped for she hoped Sir Thomas would remember her desire to see the gardens before she left. She refused to entertain the suspicion at the back of her mind that it was the prospect of spending some time with her host that excited her more than the gardens themselves. She knew it was improper for a single woman to be alone with a man, but she wanted to tour the gardens without James. She could not bear the thought of her brother making more of his belittling remarks.

She decided to go downstairs and descended the spiral staircase to the passage. She liked the feel of her skirts sweeping around the sinuous curves of the spiral. Wondering if she should sit in the parlour, she went to the door, but inside she saw her host and his wife. Thomas had stripped off his wet shirt. It lay on the floor by the fireplace. He was bending forward so that Dawn Light could rub his hair dry with a towel. She was rubbing vigorously and they were laughing. Lizzie saw a livid scar on Sir Thomas' right arm, just below the bicep and another across his back. She felt a desire to run her fingers over the length of the scars, feel his muscles move under her touch. Alarmed at the sensation she drew back from the door. They were so intent on their task in the parlour that they did not see her as she hurried away.

She was struck once again, as she had been the previous evening, by the easy intimacy of their relationship. How good it would be if her relationship with her future husband could develop that way. What little she had seen of Anthony Hanham so far did not encourage her to imagine that he would allow himself to get soaked, let alone strip his shirt off in the parlour.

She tried to recall Dawn Light's native name, murmuring it to herself. Waaseyaaban- it had a rhythm like music.

Joan Bushy emerged from the kitchen asking if Elizabeth and her brother would like some breakfast.

"James is still asleep. I think the storm kept him awake during the night. I will wait until he comes down. You mentioned Sir Thomas' library yesterday. May I see it?"

Joan nodded approvingly. "Of course. He has a goodly number of books. He was always one for reading and studying despite his desire for adventure. He was quite the stellar scholar at Oxford. We were all so proud of him."

She stepped across the passage and opened up the library door. "You go on in there and look at some of those books. He will be pleased that you have an interest in them."

Lizzie, as Joan pulled the door shut behind her, realised that the window in this room was directly below the one in her bedchamber through which she had watched Tom run from the garden in the rain. Long rows of shelving took up one whole wall of the room and every shelf was stacked with books and manuscripts. Some were bound in handsome leather, their titles tooled in gold lettering, others cased in stiffened card covered in fabric. Some were just loose pages tied together with ribbons. This was not one of those libraries intended only for show, the books never opened. It was clear that the volumes were well-used. Two books were left open on a stool and a pile of them were spread across a bench under the window.

His desk stood near the window, sideways on to catch the most light. An inkwell and a pot full of quills stood on the desk amid sheets of paper strewn around in disorder. She picked up a sheet. The text was written in a bold, legible hand, but several ink blots decorated the page where the end of the quill had split through too much pressure by the writer. It was a description of the vegetation of an island and the creatures that lived within it, the detail brought vividly to life. Lizzie became engrossed in it and searched for the page that should follow.

So intent was she on finding it that she did not hear the door open. Thomas Mountfield stood in the doorway watching her, a thoughtful smile on his face.

"I see you have been taught to read Mistress Norrington."

He walked into the room and leaned against the fireplace. Elizabeth dropped the papers she was holding.

"I did not mean to pry Sir Thomas, truly. Your housekeeper said you would not mind if I looked at some of the books in your library, but the story written here caught my eye and I wished to read more."

"Don't worry. I am not offended. There are no secrets on that desk, only my scribbles. I am pleased that your father gave you the opportunity for an education. Not every man does that for his daughter."

He motioned her to sit down in a chair by the fireplace, but he remained standing. He was fully dressed now, but the girl's mind kept straying to the sight of his bare back and that scar between his shoulder blades.

"I have to thank my mother rather than my father," she told him. "She was an educated woman herself and insisted that I should have a tutor from the age of five. Father is inclined to believe that over much education hinders a woman's marriage prospects, but he agreed that it would do me no harm to learn the basic skills of reading and writing in English. I have no knowledge of other languages. Perhaps if mother had not died when I was seven, my education would have been broader."

"Her death must have been a hard blow for you. I met your mother once."

She looked at him in surprise.

"I must have been about fifteen- yes- it was during the vacation, before my second year at Oxford. I was with my father when he paid a call on Sir Neville. Your mother greeted us on our arrival with great courtesy. She was a very gracious lady, beautiful too. You resemble her very much. Now I come to think of it, there was a small child playing in the garden with her nurse, a girl who had only just learned to walk judging from the number of times she fell over. That must have been you mistress."

Lizzie did not know whether to laugh or cry. This unexpected memory of her mother, spoken so sympathetically, touched her heart.

"Is your father Sir Robert Mountfield of Salisbury?" she asked.

"Yes he is."

"My father has often spoken of him. They dine together sometimes in London when parliament is called."

"They studied at the Inns of Court together I believe in their early days," Thomas told her. She was expecting him to say more about the relationship, but he seemed reluctant to expand on that subject. He bent over and picked up the sheets of paper she had dropped, which had floated to the floor and placed them back on the desk.

"I hope I haven't disordered them," Lizzie said anxiously.

He laughed. "Did you see any order there in the first place? I am notoriously untidy. I drive Joan to distraction."

"These are your writings then."

"I am trying to write an account of our expedition to the Americas and also to put down the true facts, as I experienced them, of the campaign in the Low Countries in 1586. I make slow progress because although my ideas flow fast, when I read back what I have written, I am so dissatisfied with it, I tear half of it up and have to start again."

He gave her a self-depreciating smile. Elizabeth studied his face. His features were strong, well-defined with high cheek bones and dark brows. His gaze was very direct, the eyes expressive. They reflected so many different things; intelligence, humour, sympathy, but she also detected frustration and sadness in their depths. She was certain he had known suffering.

"The island you describe here, is that where you met Dawn Light?"

She wanted to say Waaseyaaban, but feared she would mispronounce it.

"Yes, Roanoke Island. A group of us sailed in five ships from Plymouth in the spring of 1585, under the leadership of Sir Richard Grenville. The whole thing almost hit disaster at the start. I was on board "The Roebuck" but we were caught in a fierce storm off the coast of Portugal and Grenville's ship, "The Tiger" got separated from the rest of us. We thought we might never see them again, but by good fortune we were re-united on the coast of the Americas. Then coming into the shore the Tiger struck a reef and was holed. We managed to repair her, but most of the food supplies were ruined, which didn't do much for our morale."

"Were the native peoples hostile to you?"

"Not on Roanoke Island- on the contrary- they were most friendly at first- without their help we would have starved. Most of the men in our party were not farmers. They were adventurers hoping to find wealth of some kind. I knew very little about agriculture myself then and although the mainland was fertile, the soil on Roanoke was sandy and dry. Grenville decided to go back to England for supplies, leaving around one hundred of us there to fend for ourselves."

"What did you do?"

"We built a wooden fort and explored the island. I spent much of my time in the native villages observing their customs and became friendly with two Croatan brothers who invited me into their home. There I met Waaseyaaban, their sister and we- became very fond of each other."

"Did her brothers object?"

"No, they encouraged our relationship. It was if they were offering her to me as a gift of friendship. It turned out to be the most precious gift I have ever been given."

"Why did you leave the island?"

"We all left it. We had little choice. Almost a year went by and Grenville did not return with the supplies. Unskilled farmers as we were, we came to rely more and more on the Croatans to feed us, which put too heavy a burden on them. Then we were attacked-"

Lizzie gave an involuntary gasp and he smiled at her complete involvement in his tale, before he continued, "Not by the local Croatans. When we arrived on the coast the previous July, a party of men were exploring the mainland and got involved in a brawl with some Secotan people. I was not there. I was helping to repair the Tiger, so I don't know the rights of it, but it was probably the fault of our men. It was something to do with the theft of a silver cup. Whatever happened, Ralph Lane who was in charge, reacted too fiercely and burned the Secotan village to the ground. The natives brooded on their resentment for almost a year, then came across to the island and attacked the fort. We succeeded in driving them off but several of our men were killed and others wounded. I took an arrow in my back."

Elizabeth just managed to prevent herself from telling him she had seen the scar.

"I was fortunate. The missile hit me at an angle, so it did not sink in too deep, but I developed a fever as a consequence. Dawn Light treated my wound, nursing me through the fever and refused to leave me from then on."

He ran his hand through his hair, disturbed by the memory of those tense days at the fort, wondering when the next attack might come.

"But how did you get home again?"

"Our saviour was none other than Sir Francis Drake. He had been privateering in the Caribbean Islands and called in at Roanoke on his way home, laden with booty as usual. He offered to take us all home and as there was still no sign of Grenville, we agreed. The day before we left Waaseyaaban and I were married in her village, after their custom and she came back to England with me."

"Your father must have felt such relief to see you safe home again Sir Thomas," Elizabeth said with sincerity. He did not reply and when she added, "I expect you visit the house at Salisbury often," he answered curtly,

"My father and I are not on good terms."

There was an edge of bitterness in his voice, but seeing that she was embarrassed at the thought of saying the wrong thing, he said more gently,

"My mother and my youngest sister, Cecily, sometimes venture into the fearsome forest to see if I am still alive."

"You have other sisters?"

"Two older ones, both too comfortably married to bother with their troublesome little brother."

She guessed that she had trespassed on a sensitive subject and wished she had been more diplomatic. Eager to pass on to something else, she pointed to some more papers on the desk, asking,

"Those poems, are they your work too?"

Thomas sat down in the high-backed chair at his desk, turning it to face Elizabeth. He picked up a sheet of the poetry, tracing the lines with his fingers, a gesture full of affectionate regret.

"These were written by a man with far more skill in verse than I shall ever have. These are Philip's poems, Philip Sidney."

"Sir Philip Sidney?" Elizabeth repeated, unable to hide her surprise.

"Yes, he often gave me copies and sought my opinion. I spent some time in his household and he became my friend. I was with him in Arnhem when he died."

She did not know what to say. Sir Philip was England's shining example of a gentleman; the whole nation mourned at the news of his death. Thomas wondered if she believed him; it must have sounded so unlikely. The grief that filled his heart at Philip's loss was profounder than he could explain in words. It would be three years come September, but the feeling that the quality of his life was forever diminished was still as strong as it was on the day he had held his hand and watched that great soul part from his body.

"It was Philip who encouraged me to go on the voyage to the Americas. He was always taken with the idea of spreading England's influence to far parts of the globe and eager to support Frobisher and Raleigh's schemes. Part of him wished to go himself, but he was convinced that the Queen would call him to do some great work on her behalf. He was forever waiting for a great purpose to fulfil his life."

He rested his head against the back of the chair, wondering why he was telling all this to Elizabeth. He mocked himself inwardly for responding with such willingness to her eager innocence, but there were times when he needed to talk, when all the frustration he suppressed threatened to burst through his chest like some parasite that had out-grown its host.

"When Her Majesty finally gave in to Lord Leicester and Walsingham's pressure to support the Netherland states in their rebellion against Spain with troops and not just money, Philip believed his great moment had arrived. He had a vision of a great Protestant crusade against the forces of Catholicism. It was almost a cosmic struggle in his eyes.

When we came back from Roanoke, I was restless, not sure what to do and I re-joined his household in the Netherlands. His enthusiasm could carry all before it. He persuaded me that the cause was just, but the reality did not match the vision. It rarely does. I was soon disillusioned, but despite all the frustrations and disappointments, Philip stayed true to his vision right to the end."

He closed his eyes for a moment, images from those days still vivid in his mind. The Earl of Leicester, against the Queen's express wishes, had accepted the title of Ruler of the Netherlands as soon as he arrived in the country. Queen Elizabeth had never wished for open war with Spain. She supported the rebels with money, but her aim was different from theirs. She did not wish to destroy Spanish sovereignty over the Netherlands, but wanted the States ancient rights restored. She had no lust for glory at the expense of the economic ruination of her country and widespread social distress. Thomas had come to evaluate the situation differently at a distance, after much thought. He could see how she walked a diplomatic tightrope trying to keep a balance and ward off possible invasions.

She had been offered the sovereignty of the Netherlands by the rebels and flatly refused it, issuing a pamphlet in several languages declaring her desire for peace and that she did not intend to seek territory and authority in the Low Countries. Leicester's action made a nonsense of that statement, jeopardising her whole policy.

Robert Dudley had always seen himself as a great Renaissance prince. In his eyes he was the premiere nobleman in England, a man who had once aspired to marry the Queen. He set up a court in The Hague that rivalled the royal court at home. The Earl was Philip Sidney's uncle and Philip had always admired him, but when he and Tom paid a visit to Leicester in The Hague, even he was astonished at Dudley's affrontery. Thomas was disgusted. Lady Leicester was driving around The Hague in a luxurious coach, attended by a phalanx of servants and gentlewomen. She wore cloth of gold dresses and was weighed down with ropes of pearls. She acted as if she was a Queen herself.

It was little wonder that Elizabeth was incandescent with rage. She wrote a furious letter condemning his actions, which she insisted be read out in front of the Netherlands States General with Leicester in attendance. He was humiliated and it undermined his position. The Queen however was caught in a cleft stick, for to force him to renounce the title might cause such dismay amongst the States that it would be more trouble than it was worth.

Philip was appointed governor of Flushing. He had expected to be in the thick of the action, not sitting in a garrison, the morale of the poorly supplied troops getting lower and lower. Money was always a problem. Looking at it from their position then, it seemed as if the Queen was too parsimonious to pay her troops adequately. Philip feared that the men would mutiny, although he vowed that he never would waver from his original resolution. He held true to his vision of the great work. God's work he called it.

It was a hopeless situation, doomed from the moment Leicester made that initial mistake of over-reaching himself. His position was uncertain because he had gone against royal policy and the instructions sent to him afterwards were contrary to the expectations of the States and his own desire. The army suffered a series of dismal failures as the Duke of Parma's troops, some of the best in Europe, continued to gain ground.

Thomas realised now that they had been mistaken to blame the Queen. The campaign was costing the nation £126,000 a year and she knew she must keep some finance back to support the French Huguenots if necessary. There were two English armies in the Low Countries. The one not under Leicester's command was supposed to be paid by the Netherlands States, but they failed to do so. Wealthy Dutch merchants were selling supplies to allies and enemies alike at extortionate prices. Some of the troops were close to starvation, sullen and bedraggled.

Thomas suspected that there was much corruption in the army itself. When a captain raised a company to fight he was paid a sum of money to equip the troops and pay them a certain amount per day. Some were greedy and saw it as a way to get rich quick, buying inferior equipment and inadequate supplies, sending the men off to war in a poor state while they flaunted themselves in society on the proceeds. It was even suggested that the Earl of Leicester had indulged in this game, increasing his own pay and that of his officers to the detriment of the men at arms. Philip, who would never have done such a thing himself, would not believe it of his uncle, but Tom was not so sure.

They had chafed at the inactivity forced on them at Flushing. Philip believed that the way to victory would not be found in the Low Countries. The army must drive on into the very heart of Spain. It was his thirst for action that prompted him to join the fateful engagement at Zutphen.

To Thomas now, the campaign was a tragic farce, the only result of which was to persuade the King of Spain to launch his invasion of England at last and put the country in even greater danger.

He sat there with all these thoughts flooding through his mind, his attention momentarily diverted from Lizzie Norrington. Her large blue eyes were intent on his face.

"I lost two more good friends in that campaign," he murmured, "That is part of the reason I am trying to write about it. Philip will always be remembered and rightly too. Places of learning all over Europe have paid tribute to him and when his writings are printed, which I have every expectation they will be soon, his reputation will grow. But Harry and Joshua and others like them, who made what I now believe to be a pointless sacrifice, who will remember them? I have this perhaps foolish hope that in the future someone will read what I have written and spare a thought for them too. I bear no resentment against enemy soldiers. I killed several brave men at Zutphen, so I have been the cause of sorrow and loss amongst families in Spain. I hope perhaps someone will write about them also."

No man had ever spoken to Elizabeth with such emotional candour before. She had an overwhelming urge to touch him, but sat very still in her chair.

"I have Harry Carthew to thank for this house," he told her. "We were at Oxford together. He had bought this piece of forest and intended to build a house here as a refuge when the noise of London got too much for him. The ground had already been cleared in this area in preparation, just before he joined the Netherlands campaign. He had no family and he left it to me in his will. I decided to carry out what he had intended."

He gazed out of the window as a pale sun lit the back gardens.

"You may have heard that another expedition was sent to the Americas in 87. They intended to go back to Roanoke. John White, who was on our expedition, was to lead it and he sent word to me asking if I wished to join them. I had been wounded at Zutphen, not severely but I had suffered several bouts of fever since my return and was low in body and spirit. I could not face it. I did offer Waaseyaaban the chance to go back to her people. She would have taken what was left of my heart with her, but I felt that it was only fair. She refused. She told me I was her home. So we came here and I built this house instead, not single-handedly of course. She loves it here. She has given everything up for me. She has faced an alien environment, shared the discomforts of a war campaign; it is only right that I provide her with a home where she can be free to live a life as close as possible to the one she came from."

He stood up, banging the flat of his hand on the desk with a show of resolution.

"I fear I have bored you to your very soul with my melancholy ramblings Mistress Norrington."

"Oh no," Lizzie stood up also, "No indeed. I am honoured that you choose to

speak of things that mean so much to you. It is my experience that many men think women incapable of understanding weighty conversation."

"Then we men are very foolish. Where is that young brother of yours?"

"He was still asleep when I came down stairs. I think he had a restless night."

At that moment, as if on cue, James opened the door.

"Are you in there Lizzie?" he demanded, but stopped when he saw Sir Thomas. He dropped his gaze, ashamed to look in Tom's face.

"Good morning Master Norrington," Thomas said cheerfully. "Your sister was just telling me you did not sleep very well last night. I'm sorry to hear that. The thunder kept you awake no doubt."

"Yes it did sir," James muttered. He was relieved however that clearly Sir Thomas had not told Lizzie about his adventure the previous night.

"You must have something to eat before you leave." Thomas ushered them both out of the room. "Joan makes the most delicious savoury pancakes."

After breakfast James went down to the barn to roust out the servants. Jacob Whyte had everything in hand already, but he maintained the fiction that James was in charge of the party. Elizabeth asked Thomas if she might have the promised tour of the back garden. Dawn Light was standing in the kitchen doorway watching them talk. Lizzie was gazing up in to his face, hanging on his every word. Tom looked across at his wife, saying, "I am just going to show Mistress Norrington the results of your hard work and care."

A mischievous smile spread across Waaseyaaban's face. She puffed out her chest and flexed her biceps, emulating a masculine manner. Then she patted her husband's chest with the flat of her hand.

"Makwa," she said in a low but distinct voice, her teeth showing white in her tanned face and then she danced away into the kitchen laughing her guttural laugh before Tom could respond.

As they walked down the path, the flagstones glistening wet from the recent rain, Elizabeth asked, "What does that word mean Sir Thomas – Makwa?"

He gave her a self-conscious smile. "It is the word for bear in her language. Croatan men are very smooth skinned. They don't grow hair on their faces and bodies. When I first met Waaseyaaban my beard was more abundant than it is now," he ran his hand over his neatly trimmed beard, "And she was fascinated by my chest hair, so I became her bear and have been ever since."He was not sure that Elizabeth had understood the full implication of his wife's gesture and changed the subject before she had time to dwell on it, pointing out a fine bed of carrots and radishes. Elizabeth was impressed by the orderliness of the plots, each one surrounded by a path of tiles for easy accessibility.

"Croatan society is very orderly. Their chiefs are dictatorial and keep order ruthlessly. You should see how neat their villages are. They live in woven fibre houses with rounded roofs and their knowledge of husbandry is extensive. All their gardens are laid out in this regular pattern and contingents of men are assigned the task of scaring the birds away from the crops and seeds when newly planted. They dance around in a row or circle and sing –much more effective than a straw scarecrow- more entertaining too."

Lizzie laughed at the thought. "I should very much like to see that."

"They are called heathens by us, but they believe in a supreme being and life after death, with their own version of heaven and hell. They are a religious people. I think we make a grave mistake when we fancy ourselves far superior to them."

Elizabeth was sure this would be considered a dangerous opinion, one her father would disapprove of strongly.

"What plants are these?" she asked quickly in case he intended to enlarge on it. She pointed to a bed of tall plants with thick stems, feathery leaves and small cream-coloured flowers.

"Potatoes," he replied. "I brought some seeds back from Roanoke. We stayed with a friend near Oxford before we went to the Netherlands and I gave them to him. He grew them successfully and when we started work on the gardens here, he supplied me with some. They are easy to grow and are a substantial food- be a good addition to the diet of folk who struggle to feed their families sufficiently. I am trying to persuade Ned and Toby to grow them. Spread the idea around the village."

Lizzie wrinkled her nose. "I tried some once. We were visiting and the host served some as a novelty. I didn't like them. They were hard and tasteless."

"Ah, that's because the English do not know how to cook them properly. They boil them in their skins. If you wish to retain the skin you must roast them slowly and the skin will become crisp and the flesh inside soft, excellent topped with butter. Whereas, if you boil them you must first peel off the skin. You see, I even give lessons in cookery."

He flashed her a disarming smile. She had known him less than twenty four hours but already she was well versed in the range of his smiles. There was the one she had just enjoyed which lit up his face, but he also had a formal, courteous smile with his lips pressed close together. That one was enigmatic and did not reveal what he was thinking. She imagined that if he was angry a sardonic edge would creep into that smile. Perhaps the one she liked best was the slow, sensuous smile that began at the corners of his mouth and slowly widened, betraying his amusement or pleasure.

They walked to the end of the garden where soft fruit bushes grew, raspberry, gooseberry, red currant and blackberry. Beyond them, protected by a semi-circle of hawthorn and wild roses, were two small grave stones. He saw her looking at them and indicated that she could go closer if she wished. Engraved on each of them were one word and a date- Adjidamo January 1587 and Wawackechi March 1588. She looked up at him questioningly, but could not bring herself to ask. He touched the top of each stone.

"Our children. The boy Adjidamo was still born. Dawn Light called him her little squirrel, so that is his name. Our daughter lived for five days, so at least we had the joy of her company for a brief while. Wawackechi is a young deer, a fawn."

Lizzie's eyes filled with tears.

"The loss of children is a very common sorrow Mistress Norrington. You are very tender-hearted. The world is a hard place, but it would be even harder without those with a tender heart. Thank you for your compassion."

She knew now why there was often sadness in his eyes. He was estranged from his family, had lost close friends in circumstances that troubled his conscience and both his children had died.

A stray piece of hair had escaped from beneath her French hood. It was the current fashion for women to part their hair in the middle, plait it and pin it in a coronet around the head beneath the hood so that very little of it showed. The loose strands caught Tom's attention.

"Your hair is a very rare colour Mistress. It reminds me of ripened corn."

He said this so naturally, as if it had just occurred to him and Lizzie did not consider it too forward a comment. It was Tom himself who was aware that he had spoken without thinking. Down by the barn the Norrington's servants were leading out their horses.

"It seems your party is ready to leave. We had best join them. Sir Bartholomew's household will be anxious if you are very late arriving."

"He did not know on what exact day we were setting out, only that we should come this week."

"Then you could have met trouble on the way and he would not have sent anyone out to look for you." Thomas frowned at so casual an arrangement.

"To be frank, I was surprised that Anthony Hanham did not take the trouble to escort you to your future home himself."

Elizabeth flushed at the criticism in his voice. She had thought the very same thing when she first heard they were travelling without any escort from the Hanham household, but she did not want Sir Thomas to perceive her doubts and defended her fiancé.

"Anthony has many business interests in London. I believe he was called away to deal with them."

Thomas did not comment further. He intended to set the travellers on the path to Westbury. The road from that town to Frome was a direct one. Jacob Whyte watched Tom lead his powerful chestnut stallion out of the barn. The steward was a good judge of a horse and admired this one.

"That is a magnificent animal Sir Thomas. I could not prevent myself from studying it in the barn- such power and grace."

"Thank you. He has a good lineage. He is young and rather fiery as yet, but we get on well together. I call him Hope, for it is something we all have a need to hang on to."

Mark Wheeler, quick to comprehend the pun, let out a yelp of laughter.

Jacob frowned at him and the Smith twins stared in puzzlement ignorant of the joke.

"Ox brains," he mouthed at them wordlessly.

Thomas had just mounted when Dawn Light came out of the house. She was dressed in her sleeveless smock again, unadorned except for the turquoise pendant and earrings made of copper disks. Jacob had warned the servants that this was a strange household, but they must give Sir Thomas due respect. They had spent most of their stay lolling around in the barn, playing dice and stuffing their faces with the excellent food Joan brought them. Dawn Light had kept well clear of them. This was their first sighting of her. James turned away, Jacob's face was impassive, but the others goggled openly.

"I come with you."

She held out her hand to Mountfield and he swung her up on to the saddle in front of him. Mark Wheeler ran his tongue over his dry lips as he watched her garment ride up over her thigh.

It took less than an hour to lead them by various paths on to the main road way. Jacob Whyte recognised the territory now and was confident that the rest of their journey would run smoothly. He thanked Sir Thomas, so did Elizabeth. James felt that was thanks enough. He did not want to speak in case it drew him to Dawn Light's attention. She may not be a witch, but he was still uncomfortable in her presence.

"We wish you a happy future as a married woman Mistress Norrington," Thomas said. "Young Hanham is a fortunate man. I hope he will come to appreciate the fact."

As they set off on the Westbury Road, Elizabeth wanted to turn and get a last look at him, but the servants were riding a little way behind her and her view was blocked by the combined bulk of the Smith twins.

"He was flirting with you," James accused.

"He was not. He was just being courteous. Gentlemen are supposed to flatter ladies."

Jacob pretended that he had not heard James' remark although it was loud enough for the rear guard to hear. Giles and Peter grinned at each other. Mark Wheeler was still dwelling on Dawn Light's legs.

"I bet that Sir Thomas has had a few women in his time," he conjectured with some admiration in his voice. "He has that air about him. I wouldn't mind a turn with that whore of his myself. Did you see her legs? God's death, I reckon she's a hot one between the sheets."

The Smiths sighed in unison.

"That's all you ever think about poxy," Giles rumbled.

"Well at least I have the capacity to think," Mark shot back at him.

Tom and his wife watched the riders until they had rounded the bend and disappeared from view.

"Pretty girl," Dawn Light said. "You want to bed her?"

There was no indication in her voice that an answer in the affirmative would distress her- quite the opposite.

"You would not care if I did would you?" he replied, laughing.

"No. Only the heart matters and your heart is mine."

"True enough. She is almost a child still. I just pray that life does not disappoint her too much."

"She is no longer child. She want you. I see her eyes. I see her heart beat in her breast- like this- boom, boom, boom."

"Behave yourself, you wanton woman." He kissed her neck. Laughing, she sprang off the horse and began to run, calling out, "Catch me Makwa, catch me."She was lithe and athletic, covering the ground at great speed. He let her get a decent start and then urged his horse after her. When he was level, he leaned out of the saddle, grabbed her around the waist and swung her back on to the horse, threatening to hang her upside down. He could not help reflecting as they rode home that Elizabeth Norrington would not find much to laugh about at Hanham House.

Chapter Two

SIR NEVILLE NORRINGTON WAS right about the cutlery at Hanham House. It was silver. Every utensil on the dining table was wrought of high grade silver, knives, forks, spoons, goblets, plates, salvers, even the finger bowls. Both the interior and the exterior of the house had a showy opulence that spoke of an owner who had climbed the social ladder and wished everyone to know it. His mother's noble lineage entitled Bartholomew Hanham to a coat of arms from the College of Heralds and a huge version of it was emblazoned over the main entrance to the house with a smaller one above the fireplace here in the dining room.

James Norrington contemplated it with pleasure. Hanham House lived up to his expectations in every part. He was proud of his own home, Norrington Hall, but it was a much older building, built in a previous century when defence was still thought essential. It was surrounded by a high wall and based around a central hall facing the main gatehouse, with smaller wings opposite each other across the courtyard. His grandfather had begun to extend it and his father had made further additions, re-siting the wall at the back of the house to make room for a garden.

Hanham House on the other hand was only ten years old. It had a long, symmetrical frontage, with a wealth of windows that blazed in the sunlight. Facing west, a red sunset reflected in those windows made it seem as if the house was on fire. Built of finely dressed ashlar, the exterior incorporated some of the classical details fashionable on the continent. Each corner of the house was rounded like a tower, with angled bay windows. The gable above the central entrance was fashioned in the curved Dutch style and topped by an elaborate finial.

It differed from Norrington Hall in another way. The older building was an integral part of the village of Norrington, standing close to the church.

Hanham House was set apart in its own park land, approached along a drive lined with elm trees. This reflected the growing philosophy amongst the wealthier gentry that their elite position entitled them to as much privacy as the nobility. It underlined their status. Sir Bartholomew had engaged the master mason Robert Smythson, perhaps the finest craftsman in the country, to design and build his new house. The cost was enormous; he used up all the money his mother had left him in her will, but for him the result was well worth it.

James was in his element and Lizzie had grown rather weary of his pointing out every opulent feature of the house with such enthusiasm. Sir Bartholomew and his wife had greeted them with great courtesy and Lady Agnes was kindness itself when showing her the apartments made ready for her future niece-in-law, but Elizabeth could not rid herself of the disappointment she felt because Anthony Hanham was not there. The fiction she had invented to excuse his failure to escort her from Norrington Hall had turned out to be a reality. He was away on important business. She had hoped that receiving his future wife might take precedence. Surely he could have stayed at home this week, knowing that she was coming. She tried to convince herself that she was expecting too much and she should be grateful to be welcomed into such a distinguished family, but she remembered the concerned expression in Thomas Mountfield's eyes at Anthony's lack of gallantry. If he had been in Anthony's place, he would have come to fetch her, she was sure.

She had not mentioned their adventure in the forest and neither had James, fearing it would cast doubt on his leadership skills. Sir Bartholomew had learned of it from Jacob Whyte. The steward was an honest man and should the Norrington children mention it, his silence might suggest he was trying to disguise his own lack of judgement in deciding to take the path through the forest. He was not a man to dodge responsibility.

Hanham was holding forth on the matter as he leaned back in his chair, replete with generous helpings from a four course meal.

"Of course we must be grateful to young Mountfield for offering you hospitality, but it is best not to mention to others that you have stayed in that house. He has put himself outside polite society with his radical ideas and way of life."

"Respectable people don't visit that household," Lady Agnes confirmed, spreading her hands, palms outwards, to emphasize the impossibility of it, "I mean, how can they?"

James gave his sister a triumphant look, but Lizzie would not let Sir Thomas go undefended.

"Sir Thomas was very courteous and kind to us during our stay," she declared. "He behaved most properly."

"Well I am pleased to hear that he can still behave like a gentleman when the circumstances demand it. However, you must have no more contact with him."

Elizabeth was not sure which hurt most, the thought that Anthony did not care enough to be present to greet her or that she might never see Tom Mountfield again. At that moment she knew she would rather be in his quirky house with its modest beauty, than in this place with its pretentions to be a palace.

James was saying, "He does not always dress like a gentleman and he boasted to Elizabeth that he was a friend of Sir Philip Sidney's. I didn't believe it for a moment. "

When Lizzie, knowing that Sidney was a great hero to James, told him about Thomas' relationship with the nation's shining example of chivalry, she hoped to make her brother see Mountfield in a more sympathetic light. He was convinced however that it was a fiction to impress her. He wondered how long she had been alone in the library with him and what else he had said.

"Oh no, my boy," Bartholomew contradicted to James' surprise, "He may act waywardly, but he is not a liar or a boaster. That is what makes his behaviour so puzzling. He has connections with some very important people. He was a close friend of Sir Philip's- was with him in the chamber when he died at Arnhem. When he came back from the Low Countries he was summoned to the Queen's presence and she knighted him in person as a reward for his friendship to Sir Philip and his services to the country. Great men like Walter Raleigh and Francis Drake speak well of him. He could be a favourite at court. He is a handsome, well-set fellow. The Queen has always had an eye for a good-looking man. But what does he do? Shut himself away in the middle of a forest with a ---"

He was about to say heathen whore, but thought better of it in front of Elizabeth and Lady Agnes stepped in with, " Such a shame. Such a waste. It has broken his poor father's heart you know."

Elizabeth knew that it had not left Thomas unscathed.

Hanham continued,

"I was talking to his father only a few months ago, when we were on the circuit together. The subject of Thomas came up and he unburdened himself to me. The boy's behaviour has caused him much grief. He is his only son after all- his heir. Started off so well too. Robert told me Thomas did well at Oxford- studied Greek, Latin, even Hebrew. He sent him to the Inns of Court afterwards just to pick up a bit of law to stand him in good stead in the future, but it was too dull for him. He craved some adventure, which is normal in an active young man. Robert said he was far from disappointed to see a son of his enter Sir Philip Sidney's household. He accompanied Sir Philip on an embassy to the courts of the German Emperor and the Elector Palatine once and Sidney entertained princes and ambassadors in his house here in England. No doubt that is where Sir Thomas picked up his skill with languages. According to his father he speaks good French, Italian, Spanish and Flemish."

Elizabeth felt like adding "And Croatan," but decided that it would not be appreciated. She watched Lady Agnes shaking her head gravely at the tragedy of it all, in full agreement with her husband, who continued,

"Robert was less delighted with that trip to the Americas- couldn't understand why he should put himself in such danger when he was so well placed with Sidney."

"Sir Philip encouraged him to go on his behalf," Lizzie explained.

"He told you that did he?"

"Yes. He is writing an account of his travels there and also about the campaign in the Low Countries."

"Is he indeed?" Hanham raised his eyebrows at the positiveness of her assertion, "Well that will afford little comfort to his father. Robert confessed to me that he and his wife were full of relief when he came home safe the year after, hoping he would settle down, but far from it. He brought that native woman home with him, insisting that she was his wife and expecting his parents to accept her. They quarrelled and he went off to fight in the Netherlands barely two weeks after he had arrived back from the Americas. When he returned and was so highly honoured by Her Majesty, Robert hoped the boy might suffer a change of heart. He had his eye on a fine young widow who would have made Thomas an excellent wife. He is a broad-minded man. He would have overlooked Thomas keeping the native woman in the household as a mistress if he really desired it, but the boy was stubborn. Insisted the woman was his wife."

"But she is," Lizzie could not prevent herself from interrupting. "They were married before they left the Americas."

"By a Christian minister, in a proper ceremony?"

"No, in the custom of her own people."

"Exactly- no true marriage at all. Sir Robert is not an unreasonable man. Seeing his son would not be shifted, he agreed that if the woman would convert to Christianity and they would marry in church and he would teach her to dress and behave like a respectable English woman, she might be accepted in the house."

"Threw it back in his face," Lady Agnes joined in, waving her hands dramatically, the gems in her rings flashing, "Did he not Bartholomew?"

"Indeed he did my dear. Told his father she was not a dog to be led about on a leash until she learned obedience- that she had a right to her own customs and freedom of dress. He declared that if Sir Robert would not accept her into the household as she was, then he did not feel he was welcome either and has not been over the threshold since."

"I have wondered," Agnes murmured to Elizabeth, laying a hand on the girl's arm in a confidential manner, "If some fever he picked up abroad has turned his brain or if this creature has cast some spell over him. We have no idea what powers these foreign heathens possess do we, what devilry they can command."

Elizabeth itched to tell them what she really thought, but knew it would be ill-mannered to argue too strongly in her circumstances. She expected James to agree with Lady Agnes, but he kept quiet. He would have done so before his experience of the previous night. Now he had an image in his mind of Waaseyaaban's perfect body and remembered that Sir Thomas had acted honourably by not exposing his behaviour to Elizabeth. He felt ashamed. He did not want to, but the feeling came unbidden, especially as he had been so convinced that Mountfield's claim to be a friend of Philip Sidney's was just bragging and now he knew he was wrong about that too. Never-the-less, that night he felt safe enough to undress and get inside the bed covers. He slept well. It was Elizabeth who had a restless night.

Two days went by before Anthony Hanham returned to the house. Elizabeth was sitting in the garden watching a gardener clip the box hedges into shape. The garden was a formal one, similar in design to their own at Norrington Hall, but much larger. It was elegant and there was a fine rose arbour.

Despite Lady Hanham's careful attention Lizzie felt lonely and out of place, missing the familiarity and security of her own room at home.

Jacob Whyte and the servants had set off for Norrington Hall the day before and she so wished to go with them. She rebuked herself for such childish feelings. She closed her eyes, listening to the drone of a bee nearby, but her contemplation was interrupted by James running across to her, calling, "Anthony's back Lizzie. He's in the parlour."

She jumped up, straightening her bodice and smoothing down her skirts before hurrying across the lawn. She wanted to run, but checked herself. It would not be a good beginning to be out of breath and flustered when she met him. She was certain an appearance of lady-like self-possession would impress her future husband.

Anthony Hanham was lounging in a chair when she entered. He had thrown his cloak and riding gloves down on the floor.

"Ah Elizabeth." He stood up with a languid grace and bowed. Then she noticed that Sir Bartholomew and Lady Agnes were also in the room.

"You look charming," Anthony continued in an affected drawl. "Did you choose that garment or is it my Aunt's taste?"

"I did."

"Good, that promises well."

Anthony Hanham looked nothing like his uncle. Sir Bartholomew was a man of middle height, who had been muscular and athletic when younger, but was now running to fat. His increasing girth bulged beneath his doublet. He had a rosy face with an amiable expression tinged with self-satisfaction. His nephew was also of middle height, but very slender with a long neck. The large eyes in his pale face were light grey and his hair silvery blond. A cursory glance gave the impression of angelic beauty, but there was a look of bored insolence in those eyes that did not accord well with angels.

James was standing beside Bartholomew, who taking the boy by the shoulders, pushed him forward to meet his nephew. He was about to make an introduction when Anthony demanded, "Who is that?"

Encouraged by Bartholomew to speak up, James replied, "I am James Norrington, Master Hanham, Elizabeth's brother."

"Oh- why have you not returned home?"

"Don't you remember?" Lady Agnes prompted, "We discussed it with Sir Neville and agreed that James could join our household."

"Did we? Must have forgotten. Well I suppose he can stay until after the wedding, as long as he doesn't trail around behind me getting under my feet and pestering his sister."

James looked crest-fallen. Agnes was about to say something when Anthony cut across her, quite rudely Lizzie thought.

"Where's Goodship? I need him to take a message for me."

His uncle was not sure where Goodship might be at that moment. Anthony gave a tired sigh. "Never mind. I will find him myself. I suppose my

Aunt and Uncle have already showed you around the house Elizabeth?"

She nodded.

"Good, that will save me the bother. Such a tedious business, describing everything. I will see you later." He strolled out of the room, his walk as affected as his accent.

Anthony was the son of Bartholomew's elder brother. Both his parents died young. The Hanham's had no children of their own and welcomed him into their house. They spoiled him outrageously, giving in to his every whim, so that he had grown up believing that there was no right opinion but his own and that his every desire should be satisfied. He wanted a beautiful young wife, a virgin, not a widow who had been soiled already. She must be exclusively his property. His uncle had found him what he wanted. He was pleased with Elizabeth's beauty and she seemed demure enough. At that moment his mind was on other things. He would begin the process of wooing her later.

Lady Agnes could see that both the Norringtons were unhappy with her nephew's manner.

"Anthony is tired after his journey from London. He has so many business interests to attend to that it makes him forgetful of other things. He is perfectly at ease with you staying here James. Don't mark what he said. He meant nothing by it."

"What kind of business is he occupied in?" Lizzie asked.

"Oh, he has so many irons in the fire, I get confused," Agnes replied.

In fact she had no idea what Anthony did in London. She was only aware that it appeared to be very lucrative. "But you need not worry your head about that my dear child. He will not bother you with business talk."

"But I should like to be of use to him, help him with his business if I can."

"A wife should never interfere in business matters." Sir Bartholomew was dogmatic in his opinion on that. "Besides you will be too concerned with being a mother before long."

Elizabeth was much encouraged when Anthony came to her later that day. He was more attentive, complimented her father and seemed more relaxed. He promenaded around the garden with her on his arm, asking about her likes and dislikes.

He talked about Sir Bartholomew's town house in Frome and promised to take her there the next day. He spoke of a jewellery maker in town where she must choose some finery to wear for the wedding. He even apologised for the way he had spoken to James.

"I have remembered since that we had agreed the boy should join our household. He is welcome of course, although it is only right that he should visit his father regularly. Perhaps half the year in each household would suit."

On the whole he was very agreeable. Lizzie wished that he would speak less artificially and was troubled by the fact that when he smiled the warmth did not show in his eyes. However, she assumed that there were faults in her that he must bear with equally.

She enjoyed the visit to the town house and that afternoon when the fabrics were delivered from which she must choose material for her wedding clothes, she felt excited. Lady Agnes had laid out sample bolts of material on Lizzie's bed. The silk, satin and velvet were such a pleasure to touch, the texture soft and sensuous. She wondered what Dawn Light had worn when she and Thomas had married on that island, countless miles across the ocean. She imagined her dressed as she had been when she joined them at dinner, but wearing a garment made out of deer skin instead of broad cloth.

Agnes Hanham was saying, "The choice is yours Elizabeth of course, but I hope you will take some advice from me. I think white satin would be best for your kirtle- plain satin- looks so virginal, but you will also need some colour- a jewelled bodice perhaps and a gown of gold or silver brocade. You are such a pretty girl, you will look well in anything."

Agnes had told her she was pretty several times a day since she had arrived. It was flattering at first but now Lizzie was vaguely irritated by it. In the back of her mind was the thought that if she had been plain she would not have received such kindness; in fact she would not have been there at all. She did not want to be regarded simply as a pretty little ornament to set off a handsome husband. She hoped Anthony would engage in proper conversation with her on a range of topics, not assume that she was interested in domestic details only. She could not forget the frank, earnest way Sir Thomas had spoken to her in his library, never patronising her. Eventually she allowed Agnes' enthusiasm for the wedding garments to draw her in too and began to look forward to her wedding day.

Tom Mountfield lay along a bench at the bay window of the White Swan tavern in Frome that projected out over the street, his back against one wall and his feet pressed into the opposite wall. The image of the swan on the inn sign was crudely painted. The sign was swinging in the light breeze, making a creaking noise reminiscent of a gibbet. Tom was watching the people below making their way to the outskirts of the town for the September fair. It was interesting to view them from above, a different perspective. They made a moving pattern in the street. Thomas noticed one man, a fellow in a green jerkin, weaving between the groups of pedestrians in an odd manner. His behaviour was more evident from above than it would have been at street level. When he came up directly behind an elderly man walking with four girls, Tom saw the glint of a knife and realised that the man in the jerkin was about to slit the cord that attached his purse to the belt of the greybeard.

Thomas leaned forward, opened the casement and called out loudly,

"Have a care for your purse friend! Green jerkin-right behind you."

Several folk turned round, including the old man, who brandished his walking stick with impressive menace. The thief backed off. Looking up at the window he glared at Thomas and snarled between his teeth, "Interfering bastard," before he fled down the nearest alley way.

The man whose purse had been saved waved an acknowledgement to Tom with his stick and ushered the girls, probably his grand-daughters, on down the road.

"Cut purses, pick pockets, cozeners and cheap jacks will all be out in force today," Tom said to his companion. "They know that even the poorest folk will have a few pennies on them at the fair."

He intended to leave the window open, but a foul smell rose up from below. The gutter at the side of the tavern was running with effluent.

"Jesu, what a stink!" He shut the window abruptly.

Simon Bailey adjusted the round, steel-rimmed glasses perched on the bridge of his broad nose and grinned at Tom.

"The landlord says the drain round the side is blocked up, offal from the shambles."

Simon's voice was loud and definite with a pronounced North Country accent.

"Perhaps you could have found a better Inn for a lodging," Tom suggested.

There was a musty smell in the room. The walls looked damp, grey mould forming around some of the cracks in the plaster and the bed linen was grubby. When he had first walked into the room, the door handle had come away in his hand."I can't afford to be profligate with money, not with four children growing like bean stalks."

"Especially when half your clients don't pay what they owe you."

There were plenty of shady lawyers, greedy men who were interested only in making money with little regard for the law. Thomas was proud that his friend Simon was not one of them. Bailey was as straight as a dye; as open and honest as his Yorkshire voice. He was ever willing to take on cases on behalf of the poor. He felt it was his duty as a Christian.

"Well, that's because half of them haven't got two farthings to rub together as you well know. How can I demand money from people who can scarce feed themselves? Somebody has to defend their rights. If you had taken up law instead of gallivanting about with Philip Sidney and sailing off to the Americas, you would have been just as bad as me. Worse I reckon."

Thomas laughed. "Yes, no doubt I would. So it is fortunate that I did not take up law or I would be begging in the streets by now."

"When did you last come up to London?" Simon asked.

The table in front of him, which wobbled when any pressure was put on it, was spread with documents that he had been studying. Thomas considered for a moment.

"It must have been Accession Day 1586 – nearly three years."

"Do you not miss the liveliness of the place, the gossip, the feeling that something momentous is just around the corner?"

Tom stood up, picking up the door handle from the chair into which he had tossed it previously. He inspected it to see if it could be fixed back on.

"I'll tell you what I do not miss Simon- the stench, the dead dogs floating down the Thames, yelling myself hoarse for boatmen at Temple Stairs because they ignore you and head for the more richly caparisoned; those rotting tenements which are not fit for animals let alone humans, children left to die in the street, kicked out of the way without a shred of compassion. London may be the heart of the nation, but part of that heart is diseased."

"Ay, I can't deny that, but there is crushing poverty in the countryside too. That is why so many country folk are emigrating into the towns- London in particular- hoping for something better."

"A false hope I fear. I admire your courage my friend. You live amongst them and strive to help them, while I hide away in my forest. I have little to offer at present. I am tired in mind and spirit."

Bailey was gazing at his friend over the top of his spectacles, his short-sighted hazel eyes sympathetic.

"That will pass. You are a strong-hearted, talented man. God has plenty of work for you to do yet. When you have finished those writings of yours, you will come up refreshed and ready to take up the struggle again."

Mountfield smiled wistfully. For a man who dealt daily with the convolutions and knotty problems of the legal system, Simon Bailey saw life in very simple terms, the struggle between good and evil. He believed that everything he did must reflect the goodness of God. His Protestantism had moved to the more extreme side over the years with a Puritan emphasis on the division between the godly and the ungodly. In a corrupt and unregenerate world men must trust in the transformative power of God's word and launch a campaign against Anti-Christ and sin.

"Although I have little desire for London," Tom reflected, "I would like to see my friends more often- you included. Are you sure that you cannot come home with me today and stay the night?"

Simon shook his head, waving a hand at the wealth of papers in front of him.

"I wish I could. Nothing would please me better than to be plied with tasty food and fussed over by Joan Bushy, but I have to see my client again this afternoon and get back to London tomorrow to prepare the case. I am also acting for someone in a case coming before the Court of Pleas next week, so I have to prepare the details to give to the Sergeant who is doing the pleading. Then I've two criminal cases at the Old Bailey the following week."

"Well at least you are not lacking work."

"Grateful for it too. We truly did intend to come to you at Christmas, but the snow was impassable. The children love coming to your house and running around in the forest with those wolfhounds of yours. My eldest reckons his ambition is to out-run Dawn Light one day."

Waaseyaaban had soon formed a bond with Simon Bailey's children. She was at ease with their natural reactions and enjoyed showing them the secret hideouts of the forest creatures. Simon's wife however was wary. She tolerated Dawn Light's differentness, but made no attempt at friendship. Bailey said that although his Ellen had many qualities, imagination was not one of them and Tom should not worry about it. Thomas knew he was too sensitive about reactions to Dawn Light, but it never ceased to sting him.

"What's that hubbub?" Simon went to the window and looked down. A crowd of men were jostling and arguing, the air thick with oaths. A woman on the periphery of the fray was screeching in a pitch that hurt the ear.

"All that profanity and violence in front of young children," Bailey shook his head. "That's the trouble with fairs and festivals- too much drink flowing, too much sin comes to the surface."

"But there is pleasure and innocent enjoyment too, especially for the labouring folk," Tom defended. "They have little variety in their lives. The pageant today will be very unsophisticated but they rarely get the chance to see something like that. I have never felt that the policy of suppressing community gatherings in the name of godliness and good order was the right one. I mean, how many riots have grown out of the May games, Morris dances or the Plough Monday festivals? Stamping on what little joy they can create for themselves will only make people more sullen. It's no wonder the authorities have met with limited success in carrying it out. Do you truly believe Simon that God is offended by dancing and football?"

"Nay, you know me better than that. I have always enjoyed a game of football, though I have no skill in dancing. I trip over my own great feet. I leave dancing to elegant fellows like you. Hey, do you remember that football game we used to play at the end of the Michaelmas term? How the lawyers used to strip off their black robes and join in with us students; thirty or forty of us, all banging around the Temple Gardens, fighting for the ball."

He put his arm around Tom's shoulder and hugged him, the memory of it all filling him with affection.

"How can I forget? We always went back to our lodgings with black eyes, bruised ribs and bloody knees."

Tom recalled that he was knocked insensible on one occasion and woke up in the back of an apothecary's shop, surrounded by sinister looking jars of coloured liquids. It was fully five minutes before he could remember who he was, let alone where he was.

"It has been forbidden now," Simon said. "There was a fear that with all the tension caused by the Spanish invasion that the apprentices might join in and it would turn into a vicious brawl. A good thing perhaps- it was rough enough even in fun."

Thomas had met Simon Bailey on the first day of his arrival at the Middle Temple. They shared lodgings and Tom took to the forthright Yorkshire man immediately. Bailey's father was a Pontefract merchant whose growing prosperity enabled him to send his son to study law. He was three years older than Tom and lacked Mountfield's background of academic study, but he had a quick mind, a sympathetic understanding of his fellow human beings and a passion for justice. He was single minded in his intention to become a lawyer. Thomas was never sure that he wanted to be studying at the Middle Temple.

He had loved life at Oxford, but beside the scholarly part of his nature there lived a desire for adventure.

He had always reacted against rigid social constrictions and there were too many artificial formalities in legal studies for his temperament.

Towards the end of his first year at Christchurch College Oxford, Tom had seen Philip Sidney for the first time. The high born Sidney, nephew of three such great nobleman as the Duke of Northumberland and the Earls of Warwick and Leicester, had completed his studies the previous year, but he returned to his old college to take part in a debate on the art of poetry. Thomas was impressed by his ardour and the breadth of his learning. He had never heard anyone expound such a consistent theory concerning the value of poetry. He did not agree with every point Philip made, but the idea that man's undisciplined passions could be persuaded to virtue and noble purposes by poetry appealed to the romantic streak in his nature. Sidney was affirming Tom's belief that an idea could be as important as reality, that literature of the imagination had a social value.

He joined in the debate with enthusiasm and afterwards Philip had talked to him about his intention to expand his theories on poetry and write them down. He also revealed that he was about to embark on a tour of Europe to improve his language skills and broaden his knowledge of European politics. Even then, at the tender age of eighteen, Sidney had the dream of a united European Christian republic. He had a fervent hatred of the corruption of the papacy.

How Thomas had wished that he too might travel in Europe. The memory of that day remained embedded in his consciousness and when a few years later he became so bored with his law studies that he could bear it no longer, he took the bold step of writing to Philip, asking to join his household. He could hardly believe it when his request was accepted. His only regret at leaving the Temple was parting from his friends, particularly Simon Bailey. The day he left they had embraced warmly and Simon promised to remember him every day in his prayers.

Bailey had always displayed an active, natural faith. His family came from a part of the country where Catholicism still had many adherents, but the Bailey's were staunch Protestants. Simon had an inclination for reform even then, but it was not extreme. In recent years he had become involved with a group whose views were more radical and they had a strong influence on him. Some of this group were Presbyterians and had supported a Bill brought before Parliament two years past, recommending the abolition of bishops and the reorganisation of the church as a presbytery with ministers elected by the congregation.

The Queen vetoed the Bill, but it made the Archbishop of Canterbury, John Whitgift more determined to root out puritanical views. He mounted an attack on what he termed the disorders in the church in an attempt to enforce conformity. Tom feared that his old friend was standing on dangerous ground.

"What grieves me," Simon was saying, "Is the growing disrespect for the Sabbath. Sports and dancing are well enough at an appropriate time and place, but I have seen groups of youths playing football in the churchyard on a Sunday while a service is in progress. Instead of setting an example, you find their fathers in the taverns gambling with dice and staging cock fights."

He had taken off his glasses and was pacing the room, running his hand through his thinning sandy hair. He always paced around when he was agitated as if he needed to reinforce his opinions with his own heavy tread.

"The Church needs to take this in hand. The Church of England is a weak compromise Thomas. Too many vestiges of papist flummery remain."

He picked up his spectacles and jammed them back on his nose with emphasis. Tom had returned to the window seat but with his back to the window. He felt Simon's view was too simplistic.

"Compromise was needed when Elizabeth came to the throne. I have studied the history of this in great detail. You know as well as I do that the country had barely come to terms with the reforms promulgated by King Edward's advisors when Mary came to the throne and in the twinkling of an eye everyone was expected to pay deference to Rome again. Instead of people being persecuted for loyalty to the old religion, steadfast Protestants went to the fire for their beliefs. Ordinary folk must have been bewildered, not knowing where they would be facing when the world stopped turning. What was needed was a settlement that made the church's autonomy from Rome clear, but did not alienate traditionalists with extreme measures. A reformer's crusade then would have been fatal. It was necessary to establish a balance. Of course it has faults, all compromises do, but by and large it has worked."

Simon sat down beside Tom and took hold of both his hands. He looked directly into his friend's eyes, the sunlight through the window glinting on his spectacles.

"Thomas, that was thirty years ago. Granted it may have been needed then, but advances in reform should be well underway by now, all that other stuff swept away. 'Behold I make all things new.' Worship should be as close as possible to the first apostolic form of worship.

The basis of the church should be the word of God as revealed to us in the Bible and that word should be spread by preaching. I was encouraged for a while when it looked as if there would be an effort to license ministers and educate them to preach proper sermons, but it hasn't been carried through. Half the licensed preachers rely on books of piddling little homilies that they read out. That's not preaching."

Tom could not help smiling at his disgust for homilies. He wondered why Simon could never see the other side of the coin. Poorly educated folk often found it hard to follow a long, learned sermon. The colour of elaborate ceremonial caught their attention and he could see how it could create a sense of awe that might elevate thoughts towards God. Many of the labouring people led dreary, colourless lives and beauty in a church, stained glass, rich fabrics, murals on the walls, could help to inspire reverence. Only the literate could read the Bible for themselves. The stories told in stained glass and painted murals could be understood by the illiterate. Ironically perhaps the stripping away of rituals, belief in the power of saints and relics and the loss of the quasi- mystical relationship between priests and God, lessened some people's respect for the church, making it seem too ordinary and was partly responsible for the increase in irreverent behaviour. Tom knew he would never be able to get Simon to concede that.

"We must drive reform on from below," Bailey was saying, "As those above have failed us. Whitgift is too intent on persecuting his own brethren. Her Majesty says she would meddle with no man's conscience, but the policy of her church meddles with mine. She has taken Whitgift into the Privy Council, which proves she supports his attempt to root out reformers."

"You have no objection to his rooting out Catholics though do you?" Tom replied with a wry smile.

"What sort of question is that? The papists endanger the country with their plots against the Queen and their support for foreign invasions. They must be rooted out."

Thomas shook his head, trying to find the right way to explain his point of view.

"I have no desire to be under the heel of Spain believe me. I was quick to turn out with the militia last summer, but those Catholics who plot against the Queen, they commit treason. Their crime is political, not religious. There are plenty of Catholics in England who are fiercely loyal to the Queen, but in your eyes they are still guilty of a crime because to you their religious beliefs are a crime."

Simon started to protest, but Tom held up his hand. "No, hear me out. I believe in complete freedom of conscience and worship. I know that in our world it is not possible to disentangle politics and religion. Yet in an ideal world that is how it should be. A government's policy should be founded on sound Christian principles- yes and an individual should lead his life in accordance with his faith, but diplomatic relations with other countries should have a secular base, not clouded by religious differences. Then there would be no fear about freedom of conscience."

Thomas was well aware that rulers would still covet the territory of other nations and conflicts would continue, but they would not be complicated by religious zeal, either real or feigned.

"How often do you attend church now?" Simon asked.

"Just enough to keep my name off the absentee register."

"That's a cynical thing to say Tom." Simon looked hurt.

"I'm sorry. I should not have put it that way. I attend once or twice a month. Sometimes I feel the need to worship with others, but more often I sense the presence of God more readily out in the forest. Waaseyaaban believes in a supreme being. She may call it by a different name and look at it from a different angle, but in my mind it is still the same God. I have told her the history of Christianity and stories from the Bible, which she enjoys, but I feel no need to force her to become a Christian."

Simon squeezed his shoulder and let his big hand rest there.

"You must take care Thomas. Such thinking may lead you into atheism."

He looked so concerned. Tom sighed.

"Oh why do you reformers always equate a belief in freedom of conscience and worship with anarchy and atheism? I assure you that I still believe, although my faith has been sorely tried at times and as I grow older, I become less sure of God's purposes. But I must believe or the world would seem a bleak place indeed."

There was silence for a moment, then he added with resolution,

"I didn't come here for a theological debate. Let's talk about something else. What gossip have you to tell me about the all-powerful ones at court? Lincoln's Inn was always a hub of gossip. You lawyers are the worst tittle-tattlers in the world."

For all his earnestness, Simon was also relieved to change the subject.

"Well, Raleigh still appears to be top favourite although his rivalry with Essex is stepping up a notch or two."

"Devereux still preening himself then?" Thomas pronounced the word Devereux with a curl of the lip that did not suggest admiration. "He and Sir Walter have moved on from trying to out-do and insult one another with verses. They are at war using paintings now."

"What!"

"At the end of last year Raleigh had his portrait painted. A colleague of mine knows the artist and saw the painting in his workshop. Walter's posed nobly dressed in black and white- constancy and purity- the Queen's colours. The whole picture is stuffed with symbols. He's wearing a pearl earring, the Queen's favourite jewel and over his motto, Amor et Virtute, there is a crescent moon painted."

"Oh very clever, Tom exclaimed with a grin, "Devotion to Cynthia the moon Goddess, who of course is really the Queen. The moon waxes and wanes but is always the same, always beautiful."

"Not to be outfaced, my Lord of Essex has had his picture painted too, also dressed in black and white, but leaning poetically against a tree entwined in eglantine. His motto is Dat Poenas Laudata Fides."

Mountfield laughed. "My praised faithfulness causes my suffering" Declaring his painful devotion to the Queen and showing off his classical learning at the same time. That phrase was originally associated with Pompey."

Walter Raleigh had always been ambitious. He was proud with more than a touch of vanity, but Tom would trust him over Robert Devereux any day.

"Had you heard that Essex is paying court to Sidney's widow?"

"Is he? Well, Philip did bequeath her to him. That may explain why she has not written to me for months. She was wont to send a letter now and then to tell me the progress of their daughter, but if she intends to accept Devereux she may think I will disapprove. It is no business of mine who Frances marries, but I would wish little Elizabeth a more stable step-father."

"You really don't like him do you?"

"He aspires to take on Philip's mantle, to be seen as the next great Protestant champion. Military glory is the only true path for an aristocrat to show his nobility. Take it to the Spaniards and hang the consequences."

"But is that not what Sir Philip thought too? Protestantism needs a champion. Surely he is made of the same heroic mould."

Thomas snorted scornfully. "Robert Devereux is not worthy of being mentioned in the same breath as Philip. Philip had a genuine humility, a grace of spirit. He sought glory not for himself, but for God and his country. Essex wants it only for himself, although he may have persuaded himself into believing it is for something nobler. He is petulant, arrogant, jealous- he can't bear to share pre-eminence with anyone."

Simon thought he had finished and was about to comment when Tom continued, "What really angers me is that he is forever swearing his devotion to the Queen, fawning around her to lend him money to fund his extravagance, but deep down he despises her, sees her just as an ageing, parsimonious woman, who is incapable of understanding the heroic need for martial glory and fumes because he has to bow to her will. That woman has more moral courage than he will ever have and she has the measure of him."

"But they say she dotes on him."

"She likes to be flattered, but she is not taken in. I think much of her patience with him is due to the fact that Leicester was his step-father and she does it for the love of Dudley. I am sure she hopes that he will grow into some common sense and be a useful servant to her with all the talents that he possesses. I know her judgement is shrewd and I hope she is right, but I fear she has miscalculated this one. Robert Devereux has the ambition of Lucifer and we all know what happened to him."

Simon whistled through his teeth. "And I thought I was positive when I get my teeth into an argument. That was a rant if ever I heard one."

Thomas puffed out his cheeks as if it was a relief to get it out of his system.

"Well I have to vent my spleen now and then."

"You might be interested to know that Essex is in hot water with the Queen. You heard that Drake went off privateering in April?"

"Yes, Matthew Collier sent me word of it."

"Essex galloped off to Plymouth to join him without the Queen's permission. Hoping to get enough bounty to pay off his debts no doubt. The rumour is that he owes £23,000. They say the Queen is furious."

"I suspect she fears that he will throw his weight around and try to take over the expedition, upsetting everyone else. I hope he suffers the consequences of his rashness."

They both glanced down into the street below as a coach rattled past scattering the crowd in all directions with no thought for their safety. There was a coat of arms on the side of it that both men recognised.

"Hanham," said Simon. "Probably young Anthony Hanham taking his new wife to the fair. My client tells me she is a pretty little thing."

"She is a very charming girl, Neville Norrington's daughter. I met her a few months ago."

"Sir Bartholomew and his nephew own half of the county now, buying up land and farms. They have too much influence in my opinion."

It was happening all over the country, the wealthy creating grazing for sheep or extending their park land. Whole villages were pulled down to make way for their plans and families left without homes or sustenance. Many of them gravitated to the towns in their desperation. London was growing at an alarming rate as Simon had already pointed out.

"Norrington's daughter may have married into money, but I don't know if she has the best of the bargain with young Anthony Hanham."

"What do you mean?" Tom frowned, recalling the uneasiness he had felt concerning the casual way the Hanhams had treated Elizabeth's journey to their house.

"Apparently his business dealings are none too savoury. He makes his money through rack-renting in London. He's also a regular visitor to a certain brothel near the docks. I took on a case for a man who wanted Hanham to act as his witness to his innocence over starting a brawl in the brothel, but of course he refused because he did not want it known that he frequented the place. I shall never understand why a man of wealth with a pretty young wife is drawn to such sinful places."

Thomas gnawed his lip. It was not what he wanted to hear. Elizabeth Norrington deserved better than that. He had a sudden desire to go to the fair in the hope that he might see her. He stood up buckling on his sword belt. He rarely wore a sword these days except when he travelled to areas unfamiliar to him or where there was the possibility of violence. Brawling often broke out at fairs and he felt safer carrying a weapon.

"I have a fancy to look around the fair before I go. I promised to buy Dawn Light a trinket or two. Will you come with me?"

"No I can't Tom. I have to see my client in less than an hour and I need to read through some of these papers first. I better see if I can fix the handle back on that door too or the landlord will charge me for it. I promise we will come to you this Christmas, whatever the weather."

They embraced, but before he left Thomas said with some urgency, "Be careful what you say in public about the need for reform. Whitgift is in deadly earnest about bringing everyone into line. There are informers everywhere. I don't want to have to visit you in the Tower."

Simon shrugged his warning off lightly, but as Tom ran down the stairs he knew in his heart that Bailey would always speak out for his beliefs when the opportunity arose. He looked up at the window. Simon was standing there waving to him. He put up a hand in response before he began to walk towards Barton Fields.

The broad, flat meadow that was known as Barton Fields lay alongside the river and in wet seasons it always flooded. This summer had been dry, rainfall sparse and there was a brownish tinge to the grass. Crowds of people wandered around amongst the stalls and booths that dotted the field in higgledy piggledy confusion. Musicians competed with each other for attention, some less melodious in their playing than others. On one side of the field children were dancing in a ring to a plaintive tune played on a pipe, the rhythm underscored by the beat of a drum. Mingled with all the human voices were the sounds of animals brought to the fair to be sold. Tom was aware of the honking of geese in particular.

He strolled amongst the stalls, stopping near a vendor selling meat pies, who was doing a good trade. From where he stood Tom had a clear view of a fire-eater. The man was standing on a plank laid across two barrels so he would be visible to the ring of spectators gathered round him. His audience gasped as the fiery brand disappeared into his mouth.

A fracas had started by the river. The splintered remnant of a stall lay on the ground and two men were squaring up, shouting abuse. A third man was trying to get between them and calm things down. Tom was watching this little drama when a soft voice close to him said, "What's a handsome gentleman like you doing here all alone?"

He turned to see a girl of about fifteen standing beside him. She was tall with a full figure. Brown curls tumbled from beneath her linen cap and the bodice of her kirtle was loosely laced at the top to reveal her ample cleavage. She was pretty, although she had applied too much rouge to her cheeks and her smile revealed two gaps where teeth were missing.

"You don't want to be lonely on such a merry day."

She moved closer and Thomas caught the sharp smell of cheap perfume on unwashed skin. She ran her hand suggestively over his codpiece.

"I bet the weapon you have here will thrust just as deep as the sword that hangs at your belt. I know a comfortable, private spot, just behind that booth.

My charges are most reasonable compared to the pleasure you will receive."

She attempted to take his hand and press it on her breast, but he stepped back.

"Thank you for the offer," Tom said with an amused smile, "But I do not intend to unsheathe my sword today."

The girl shrugged murmuring, "The loss is yours Sir."

She could see that he meant it though and walked away behind the booth she had indicated. The pie seller looked at Mountfield, laughing."I should keep away from Polly and her friends sir if you don't want a dose of the clap. They don't get many high class customers if you see what I mean."

Thomas strolled away wondering just how young Polly was when she first turned to prostitution. She seemed very practised at her trade already.

Along the edge of Barton Fields was a stream that fed into the river. Several trees grew beside it, beech, hawthorn and chestnut. A wooden seat had been fashioned all the way around the trunk of one of these trees. Tom sat down in the shade. He was disappointed that Simon Bailey could not come home with him. He saw so little of his friend and their time together that morning had been very short. He knew that it was partly his fault. He could make more effort to visit friends; it did not take an age to ride to London or Oxford, but Waaseyaaban was not comfortable outside her own domain and he hated leaving her for too long.

In this melancholy frame of mind, he was not enjoying the bustle of the fair as much as he imagined he would and was considering returning home, when he saw Elizabeth Norrington. She was quite near, browsing a stall spread with fabrics. He was surprised to see that she was alone. She moved to the next stall and after a few moments made a purchase, taking a purse from the pocket inside her gown. Tom was tempted to walk over to her, but decided it would be best not to do so. Then as she turned to join the crowd watching the fire-eater, she happened to look in his direction and recognised him at once. She hesitated briefly before walking towards him. He stood up to greet her, bowing.

"Sir Thomas, I did not expect to see you here."

"Mistress N- Hanham," he almost said Norrington but corrected himself, "This is a pleasure. You are not alone surely?"

"No, my husband and James are with me. Anthony is speaking with some business acquaintances and James is somewhere amongst that crowd watching the fire-eater. You are wise to sit in the shade; it is very hot in the sun. I think I will follow your example for a while."

She sat down on the bench and he followed suit.

"Do you always come to this September fair?"

"No this is my first visit and I did not come to Frome to see the fair at all. A good friend of mine, a lawyer, was consulting with a client here and is too busy to visit us at home, so I came here to meet him and talk for an hour or two. The fair was an after-thought."

"Then Dawn Light is not with you?"

"She does not care for towns and crowds."

He studied her face. She seemed paler, thinner than he remembered from four months ago, her eyes larger than ever.

"I see you have bought something."

She was holding in one hand a silver, heart-shaped locket with a garnet in the centre.

"Yes, it is only a cheap jewel, but it is pretty and will look well pinned on a particular bodice I have."

He smiled. "I promised Dawn Light that I would bring her back some trinket or other. I always do if I come to a town. She loves presents. She is like a child in her excitement. Watching her delight gives me equal pleasure."

"All women love presents Sir Thomas, especially when they are sincerely given. The value is not important."

She fingered the handsome jewel she wore around her neck, a string of baroque pearls with a jewelled, enamel pendant suspended from them. It was an expensive piece, finely wrought. Tom wondered if it was her husband's wedding gift to her and just how sincerely it had been given. He inquired after James.

"Sir Bartholomew has taken to James. He has given him a falcon and two hunting dogs of his own. He intended to stay until Christmas and then go back to father for a few months. I hoped that we could all spend Christmas at Norrington Hall, but Anthony feels it is more fitting that father comes to us."

"How does Hanham House suit you?"

She looked down into her lap, turning the locket over in her hands.

"I have all the comfort I could wish for. Sir Bartholomew and Lady Agnes are very kind. The garden is very fine. I spend much of my time there. I sometimes wish there was a little more that I could do. I embroider of course and sketch a little, but I miss my reading. Anthony and his uncle are not fond of reading."

She pictured Sir Thomas' library and his untidy desk covered in the pages of his writings.

"Have you made much progress with your writing?"

"Some. I write in bursts."

"I am sorry your friend could not come to stay with you," she said. "You must miss your friends, sharing the life of the intellect. Sir Bartholomew told me something of your life; how well you did at Oxford and how you never go to your father's house anymore because he will not accept Dawn Light as your wife."

"Did he now?" Thomas raised his eyebrows. He had not expected her to say this. He was offended that Bartholomew Hanham should discuss his relationship with his father. She was looking at him with such an earnest expression in her eyes and it was not her fault, but he could not prevent a sharp edge in his voice.

"How did he come to be discussing me Mistress Elizabeth?"

It was the first time he had used her Christian name. Somehow he did not enjoy saying Mistress Hanham. It did not sound right.

"Jacob Whyte told him how we got lost in the forest," Lizzie explained, pleased that he called her Elizabeth. "And he was grateful for the hospitality you gave us."

"So grateful that he proceeded to tell you what a dangerous man I am– how I broke my poor father's heart – how unreasonable it was of me to get offended when my father, the hypocrite, is happy for me to keep Dawn Light as a whore, but will not accept her as my wife. Then no doubt he told you that you must not associate with me."

The expression on her face told him he had hit the mark. He was sorry that he had sounded so bitter and added more gently,

"I fear that most of my father's acquaintances, in fact most of polite society, agree with his point of view. Very few are interested in my side of the story."

"But I understand. I admire your courage."

She stopped, hearing someone call her name. James was running towards them very fast.

"Lizzie, Anthony is looking for you. He is coming this way."

There was an urgency in his voice that caught Tom's attention. Elizabeth jumped to her feet, almost dropping the locket. Anthony Hanham was indeed sauntering towards them. He was only ten when Thomas had last seen him, a timid boy, reluctant to speak. The elegant fashion plate coming their way bore scant resemblance to the boy Tom remembered. He was dressed in a doublet and breeches of gold brocade, the sleeves of the doublet slashed to reveal blue insets. His breeches had identical blue insets and were of the puff-ball variety, standing out around the thighs as if a great quantity of air had been blown in to them. Thomas leaned back against the tree regarding this vision with amusement. From the crown of his feathered hat to the toes of his tooled leather boots he was the epitome of a courtier about to have an audience with the Queen rather than a man attending a modest country fair. He even wore the latest style of pleated ruff. Tom could feel a restriction around his own throat just looking at it.

"Mountfield." Anthony posed himself in front of Thomas, looking at him scornfully. Although he inclined his head in acknowledgement, Tom did not stand up. He did not feel like according Hanham too much courtesy.

"So you do emerge from the wilderness sometimes. Where is that brown faced whore of yours, too wild to mix in civilized company? Frighten the peasants eh?"

He paused, waiting for a reaction to the insult, but Tom remained leaning against the tree regarding him with a calm expression. The stricken look on Lizzie's face told him how much she wished to be disassociated from her husband's taunt. James looked down at his feet. Hanham took hold of his wife's arm.

"Come Elizabeth, we will miss the pageant."

Tom did rise now, to bid Lizzie goodbye with a formal bow and as Hanham turned to leave he stepped close to him, murmuring in his ear in a soft, distinct voice, too low for Elizabeth to catch, "I hear it is you who has a taste for whores Hanham."

Anthony stiffened then steered Elizabeth away.

"You coming?" he drawled at James, not bothering to look back.

James had not expected to see Thomas Mountfield that day but it was his chance to put something right.

"I will come in a moment. I have something to say to Sir Thomas."

"Suit yourself." Anthony flapped his hand in a gesture of indifference.

An elderly woman carrying a basket of goods for sale was passing. She was bent, unsteady on her feet, relying on a stick to help her balance. Her hands were gnarled and twisted like the roots of trees. She stumbled as Anthony and Elizabeth swept past her, the basket brushing against Hanham's doublet.

"Don't rub your filthy wares against me crone," he snapped, pushing the basket away from him with such force that the woman lost her balance and fell to the floor, lengths of ribbons, straw dolls, nosegays and bracelets scattering around her. Lizzie gave a cry of protest but could not stop because Anthony was gripping her arm too tightly, compelling her to move on with him. Looking back she saw Sir Thomas lifting the woman to her feet and sitting her down on the bench whilst James collected together her scattered wares and put them back in the basket.

The old woman sat on the bench for a moment or two, getting her breath back and then declared her intention to carry on.

"Are you sure you are steady enough Dame?" Tom asked. "Shall I carry your basket to your destination?"

She shook her head. "No, no, I have had worst falls than that sir." Before she left them, Tom bought two lengths of ribbon, a nosegay and a bracelet of polished pebbles for Waaseyaaban.

"May the good lord bless you sir," she said, patting his cheek with her knobbly fingers, "You and your kindly boy."

Thomas sat back down on the bench, watching her hobble away. James stood beside him, stiff and awkward, not knowing how to begin what he wished to say. Since he had been at Hanham House he had dwelt often on what Sir Bartholomew had said about Thomas Mountfield. Philip Sidney had always been James' great hero and he had not refused to support his friend Thomas when he came back from the Americas with a native wife. He felt ashamed that he had not believed what Thomas had told Lizzie and knew he must apologise. He was itching to ask him about Sidney, hear stories that perhaps only Thomas knew, but how could he bring himself to do that if he did not apologise?

"Thank you for helping to pick up her wares," Thomas said, "But I am sorry that you had to suffer the indignity of being mistaken for my son." To his surprise James smiled. "What is it that you wish to say to me? Don't stand there like a man called up for the militia. Sit down."

James did as he was bid.

"I must apologise sir," he began hesitantly. "For I have done you an injustice."

Tom raised his eyebrows in query, wondering what was coming next, but he did not comment. He could see that it was hard for the boy to find the right words.

"When we were riding to Frome from your house last May my sister told me that you were a close friend of Sir Philip Sidney's and I scoffed at it. I called you a boaster and thought you said such a thing only to impress her."

He paused, expecting Sir Thomas to speak, but Tom just regarded him with a quiet interest and James stumbled on, "I judged you unfairly sir because – well because I believed your manner of living to be ungentlemanly, even though you kept your word and told my sister nothing of my spying at your bed chamber door. But now I know it was all true concerning Sir Philip. Bartholomew Hanham confirmed it- how you had fought beside him in the Low Countries, been with him when he died, travelled back with his body and was knighted by the Queen herself. Now I am so ashamed to have doubted your honour. It is just that ---- "

Tom put his hand on the boy's arm to reassure him.

"I understand. It confuses you that a man with such connections chooses to live outside the conventional avenues of wealth and influence. Your doubts were reasonable enough. I accept your apology unreservedly. It is never easy to admit a misjudgement and you have shown courage to speak to me like this."

James' face flooded with relief. He had been fearful of Tom's reaction to his confession.

"I have always admired Sir Philip," he said with eagerness. "Even when I was a small boy I loved the stories of his prowess in the tilt yard, how no one could best him- what a wonderful horseman he was and yet he was learned too. He seemed to me the noblest gentleman in England."

Tom nodded. "Chaucer's knight embodied eh? Sans peur et sans reproche. Well every bit of your imagining was true. His fame was not exaggerated; he was everything you believed and more. He may not have achieved as much in his short life as he wished, but he will be remembered for what he was, not what he did."

James was beginning to see Thomas Mountfield in a different light. When he and Lizzie had stayed at his house, he had been irked by Tom's mocking manner, the casual way he dismissed all James' cherished beliefs inculcated into him by his father. It seemed to him as if the man was indirectly mocking his father. He judged him to be frivolous and light weight to flout society so brazenly. Now, listening to the emotion in his voice as he spoke of Sidney, James realised that he was dealing with a profoundly serious man, despite his strange ideas. It prompted him to confess something he had told no one before.

"I wept when I heard the news of his death. I shut myself in my chamber and wept."

"Oh so did I James. I was holding his hand at the last and I could not believe that he had left us. It seemed impossible that the fire of his spirit should be extinguished. I wept like a child. I managed to maintain my dignity at the funeral- the pomp and ceremony of it, the fact that the nation was paying tribute to him- made it seem less real. But in November at the Accession Day Tournament, when they led out his favourite horse caparisoned all in black, that riderless horse moved me more than all the funeral speeches. I could not hold back my tears then, not only for Philip but for other good friends who had died in the campaign. There is no shame in weeping if the cause be true."

"Would you tell me about Zutphen Sir Thomas, what it was like?"

Tom did not want to dwell on the details of that day right then. The memory of it and its consequences had oppressed his mind for three years and he was trying to let go of it. He hoped that once he had committed it to paper he would be able to let go. Yet James was looking at him so hopefully and he did not wish to disappoint him.

"It was very confused and you only see the part of the battle you are involved in yourself, not the overall shape of it. I will try to explain how it came about. You know that the Prince of Parma was the commander of the Spanish troops?"

James nodded. He had tried to follow all the news from the Low Countries, piecing together what his father passed on to him.

"Well, Parma was besieging Rheinberg and the Earl of Leicester decided to counter this by laying siege to Zutphen. The town is on the banks of the River Ijssel and was strategically important to Parma because it gave him access to the Veluwe region, a very prosperous area that contributed a lot of money to support the Spanish campaign. The Earl thought that if he could take Zutphen it would cut Parma off from that valuable source of income."

"Was it a good strategy?" James asked.

"It seemed so at the time. Philip, my friend Harry Carthew and I were in Flushing. My other close friend, Joshua Standing was killed before I arrived in the Netherlands. Philip had grown restless cooped up in Flushing, so he decided to join his uncle Leicester at Zutphen. Harry and I and few others went with him to swell the ranks of the cavalry."

Tom as he looked at the boy's eager face paused for a moment, recalling how enlivened Philip had been at the prospect of action. He could hear in his head the drumming of their horses' hooves as the small band galloped headlong over the flat countryside towards Zutphen.

"Had the fighting already begun?" James prompted. He could sense a reluctance in Mountfield and did not want him to stop.

"No, we found that the earl had thrown a bridge over the river and our forces had completely surrounded Zutphen. He was in a very favourable position with every chance of forcing the town to surrender as long as relief supplies were prevented from reaching it."

He sighed, thinking how easily things had gone wrong, as they did too often in that confused campaign.

"The day after we arrived some of our troops captured a messenger trying to get into the town. He was bringing news to Verdugo, the commander of Zutphen, that Parma was sending a convoy with supplies under the Marquis Del Vasto. Leicester decided to set an ambush for them. He was confirmed in this idea by one of his captains, Rowland York, who was a seasoned campaigner with much experience of enemy tactics. York was confident that the convoy would be lightly guarded and he convinced the Earl."

Tom could not think of Rowland York charitably. In the aftermath of the fight at Zutphen the Anglo-Dutch army had withdrawn, but when the main Spanish forces went into their winter quarters Leicester had resumed the siege. He failed to take the town, but left commanders in charge of garrisons in smaller towns nearby. Rowland York was one of them. The following year York and Sir William Stanley surrendered their charges and joined the Spanish cause. Tom was back in England by then struggling to throw off a bout of fever and come to terms with his disillusionment. When he heard the news of York's desertion he wondered if his miscalculation at Zutphen had been deliberate.

"York was sorely mistaken. The convoy was about three thousand strong and they were fresher, better armed and better trained than our levies. We were outnumbered too because trusting to York's advice the Earl had detached less than two thousand men from the main force to lay the ambush. But the dye was cast. We took position around a small village about half a mile from Zutphen with the infantry in one large battalion, a force of pike men at the front and the cavalry divided into two squadrons. Rows of musketeers were positioned along the sides of the road. It was a very misty morning and we just waited for the convoy to appear."

James was there in his imagination, sitting astride his horse beside Sir Thomas and Philip Sidney, staring into the mist. He was honest enough to admit to himself that he would have been afraid. He could taste fear on his tongue just thinking about it. He wanted to ask Thomas if he felt fear before a battle but did not like to be so bold.

"When the convoy did appear we could see it was heavily guarded. The

Earl of Essex was in command of the cavalry and once the convoy had passed the village, he led us in a charge."

Thomas had no love for Robert Devereux, but he could not deny that he was courageous in battle. He remembered with great clarity his shout of 'Follow me my good fellows for the honour of England and our Queen.' Essex was a month from his twenty first birthday then, imperious, confident, much admired by his captains.

"We drove their cavalry back, but their pike men formed a solid phalanx and kept us back from the wagons.

We broke through the first two ranks but could get no further. The wagon drivers abandoned their posts and fled when the fighting started. You couldn't blame them, they were unarmed- probably local men pressed into service against their wills. In an instant Spanish troops with arquebuses took their places and kept the wagons moving towards Zutphen. We were impressed by the Spaniards' discipline. They convinced us that day that they were the best troops in Europe."

"What did you do then sir?" James queried. He had never heard Spaniards spoken of with respect before. His father always referred to them as those vile papist dogs.

"We regrouped for a second charge. Philip feared that the men would be disheartened by the failure of our first assault and he made one of those wondrous, foolish chivalric gestures of his. It struck him that most of us had no leg armour comparable to his own. He did not want the men to attribute his boldness in the charge to his superior protection, felt it was ignoble to have an advantage over them. So he took his leg armour off. We protested, but there was no turning him. He pointed out that my only protection was a breast plate and helmet- which was true but not because I wanted to set a brave example. We had left England in such a hurry after our return from Roanoke, I did not have time to get fitted out with full armour."

"And his noble gesture was his undoing," James murmured.

"It was. We mounted a second charge with the same result as the first. When we reformed I realised that Harry Carthew was not with us. I had not seen him fall and I never saw him again, alive or dead."

Despite his anxiety for the severely injured Sidney and heedless of his own wound Tom had searched amongst the wounded for Harry. Finding no sign of him or anyone who had news of him, he sent out two men to look for him on the field. They had not returned by the time it was decided to take Philip to a safer position in a litter. It was the day after Philip's funeral that he learned Harry's body had been identified and buried near Zutphen.

"During our third and last charge Philip was hit in the thigh by a musket ball at close range. His thigh was smashed. He managed to remain upright in the saddle though and get off the field. His great skill as a horseman stood him in good stead."

"You must be a good horseman too sir, to charge three times with cavalry like that."

"I manage a horse well enough."

"Did you take any further part in the battle?"

"No. I had received a thrust in the upper part of my arm from a pike-not serious, but it was my sword arm and made it difficult for me to wield my weapon properly. So I decided to stay with Philip. I could see his wound might prove mortal if it did not receive proper care. He was in great pain. I went to fetch him a cup of water. There was just a cup-full left in a bucket nearby. Lying next to Philip was an infantryman, only a young lad, not much older than you. He had been slashed in the throat and chest. It was clear that the hand of death was about to touch him. He was coughing and spitting up blood. When I brought the water to Philip he told me to give it to the boy. He recognised Philip and despite his condition protested, but Philip insisted, saying he had the greater need of it. That is something I shall never forget."

James' face was alight with triumph.

"Then that story is true. I knew it must be. Father heard tell of it and my cousin Robin to irk me said it wasn't true, just a tale spread to make his fame seem greater. Robin has always scoffed at me for admiring Sir Philip."

Thomas patted his shoulder.

"Well you can tell your cousin Robin he was wrong because you have spoken to the man who was holding the cup."

"I'm sure he was brave at the end sir."

"He had to suffer for three weeks, wracked with fever through the latter part of it. It is hard to keep your dignity when the heat of fever stirs strange images in your brain. He was much troubled by something on his conscience for which he felt he needed forgiveness. Once he had confessed that he was at ease and died peacefully confident of God's mercy."

He did not think it fitting to share with James what had troubled Philip's conscience. Lying on his death bed Sidney had been reliving that day five years before when he first set eyes on Penelope Devereux. She was his aunt's ward and was brought to court to be introduced into high society before she married Lord Rich. Philip had fallen in love with her with a passionate intensity. Even after her marriage to Rich and two years later Philip married Frances Walsingham, his desire for her remained. It weighed on his conscience that he had held on to that desire through the years and had recalled it even now when he should be preparing himself for death. After he had confessed the weight was lifted.

"You always knew those sonnets I shared with you were about her," he had murmured to Thomas and Tom had nodded, his throat too constricted with sorrow to speak.

"I cannot imagine that Sir Philip could have done anything that needed forgiveness," James said, puzzled. "We have all done some things for which we are in need of forgiveness James. I know I have."

There was a short silence as James wondered what sins troubled Sir Thomas, then he said, "My sister tells me you have letters and poems written in Sir Philip's own hand. I wish I could see them- not to read your private letters sir- but just to see his handwriting."

"You could read the poems," Tom suggested.

"I am not very good with poems. They exceed my understanding."

Thomas laughed. "Probably because no one has taken the time to discuss them with you. There is another thing that might take your fancy more. I have the sword he was wearing at Zutphen."

"Oh sir, it would mean so much to me to hold that in my hand." Then James' head dropped in disappointment. "But my father and Sir Bartholomew say that I must not visit your house again because your way of life is not respectable. They are right of course," he added swiftly not wishing to appear disloyal to his father, "so I shall not be able to see those things of Sir Philip's."

"Yes, a knotty problem, but perhaps if we both think hard about it we will come up with a solution in the end. Is it not time you re-joined your sister and Anthony Hanham? He will wonder where you have got to."

"Oh he does not care what I do."

This came out spontaneously and James realised Thomas would pick up on the implication, so in a different tone of voice, he added, "I am given complete freedom at Hanham House. Thank you for telling me about the Netherlands Sir Thomas."

He bowed and trotted off to find his sister. Thomas called out after him, "My friends call me Tom."

James did not want to spend the rest of the afternoon with his brother-in-law. He would much rather talk longer with Thomas Mountfield. He was not happy at Hanham House. Sir Bartholomew and Lady Agnes were kind enough, but Anthony treated him with contempt. The man who had fought alongside Sir Philip Sidney had just offered him friendship. Anthony Hanham barely acknowledged his existence. While Sir Neville was at Hanham House for the wedding, Anthony put on an act, a pleasant face, but once Norrington had left he made it quite clear that James was beneath his notice. He would have gone home to his father if he had not worried about deserting Lizzie.

Thomas watched him go, his skinny legs looking even thinner in his dark hose, until he had disappeared into the crowds and then jumping to his feet, Tom resolved to fetch his horse from the stables and go home. He had intended his visit to Frome to be a happy reunion with an old friend, but his mind was unsettled as he rode home. He chose a route that took him up onto the downs, where he could urge Hope on to a fast pace. The stallion responded, lengthening his stride, enjoying the feel of the undulating chalk downs beneath his hooves. Tom hoped the exhilaration of the speed would help to clear his mind of his troubled thoughts. The dissatisfaction of having so little time with Simon Bailey and the nagging fear that his friend's religious ardour might lead him into danger mingled with a concern for the Norringtons. He dwelt on the way Elizabeth had jumped to her feet on Anthony's approach; there was fear in such haste. James' unhappiness was evident also, despite his attempts to mask it. Clearly the boy was beginning to experience what it was like to be the victim of arrogance and see flaws in the principles drummed into him by his father. Then there was Simon's story about the brothel by the docks. He could only wish for Elizabeth's sake that the fastidious Hanham consorted with whores free from disease.

A pheasant flapped up steeply in front of them, startled by the sudden approach of the horse, its red face and green/blue neck, ringed with a white collar, vivid in the sunlight. It landed a few yards away and regarded them with a ruffled dignity.

Tom told himself that the Norrington's problems were none of his business. There was nothing he could do about it anyway, but he could not rid himself of that feeling of unease. When he rode up to his house he saw a coach standing in the yard near the barn. He recognised the vehicle as his mother's. When he led Hope into the barn he found Jack Ross rubbing down the coach horses, drying off their flanks that were damp with sweat. Ross was one of four grooms employed by his father and he was his mother's preferred choice as a driver. Born in Scotland, Jack had come down South in his youth to look for work. He was now in his mid- forties but he had not lost his native accent. He had a natural affinity with horses and took on the task of attending to Tom's stallion, whose own flanks were steaming from the effort of the fast ride home.

Tom ran across to the house to be met at the front door by Joan Bushy, who informed him his mother was in the parlour. Lady Anne Mountfield was sitting in a chair sipping one of Joan's cordials when her son entered. He unbuckled his sword belt, threw it on the chair and strode over to his mother, who rose to greet him. He kissed her cheek and then stepped back to look at her. Every time he saw her he was struck by how little she seemed to age.

"Mother it's good to see you. I hope I have inherited your power to stave off the ravages of time."

"Ah, the grey hairs are hidden beneath my hood and I have a lotion that helps with the wrinkles," she replied with a smile. "You are looking very well yourself."

She had been very worried about Tom's health when he returned from the Netherlands. The wound on his arm was infected, weeping puss and took a long time to heal. He suffered from recurring bouts of fever and was lower in spirit than she had ever known him to be. She wanted him home with her in Salisbury, where she could nurse him back to full health, but the quarrel with his father made that impossible. Instead he was living in a makeshift hut in Selwood Forest, building a house with a crew of local builders and carpenters. He needed comfort and care, not that Spartan existence. She did not trust that strange woman he called Dawn light to look after him properly. It was this concern that had prompted her to suggest to Joan Bushy that she offer herself as housekeeper once the house was habitable. Joan had gone willingly. Waaseyaaban was suspicious of her at first, but Joan's patience and kindness gradually won her over. Anne had to admit that her fears for her son were unjustified. Looking at him now, it was such a pleasure to see how fit and healthy he was, her handsome Thomas.

"Have you come on your own?" he asked.

"No Cecily is with me. She is out in the garden somewhere, picking blackberries with Dawn Light. Joan has a fancy to make a blackberry and apple pie. Cecily is not suitably dressed for fruit picking. If she starts playing around with those giant hounds of yours she will end up tangled in the briars."

"She will disentangle herself soon enough. It's good for her to have a taste of freedom now and then before you shackle her to Godfrey Roper."

Anne shook her head as she sat back down in the chair and Tom drew up a stool to sit beside her.

"Now that is unfair Tom and you know it. Cecily is more than happy to marry Godfrey. Besides, you like him. He is steady, hardworking and he is very fond of her."

"Fond of her," Tom repeated, laughing, "He is more than that. He is besotted with her. But he is forty two Mother and very set in his ways. That cloth business of his is all his mind runs on. Cecily is lively minded, spirited. She needs conversation that will stretch her mind. She will soon get bored with discussing the varying prices of bolts of cloth."

"Nonsense, Godfrey is an alderman with every prospect of being elected mayor next year. The mayor of Salisbury is a prestigious position. She will have to attend many functions, meet all kinds of people. She will not lack for good conversation and she will enliven Godfrey. Besides, what breadth of conversation do you have with y- Dawn Light?"

It was clear that she had been about to say 'your wife' and corrected herself.

"You almost said it then." Thomas gave her a direct look. "Damnation Mother, would it choke you to refer to her as my wife just once?"

"You know it offends your father," she replied calmly.

"So it does not matter if you offend me. How is the old hypocrite?"

"Thomas don't speak about your father like that. You know he has only ever wished the best for you."

"Well he has a very strange way of showing it and to answer your earlier question, the implication of which did not escape me, my wife and I have the kind of instinctive relationship that does not always need words."

Lady Anne reached out and stroked her son's hair. She had little chance to show her affection for him, they met so infrequently.

"Oh my dear, I worry about you. You will suffocate shut away here in this forest. You may have everything you need physically, but you should be amongst your intellectual peers. Robert met one of your old Oxford tutors last month, quite by chance. He spoke so warmly of your abilities, said you would be welcome to take up a post lecturing there. This conception you have of fulfilling your duty to Dawn Light is very noble, but would it hurt her so much to dress more conventionally so you could both come out more into respectable society? I am sure she would do it if you asked her, made it clear to her that it would make you happy."

"But it would not make me happy. I admit that I would like to see my friends more and have more contact with academic life, but not at the cost of forcing Dawn Light to be something other than herself. I love what she is. There are so many false values, such empty vanity in what you call respectable society."

He stood up and walked to the window. His mother followed him and they stood together watching a cockerel strut along outside the barn. It reminded Tom of Anthony Hanham. He put his arm around Lady Anne's shoulder and said quietly, " Mother, I saw a gallant today at Frome Fair in the full heat of the sun, mincing along like a peacock in a gold brocade doublet and gold breeches that looked like pumpkins and a starched ruff. I had to shade my eyes not to be blinded by the dazzle of his glory. If that is what it takes to be respectable, then I prefer to remain disreputable."Anne could not help herself from smiling at the image he had conjured up.

"You dazzle with words Tom Mountfield."

She reached up and pulled his shirt collar out over the neck of his doublet, smoothing it down neatly. Tom felt a sharp stab of regret that his fractured relationship with his father must inevitably hurt her too. He was grateful when the door burst open and his wife ran into the room closely followed by Cecily and the two wolfhounds. Waaseyaaban threw her arms around his neck and he lifted her up off the ground. It amused him that she always greeted him in that joyful way even if they had been apart for only an hour. She kissed him fiercely, giving his mother a swift, sidelong glance to judge her reaction. Lady Anne's expression was neutral, unreadable. Dawn Light did not care if his mother disapproved of such passionate displays of affection. Tom was her Makwa, her life. There were times when her whole body ached for his touch and she had no wish to hide it.

"I hear you have been encouraging my little sister to behave in a manner that does not befit a lady," Tom said with mock gravity.

Cecily Mountfield kissed her brother's cheek.

"As if I needed any encouragement. Look, my fingers are purple."

She held up her fingers to demonstrate, delighted by the sight of it. Cecily had the kind of bright eyes that were always full of mischievous humour. They were green like Tom's but much lighter in colour. Tom's olive green eyes were dark, looked almost brown at times, but Cecily's were closer to emerald. She had dispensed with her hood to reveal a coronet of dark brown hair plaited around her head. She had a bold, confident, happy air about her.

"Joan tells me you have been visiting Simon Bailey, she said. "Is he as Blunt and Yorkshire as ever?"

"Every bit and just as eager to reform the Church of England."

"The last time he was here when we visited too, he told me I must not give in to frivolity and light-mindedness." The memory amused Cecily. "You know the way he looks at you through those round glasses of his, full of concern."

Tom nodded. He was smiling but again the fear for Simon's future came into his mind. He picked up his sword belt and detached the cloth purse laced on it.

"Which reminds me- I have a few trophies of my visit to Frome for my beautiful wife."

He tipped the articles from the purse on to the table. Dawn Light knew he would not fail to bring her a gift. He never forgot. Her face lit up.

She put the bracelet of smooth pebbles on her wrist at once and then appraised the two lengths of ribbon. The nosegay she smelt. The fragrance was still strong and she held it out to Lady Anne.

"For you."

Anne was taken by surprise. The look in Dawn Light's eyes was defiant. She was challenging Anne to accept, knowing a refusal would displease Tom. Anne however had no wish to reject the unexpected gift.

"Thank you my dear. I rarely receive gifts of flowers these days."

"My father was never one for romantic gestures," Tom commented.

Lady Anne could have told him that he did not know his father as well as he thought he did, but she did not contradict him.

"This one is for me," Dawn Light said, claiming the purple velvet ribbon. "This one for Cecily."

She pressed the blue, satin ribbon into Cecily's hand. Waaseyaaban liked to give gifts herself. No guest ever left a Croatan house without a present from the host. It was an essential element in their culture. By giving gifts to Tom's female relations, she was stating that this was her house as well as his.

She loved all of the presents he gave her, but her favourite was something he had made to protect the seeds from the birds when she first planted them. He bought a box of copper discs, pierced a hole in each one and strung them together with wire. He made four of these chains with six discs in each chain, drove a nail into the tops of four wooden poles and hung a chain on each one. When the poles were pushed into the earth near the seeds the copper blazed in the sunlight and on a windy day the discs clattered together keeping the birds on the move.

Tom had told her with a very straight face that he, Ned and Toby had first tried the Croatan way of scaring birds, dancing and singing in the garden for more than an hour, but instead of being afraid the birds were so amused by their dismal performance, they all gathered round to laugh at them, so they had to resort to the copper discs. It was not until he broke into a smile that she realised he was joking. Croatan humour was broad and visual. It took her some while to get used to Tom's dry wit, but now she was quick to appreciate it.

She loved those copper discs. Some days she would sit on the ground beside the graves of Adjidamo and Wawackechi, singing to them and telling them how beautiful the copper discs gleamed. These little lost ones were the gifts she most wished to give Thomas and they were taken away. Thomas' mother was fortunate; all her children had lived.

Dawn Light wondered if Lady Anne realised or even cared what pain that loss had given her. Thomas knew. He would sit with her sometimes while she sang to them and hold her hand, sharing her grief in silence.

Cecily was holding the blue ribbon against her dress.

"It goes very well with this kirtle. Thank you Dawn Light. Do you like my kirtle by the way Tom?" She twirled herself around. "See how the skirt stands out. I have a Spanish farthingale over my petticoat, look."

She lifted up the end of the kirtle to reveal a garment made of canvas with a series of cane hoops sewn into it.

"Everyone is starting to wear them now."

"Do you not find it ironical," Tom said with a wry smile, "That we stand on the shore ready to cut the throat of the first militant Spaniard who sets foot on our soil and yet we fall over ourselves to copy their ludicrous fashions?"

Cecily laughed. "Yes, that's true. It's a paradox is it not? You should compose a verse with that paradox at the centre of it- the Spanish paradox."

"A good idea. We will invent one together after supper little sister."

"I have been amusing Dawn Light by telling her that the ladies at court are wearing such large farthingales that they can hardly sit down. I shall instruct my seamstress to make a monstrous sized one and I shall appear in it to astonish Godfrey when he visits me next."

Tom shook his head, laughing.

"Poor Godfrey, he will never be able to keep up with you."

"Of course not. He will be my devoted slave and I will do whatever I wish. I will have a very merry time of it."

Joan Bushy appeared in the doorway to announce that supper would be ready in ten minutes. Cecily clapped her hands.

"Good, I am starving. Joan has made some sugar animals."

"You should curb your desire for sugar and sweetmeats," Tom warned. "Your teeth will be black before you reach forty- might cool Godfrey's adoration."

"Oh he would adore me if I had no teeth at all. I must say your teeth are in a very fine condition for a man of your advanced age," she teased. "All my friends and Godfrey's sisters too sigh over you, with your dark sad eyes and flashing smile."

He pulled a face at her.

"I don't have your taste for sugary food, besides Dawn Light mixes up a paste that is excellent for cleaning the teeth- a mixture of salt and sage leaves. You must take some home with you- help you to sparkle at the wedding."

Cecily was thirteen years younger than Thomas. Anne Mountfield had borne three children in the space of seven years, Grace, Margaret and Thomas. It seemed as if there would be no more. Sir Robert was happy enough, particularly when the last one was a boy. To find that she was with child again at the age of forty one was a surprise to them both, but one they welcomed with joy. Despite the age difference Tom and Cecily were always close. She was born the year before Thomas went up to Oxford. He spent much time playing with her when he was home in the vacation and later, when he joined Philip Sidney's household he came home as often as possible and held her spellbound with stories of the places he had visited and the people he met. He would render her helpless with laughter doing impersonations of the pompous foreign dignitaries who were Philip's guests.

When he declared his intention to sail to the Americas she was just 14 and wanted to go with him. Her father poured scorn on the idea and she shut herself in her bedroom for two days, refusing to come out until Tom managed to persuade her that their parents were right. She did not want him to face unknown dangers without her, feeling that somehow she could keep him safe if she was there too. She feared she would never see him again.

She did not question the choice he had made on his return, accepting Waaseyaaban without reservation, proud of her brother for defying their father and convention. She did so want him to come to her wedding though. As they went through into the dining room she said, "Tom, you will come to the wedding won't you? It is only three weeks away now and you still have not said positively that you are coming."

Thomas glanced across at his mother.

"Not without Dawn Light."

"But I want Dawn Light to come too. We were talking about it earlier."

"I do not think father will approve of that."

"Oh pooh! He will have to put up with it. The minister is coming to conduct the ceremony in Godfrey's house anyway, so you will not have to abandon your principles by coming home and father has no say over who is allowed in Godfrey's house. Godfrey is puzzled by Dawn Light, but he has no prejudice against her and he will welcome her, particularly when he sees how much it pleases me. His ancient mother, poor soul, is so confused she does not know what world she is in, so she won't mind. His sisters will be far too busy ogling you to care about the other guests. I don't blame them. Bella's husband looks like a frog. So there, you have no reason not to come.

If you and father wish to carry on your silly feud, you need not speak to each other. He can stand in a corner with Grace and Margaret and their families and look scandalised. I shall ignore them. I would rather have you there Thomas than all of them put together."

He was touched by the sincerity of that last sentence. He turned to Dawn Light. "Do you wish to go to Cecily's wedding?"

She nodded, a short, determined nod, then added, "Not in hoops."

Dawn Light could never understand why white people wore so many layers of clothes even in the warm weather. The Croatans needed freedom of movement to work, to hunt, to be ready to react to danger. When it grew cold they wrapped themselves in cloaks of animal fur.

"We will not expect you to wear any hoops," Cecily assured her. "You could wear a loose, unstructured kirtle with a similar over-gown. I have just the thing. We are about the same size and it would fit you well. It is longer than you are used to wearing, but it would not encumber you. It is made of a beautiful mulberry coloured velvet. You could plait that purple ribbon in your hair. You will look so splendid."

Lady Anne said quietly, "I would be very pleased if you both would come. It is only right that you should be there."

"Very well," Thomas agreed, "We will come. I must confess I would have been very sorry not to see our little Cecily on her wedding day."

His sister kissed him on both cheeks.

"You have made me truly happy Tom. It would not be the same without you. It so happens that I have brought that kirtle and gown I mentioned with me, just in case you agreed. Dawn Light can try it on after supper."

Tom had a deep affection for Cecily. Her vivacious enthusiasm was always hard to resist and it pleased him to see Waaseyaaban respond to her friendship. As he sat down to supper, although he was apprehensive about the reception his wife might receive from some of the guests, he was convinced that they should go.

Chapter Three

THE EARLY MORNING FROST was sharp. It glistened white on the remaining hawthorn berries and rose hips. The grass crunched under Samson's great hooves as Ned Carter and Toby Aycliffe rode the shire horse towards Sir Thomas Mountfield's house. Apart from a few frosts like this one it had been a mild winter so far. After a hot September, October had been kindly; blue, misty mornings and evenings with soft days that saw the forest ablaze with colour, the leaves red, yellow and russet. Rough winds at the end of the month had torn the leaves from the trees and a carpet of them, crisped by the frost, lay on the ground, but the darkness of November was less chill and dismal than usual. Now it was the second week in December and there was no sign of any snow. The previous winter the snow had begun to fall at the end of November and lasted all the way through to February.

Toby sitting in front, in charge of the reins, was whistling an old tune his grandfather had taught him when his cousin demanded he stop the horse. Ned's sharp eyes had spotted something amongst the fallen leaves that he wished to investigate. It was at the base of a tree, originally camouflaged by the leaves, but the covering had been blown partly aside. Ned grabbed hold of it and pulled it out of the ground, waving it at Toby.

"Look, a snare. Master Tom will not be pleased to see this."

Thomas Mountfield had made it clear when he came into possession of a large area of the forest that he was happy for the local population to hunt on his land. He had a different conception of ownership from those landlords who were eager to see peasants mutilated or hung for trying to provide for their families. He stipulated however that they should do so with their crossbreed lurchers and terriers or with weapons, not by laying snares. Wire snares were indiscriminate and could catch creatures not designed for the cooking pot. He had known a fox chew off its foot to free itself and die a painful, lingering death. When animals hunted each other for food they killed quickly.

In the chain of being man was above the animals. The Book of Genesis spoke of God giving man dominion over the fish of the sea, the fowls of the air and over every living thing that moved upon the earth. In Tom's mind the concept of dominion included with it the corollaries of responsibility and care. He hated to see a creature ill-treated or made to suffer unnecessarily. When he was nine, his father took him to a bear baiting, confident that his bold son would enjoy the spectacle.

In truth Tom felt sick to the very pit of his stomach to see handsome mastiffs dragged away with their skulls smashed and their bellies ripped open by the bear's fearsome claws and the bear itself, so magnificent a creature, finally pulled down by the weight of numbers, bleeding from wounds all over its body. What made him even sicker was the savage exultation of the crowd, their screams and yells more primordial than the sounds of the embattled animals. He vowed never to attend another bear or bull baiting.

The following year his father was invited to a baiting arranged by an important official in the judiciary and insisted that Thomas come with him. Just before they were due to leave, Tom sneaked his horse out of the stable and rode off across Salisbury Plain, not returning home until late in the evening. His father, who was sparing with corporal punishment in most circumstances, gave him a thorough caning for his disobedience, but though his backside stung for days, Tom never regretted his action.

Ned Carter walked the rest of the way to the house, looking for more snares. He found three, all empty, indicating that they were recently set. He pulled them all up. The cousins were both annoyed that someone had chosen to disregard Sir Thomas's instructions. Neither of them could understand why a man who had fought natives in the Americas and killed Spaniards should be so tender towards creatures, but they respected him and were keen to insure the villagers complied with his wishes.

They found the man in question in the barn with his wife. They were sitting on stools packing apples into wooden pallets filled with straw. It was essential that the apples should not touch each other if they were to be preserved through the winter. The crop was excellent this year and there would be many pallets to store on the shelves in the brew house. Thomas was intending to make plenty of cider. Ned showed him the snares.

"They were all planted within a mile of the house- couldn't have been set long for they were all empty. I can't believe twere any of our lot – unless-"

He had a sudden thought and Toby had it at the same time for they both said in unison, "Isaac Salter."

"He is back in the village living in a tent the other side of what's left of the common pasture." Ned continued. "He's not right in the head- don't understand half what is said to him."

"Could you try to discover who is doing it?" Tom asked, "And explain why I won't allow it."

"I bet it is Isaac." Toby stood eyeing the apples, contemplating what fine cider they would make and tasting Joan Bushy's apple pies and crumbles already. "If it is, we will put the fear of God into him Master Tom, don't you worry."

"There is no need for intimidation, particularly if he is slow-witted. If you have problems with him, bring him to see me. Let me talk to him."

They agreed, but were sure that they could handle Isaac Salter

"Shall we take that last load of timber to Pocock's yard while the weather still holds?"

Ned stowed the snares away in the saddle bag thrown across Samson's back. They could not afford a saddle, for one would need to be custom made to fit the shire's broad back, but they did possess a pair of saddle bags joined by a leather strap.

"That's a good notion. We have almost finished packing these apples. I will come and help you load up when we have."

Thomas supplied three timber merchants from his forest land, replanting areas where the trees had been felled with new saplings. He had spent very little of his pay from the Netherlands campaign and there was money left over from Harry Carthew's legacy even after the house was built. They grew much of their own food and the money from the timber sales was enough to pay Ned and Toby's wages and buy the extras the household needed. Sir Thomas and Lady Mountfield did not have extravagant tastes. Tom was determined never to put himself in a position where he needed financial help from his father. He would show Sir Robert that he could live comfortably without his support.

He tried not to dwell on that last argument, when he had walked out of the family home vowing not to return, but there were times when it ran through his head and he could not block it out- his father shouting after him, "Thomas, Thomas come back here at once." – then when Tom did not even turn round- "You will regret this young man. You will not manage cut off from your family and friends. It is you who will suffer. It will not be long before you abandon that woman and come back to me with your cap in hand, asking to be forgiven."

"I'm damned if I will," Thomas called back as he slammed the door and every time his father's words came into his head, he repeated "I'm damned if I will" sometimes out loud.

He had not seen Sir Robert since that day until Cecily's wedding in September.

He did not regret attending the wedding, but it was not a comfortable day. He recalled the events in his mind as he and Dawn Light carried the trays of apples over to the brew house. Cecily was right about the mulberry kirtle and gown; they suited Dawn Light as if they had been made for her. She wore her own exotic jewellery and with a band of that velvet ribbon around her head and woven down into her plait, her beauty took the breath away. She looked more vital, more alive than most of the pallid, formal women guests. She stayed close to his side and he held on to her hand.

Godfrey was affable as always. His beloved Cecily called Dawn Light her friend, that was good enough for him and he had always liked Thomas.

"My dear fellow," he said with genuine admiration in his voice, "How splendid your wife looks- almost a match for my Cecily."

Tom warmed to him as he watched him bustle around greeting everyone, his round face flushed in the hot, crowded room. Cecily might lack for sparkling conversation but she would be loved and cherished by an honest husband. He was moved by how beautiful, elegant and self-possessed his little sister looked in her wedding gown; how gracefully she played her role during the wedding ceremony, encouraging Godfrey with her bright eyes.

The awkwardness came after the ceremony, when the guests mingled. Godfrey's sisters were dying to speak to Tom, but held back in case their husbands disapproved. Bella's husband did indeed resemble a frog with his bulging eyes, wide mouth and warty, sallow skin. Catherine's husband was thin with dark rings under his deep set eyes. He had a melancholic air about him. Both couples had left their numerous children at home in the care of servants.

Tom's older sisters however were accompanied by their offspring. Grace and Margaret greeted their brother with a peck on the cheek and a fleeting, nervous smile at Dawn Light. His four nephews and four nieces, none of whom had he seen for three years, came up one by one and murmured a greeting to their uncle, the boys bowing, the girls giving little bobbing curtseys. Not one of them dared look Dawn Light in the face. Tom's two brothers-in-law contented themselves with raising a hand to him from a distance before they sat down to start on the wedding feast, their wives and children hurrying over to join them.

Robert Mountfield had avoided eye contact with his son before and during the ceremony, which suited Thomas fine, but now his father and mother,

Lady Anne looking cool and dignified, were walking towards them.

He took a deep breath, squeezing Waaseyaaban's hand tighter. This was the first time she had seen Sir Robert. She appraised him with curiosity in her dark eyes. Although in his mid-sixties, he was upright and moved freely without the appearance of stiffening joints. He was a similar build to Thomas and she saw a resemblance in his strong features and direct gaze, but his mouth was severe, unsmiling. Her Makwa had a smile like his mother.

"Thomas," Robert acknowledged his son in a brusque voice. "You look healthier than when I saw you last. At least you had the courtesy to attend your sister's wedding, although I doubt if Godfrey's relations think very highly of your manners, bringing that woman with you."

Tom has been prepared to be civil to his father, but after that remark he felt like hitting him. He bit his lip to prevent himself from making an equally hurtful retort and walked away, his arm around his wife's waist.

"He hates me much. I see it in his eyes." Dawn Light looked up at Tom, sensing his struggle to control his anger.

"He is a narrow-minded old fool," he said bitterly. "He knows nothing about you. Don't let his words hurt you."

"They do not hurt me. It is you they hurt."

She was well aware of the pain the estrangement caused Thomas and it made her devotion to him even fiercer. "He will not drive me from you –never."

"Do you want to go home now?"

"No, we must eat food. We insult Cecily if we do not eat food."

He smiled and kissed her, causing a murmur amongst the nearest group of guests.

Unknown to Thomas, Lady Anne was reproving her husband for his harsh words, as she gazed after her son. "Robert, I begged you not to speak unkindly to him today. Could you not let it pass for one day? No matter what we feel about it, Tom regards Dawn Light as his wife and how would you have reacted if someone had spoken of me in that dismissive way?"

Sir Robert snorted. "Dawn Light- what foolish nonsense of a name is that?"

"It is an English translation of her Croatan name Father dear," Cecily was at his shoulder, bubbling over with high spirits, "And that would tie your crabby tongue in knots. I will not permit such a sour face at my wedding. Now sit down with Mother and be merry."

Cecily was the only one of his children who could get away with speaking to her father so disrespectfully. He would forgive her anything. Tom would have enjoyed that exchange if he had heard it.

What he did recall as he stacked the last pallet of apples on the shelf, was Cecily coming between him and Waaseyaaban and linking her arms in both theirs.

"Only Father could be such a pompous misery on a day like this. You come and sit at the bride and groom's table. We shall be as snug as four bugs in a rug. I reserve the right to have the handsomest couple in the room at my table."

As Cecily steered them over to a small table set apart from the long oak dining table where most of the guests were seated, Dawn Light said seriously, "You are right about Bella's man. He look just like frog."- and all three of them laughed.

Thank Jesu for Cecily's merry, loving heart Tom thought as he went to join Toby and Ned stacking the wood cart. When the cart was filled to capacity and the load secured with ropes, Toby backed Samson into the shafts and the cousins were ready to set off for Pocock's yard. The horse pulled the heavy load with ease. Sarah Bushy ran out of the house with a bag of provisions her mother had prepared and handed it up to Ned. It would be well into the afternoon before they returned and Joan believed men needed sustenance when they had been engaged in hard physical toil.

Sarah smiled prettily at Toby and Ned, waving them farewell. Thomas suspected that the girl had a fancy for Ned Carter, who was always ready to laugh with her and compliment her work. He was married with five children and did not flirt with her seriously, but Sarah magnified the significance of his every gesture. Tom watched her walk back into the house, smiling to herself in a dreamy way. She was a buxom girl with a stature like her mother. A willing worker, she was always ready to smile, showing her deep dimples. There was a simplicity about her, an innocence more fitted to a child than a nineteen year old.

Joan Farrow was twelve when she became a servant in the household of Sir Robert Mountfield. Lady Anne was taken by the girl's practicality and cheerful nature. Joan had infinite patience with her mistress' one year old daughter Grace and Lady Anne promoted her to be her personal maid. Two years later there was second daughter to keep an eye on. When Thomas was born, Joan was seventeen and being courted by Roger Bushy, a well favoured young stone mason. She refused his offer of marriage because she feared she would have to leave the Mountfield household if she wed. When Lady Anne

assured Joan she would not part with her even if she did marry, she accepted
Roger Bushy.

She spent her days at the Mountfield's commodious house in the centre
of Salisbury and went home in the evening to a modest cottage nearby.

Roger Bushy was killed in an accident. He was working on a building
in Salisbury when the scaffolding broke and he fell forty feet, breaking his neck.
This left Joan in her late twenties with a two year old daughter, but her job gave
her the security she needed. She loved the Mountfield children as if they were
her own and although she had several offers to re-marry, she was content with
her life. Her only worry was Sarah, who as she grew older did not develop
much understanding of the ways of the world. She was eager to please and too
ready to respond to the flattery of a handsome young man. Her mother's fears
were justified when Sarah was got with child by an itinerant peddler with a
honeyed tongue. She suffered a miscarriage before her condition was evident.
Lady Anne knew, but did not tell her husband, fearing he might have turned the
girl out of the house. Joan would consider herself forever in her mistress' debt
for her kindness. When she came to look after Thomas, she brought Sarah with
her, believing she would be safer in that remote house. The girl seemed happy
enough but Tom often wondered if Joan's understandable protectiveness isolated
her daughter too much. Perhaps it would be better to find her a decent husband.
He knew Joan feared Sarah would not cope with running a household and
that she would be put upon by others, but the fact that the girl spun romantic
fantasies around Ned Carter and cast longing eyes on male visitors suggested to
him that she was eager for a sweetheart.

He stood reflecting on the complicated concept of freedom; how a man
could be bodily free yet enslaved in mind and spirit, often by self-imposed
restrictions. The reverse could also be true that those in physical bondage
sometimes displayed a lightness of spirit to be envied.

"You think too much, too deep. Make head hurt."

Waaseyaaban stood beside him holding out a tankard of small beer. He
took it gratefully. Loading wood was thirsty work.

"Two ducks missing," she said, angling her head in the direction of the
poultry pen. "Many feathers. Fox I think."

Tom nodded. "I heard the vixen calling last night. She was fortunate not
to step into one of those snares. I'll take a good walk around later to see if there
are any more of them. Let's see where the fox got into the pen."

They were about to walk in that direction when a rider on a bay horse trotted up to the house from the front approach. He did not see them at first and slid off his horse with a groan, rubbing his backside ruefully. It was Simon Bailey.

He was wearing his black lawyer's robe and looked distressed. He took off his glasses and wiped the lenses on his robe, then mopped his brow.

"Simon!" Thomas was striding towards him, a puzzled smile on his face. "This is unexpected. You are a trifle early for Christmas."

He felt uneasy as he gave this light-hearted greeting. Simon had nothing with him- no saddle bag, no water bottle- none of the things a traveller took with him on a journey. Simon began rubbing his lower back again complaining,

"I do not have your skill in horsemanship Thomas Mountfield. If I ride more than twenty miles at a decent pace my backside gets numb."

"What's wrong? Has anything happened?"

Simon was eyeing the empty tankard in his friend's hand. "I could do with one of those."

"Of course, go on into the house and I will see to your horse."

Dawn Light took the reins. "No, I stable horse. You go with friend."

She smiled at Simon. She liked Bailey the best of all Tom's friends because he spoke plain and had simple tastes. She had been looking forward to his children coming at Christmas, though she wished the sharp-faced Ellen did not have to come too.

Thomas took Simon into the parlour and offered him the chair with the plumpest cushion out of kindness for his sore backside. Bailey laughed uneasily. When Tom fetched him a tankard of beer, he drank it straight down.

"You look like you could do with another."

Tom refilled it from a jug on the table and Simon drank half of that before he felt able to reveal his reason for being there. Although there was a chill in the December air Bailey was sweating. He had no inclination to sit close to the fire.

"I am in trouble Tom. I don't know my own mind. I need your advice. There is an arrest warrant out for me and I am confused as to what God wants me to do- whether to give myself up or save myself."

He took another draught of beer and shook his head in a bewildered way that was unlike Simon.

"What is the reason for the warrant? Is it your connection with that Presbyterian group?"

"No, not directly, although I suppose they know of the connection. Last

Sunday, John Aylmer, the Bishop of London was preaching at St.Paul's Cross.

I went hoping to hear an inspiring sermon, but all his so-called sermon consisted of was a condemnation of reformers and a call to obedience. So I shouted out and told him we wanted to hear the gospel preached not listen to him support Whitgift's oppression of good Christians."

Thomas felt his heart sink. "What else did you say?"

"No more than what I often say to you- that the church should be based on the word of God and the dissemination of that word by preaching and it was high time all the remnants of popery were swept away."

"Is that all you said?"

"Well- no. In the heat of the moment I said that the Queen herself does not set her people a good example by keeping such papist objects as a silver cross and candles in her own chapel."

"Jesu Simon, you spoke against the Queen in public? Don't you realise that could be interpreted as treason?"

Bailey buried his head in his hands. "I did not mean to speak against the Queen. You know I love and respect her as much as any man, but when zeal for the true religion takes hold of me I have to speak the truth. There were plenty in the crowd who agreed with me, though others tried to shout me down."

Thomas ran his hand through his hair and let out a long exhalation of breath, not sure what to say next. He felt as if he had received a punch in the stomach. The parlour door came open and Joan Bushy looked into the room.

"Dawn Light said Master Bailey was here. Oh- I see you have fetched him something to drink already. Shall I bring in sweetmeats or cakes?"

"No thank you Joan, not at present."

She sensed a tenseness in the atmosphere and withdrew without another word.

"When I got home that Sunday and dwelt on what I said, I realised I could be in trouble."

Simon took off his glasses, fiddled with them and put them back on again. Tom had never seen him so agitated, but it was not fear that gripped his friend. It was indecision and anguish of spirit.

"Ellen and the children are in Colchester visiting her brother. As we were coming to you for Christmas she decided to call on her family early. So knowing they were safe I thought I could face up to the consequences with an easy mind and if God wished me to suffer in His cause, to test my faith in the fire of affliction, I would be ready."

He got out of the chair and began to walk round the room. Tom stood watching him in silence, waiting for the rest of the story. "Monday I went into my chambers, prepared some cases as usual, had dinner with some colleagues- I was very calm and settled in my mind, but when I went in early this morning, my clerk came running in great excitement saying he had heard news that there was a warrant out for me and the archbishop's men would be coming to arrest me today. I told him not to fear, that I had expected it."

He came across to Thomas and took hold of both his arms in a firm grip as if he needed something to anchor himself.

"My clerk is only a young lad. He was in great distress and as I waited I began to have doubts. I asked myself if God really wanted this kind of sacrifice. Perhaps instead he wished me to leave my profession and testify to him by preaching the word. Then I could not be sure if God was speaking to me or if it was my fear of what was to come that put these ideas into my mind. I sorely needed to talk to someone- someone with a logical mind, who would understand my predicament and who was better than you Thomas?"

He was still gripping Tom's arms, increasing the pressure as he spoke.

"Help me Tom. Help me understand what God wants of me. Tell me it is not cowardice that brings me here."

"Oh Simon, I am perhaps the last person to know what God wants, but I do know that you are no coward. Come, sit down."

Bailey stared at him intensely for a moment and then relaxed his fierce grip on Tom's arms, allowing himself to be steered back to the chair. Thomas sat down beside him, encouraging him to finish the tankard of beer.

"Now listen. Any advice I will give you springs from a desire to see you safe in body first and foremost, for your family's sake as well as your own."

He understood now why Bailey had arrived with only the clothes on his back, still in his lawyer's robe. He had come straight from his chambers that morning.

"How did you escape them?" he asked.

"Once I had decided to come to you, I told my clerk to get a message to my wife's brother to take the family up country to my parents in Pontefract. My horse was stabled at my house and I dare not go back there. I reckoned they would come to take me either from the archbishop's residence at Westminster or from the Tower. The first lot would come by river, the second along Thames Street. So I went into Fleet Street, up Shoe Lane and hired a horse from an ostler on Holborn Hill. You know what a mild, slow moving beast my own horse is, but this one was far more lively. Twas as much as I could do to stay in the saddle at times. Then I nearly lost myself in this damn forest. The paths always confuse me."Despite the circumstances, Thomas could not help smiling. Simon had never been a keen horseman.

"I thought I would be safe down here for a while. Give me time to sort out what I should do, with your help."

"You will not be safe here for very long. Whitgift has Walsingham's legion of spies and interrogators to call on. They will be finding out who your friends are even now. They can be very persuasive. It will not take much effort to uncover your link with me."

"I never meant to endanger you. Perhaps my first instincts were the right ones. I must give myself up and suffer the consequences."

"No- no, you must not fall into their hands." Thomas had no doubts about that. "Do you not realise that if they interpret your words as treason, you will die for it? On the other hand, if they charge you with a lesser offence it is likely that you will be locked up in the Tower or Newgate and left to rot. I consider myself fairly strong-hearted. I have faced up to dangers at sea, on a foreign shore and on the battlefield, but to be shut away from the light and air in a damp, foul- smelling cell, left to sit in your own piss and ordure for years and years with no hope of release, I tell you Simon, that terrifies me. I doubt if I could retain my sanity. I do not pretend to understand God's purposes, but surely he cannot want that for you. How would that help your cause? Far better that you escape to safe place and spread the gospel. Is there nowhere you could go?"

Simon had seen a shudder pass through his friend's body as he contemplated imprisonment. He made the horror of it seem very real.

"I have friends who would welcome me in Scotland, in Kilmarnock. They have links to the group whose meetings I attended."

"Scotland is your best bet then- not too far from your family either. They could cross the border and join you."

"But how am I to get there?" Simon spread his hands out helplessly. "I could never ride all the way to Scotland. I should have to stop so many times someone is bound to notice me. I shall be discovered."

An idea was forming itself in Tom's mind, vague at first, but rapidly clothing itself in detail.

"You could go by sea."

Simon shook his head. "They are keeping a close watch on the ports since the Spaniards tried to invade. They are also looking out for Jesuit priests coming over in disguise."

"The main ports yes, but they cannot watch every little bay and harbour. You have heard me speak of Matthew Collier?"

"Aye often times. He was with you at Roanoke."

"He now lives beside a remote bay on the Dorset coast. It is very near Weymouth, but it is hidden out of sight. Besides Matthew's boatyard, there are only a few fishermen's cottages nearby. He and his two sons build and repair fishing boats and do some fishing themselves. They also have a cargo vessel which they use to collect and deliver goods for local merchants. She is only a small vessel; the three of them can handle her at sea, but she's very sturdy. He sails up to Newcastle to collect coal in her twice a year."

Simon had forgotten that his friend was an experienced sailor and had picked up the habit common to all seamen of assigning a feminine gender to their vessels. Tom was saying,

"It would not be safe to sail through the narrowest part of the channel and up the East coast – the route is too busy, but the Western route might work. He would sail around the Lizard and on into the Irish Sea, keeping the coast within sailing distance should storms blow up. There are many bays and inlets along the Welsh Coast where a boat can seek temporary safety. If the weather prevented him from entering the Forth of Clyde and landing you on Scottish soil, he could drop you off at Carlisle, where you could buy a horse and cross the border there."

Simon began to believe that this was possible because Tom spoke so positively about the prospect.

"But would he do this, risk the dangers of a winter sea for a stranger?"

"Matthew is sixty now, but he still has a taste for adventure. His sons are made of the same stuff. They go to sea in all weathers. They have a need to challenge the sea. It is in their blood. They are also of your mind concerning the need for reform in the church, although they are more inclined to keep their opinions to themselves. Matthew thinks they can do more good keeping their heads down so they will not be noticed. They have helped a number of people get abroad safely because of that."

"I see there are many different ways to do God's work," Bailey said.

He had defended his own bluntness, but had a sense of shame that he had been so foolish as to criticise the Queen openly, as he saw now how it put others in danger. Tom read his embarrassment in his face. Simon could never mask his feelings.

"We are what we are Simon." Thomas patted his arm reassuringly, wishing he felt as confident as his plan sounded. At least there was a plan. Many things could go wrong, but it had some chance of success.

"I would not expect him to attempt the trip without payment because of the danger involved," he said, knowing that Matthew would be willing to do it for nothing. A look of dismay came into Simon's eyes.

"But I have no money Tom- at least none on me. I gave what I had to the ostler to hire the horse and there is precious little at home, which is out of reach now anyway. I am due payment from two clients, but I'll never collect that now."

He had given what surplus money he had saved up to Ellen for her visit to Colchester. He was pleased that he had done so for she would need it to journey to Pontefract. He was sure her brother would find a way to get the family there safely.

"Don't worry about that," Thomas told him. "I can deal with that. Ned and Toby will be back this afternoon with the payment for a load of timber they delivered for me. Once I have paid them their wages, we can use the rest to offer Matthew Collier for his services."

Simon wanted to protest yet he knew he had no choice other than to accept his friend's generosity.

"I will pay you back somehow I swear."

"We have no need to consider that just now. Besides, I will be repaid in full if you get to Scotland safely."

"Just how far away is this bay?"

Despite the cushion beneath him, Simon was still feeling the effects of his ride from London.

"Sixty-sixty five miles. I know a direct route along the edge of the plain down past Warminster and then Shaftesbury. Not many travellers either, just farm workers and carriers on those tracks. I have done it in three hours before, riding Hope at a fast pace."

Bailey grunted dubiously. "Aye, well, I don't ride as fast as you and that creature I got at Holborn Hill pays little heed to my commands."

"If we take it steady and allow for you to fall of at least twice, we should make it in four hours."

Simon began to laugh. It was such a relief to have made up his mind. He was convinced now that God wished him to be free to preach His word. If it was not so, Thomas would not have been inspired to devise a workable plan. His friend's assurance that he was not a coward strengthened this resolve.

"We need not start until early tomorrow morning." Tom was also relieved that there was some action he could take to help. "The human blood hounds won't scent our connection out for a while yet. At least you can get a night's sleep, give your sore backside the chance to cool down a bit. Come through into the kitchen. I know Joan is eager to feed you."

Now the answer to his spiritual dilemma seemed clear Simon was ready to eat a hearty meal. When Ned and Toby returned with the money that would fund the voyage, Tom gathered everyone together in the kitchen and explained to them that Simon was in danger and needed to find a safe refuge for a while. He did not reveal what Simon had done, nor did he mention any details of his plan, no names or locations, but he did ask them all not to tell anyone else that Bailey had visited them.

He was restless that night, finding it impossible to sleep. Dawn Light lay curled against him in bed, her head resting on his shoulder as he lay on his back gazing up into the darkness. She often used his chest for a pillow, letting the rhythm of his breathing lull her to sleep. Tonight she felt the tenseness in his body.

"You cannot sleep Makwa," she murmured. "You worry about tomorrow?"

He sighed but did not reply. Simon had asked him what they should do if Matthew Collier was already out to sea carrying goods in his cargo boat. The possibility bothered him too. They had to take that chance but at present he was at a loss to provide an alternative solution if such a situation arose. Also his mind kept dwelling on how wild the Irish Sea could be at any time of year. Fierce squalls blew up without warning out of nowhere. They had visited their fury on the Spanish galleons retreating from the swift, agile English ships last July, driving some of them into the rocks on the Irish coast. Those men who managed to struggle ashore were handed over to the English authorities for execution, while others were murdered by the local inhabitants. Less than half of the one hundred and thirty strong fleet limped home to Spain in October, the crews ragged and starving. They had lost nine thousand men in the engagement.

In his mind's eye Thomas sailed the route Simon must take over and over again, as if his rehearsing it could make the journey safer.

"Why do you not tell me where you go?" Waaseyaaban asked.

"Because it is best that you do not know. Then if men should come asking, you can tell them in truth that you do not. I do not want to involve any of you too deeply in this."

"Men will come to ask?"

"Perhaps."

"Then there is danger in this for you?"

He ran his hand along the smooth length of her thigh. There was something almost organic in the way their bodies fitted together so perfectly.

"A small chance," he admitted. "But a much greater one for Simon. I won't be gone long. If all goes well, two days at the most."

"And if it does not go well?"

"Then I may be away longer- or not so long," he added as an after-thought, for something might prevent them from reaching their destination. "If you are worried, I am sure Toby or Ned would stay overnight until I return."

"I am not afraid. I protect the house."

He laughed, knowing that there were plenty of men who would hesitate to face up to Dawn Light when she was combative.

"No, I know you are not afraid, but perhaps Joan and Sarah might feel more at ease."

"You must sleep now," she urged. "You need strength for tomorrow. Simon is sleeping. I hear noise like pig snorting."

"He always did snore. That was the one disadvantage of sharing a lodging with him at the Middle Temple."

He tried to soothe his thoughts by recalling all the good times he and Simon had shared and eventually drifted off to sleep. He intended they should leave soon after first light, but when the winter light penetrated the window he was in a deep sleep and had to be woken by his wife, who sprinkled water on his face from the wash bowl. He roused himself and grabbing hold of the bowl, chased her around the room flicking water at her. Laughing she ran out on to the gallery. He was about to follow her when he remembered that he was naked and thought better of it, which made her laugh all the more.

"Pretty Elizabeth girl like to see you now," she teased.

"Oh go away wife!"

He shut the door on her and she ran downstairs still laughing.

Simon's problems had put thoughts about Elizabeth Norrington out of his head and that was where he wished them to stay. He needed to concentrate on the task in hand. He wondered however why Dawn Light had mentioned her now. Then he recalled that at supper the previous evening Simon was talking about their last meeting at Frome and how the Hanham coach had driven people off the road on its way to the fair. Tom had not told her that he met the Norringtons at Frome Fair. It was not an intentional omission, but the fact that his mother and Cecily were there when he arrived home, staying two days and all the conversation centred on his sister's wedding, meant that he did not get around to relating the happenings at the fair to his wife. Apple picking filled up the October days and the orchard was invaded by Ned and Toby's children clambering up the apple trees, throwing the fruit down to their siblings waiting below with baskets. Dawn Light's conversation tended to focus on immediate things, recent happenings, so discussing the children's antics was uppermost then and the events at the September fair seemed too distant for Tom to mention. However when Simon spoke about the coach and how Hanham was fond of parading his beautiful young wife in public, Waaseyaaban speculated on Tom meeting her there, but she did not ask him.

Simon Bailey had slept well and was in a better frame of mind to face the ride to Dorset. They were ready to leave by seven o'clock and the household assembled at the front of the house to bid them God speed. Toby and Ned had not yet arrived but had promised the day before to keep a close watch over the womenfolk. It was a cold morning, the light murky. Tom wore a jerkin lined with sheep's fleece over his doublet and had found another that fitted Simon-just about. Bailey was wider in the girth than the lean Thomas and was obliged to leave the last few laces of the garment undone. They had packed into a leather satchel some things he would need for the journey; his lawyer's robe, a thick woollen cloak to resist the cold winds at sea, enough money to hire a horse if needed and some provisions. Thomas tied the bag of gold and silver coins to pay Matthew on to his sword belt and offered to help Simon on to his horse.

"There is no need for that much mockery Tom Mountfield. I can manage that on my own."

Waaseyaaban slipped her hand inside the neck of her husband's shirt and touched the piece of turquoise that he wore. Then she fingered the similar pendant that was around her own neck.

"These keep you safe Thomas. Protect you."

He stroked her hair for a moment, kissed her and swung himself into the saddle.

"Do take care both of you," Joan Bushy advised. "God go with you Master Bailey. May you find a safe refuge."

The three women watched them ride into the trees accompanied by the deep baying of the wolfhounds who had been hut in the barn to prevent them from following Thomas. Sarah began to cry.

"Stop that crying you silly girl," her mother scolded. "Master Tom will find a safe place for his friend to stay and be back tomorrow. There is nothing to cry about."

The look in her eyes was far less assured than her tone of voice. "But I thought the gentleman and his family were to come for Christmas Mother."

"Well so they were and it seems they will not be able to now, but I am sure Mistress Cecily and Master Godfrey will call on us during the Christmas season and we will have a merry day with them."

This seemed to cheer Sarah. As they went back into the house, grateful to be out of the cold air, Joan asked Waaseyaaban, "Did Master Tom tell you in what kind of trouble Simon finds himself or where they are going?"

"No. It does not matter. My Makwa make it right."

Joan smiled indulgently. "Oh you believe he can sort out anything, don't you my dear? He is very special I grant you, but he cannot solve every problem that arises and he can make mistakes like anyone else. I was there when he took his first breath, handed him to his mother to hold in her arms. When you have cared for someone as a child, no matter how strong and capable they grow, you always have a sense of their vulnerability."

There was a puzzled frown across Waaseyaaban's brow and Joan was uncertain that she had understood what she had tried to explain to her. She patted her arm.

"Never mind my ramblings. Of course he will make it right. He will be back tomorrow, you see."

Thomas Mountfield was the last person to believe he was capable of solving everyone's problems. He would not be sure he had solved this one until he saw Simon Bailey sail away from the coast of Dorset and even then it could be months before any message reached him to confirm that Simon had made it safely to Scotland.

They made good progress in the first hour's riding, passing through several small villages nestled beneath the contours of the downs, then out on to the open plain past Westbury and Warminster to enter the valley and woodlands of the Wylie. The air was biting. They pulled their felt caps down over their ears which were turning red with cold. The breath from the horses' nostrils billowed out in clouds. They saw few people, only labourers trudging to work and a cart pulled by oxen goaded on by a sleepy lad so ragged he could have doubled as a scarecrow.

By the time they had ridden out of the valley up on to the high plain again Simon was beginning to slow down. They skirted around Shaftesbury and at the far end of the town stopped to let the horses drink from a stone water trough outside a seedy-looking inn.

Simon wondered if they might go in to see if there was any hot pottage on offer, but Thomas did not like the look of the place and after they had stamped around for a while to get some feeling back into their frozen feet, they rode on. The track they followed plunged them down into a series of deep valleys, linked by varying lengths of flatter terrain, often wooded. A weak sun struggled out to brighten, if not warm, the morning. The steepness of the track was hard on the horses and they paused in the middle of a ford to let the animals put their heads down into the water and drink again. A row of cottages, little more than hovels, lined one side of the road and two men carrying hurdles for fencing splashed through the shallow water of the ford, bidding them good day as they passed.

They were well into their third hour of travelling when they saw a town to their right, the largest settlement they had seen since passing Shaftesbury.

"That is Blandford," Tom said. "Not too far now."

"Thank the Lord for that," Simon replied with gratitude. He was weary of his jittery horse jerking sideways without warning every time a rabbit scuttled out or when it spied an unusual shape ahead. He envied Tom's easy striding, confident stallion and the way his friend could control its power.

The last part of the journey was through thick woodland until they emerged on to the road that led straight to Weymouth. This was a broader, more well-used road than most of the tracks they had ridden along that morning. The fields either side of it were ploughed and cultivated. They had travelled less than a mile along the road when Tom said, "Here it is." He pointed to a narrow lane on their left that dipped down steeply from the road. There was an edge of excitement in his voice. Although it was not yet visible, Tom could sense the presence of the sea; smell the salt in the air.

Climbing out of the hollow they followed the lane that now ascended gradually until Tom directed his friend to turn right, up another hill flanked by grassy hillocks grazed by a few sheep. They reached the brow of the hill and there it was spread out before them, the sea. Thomas always felt a stirring in his heart when he saw the sea. It was calm this morning, a pearl grey under the clouded sky, laced with bands of dark green. There was just one spot, where the sun had pushed itself through the cloud cover that glittered in the beam of light.

They reined in their horses and stopped to gaze for a few moments, looking towards the horizon where the sky and sea appeared to touch each other.

"I still find it hard to comprehend that you have sailed all the way to the Americas," Simon murmured, seeing the memories in Tom's eyes.

"I was at ease on board ship having sailed across to Europe with Philip on several occasions, but trips across the Channel do not prepare you for the journey we took to Roanoke. When there is nothing around you but the ocean for days on end time seems to stand still. You feel very insignificant. It strips away your vanity and pretentions."

"Were you fearful?"

"At times. When that storm hit us off the coast of Portugal on the outward journey I thought we must surely sink, but a well- built craft is less fragile than it looks."

He added this assurance because he knew Bailey had no experience of travelling by sea and did not wish to make him nervous. They could not see the shore of the bay from their vantage point, only the cliff tops, but they did see something that raised both their hopes. A two- masted crayer swayed at anchor farther out to sea, Matthew Collier's cargo boat. It was broad and sturdy; the masts fore and aft, leaving a wide central space to stow the cargo.

"We are in luck Simon. Come, let us find Matthew."

They urged the horses down towards the bay past three ramshackle fishermen's cottages. Outside one of them a woman in a thick shawl was sitting on an upturned barrel mending a fishing net. Another woman was brushing dirt out of her cottage with a long handled besom. They both stared at the riders with suspicion. Matthew Collier's boat yard consisted of two long barns positioned on the cliff overlooking the bay. They were angled with one end facing the sea with double doors at each end. The doors of one barn were closed, but on the other they were wide open at both ends revealing the ribs of a boat in the process of construction and beyond it the grey sea. A ramp led down from the barn to the beach below fitted at the top with a sledge-like contraption on wheels, a device to get boats from the barn down to the water's edge.

Farther back from the cliff was a timber-framed house with a thatched roof. It was bigger than the three fishermen's cottages put together and in good repair. A man came out of the house wearing a leather apron covered in curls of wood shavings. Keen grey eyes appraised them and then a smile split his weather-beaten face when he recognised Thomas.

"God's teeth, Tom Mountfield! I did not expect a visit from you until the spring."

Tom dismounted and Matthew Collier grasped his hand with warmth.

"Although it is always a pleasure to see you, I had not intended to come until the spring, bringing Waaseyaaban with me. This is a visit from necessity. My friend here is in danger and we need your help."Simon had slid out of the saddle and was stretching his stiff back. Tom introduced him to Collier who gave him a brisk nod.

"Well you both best come in and warm yourselves and tell me your troubles. You have had a cold journey."

Matthew seemed to be impervious to the cold himself for beneath the apron he wore only a shirt and the sleeves of that were rolled up to the elbows. Clearly he had been working on something when they arrived.

"I must attend to the horses first," Tom said. "Despite the cold, they are sweating from the journey. They need rubbing down and feeding."

Matthew smiled again, his eyes creasing at the corners. His hair was white and his face very lined, but he moved with the confidence and strength of a much younger man.

"I do not know another man who cares so much for the comfort of horses as Thomas," he told Simon. "My sons will look after them. Caleb! Micah! "

He shouted the names in a stentorian voice. The doors of the second barn swung open and his sons came trotting over to him. They were as pleased as their father to see Thomas and led the horses down to the barn from which they had just emerged.

Tom and Simon sat before the fire warming their hands and feet in Collier's small kitchen. There was an iron cooking pot suspended over the fire and Matthew filled a bowl with steaming pottage from this utensil for each of his visitors.

"You get that down you while I clear away all these wood shavings before Esther comes back. She has gone into Weymouth market in the donkey cart. She hates me to work indoors, but I thought while she was gone I would take advantage of a comfortable chair."

On the floor in the corner was a square canvas covered in wood shavings and the half-finished carving of an eagle. Simon commented on how life- like it looked.

"Tis a figure head for a ship, commissioned by a merchant down in Poole. Offered me a handsome sum to do it. I can turn my hand to anything to do with wood."

Collier's sons joined them and helped themselves to pottage, sitting down next to each other on a bench along the kitchen wall. Thomas told them Simon's story and the plan he had conceived, hoping that Matthew would agree it was possible. Matthew and his sons listened with quiet attention to the story, not interrupting at any stage. Caleb and Micah were both short and wiry like their father.

All three of them, despite their lack of inches, gave the impression of great strength and endurance, particularly in their brown, sinewy arms. Caleb the elder brother was blonde with grey eyes very like Matthew's. Micah had curly chestnut hair and brown eyes, but their features were very similar. It was easy to see they were siblings.

"I know it is a long journey up the west coast and not a propitious time of year, but I feel it is Simon's only hope," Tom said. "And I know you have helped those of a like mind to you before."

"I am ready to do it." Caleb Collier slapped his hand down on his knee with decision. "Tis sinful that a god-fearing Protestant should be harried by his own church."

Micah added his agreement. Simon looked at them gravely.

"I want you to be sure. I have no wish to put others in danger. I have already involved Thomas and feel guilty about it. I have no right to expect a welcome here or that you should embark on a dangerous course for a stranger."

"Any friend of Sir Thomas is no stranger to us," Caleb declared.

Matthew smiled at Tom. "I vow, I always forget to address you respectfully."

"Tom is good enough for me," Thomas replied. "It was Tom when we first met and so it shall remain, No touch on the shoulder with a royal sword can make any difference to that and there is no need for Caleb and Micah to call me Sir Thomas."

"Ah well, I think they take pleasure in the notion that their old father has a friend who was knighted by the Queen's own hand. Let them call you sir."

"I never do." Simon Bailey said this as if the fact had just occurred to him and Tom gave him a look that plainly showed he was glad of his friend's omission.

"Sir Thomas is always welcome in this house," Caleb told Simon. "He saved my father from a native spear in Roanoke and took an arrow in his back for his pains. We were full of joy to see them both back safe from that wild place."

Matthew explained that he had intended the rest of the family to join him at Roanoke should the settlement succeed.

"Mother was mightily glad that it failed," said Micah. "She had no desire to live in the Americas. But Father, we must help Master Bailey."

Matthew nodded thoughtfully. "Yes, I agree. If we are fortunate and this weather holds for the next two weeks, we should do it easy enough. We must not delay, but prepare to leave on the tide tonight. Tis best we start in darkness. The coast watch has been vigilant since the Spaniards got so bold.

They fear that Spanish spies, Jesuit priests and smugglers are hiding behind every rock. They were here two nights ago, so I doubt if they will come again tonight."

Thomas and Simon exchanged relieved glances. Tom untied the money bag from his belt and held it out to Matthew.

"You must take this for your services."

Collier weighed the bag in his hand.

"Too much Tom."

"No, it is commensurate with the danger of the task. Should-God forbid-any ill befall you, Esther will need some money put by. I think when she returns and hears of this plan, she will be far less enthusiastic than you."

"Every time we put out to sea there is a chance that we will not return. Esther's family have been fishermen and sailors for generations. She knows how unforgiving the sea can be and is prepared for it."

Thomas wondered if you could ever be truly prepared for bereavement. Facing up to the possibility was very different from experiencing the reality. He knew that only too well. When Esther did arrive home, laden with baskets of provisions, it was evident that she was not as pleased to see the visitors as her menfolk, though she passed no comment on her husband's intentions. Her sons were keen to avoid her gaze however and all the men drifted out of the house.

"Listen to her banging the cupboard doors," Micah said with a grin. "Mother has no need to speak to show her displeasure."

Thomas suggested that she must feel lonely when they were away at sea for long periods of time.

Caleb laughed. "Oh she says she is. She is always chiding us for not marrying yet and providing her with grandchildren to keep her company, but as soon as we set sail, she calls on our cousin Ephraim's youngest son Joseph to come and stay with her. Poor Joe, she orders him around like a servant and he is fool enough to do her bidding. Women are full of wiles."

"How is that comely, spirited wife of yours Tom?" Matthew asked.

"Just as comely and full of spirit as ever."

"Pleased to hear it."

They spent most of the afternoon taking provisions for the journey over to the crayer in a rowboat. Thomas and Simon went with them to inspect the vessel that would be Bailey's home for the next few weeks.

As they helped to secure the barrels in which the provisions were stored in the cargo space, it dawned on Simon that there was no lower deck and no cabin on the Dorset Maid. Tom was gazing up at the highest point of the cliffs farther along the coast, watching the seagulls wheeling over it, white against the grey sky. Bailey plucked at his sleeve and murmured in a low voice so the Colliers would not hear, "Thomas, where does a man sleep on this boat, or get shelter from rough weather?"

Mountfield pointed to a roll of canvas attached to a series of rings fixed to the level of the deck above the cargo space.

"That canvas will be pulled over any cargo to protect it from the elements and attached to the rings on the other side. When there is a small crew like this, men take it in turns to sleep. They get down under the canvas, wrap themselves in a cloak and sleep beside the cargo. It is like being in a tent. You can roll up your lawyer's robe and use it as a pillow."

Simon looked dubious. He did not fancy lying for hours on those planks. He imagined he felt the stiffness in his back and legs even then just contemplating it.

"But when there is a big swell, does not the water get under the canvas?"

"I can't promise you a dry journey," his friend replied.

Thomas could understand Bailey's apprehension for the lawyer's only experience of boats was being rowed across the Thames in a wherry.

They were securing the last of the barrels when Caleb spotted a rowing boat with a crew of four coming from the direction of Weymouth. As it drew closer, it headed in towards the bay. Thomas glanced anxiously at Matthew.

"That's Amos Jackson and his brothers. They live in the cottages yonder. They hire themselves out to work on the bigger fishing boats that operate from Weymouth harbour. They row across to Weymouth early in the morning to see what work they can pick up."

"Their women folk gave us some keen looks when we rode past this morning," Tom said.

"You have nothing to fear from them," Collier assured him. "That family has no love for the long reach of the government. They indulge in a bit of smuggling when the chance arises. They ask no questions about any of my visitors and I turn a blind eye to theirs. Besides, strangers often come to my yard, merchants' agents with haulage commissions or to arrange for boat repairs."

The fishermen had hauled their rowing boat up the beach into the shelter of the cliff and were trudging along the pebbles carrying some lobster pots.

"Looks as if they will have a tasty supper," was Micah's observation. The winter darkness descended by four o'clock and it was an uneasy time for Simon and Tom sitting in Collier's house waiting for the right hour to embark. The plan was for Thomas to go out to the Dorset Maid with them and then bring the rowboat back to shore. He would pull it up alongside the Jacksons' craft, collect his horse and ride home through the night.

As he sat staring into the fire, Tom had an unsettling thought. Simon had hired his horse at Holborn and ostlers often branded their hire horses to discourage customers from acquiring them permanently. Should Bailey's escape route be traced and the horse found on Matthew's property, he would be incriminated.

He and Simon went down to the barn with lanterns, both grateful for something to do besides waiting and inspected every inch of the horse for distinguishing marks. It was a relief not to find anything. The animal did not take kindly to such intimate attention and aimed a kick with a back leg at Simon as he moved away.

"I tell you Tom, this creature took a dislike to me the moment I got on its back," he complained. "I swear I fear the sea less than the thought of riding this horse any distance again."

The horse turned its head and looked at Bailey, its eyes shining in the lantern glow, with a malicious expression in them that suggested it had no desire to bear him on its back again anyway. Thomas burst out laughing and it lifted the tension somewhat. Before returning to the house Tom saddled Hope and led the stallion out of the barn, tying him to the hitching rail outside, ready for a swift get-away. He patted the horse's neck murmuring assurances that they would be riding back home soon. Simon admitted that he felt guilty that the ostler would not get his mount back. The honest Bailey had never stolen anything in his life and hated the thought that the Holborn ostler would regard him as a thief, but there was nothing he could do to remedy it. Caleb suggested that his mother should tell her nephew's son Joseph that the horse was left in part payment by a customer and ask him to take it to the local horse dealer and sell it. This idea was welcomed by Esther, who had no desire to feed an extra horse.

When the hour for departure finally arrived, Esther Collier gave her husband and sons a restrained kiss each, with no show of emotion.

"I am going to bed now. I will lock the doors behind you. I hope you find a safe haven Master Bailey."

She gave Thomas a long, enigmatic look. He felt she was asking him what was the use of bringing her husband back safely from Roanoke when he was now putting him and her boys in more danger. Perhaps it was the reflection of his own uneasy conscience that he saw in her face rather than any rebuke of her own, but he could find nothing to say to her and she turned away.

They needed their lanterns to find their way down to the rowboat for although the moon was in its second quarter and growing fuller, it was obscured by banks of cloud and it was only when the stiff breeze parted the cloud at intervals that the path was illuminated by moonlight. They rowed to the Dorset Maid without speaking, the sound of the oars cutting the water exaggerated by the silence. Climbing aboard the crayer, the Colliers lit the fore and aft lanterns and prepared to cast off. There was no time for elaborate farewells. Thomas shook hands with Matthew and his sons, thanking them once again for their help and courage, then he embraced Simon. Bailey felt tears well up in his eyes which misted the lenses of his spectacles as he held Tom firmly in his arms.

"I shall pray for you Thomas and I hope you will do the same for me. Tis truly said that a good friend is worth more than all the world's riches. If God wills it we shall meet again. If not, you will always be in my heart."

"I will miss you Simon Bailey. Try to get a message to me somehow when you are settled in Kilmarnock."

Simon promised he would do so and Tom clambered back into the rowboat. He could see the dark shape of Simon on deck, waving to him as he pulled away from the crayer. He swallowed down the lump in his throat and put much effort into his rowing in an attempt to fight off the sorrow he was feeling. He knew there was every likelihood that he would never see Simon again. As eager as he was for Bailey's safety, he could not help feeling sorry for himself. Over the last few years all his close friends were taken from him, Philip, Joshua, Harry and now Simon. At that moment he was flooded with a stinging sense of loss. Reaching the shore he pulled the rowboat up the beach to rest in the hollow under the cliff next to Amos Jackson's. He gazed out to sea trying to make out the Dorset maid and fancied he could just see the glow of her lanterns, but that too soon disappeared.

He turned to walk back to the house to collect Hope, when he heard shouting and saw two lights approaching along the beach from the Weymouth direction. He put out the candle in his lantern and hooking the lamp on to his belt, scrambled up the cliff directly behind him, cursing under his breath,

"Damnation, coast watch!"

He was sure they could not have seen the Dorset Maid, but must have spotted his lantern as he rowed to shore.

Perhaps they were acting on information that smugglers were in the area. Whatever it was, he could not risk being caught. He had no feasible excuse to offer for his presence there in the darkness. The shouting grew louder and he could make out the words, "Who is up there? Stop, stop for the constables."

Ascending the narrow path in the dark was no easy task and took longer than he anticipated. He was almost at the top when a figure loomed at the side of him. He must have come up another path with an easier ascent. Coming some way behind was the light of a lantern, presumably held by another constable. It was too dark to see any faces. The nearest constable struck out with his cudgel into the darkness and more by luck than aim caught Tom a hard blow on the side of the head. The force of it knocked him down on to his knees, but before the man could strike again, Thomas rammed his shoulder into his legs, taking him off balance. He waved his arms in an attempt to stay upright to no avail and tumbled down the path right into his colleague carrying the lanterns. The second constable lost his footing as a consequence and they both crashed down on to the beach, the lantern glass smashing on the rocks. Tom got to his feet and managed to haul himself on to the cliff top. His head was ringing as if a church bell had been striking right next to him and blood was running into his eye and down on to his jerkin. He could hear groaning below. One of the constables was moaning in pain.

"Oh my leg, Jesu, I've broken my leg."

Thomas stumbled across the flat stretch of ground to Collier's house, untied Hope, swung into the saddle and urged the stallion up the steep track away from the bay. He did not look back once, but rode the horse as fast as he could go for about an hour to make sure he was well away from the area. He thought he knew the way home well, even in the dark, but he was beginning to feel the effects of the blow on the head and was forced to slow down to consider the direction with more care. He was losing a quantity of blood and felt very sick. When he looked upwards, the tops of the trees seemed to be moving down towards him and he realised that he was swaying in the saddle. He pulled Hope to a halt and almost fell to the ground.

"A dismount worthy of Simon Bailey," he told himself. He fumbled in the darkness for his saddle bag intending to take a drink, but the horse appeared to be moving away from him in slow motion and a blackness profounder than the night closed in on him.

Tom Mountfield opened his eyes to stare up at a dawn sky smudged with traces of pink. He had no idea where he was or what had happened. He lay on his back listening to the song of a thrush, one of the few birds to sing in the winter months. When he sat up he felt a fierce pain in his head and putting his hand up to it found his hair, the side of his face and the front of his jerkin sticky with partially dried blood. His whole body was chilled and he began to shiver. Then his memory flooded back. He looked around to see that he was lying in a shallow, dry ditch beside a field. He must have been insensible for some time. He heard a cough and turning his head painfully saw two children, a boy and a girl, standing on the track nearby, staring at him. They were thin and dirty, their clothes patched and too inadequate to withstand the cold weather. The girl was constantly scratching under her arms and in her hair as if she was badly infested. She wore no shoes; her feet were wrapped in pieces of cloth.

"We thought you was dead," the boy announced. "Did you fall off your horse Master?"

"Horse, where's my horse?" Thomas pushed himself up out of the ditch. There was little sensation in his feet and he stamped on the floor to bring some life back into them. He was forced to stop however because the stamping made him feel dizzy. The boy jerked his thumb in the direction of a copse of trees on the edge of the field.

"There's an 'orse over there Master. Might be yourn- has a saddle on him."

Much to his relief Tom saw Hope grazing on some sparse tufts of grass beneath the trees.

"You're bleeding," said the girl, her pink rimmed eyes fixed on the wound on his head. "You need an apothecary. There's one in the next village. His charges are too high for the likes of us my mother says, but you may be able to afford him."

"What is the next village called?" Tom asked.

"Sturminster Master.

He sighed with relief. At least he was on the right road, although he was some miles away from Shaftesbury yet. He intended to walk over and fetch Hope, but his legs did not feel too steady, so he whistled a shrill call to the stallion. Hope's ears came up, he turned and began ambling in their direction. The children exchanged impressed glances. Thomas leaned against the horse, stroking his ears and neck, praising him for staying close by. He was pleased to discover that the contents of his saddle bag were still intact. Reaching inside, he pulled out some coins and gave the children two silver sixpences each. "That is for your kind advice, but I doubt if I will be calling on your expensive apothecary."

He hauled himself into the saddle and rode off towards Sturminster. The boy bit both sixpences to make sure they were genuine. His sister followed suit.

"They'm real," she said, hardly believing their good luck. They were both pleased that the man in the ditch turned out not to be dead after all.

The rest of the journey home was a blur to Thomas. He had to concentrate to stay in the saddle for nothing around him appeared to be in the right place or at the right angle. A stone way marker that said Warminster two miles doubled itself when he looked at it. One way marker moved behind the other, then they stood side by side and finally morphed into one again. He feared he was about to pass out once more, but pulled himself together with an effort. He was grateful that Hope knew the path home through the forest because by the time he reached his own domain, he could not tell one path from another. Hector and Ajax came loping out of the trees to escort them to the house, barking a greeting.

Dawn Light was sitting in the front porch peeling and coring apples when she heard the dogs barking. She saw her husband ride towards the barn and perceived something was wrong for he was leaning forwards over his horse's neck. She threw down her knife and ran across to him as he slid out of the saddle, holding on to Hope to steady himself.

"Makwa, you are hurt. What happen to you?"

"Just a blow from a cudgel. I have suffered worse."

She put her arm around his back to support him. Joan Bushy opened the side door into the kitchen at that moment and hurried over to them. The sight of all that blood horrified her.

"Oh Master Tom what have you done now?"

He smiled thinking of the countless times he had heard her say that. She went to the other side of him for extra support for she could see how unsteady he was. In the kitchen Sarah screamed and dropped the saucepan she was holding when she saw the state of her master. Then she ran outside to find Ned Carter. Tom's stallion left standing alone, walked into the barn to his regular stable, hoping to be fed.

Dawn Light and Joan took Thomas into the parlour and eased him into his favourite chair. He ran his hands over the familiar smooth wood of the chair arms, grateful to be home. He must have lost consciousness for a few moments because the next thing he knew was that Joan was bathing his head and his wife was sitting on the floor beside him rubbing his icy hands to restore the circulation in them. "This wound is worse than the one he got when he fell out of the oak tree," Joan was saying. "He should never have climbed to the top of that great tree." She stopped when she realised Tom was stirring. "Thank goodness you are with us again."

"I was trying to reach Meg's kitten," he murmured as he sat forward endeavouring to clear his blurred vision, "When I fell out of that oak tree."

Tom's sister Grace, who was six years his elder, was a quiet girl who kept her feelings to herself. Margaret, three years older than Tom, was the exact opposite. She was noisy, excitable, always ready to turn the smallest incident into a major drama. He was seven, skimming stones across the lake in the garden when Meg came weeping and wailing because her new kitten had climbed into the oak tree and could not get down. She was convinced it would fall out and die, insisting that Tom climb up to rescue it. He loved climbing trees and did not hesitate, but he was the one who fell. He had almost reached the kitten when the branch beneath him broke. He remembered the sensation of falling but nothing else until he woke up in his own bed with his mother sitting beside him, her face white and anxious while his father spoke to a physician. Meg was still wailing although the kitten, startled by the commotion, had climbed down on its own.

"He was insensible for nigh on two hours. We were afraid he had broken his skull." Joan worked away at the cut, cleaning the dried blood from his hair.

"Fortunately I have a thick skull," he said and then winced as she pressed on the deepest part of the wound.

"This is a deep wound. It needs a stitch or two."

"Then stitch it Joan."

Dawn Light nodded her agreement and Joan went to fetch her sturdy tapestry needle and some thread. While she was gone Dawn Light asked if

Simon was safe. It would be some while before Tom knew the answer to that question, but he replied, "He is on his way to a safe place."

Joan sterilised the needle in the fire, greased the thread with a herbal balm and Thomas gritted his teeth while she put three stitches into the wound. She then put a pad impregnated with the balm over it and bound his head with a strip of cloth. The balm had a very pungent scent and he wondered vaguely if he would ever get the smell out of his hair. He felt very sleepy and was willing to accede to Waaseyaaban's suggestion that he go to bed and rest, but when he tried to stand the room revolved alarmingly and he sat down again.

"No, I shall never get up those stairs. Leave me here. It's comfortable enough."

They took off his blood-stained jerkin to find that the blood had seeped on to his doublet and shirt, so they helped him to strip those off too. He could scarce lift his arms above his head he was so drained of energy, but the clean clothes they brought for him smelt fresh and comforting. His wife pulled off his boots and lifted his feet up on to a foot stool, while Joan put a pillow behind his head. He drank a glass of wine, declaring that it was time they both stopped fussing over him and they left him to sleep.

When Joan went into the kitchen with the bloody cloths and the bowl of water tinged red, she found Sarah, her face streaked with tears, with Toby and Ned standing anxiously by the cooking range.

"Is he going to die Mother?" Sarah asked. "And has Master Bailey been killed?"

"No, you foolish girl." Joan looked across at the cousins, both of whom were screwing up their caps in their hands in agitation. "Has she been alarming you? Master Bailey is well on his way to his destination and Sir Thomas has suffered a blow on the head which needed stitching. We have not quizzed him over the circumstances yet because he is very tired and needs to sleep, but when he has rested he will be well enough. He is not badly hurt. His life is not in danger."

She picked up the saucepan which her daughter had dropped when they brought Tom through the kitchen. There was a large dent in the side of it and Joan frowned at Sarah. The girl did not notice because she was too busy describing to Ned Carter how her heart nearly leaped out of her breast when she saw all that blood. Ned was sympathising with her far too much in Joan's view.

"I'm sure Master Tom would want you to get on with your work. His horse needs attending to for a start."

She gave them sharp looks and they did not need telling twice.

Thomas slept soundly for several hours until he became part of a troubling dream. It was a version of his recent adventure, but more fearful with a sense of pursuers always close behind. It culminated in himself and Simon Bailey alone on the Dorset Maid in a ferocious storm. The wind howled like a thousand souls in torment and the boat was thrown around by giant waves. Simon stood in the cargo space clutching to his chest a bible, half as big again as the large bibles placed on lecterns in churches. The ship lurched and Simon was washed overboard. As he struggled in the water it was clear that the Bible was weighing him down, but he would not let it go.

Tom begged him to loosen his hold on it. He threw a line of rope out to him, but Simon could not take it because of that bible. All Thomas could do was watch his friend disappear beneath the angry sea, still holding on to the Word of God. He woke abruptly, shouting out Simon's name, his eyes wide with horror. Waaseyaaban was sitting on the floor, her legs tucked up beneath her, resting her head against his thigh. She squeezed his hand.

"Peace Thomas. You dream bad things, but you are safe at home."

He stared at her without comprehension for a moment, breathing heavily.

The wolfhounds, who were lying on the other side of his chair, both stood up when he shouted and now they pushed their heads into his lap, vying for attention. He stroked them, comforted by the familiar feel of their shaggy coats beneath his fingers.

"Thank Jesu it was only a dream"

The door came open and Joan Bushy hurried in asking if all was well. She had heard him shout Simon's name.

"It's nothing Joan. I was dreaming –that's all."

"Are you sure you are not feverish?" She put her hand on his forehead. "Perhaps I should send for that little Italian physician, Doctor Rienzi, who lives at Pewsham."

"No, I do not need a physician."

Tom had visions of Joan confusing the poor fellow, whose English was limited, with tales about him falling out of trees and other childhood escapades.

"I am not feverish. It was just a troubling dream- nonsense as dreams often are."

He knew it was not nonsense. The symbolism of it was plain enough.

"Will you tell us how you came to be injured?" Joan asked. "Just what happened?"

"I told you before we left that I cannot reveal the details of the plan for Simon's freedom, so I will not describe to you where we went or exactly what happened. It is safer for you if you do not know. But on the way home I was struck by a constable with a cudgel because in the darkness he mistook me for a felon. It was so dark I did not see his face, nor he mine and I managed to ride away. Now stop fussing over me Joan Bushy. I am not seven years old anymore."

"You get yourself in just as much trouble," she retorted," But I must admit you are looking a little better."

"I feel much better. My vision has cleared and the room has ceased to spin and I promise not to fright you with any more shouting."Satisfied, Joan went back to her work. All this while Dawn Light was sitting quietly, her head still resting against his thigh. Her calm, wordless presence was soothing, like cool water to a dry throat. Her hair lay across his knee and he stroked the glossy black curtain absently as they sat in companionable silence. He was wondering where the Dorset Maid was now- hopefully up past the Bristol Channel. His mind also dwelt on those exciting, stressful months at Roanoke and he was eager to take up his pen again to complete his description of the experience.

He had intended to ask Matthew Collier if he had heard any news of the more recent settlers in the colony, but the urgency of Simon's situation had put it out of his mind. When he and the other colonists, despairing of Richard Grenville's return with supplies, had sailed home with Drake, Grenville had arrived not long after their departure. He had no choice but to return to England, although he left a small detachment of men to maintain an English presence on the island.

The expedition organised by Raleigh in 1587, led by John White, was instructed to collect the men on Roanoke and set up a new colony on Chesapeake Bay. When they arrived at Roanoke all that was left of the garrison was one skeleton. The rest had disappeared without trace. For a reason that he did not have the courtesy to explain to the colonists, the commander of the fleet insisted that they should remain at Roanoke and refused to let them back on board the ships. White had no choice but to attempt to re-establish the colony and reopen friendly communications with the Croatan. The previous conflict had not been forgotten by the Secotan however who were still hostile and murdered one of the colonists, George Howe, while he was fishing for crabs. Uneasy, the settlers persuaded John White to sail back to England for re-enforcements. He was reluctant to do so: his daughter had just born a child, the first baby to be born at Roanoke, Virginia Dare. Eventually he was persuaded and sailed in dangerous winter seas back to England, leaving one hundred and fifteen colonists behind, including his own family. All this information had been passed on to Thomas during previous visits to Matthew Collier's boat yard.

White hit a snag when he reached England because the country was gripped by the fear of a coming invasion, every available ship being called on to be ready to fight the Spaniards. The only ships he could hire were two small vessels that were inadequate for his purpose.

To make matters worse the captains in charge of the vessels were only interested in booty and tried to attack some Spanish ships on the outward journey. They failed and were captured themselves, losing all the supplies and some of the re-enforcements intended for the colonists. The ships sailed back to England. As far as Tom knew, White had made no attempt to return since and there had been no news of the colony. He could well imagine what the colonists were going through, threatened by hostile natives and short of supplies. He had experienced a taste of that himself, but these unfortunates had been abandoned for two years. They may not have survived. He was thankful that he had refused John White's appeal to join them when they sailed in 87.

"What is in your mind Makwa?"

Waaseyaaban was familiar with that distant, absorbed look in her husband's eyes.

"Oh, I was thinking about your country. Although it was hard for us colonists there I consider it a very beautiful land. You must long to go back there sometimes. I often think of the nights we sat out under the stars watching the beavers-how vast the sky seemed."

"Some things I miss, my brothers, the cry of the wolf, but I have many things here to love, the garden, the forest. I tell you before, my home is where you are."

Thomas often asked himself what he would have done if she had refused to come to England with him. He liked to think he would have risked everything and stayed with her, but he could not be sure. After four years together he was certain now that he could not live without her.

"The men who ask questions about Simon, "she said looking up into his face, "When will they come?"

"Soon I expect," he replied.

Thomas was right about the men who ask questions. It was the 2nd of January and he was in the village visiting Nathan Pocock the timber merchant. There was a one room cottage belonging to Pocock backing on to the stream that ran past the timber yard. He had been in the habit of renting it out to tenants for years now but at present it was empty. Tom was hoping to rent it himself as the first step in fulfilling one of his long cherished desires- to open a school in the village. The nearest school was ten miles away and the poorest of the villagers had no transport.

In fine weather some children might be persuaded to rise at the crack of dawn and walk to school, but in heavy rain or the winter snows they would sit all day in wet clothes and boots. Many of their cottages were damp and poorly heated so their wet apparel did not dry out at home overnight. Few children had two pairs of boots or shoes and some did not have a change of clothes, which obliged them to put the same damp garments back on again in the morning. This state of affairs meant that very few children from the village attended school in bad weather. A school in their own village would make all the difference. Pocock's empty cottage was ideal. It needed some repair but it was basically sound.

Once it was ready, Tom intended to offer as an incentive, two pairs of new boots to every child who attended school regularly. His brother-in-law Godfrey Roper was always eager to support charitable causes and had promised to talk to his fellow clothiers in Salisbury to persuade them to join him in contributing money to buy desks and chairs. Thomas had almost convinced Pocock to offer the house free of charge. The timber merchant was still thinking about it.

Mountfield was looking around the empty house gauging how much work needed doing on it. Hector and Ajax had followed him down to the village and were sniffing around the wood pile beside the house, perhaps picking up the scent of rats. Hope was tied to the gate post. The gate itself had fallen to pieces long since and lay in fragments around the posts. Tom finished his inspection and was about to mount Hope when he saw a party of horsemen reined in outside the timber yard talking to one of Pocock's workmen. There were two men in sombre garments and black cloaks accompanied by four armed soldiers wearing the livery of the Westminster Palace Guard. Tom was in no doubt who they were. The man talking to Pocock's labourer seemed to be growing impatient with his answers. Thomas swung into the saddle and rode over to them, the wolfhounds in close pursuit.

"Excuse me gentlemen, are you asking the way to Sir Thomas

Mountfield's house by any chance?"

He nodded at the labourer who made off into the yard, glad to be free of the questions. The man in charge of the party gave Tom a surprised look, not expecting to be thus addressed.

"I happened to hear the name mentioned as I rode up. My house is rather off the beaten track. I am Sir Thomas, so if you wish to speak to me it will save you a journey. What can I do for you?"

The man looked at him as if he was calculating whether Tom was telling the truth. He must have decided in his favour because he said, "Good day Sir Thomas. I am Walter Amor, special commissioner for His Reverence, the Archbishop of Canterbury. This is my assistant William Paul. We are investigating the disappearance of a lawyer by the name of Simon Bailey, who we believe is a friend of yours."

"Well, that is a coincidence. I am worried about his whereabouts myself. He was due to stay with me at Christmas, he and his family, but they did not arrive and I have received no word to tell me why. I was about to ride over to Devizes to send a message by courier to his chambers at Lincoln's Inn to try to discover what happened."

He looked the commissioner straight in the eye as he said this. Most of it was true anyway, except the bit about riding to Devizes. Walter Amor had an impassive face with the steely gaze of a man used to interrogation.

"You will not find him in his chambers." His voice was crisp and business-like.

"There is a warrant out for his arrest and he has fled."

"What is he accused of?"

"The offence is a very serious one. He criticised the person of her Majesty the Queen in a public place and wishes to subvert the Church of England. Are you not familiar with his views?"

"I know Simon to have an honest Christian desire to reform the church, but not to subvert it. He has a great love for his country and the Queen. He would never speak harm against her."

"Do you share his religious views Sir Thomas?"

Amor snapped his fingers at his assistant who handed him a sheaf of papers in a leather folder.

"I do not think my religious convictions are at issue here," Thomas replied evenly.

"Indeed?" Amor was flicking through the papers and found what he was looking for, "But I see here that you do not attend your local church every week. Is that because you have a quarrel with the order of service?"

Tom smiled. "You have been checking on me I see."

"It is my job Sir Thomas. You have a heathen wife and an unconventional manner of living. Perhaps you have no religion at all."

"Are you in holy orders Commissioner?"

"No, mine is a secular post. Why do you ask?"

"Oh- just interested. I presume you have come to discover if I have seen Simon Bailey recently or know where he might be"

Amor inclined his head. "Well, as I have just told you, I wish I knew myself for I am concerned for his welfare. I saw him last September in Frome, where he came to meet a client and he assured me he and Ellen were coming for Christmas. I have had no word since."

Amor handed the folder back to his assistant.

"I have no wish to infer that you are a liar Sir Thomas, but we have instructions to search the property of all Bailey's acquaintances. Here is my seal of authority."

He took from inside his cloak a document stamped with an elaborate red seal. Thomas glanced at it and handed it back.

"You must admit that your house would serve as a good hiding place, for I gather it is in the midst of the forest. I was troubled by that fellow from the wood yard's reluctance to tell me the way and his failure to mention that you were nearby."

"I suppose your job makes you suspicious of everything Master Amor. The folk around here are wary of armed soldiers and prefer not to get involved. Besides, he may have no notion of the way to my house, beyond knowing it is in the forest. It is only when you have followed the paths often that they become familiar to you and remain in the memory."

Walter Amor was used to men becoming nervous and confused when he questioned them and searched their faces with his passionless eyes. This Thomas Mountfield is at ease, amused, on the edge of insolent, he thought to himself. He pondered on whether it was the confidence of a man telling the truth or of a brave, defiant man, shielding a friend.

"This is a serious matter," he warned. "Not to be taken lightly."

"I assure you I do not take it lightly and you are welcome to search my house and the part of the forest that belongs to me. I do not live in a great mansion; there are few places to hide in my humble dwelling. It will not take you long. Come, I will escort you there myself."

So saying, he turned Hope around, whistled to the wolfhounds and set off through the village.

"He is a cool fellow Master Amor," William Paul said to the commissioner. "I don't think he has anything to hide."

"Hmm, perhaps not. He has style I grant you. You must remember that he spent some years in the service of Sir Philip Sydney. That sort of man can be very loyal to his friends. I shall be interested to judge the reaction of his household to my queries."

The party moved off to follow Sir Thomas. Amor observed how readily the villagers they passed greeted Mountfield. He appeared to be well respected. On the other hand, the looks they gave the soldiers were surly, bordering on hostile. The forest in winter without its thick canopy of leaves seemed less impenetrable, but there was still an air of mystery about it. The bare branches twisted above their heads forming a dark lattice. The soldiers grew uneasy the deeper they rode into the trees, looking around them at every noise as if they expected an ambush. Thomas kept a short distance in front of them, not wishing for any conversation with Amor. He was leading them by the longest, most circuitous route. There were shorter paths to his house, but he wanted them to feel the power of the forest, taking pleasure in their obvious discomfort. He knew it would be difficult to unsettle Amor; from his demeanour it was clear that he was an experienced interrogator who could pick up on the smallest sign of hesitation or weakness. Tom's one worry was Sarah Bushy. She was easily intimidated, breaking into tears at the slightest provocation. He had to make sure that Amor did not question her on her own.

Walter Amor noticed that they now passed through areas of the forest that was managed; sections cleared and re-planted, others coppiced. He urged his horse up to walk beside Sir Thomas.

"You practice forestry here Sir?"

"On a small scale yes. We supply three local timber merchants."

"So you employ workers?"

"There are two men from the village who help me with the forestry and general labour."

"I shall need to speak to them."

"Of course."

The house now came into view. The dead stalks of lavender had been cut back to ground level, but the beds either side of the path still held some colour for winter heathers, white, purple and pink decorated the borders. Amor had not been sure what kind of habitation he would find here in the forest and he was pleasantly surprised by the house. It was modest by wealthy standards, but well-proportioned and in good order.

"I must compliment you on your house Sir Thomas. The whole aspect is most pleasing."

"What did you expect, a mud hut between the trees?"

Amor's mouth tightened. "There is no need for this antagonism. My compliment was genuinely meant."

He turned in the saddle and motioned two of the soldiers to come forward.

"Search the out buildings thoroughly and report to me when you have done so." As they rode over to the barn Ned Carter came out of the orchard carrying a spade.

"Can I help Master Tom?" he called out, giving the soldiers a wide birth.

"Could you see to the horses please Ned? You can stable Hope but our visitors will not be here long, so you can tether their mounts to the rail."

He looked pointedly at the commissioner as he said this. Amor thought 'he likes to challenge me, to stand on favourable ground- not a man to retreat.' He had trained himself to analyse the actions and gestures of others, to interpret their significance and he was aware of Tom's tactics.

Thomas waved them to proceed him into the house; the soldiers followed and were instructed by Amor to stay in the cross passage when he and William Paul were shown into the parlour.

"How do you wish to proceed?" Tom inquired, taking hold of the collars of both the wolfhounds to prevent them from sniffing at the robes of his visitors. He could see that the commissioner's assistant was afraid of them.

"I would like you to assemble your whole household."

Thomas laughed. "Well, apart from Hector and Ajax here, my household consists of my wife, my housekeeper and her daughter. They are in the kitchen where it is warm. Perhaps you would speak to them there, then your officers can look up the chimney and on the pantry shelves for fugitives."

He was indeed playing the game of taking the initiative, holding that favourable ground. Rather than bidding the members of the household to come to Amor he was obliging the commissioner to go to them, lessening his importance, playing down the menace. Joan Bushy was always mistress in her own kitchen no matter what confronted her there. The commissioner had little choice but to accede to Tom's suggestion.

Dawn Light was mixing some sage and salt toothpaste, Joan and Sarah scouring out pots, when Thomas showed the visitors into the kitchen. She had seen them arrive and had said to Joan, "They are here, the men who ask questions."

She was not afraid of them, but worried that Tom might be in danger. She put down her mixing bowl and went to his side slipping her arm through his. She was wearing her knee-length smock still, but wore over the top of it a man's sleeved jerkin lined with fleece. Soft deerskin boots came up to her calves. The only restriction on her flowing hair was a sheep-skin headband decorated with bead patterns.

William Paul gave his master a startled look, but Amor's face remained impassive. He explained the reason for their visit in succinct terms, stressing the seriousness of Bailey's crime and the urgent need to find him. He then addressed Waaseyaaban with careful courtesy.

"Lady Mountfield, can you recall when you last saw Simon Bailey?"

She thought for a moment before replying, "Two springs, not this spring, the one before."

"So he came here in the spring of 1588. Was he alone?"

"No, with wife, with children."

She remembered that April so well. Wawackechi had died the month before and Simon's children had filled her with joy and sorrow in equal measure.

"And you have not seen him since?"

She shook her head looking directly into his compassionless eyes. She would never betray her Makwa's friend. Amor turned to Joan Bushy.

"Do you remember that visit Mistress Bushy?"

"I do indeed- such happy, laughing children, excited by the forest. Sarah and I were looking forward to them coming at Christmas. The heavy snow prevented it last year, but we fully expected their arrival this year. We have been worried. Have you spoken to Ellen about Master Bailey's whereabouts?"

Tom smiled to himself. Trust Joan to quiz the inquisitor.

"His family have disappeared Mistress."

"Disappeared- oh Dear Lord! I hope nothing has happened to those poor children."

Tom was so pleased that he had not revealed any details of the case to the household. Joan's distress at the news of the family's disappearance was genuine and it showed.

"You have not seen Master Bailey this year- on his own perhaps?"

"No Sir. He did come to Frome and Sir Thomas went there to meet him. That was in September. We hoped he might visit us then, but he was too busy and had to return to London."

Sarah Bushy was gazing at one of the soldiers. He was a muscular young man with wavy fair hair and bright blue eyes and Sarah was immediately smitten. He winked at her as he stood behind the commissioner. She was so hypnotised that when Amor asked her when she last saw Bailey she hardly heard the question.

"I did so want them to come at Christmas," she said looking over Amor's shoulder at the soldier. "The children make it such a merry time, but Mistress Cecily and Master Godfrey came instead and we had a fine time playing games by the fire."

"The Commissioner is not interested in our Christmas merriment Sarah," Joan chided gently, "Only if you saw Master Bailey here."

"Oh no Sir, because he didn't come," Sarah answered truthfully, thinking her mother meant at Christmas.

Tom gave an inward sigh of relief, silently thanking the soldier for his handsome looks. On Amor's orders the kitchen, pantry and Joan's parlour were searched.

"Joan will show you the upstairs rooms," Tom said, "Please ask your men to be respectful and not disorder anything. If you come with me you can search the dining room and the library."

At this point Toby Aycliffe and Ned Carter, both wearing disgruntled expressions, were hustled into the kitchen by the two officers who had searched the outbuildings.

"There's no need to push," Toby grumbled. "Don't think you can bully us around just because you are wearing a uniform."

He shoved the man away from him with a truculent gesture and straightened his jerkin in a purposeful way. The soldiers reported that they had found nothing. "And these two say they have not seen Bailey for some time."

Amor directed them to stand guard outside and be vigilant lest anyone hiding in the trees slipped back into the outbuildings. He then quizzed the cousins himself but got no more out of them than the soldiers.

Thomas took him and his assistant across the passage into the dining room, where the only place to hide was the sideboard. Tom was very amused imagining the hefty Bailey trying to squeeze into the cupboards beneath the sideboard. He did not share his amusement with Amor however for a sense of humour did not appear to be one of the commissioner's qualities.

Amor was impressed by the extent of Sir Thomas' library. His research had revealed that Mountfield was a learned man. His gaze fell on the untidy piles of paper on Tom's desk.

"What are those?"

"Not seditious tracts Master Amor, nor letters from Simon Bailey. I am writing an account of the voyage to Roanoke in 1585. I do have the last letter I received from Simon last September telling me he was coming to Frome. You are welcome to read that."

He began to search in one of the desk drawers, but Amor stopped him. "There is no need. You would not offer it to me if there was anything in it you did not want me to see."

He picked up one sheet of paper from the desk and read a few paragraphs. Then he began to leaf through the rest, murmuring, "Perhaps I should take these with me for checking by the Lord Chamberlain's office."

"Oh no," Thomas put his hand down firmly on the pile of papers, so that Amor's fingers were trapped underneath it, "These are private writings. I am not submitting them for publication. You have no authority to take them. There is nothing in them to interest His Reverence the Archbishop. They are not leaving this house. You are welcome to sit down and read through them if you are so minded. It will delay you somewhat but I have no objection to it."

William Paul fidgeted nervously as Thomas stared at Amor with an intensity that made even the hardened commissioner feel uncomfortable. Amor wriggled his fingers out from under the papers and smiled a thin smile that was sour round the edges.

"Well I have no reason to take them at this time. I think we have seen enough in here."

The soldiers had found nothing incriminating upstairs.

"Have you looked in here?" Tom asked, opening the cupboards under the staircase with an obliging flourish and flashing them a smile.

Three soldiers were then dispatched to search the immediate forest while the fourth remained to watch the outbuildings. Ned and Toby went back to their work, forking over the garden plots ready for early planting, Toby making obscene gestures at the officer every time he turned his back.

Amor and Paul sat in the parlour drinking small beer and eating cheese biscuits while the sweep of the forest was being conducted,

"At least he was civil," Joan said to Dawn Light, "Asked his questions with courtesy. I had to rebuke those officers though for throwing clothes about in the bed chambers."

"I do not like him." Dawn Light had returned to her mixing bowl. "His eyes are dead. I think his heart dead too."

The search of the forest proved unproductive and Amor declared his intention to leave. Tom stood, arms folded, outside the front porch as the commissioner mounted his horse.

"I trust you are satisfied Master Amor?"

"As far as I can be, yes, but I warn you Sir Thomas if you have been involved in helping Simon Bailey to escape, you will pay for it. Any connections you have in high places will not save you. I have given the same warning to all Bailey's friends and colleagues. If he contacts you, you must send word to my office at Westminster immediately. Is that clear?"

"Very clear."

"Then good day to you Sir Thomas."

As the party rode away Tom was joined by Ned and Toby, who watched them leave with satisfaction.

"Poxy arseholes them soldiers," Toby snarled, "Talked to us as if we were idiots just because we are country born- tried to frighten us, particularly that bald one with the big ears. For two pins I could have banged his pate with my spade."

Thomas patted his shoulder. "Well I am truly glad you did not Toby. We would have been in the mire then for sure. As it is, I think we have got away with it."

"Did he believe us do you think?" Ned asked.

"He's shrewd. He may still be suspicious but he has no evidence to act on his suspicions."

"You can rely on us," Toby affirmed. "I wouldn't tell them anything, not even if they tortured me."

Tom's smile was wistful. "Oh yes you would Toby Aycliffe. An experienced torturer knows just how to cause the maximum amount of pain each man can bear without his fainting. When your teeth are twisted out of your jaw and your finger nails extracted and the bottoms of your feet beaten with red hot iron bars you let go of your secrets. Never underestimate the power of torture to loosen the tongue."

"They may have done such things in old King Harry's days and under the popish Queen," Ned asserted, "But not now. The Queen does not allow such things."

"True, the Queen has no love for cruelty, but there are things that happen in the tower that Walsingham and company do not discuss with Her Majesty."

Both cousins were looking at him with troubled expressions, knowing that when he was in Sir Philip Sidney's household he must have heard and seen many things it was best not to dwell on. Tom guessed what they were thinking and said, "Not a subject we need contemplate now. I will come and help you with that digging."

Two weeks went by and Thomas heard no more from the Archbishop's commissioner. He did receive a welcome message however. He had given instructions to all his friends to send letters to Toby Aycliffe's house in the village. Couriers got lost in the forest. It was much easier for them to deliver to the village. Toby brought any mail for Tom with him when he came to work. One morning in mid-January he gave Thomas a letter, the address written in a familiar hand. Tom opened it and read, 'Cargo delivered safely without incident. Journey back rougher than outward one but all here in good health, thanks be to God. Hope to see you and your wife in the spring.

Matthew.'

Chapter Four

ELIZABETH TURNED THE LOCKET over in the palm of her hand. It was bent out of shape; the original heart outline twisted grotesquely where Anthony had ground it under the heel of his boot. The cabochon garnet still clung with tenacity to its silver collet and she ran her fingers over the smooth stone, wishing that somehow she could be drawn into the depths of its rich colour and find herself in a different existence.

She was sitting in the rose garden wrapped in a fur lined cloak, the hood pulled up over her head. The March wind was blustery and chill, but it was warm enough now to sit outside if adequately dressed. It was a great relief to Lizzie to be in the garden again, away from the oppressive atmosphere inside the house with its ornate trappings of wealth. As she sat there she realised that she was weeping and chided herself for such foolishness as to weep over a broken trinket, but she knew the cause lay beyond the damaged locket.

Nothing she did or said pleased her husband. He disapproved of her choice in garments, poured scorn on her opinions, insisted that she wear only the jewels he had given her. She was fond of the locket although it was of no great value. She liked the simplicity of it and how well the blood red garnet contrasted with the silver setting.

One evening when she was wearing it on a delicate chain, Anthony, who was in a vile mood, snatched it from her neck, snapping the chain and throwing the locket on the floor, he stamped on it. He told her he did not expect to find his wife wearing a kitchen maid's cheap trinkets and that she had no true understanding of her status. Then he ordered her to go to her chamber and put on the pearls he had given her. Elizabeth did not protest, but she scooped up the remains of the locket before she did as she was bid. What made the incident doubly painful was that Sir Bartholomew and Lady Agnes were seated at the table and ignored it. James started to rise from his seat in defence of his sister, but Bartholomew put his hand on the boy's arm and encouraged him to sit back down, as if to indicate that it was not customary to interfere in a man's dealings with his wife.

Lizzie knew that James longed to go back to Norrington Hall. Only his loyalty to her prevented him. She wanted her little brother to be happy. She knew she should encourage him to return to their father instead of being forced to watch her be humiliated by Anthony Hanham and suffer humiliation himself, but she would have missed his comfort so much and was not sure she could survive without it. James had not grown much in physical stature during the ten months they had spent at Hanham House, but he had matured in mind and understanding in great measure. Although he still believed in the importance of status and being a gentleman, he was beginning to understand the full implication of the term, that it went far beyond wealth and appearance.

Snuggled up inside her cloak Elizabeth let her tears fall. She thought of that hot day in September, sitting under the tree with Thomas Mountfield and showing him that locket. She wondered what he had bought for Waaseyaaban and imagined her pleasure when she saw her gifts. She had an image too of Thomas helping up the old woman whom Anthony had so roughly brushed aside as if she was a piece of detritus from the highway. She could not get Mountfield out of her mind; no longer wished to do so. She had begun to withdraw into a fantasy world when she had the opportunity to be alone, a world where she was safe and leading a useful life. In this imaginary world she lived in Tom Mountfield's household, helped Dawn Light with the gardens, fed the chickens, spent hours reading the books in the library. Thomas would discuss poetry and politics with her, play the lute she had seen in his study. She would fill his inkwells, sharpen his quills and tidy his papers. She would be like a sister to Dawn Light because even in this fantasy world she dare not imagine what she wanted most- Tom stroking her hair, taking her in his arms and lowering her gently, caressingly down on to his bed.

Her experience with Anthony had not soured her belief that true sexual union was joyful and fulfilling. On their wedding night Hanham had taken her with an angry brutality that shocked her whole being. It was as if she was an enemy to be besieged- not one gentle word or intimate gesture- but a fierce attack that left her bruised and sore.

Every time it was the same. If she protested or struggled in any way he would grow more violent, twist her arms, kneel on her and even punch her. So now she just lay like a statue and submitted to it, trying to detach her mind. It was worse when he had been drinking but bad enough when he was sober. She came to dread the moment when he announced that it was time they retired to their bed chamber. Her only relief was the fact that he was frequently away on business. It was a hollow relief though for anticipating his return filled her with dread. If his dealings had not gone his way he would take all his frustration out on her. He was full of anger and bitterness towards the world. The surface veneer of a languid dandy was a thin one. Beneath it he was seething with a fierce hatred that she could not understand, hatred that found release in cruelty. He would spur his horse until the unfortunate creature's flanks streamed blood and whip the hunting dogs if they displeased him. All the servants were afraid of his temper because they had all suffered verbal and physical abuse for the smallest errors.

What puzzled Elizabeth most was the equanimity of his uncle and aunt regarding his behaviour. Bartholomew and Agnes could be self-important and shallow, but they were reasonable in their general attitudes. They both treated Elizabeth and James with kindness. Granted they did not know what happened in the privacy of the bedchamber, how her body was a mass of bruises, lacerations and sore patches where he held a candle flame to her arms and back, yet they observed daily how their nephew enjoyed humiliating the Norringtons and how he bullied the servants, cursing them in language befitting a sewer. There were times when he treated even them with a barely disguised contempt, sneering at their suggestions with a sarcasm they did not deserve, but they accepted it all. Bartholomew let it pass with a jovial disregard. Sometimes Agnes made excuses for Anthony, but even as she did so suggested that the offence was too trivial to worry about. He could do no wrong in their eyes. Lizzie had never heard either of them reprimand him in any way. She knew therefore that it would be pointless to turn to them for support. Even if she submitted to the shame of revealing her bruised body, he would make up some story that they would believe rather than hers.

James was unaware of the extent of the physical abuse. He was unhappy enough as it was; she had no wish to add to it. She always made sure that she was wearing her under-smock before Charity, her timid little maid, came to help her dress.

She feared that if the girl saw the bruises she would talk to the other servants and it might get back to Anthony which would make her situation worse. She was at a loss to account for her husband's behaviour. Was he born with the seeds of that evil temper within him or had something in his life turned him that way? She knew that both his parents had died within a year of each other when he was eight and well understood the sorrow and bewilderment that could bring from her own experience with the loss of her mother. Yet he was not abandoned and neglected. His uncle had taken him into his house, treated him like his own son, given him every opportunity to prosper. Now he was handsome and wealthy; he could hardly accuse fortune of turning against him, quite the opposite. It was a commonplace that deformity and evil were equated. A twisted body was the reflection of a twisted soul. Ugliness and wickedness were twinned. The deformed had been touched by the devil, either for their own sins or the sins of their parents. Anthony Hanham was outwardly beautiful but deformed within; the mark of the devil deep inside him. She was sure it was more than just an imbalance of the humours. He was full of a bitter poison that he spewed out on the people around him. She had debated long and hard with herself concerning how much she was to blame for the way he treated her and came to the conclusion that she could have done nothing other than she did. She came to Hanham House eager to offer her love and abilities to her new husband and they did not please him. She had stopped offering her opinions on anything now, just did as she was bid with a listless obedience. When she said her prayers she tried to pray for Anthony, but the words died on her lips. What she prayed for most was that she should not be infected by his poison. She had no wish to learn to hate.

"Ah, there you are Lizzie!"

Elizabeth had been so absorbed in her thoughts that she had not noticed James come down the path. He stepped into the arbour and sat down beside her.

"I have been looking all over the house for you. Why are you sitting out here in the cold?"

"It's not that cold. I can breathe more freely out here in the open air."

When she turned to look at him he exclaimed, "You have been crying. What's wrong? Is it your locket?"

He could see the battered remnants of the locket in her hand. He was worried about his sister, how ten months could have such an effect on her appearance.

She had grown so thin, which was not surprising for she ate so little. He watched her at meal times taking a few mouthfuls before pushing the dishes away from her as if she lacked the energy to eat more. He was sure that she slept badly because she was always up so early in the mornings. She was hollow eyed and the natural bloom of her cheeks had faded to a pallor.

"It's so foolish of me to be upset over such a trifle, but I had grown fond of it and Anthony had no need to destroy it even if it offended him."

"Everything offends him. The very sight of me offends him," James said." He is so particular that he dislikes anyone to stand too close for fear their breath will mist the shine on his gold buttons. His temper is vile. He says such cruel things. He has no reason to speak to us like that, especially to you."

"Well James, he seems to find no pleasure in anything I do or say. I am at my wit's end to know how to please him. I am a complete disappointment to him."

"You have the greater cause to talk of disappointment," her brother defended. "You have done nothing wrong. I hate to see you so quiet and sad. I was looking for you because Lady Agnes is going into Frome in the coach to collect some furnishings from the town house and thought you might wish to accompany her."

She shook her head. "No, I like it here wrapped up in my cloak. I can dream of happy things."

"Oh please Lizzie. It will be good for you to go. You will catch a chill sitting here all morning. You have grown so thin you will feel the cold all the more. I will come with you if you like. We can look at the market stalls and the shops. Oh come on!"

He took hold of her hand to encourage her to stand up and as he pressed against her wrist he noticed that she winced.

"Did I hurt you?"

Before she could prevent him he turned back the sleeve of her gown to find a blistered patch of skin, inflamed and sore, just above her wrist.

"It's a burn. How did you do that?"

"I brushed against a candle."

She did not look at him as she replied, drawing her face back into the protection of her hood and James was filled with a horrified realisation.

"No brief touch of a flame would do that. He did that to you Lizzie didn't he? He burned you with a candle. Why?"

She could not deny it now; her distress was all too clear to her brother.

"I ventured to argue with one of his opinions which I considered unreasonable. He sought to teach me not to do so again."

"Has he hurt you before? Tell me!"

Because she did not reply, he pushed back the loose sleeve of her gown, unbuttoned the sleeve of her kirtle and rolled it back up her arm. She did not try to stop him. There was no point now that he knew. Her arm was a mass of bruises in various stages of development, some deepest purple, others fading to yellow.

As much as James resented Hanham's cruel tongue, he had never imagined that he would do this. His close study of the career of his hero Sir Philip Sidney had taught him that chivalry towards a woman was an essential part of the honour of a gentleman. When he was younger he thought that it applied only to ladies of his own status and upwards. Peasants and servants must be treated as such whether male or female. More recently he had begun to revise that opinion. Like his sister, he too remembered how chivalrous Tom Mountfield had been to that old peasant woman at the fair. He afforded her the same courtesy he would have given a duchess. No doubt Sir Philip would have done the same. His father had told him that it was permissible for a man to beat his wife within reasonable limits if she was rebellious or her fancy strayed towards another man. Elizabeth however had tried her hardest to be an obedient wife and this abuse was far beyond any limit. He was appalled and angry.

"You must not suffer this bullying in silence. We must tell Sir Bartholomew."

"It will do no good. He will not believe it. You know how he and Lady Agnes ignore every unpleasant aspect of Anthony's nature. Even if they saw my bruises- and I would feel great shame to have to show them- he would make up some story to explain it and they would believe him."

James knew she was right. He had been in the stables with Sir Bartholomew when Anthony had kicked a groom, a boy younger than James. The unfortunate lad had been too slow saddling Anthony's horse. Hanham had pushed him aside so that he staggered against the horse's stall and before he could right himself, kicked him hard in the stomach, leaving him writhing in pain on the floor. James had gasped at the injustice of it, expecting Bartholomew to say something, but he acted as if nothing had happened. James was so frustrated. It was his duty to protect his sister. He would be fourteen in June. Youths had gone into battle at his age. He cursed his puny frame and lack of inches, knowing that he would not be able to stand up to Anthony physically.

"Then I will tell Father. I will ride back home tomorrow. I tried to tell him when he came at Christmas that I was not happy here and that Anthony did not respect you properly, but I never had the chance to be alone with him. I thought he was going to stay all week not just three days. Twice when I began to tell him Lady Agnes interrupted and took his attention on to other things. I went into his chamber on both nights but he was fast asleep. It was all that wine he drank. He never drinks that much in the evening at home."

James had even gone so far as to shake Sir Neville in an attempt to wake him, but he barely stirred.

"I dread to suggest this James, but I fear Father would not believe it either. Anthony was all charm when Father was here."

James nodded. "Yes, just as he was before the wedding, smooth and deceitful."

"Exactly and Sir Bartholomew has been Father's friend and trusted colleague for years. He would never accept that he would countenance such behaviour. He is more likely to be persuaded that any story of Anthony's is the truth and that I have been an undutiful wife."

"Surely not Lizzie- not Father. He would not accuse us of lying."

Elizabeth wished she did not feel that her father's friendship with Hanham and his regard for both their reputations was more important to him than his own children, that it would cause him to shut his eyes to the truth.

"I told Jacob Whyte," James said. "I spoke to him while he was preparing Father's horse for the journey home. I told him how Anthony sneered at us both and called me worthless and stupid. How I wished with all my heart that I was back at Norrington Hall and that I had not found the opportunity to tell Father."

"What did he say?"

"Oh you know how correct and careful he is. He said it was not his place to pass any opinions on the Hanhams, although he was sorry I had not settled and perhaps things would improve in time. He did agree to tell Father what I had said should his opinion be sought on how we were faring. He promised he would if asked, but I know he won't broach the subject himself."

"You can't blame him. Father trusts him as an honest steward, but he would not hesitate to dismiss him if Jacob really displeased him. Oh there is no way out James! I must bear it."

"When is Anthony coming back from Bristol?"

"Today- tomorrow- I am not sure. Whenever it is will be too soon." She stood up decisively. "I have changed my mind. Let us go into town; be happy brother and sister for a while as we used to be. Buy some handsome collars for your hunting dogs- you said last night you wanted some – and some sugared fruits from that shop where the shopkeeper's daughter makes eyes at you."

"She doesn't Lizzie." James blushed. "Anyway, she can't be more than eight years old."

He was pleased however that his sister was making an effort to be more herself and they went into the house arm-in-arm.

Anthony Hanham was sitting in the corner of the Mariner Tavern, a ramshackle inn standing beside the road that led down to Bristol harbour. His feet were resting on a table as he leaned back against the wall. His normally pale face was flushed and he was in a nasty frame of mind. By the time he had downed his fifth beer he was feeling aggressive enough to stab the next customer who walked into the room. He looked with mounting disgust and hatred at his fellow drinkers sitting at the other tables. Their sociability and laughter infuriated him.

He had come down from London to Bristol to complete a deal that would have been very profitable. He was negotiating through an agent to buy two warehouses beside the harbour which he intended to convert into dwellings, divide them up into tiny, one room accommodations, lacking adequate facilities and rent them out at rates far above their worth, just as he did in London. Unknown to him his agent was also acting for another businessman interested in the property and at the last moment negotiated the sale on his behalf because he was offering a larger commission than Hanham. When Anthony arrived in Bristol he found that his agent was not there to meet him and the deal had already gone through. He tried to discover the name of the purchaser to no avail and he was beside himself with fury.

He had left London in a dark mood anyway. He called at the brothel by the docks before he left to find that his favourite whore, Uta the Dutch girl, was nowhere to be found. The brothel was at the back of an inn and run by the innkeeper Gideon Barlow. The inn and Barlow himself had all the appearance of respectability and the brothel was frequented by the better sort of customer. The girls were well looked after by Barlow, living in clean conditions compared to the average whore house.

The innkeeper swore he had no idea where Uta had gone. She had mentioned to no one that she was going out. Perhaps she had gone to the market or was visiting a friend. He looked Hanham in the eye when he said this but Anthony was suspicious. He demanded to see her room and when Barlow suggested that was inappropriate, he pushed past him and ran upstairs. The room was empty; just the bed and the furniture remained, none of her personal things. There were no clothes in the coffer. Anthony felt beads of sweat break out on his forehead. The last time he was with her he may have gone too far. No one had ever responded to him the way she did. She was willing to tolerate his sadistic tendencies and he was convinced that he was special to her, that he owned her body in a way no other customer did. Then that last time, two nights before, she had complained that he was hurting her and that she would prefer not to service him again. She indicated that she always tailored her responses to the needs of the customer and there were other gentlemen now whose needs were less demanding. He vowed he would give her something to remember him by and tying her arms to the frame of the bedhead, he cut the shape of a heart split in twain on her breast with the point of his knife. He stuffed the end of the bed sheet into her mouth to stifle her cries.

When he had finished, half appalled but also aroused at the sight of his work, he dressed hurriedly, untied her and begged her not to say anything, thrusting a whole purse of money into her shaking hands, although he had paid her already. Dwelling on what he had done the day after, he regretted losing control, fearing that he would never find another whore who satisfied him like Uta. He went back to apologise, but it seemed that he was too late.

He cursed Barlow and demanded to know where she was, threatening him with his sword. The innkeeper smiled calmly and reminded him that he was in no position to make threats if he wished to keep his reputation intact.

Anthony sat in the Mariner grinding his teeth, recalling the confrontation. At least he could punish his traitorous agent. He had sent out his three bully-boy bodyguards to find him and teach him a lesson, as painful as possible without killing him. He was waiting for them to report back.

A girl was collecting empty tankards from the tables. He looked her up and down. She was in her early twenties, pretty enough, fine breasts. He caught her arm as she passed demanding, "What do you charge? Cheaper down here than in London I'll warrant."

She pulled away from him. "I beg your pardon Sir. This is not a bawdy house. I am a respectable married woman."

He laughed at her indignation. "Oh come now, spare me your feigned propriety. All you wenches do it if you are offered enough."

"Not this one my pretty boy," she countered sharply, "Mayhap you would care to say that to my husband. He owns the Mariner."

She pointed in the direction of a hefty, bearded man in an apron who was talking to some of his clientele. He had a barrel chest and muscular arms and did not look to be a man who could be easily intimidated. Anthony shrugged.

"You would not be worth it anyway you malapert bitch."

She resisted returning the insult and swept away, the tankards clinking together as if to express her irritation. Anthony sighed and swat at a fly that was buzzing around a pool of beer spilled on the table. He missed and swore ferociously. It was another half an hour before his strong-arm squad arrived with the news he had been waiting to hear. They had found the agent at his house packing a satchel, intending to leave on a business trip, no doubt anticipating some retribution for his actions. They dragged him into the garden and beat him senseless.

"Are you sure he will not die?" Anthony asked. "That would be too easy on him. I want him to feel pain for a long time."

"He will survive." Ralph Lawrence, the leader of the trio, was very confident in his skill to maim without killing. "But you can be sure he will be in pain. I heard his arm crack, several of his teeth flew out and we closed both his eyes. His wife ran out screaming like a maniac, but Dick grabbed hold of her and held his hand over her mouth while we finished the job."

"The harpy bit me," Dick complained, examining the teeth marks on his hand.

The others laughed at him.

"That will teach the fellow not to cross me." Anthony stood up. "Now let us get out of this shit hole. Remind me never to visit Bristol again."

Just inside the main door two elderly locals were reminiscing and enjoying their beer at a table just big enough for the two of them. As he passed Anthony upended the table. The old men jumped to their feet astonished as their beer tankards flew across the room, the contents of one emptying itself on the feet of a nearby customer. There was shouting and swearing. The landlord came out just as Anthony and his cronies were riding away. He shook his fist and called them some choice names but that was his only possible redress as they disappeared into the town.

It was early evening when Anthony arrived back at Hanham House. The dusk had already descended and the lights were lit both outside and inside the house. His companions, two Londoners and a Frenchman, were not refined enough to be offered hospitality there. Although Anthony wanted them on hand to do his bidding when necessary, he respected them only for their capacity to intimidate and he did not want them hanging about around the house. When he was in residence, they stayed at the White Swan in Frome. They parted with their master at the ornate gateway and rode on into town.

Lady Agnes came out to meet him as he walked into the hall, stepping close to kiss his cheek, but he moved away from her, not wanting to be touched.

The last thing he wanted was his foolish aunt fussing over him. Her excessive affection repelled him.

"Oh Anthony, such an unhappy face, did your affairs not go well my dear?"

"God's Death Aunt, does it look to you as if they did? Where's Elizabeth?"

"Up in her chamber I think. We had a fine day in Frome today, Lizzie, James and I"

"Please don't call her Lizzie. It's so vulgar. And what merry thing were you all doing in Frome?"

"Bringing some curtains and drapes from the town house and looking around the shops. We talked and were most companionable."

"Really, well let us see if she will be companionable with me.

He sauntered up the main staircase and threw open the door to their bedchamber. There was no one in the room, but he heard voices coming from her dressing chamber at the side. He took off his outer coat and sword belt, then called her name. She emerged from the side chamber followed by James.

"Oh, I might have known you would be clinging to your sister's skirts. What have you two been plotting in there eh, you two thick as thieves?"

His frayed temper was aggravated by the sight of them so easy together, so united. Anthony Hanham did not believe in love or friendship. He considered the world to be a filthy, loveless place, full of pain and ugliness. He saw that confirmed every day in the people he met, the deals he did. Both his parents had died in the same year when he was eight. What had gripped him at their deaths was not sorrow but disgust. His father was a drunkard, who had dissipated his fortune and died a mass of suppurating, syphilitic sores. His mother died six month later of a malady of the lungs, coughing up blood and sputum. He had never felt any real connection with either of them from about the age of five and was embarrassed by the manner of their deaths.

His uncle and aunt treated him as if he was precious and taught him that he was better than everyone else, not disgusting like his parents. Yet he felt they did so only due to their desire for an heir. They did it for themselves, not for him, so he decided they deserved no gratitude from him. He remained cold in response to their warmth because he did not trust it. The only way he knew how to feel truly safe was to impose his will on everyone around him, control every situation and it could throw him into paroxysms of rage if he was thwarted. There were days when he hated the whole world and everything in it so much he did not know how to cope with it. He felt it was consuming him like a fire and it frightened him. Reeving pains would stab in his head like knives and his only release was violence.

Elizabeth stood there regarding him in silence. Why had he thought her so beautiful, he asked himself, this girl who now looked so thin and pallid with her sorrowful, accusing eyes?

"Well, say something."

"What do you wish me to say?"

She could smell the drink on his breath from a distance and braced herself.

"Welcome home dear husband might be a start."

"Welcome home Anthony. I hope you had a good journey back."

"No, I did not and what in the name of the devil are you wearing? You know I detest that dull grey colour- like some merchant's wife at church. I have told you time and time again, I wish you to wear blue, silver, gold or ruby colours because they set you off to advantage. Go and change into that blue kirtle I bought you at Christmas."

She tried not to sigh, but a faint expulsion of breath escaped her lips and he picked it up instantly.

"Don't you sigh at me. Just to make sure you will never wear this frightful garment again-" He stepped across to her, took hold of the neck of her kirtle and ripped it right down to the waist, exposing the white linen smock beneath.

"Stop it," James shouted, shoving at Anthony with his shoulder. "Don't treat Lizzie like that. You think you are a gentleman, but you are not. You are a vile brute. You are not fit to call yourself a gentleman."

"You skinny little whoreson, what would you know about it?"

"I have seen the highest example of a gentleman that ever lived."

"Ah yes, "Anthony sneered. "Your adoration for Sir Philip Sidney. Well he is dead before his time is he not? Much good his foolish chivalric gestures did him."

James threw himself at Hanham, balling up his fists and thumping him on the chest with a barrage of punches. Anthony stood back and smacked the boy across the mouth with his hand, knocking him against the wall. Just as he had served the boy in the stable, he attempted to kick James in the stomach, but Elizabeth ran between them pleading with him not to hurt her brother. He hurled her away from him with such force that she crashed into the bottom of the bed. She felt a sharp pain in her side and lay there struggling for breath. Anthony grabbed hold of James by the collar and the seat of his breeches and thrust him out of the chamber, shutting and locking the door behind him. The boy hammered on the door, hot tears of frustration coursing down his cheeks, desperate for his sister's safety and humiliated by his own inadequacy.

"Don't you hurt her. Let me back in you swine. I hate you. You only bully those not strong enough to fight back. I hate you. I hate you."

He pressed his head against the door in despair. Lady Agnes came hurrying along the landing.

"Why James, whatever is this noise about? Why are you so distressed my dear?"

"It's Anthony, he is hurting Lizzie. He tore her dress and knocked her down. Please stop him, please."

Agnes put her arm around his shoulder in a soothing gesture.

"You must not upset yourself. You make too much of it. When you grow older and have a wife of your own, you will understand that husbands and wives have these little disagreements from time to time. Young wives often take a while to learn when to submit to their husband's wishes. It rights itself in the end."

She could not fail to notice that his lip was bleeding and beginning to swell.

"How did you hurt your face my dear?"

"He did it," James flung at her, "Your nephew. He hit me in the face because I tried to protect my sister."

"If he did hit you James, I am sure he did not mean to. You really must not interfere between a husband and wife, although I am sure you have the best intentions. Now come downstairs with me and we will put a cold compress on that mouth."

Elizabeth was right. It was hopeless. Any accusation against Anthony just bounced off her and was lost. Deflated, he allowed her to steer him away from the door, his shoulders hunched helplessly.

Inside the chamber Anthony lifted his wife from the floor and lay her down on the bed. "Why does that lack-wit brother of yours not go home to Norrington Hall instead of hanging around here making me lose my temper?" he demanded.

Elizabeth shifted her position to try to relieve the pain in her side. Before she could reply her husband continued, "Look at you. You grow thinner and less comely every day. I swear to God that you refuse to eat on purpose to spite me, so I will end up married to a skinny, wrinkled creature that t'will shame me to be seen with."

"I eat little Anthony because I have no appetite and I have no appetite because I am constantly dwelling on the fact that nothing I do pleases you and I am at a loss how to mend it. What have I done or failed to do that makes you treat me so?"

When Anthony agreed to take a wife, he had no day dreams about love and devotion. He wanted a girl to complement his own beauty, but more than that, he desired someone young and unformed in mind, so he could mould her to his will. He wished to own a woman completely, so that her whole world revolved around and depended on him. Her opinions, her tastes, her likes and dislikes must be as he dictated. He would brook no other influence.

It was vital for him to dominate during intercourse for he knew women to be subtle, to have ways of asserting their power during the sexual act in a way that could hold men in thrall. He feared being a slave rather than a master. He had suffered a shock those few days ago when he discovered that he did not control Uta, but he had already learned that he was never going to own Elizabeth, absorb her within himself. Although she had ceased to voice contrary opinions and argue with him, he was aware of an inward defiance. Despite her demure manner, her quiet obedience, she clung on to an internal life of her own that shut him out. She remained stubbornly Elizabeth Norrington, judging him against other standards beyond his own. It infuriated him because no amount of bullying, verbal or physical could penetrate it. He could not answer her question because he could not explain adequately why she made him so angry.

"You do not try to please me, not truly. You accede to my wishes only when I am here. As soon as I am away you behave as you like, not as I like. You walk around in clothes fit for scullions the minute I am gone. If you had a true regard for my desires and had learned what good taste was, you would continue to abide by them in my absence. But you have a secret life. I forbid you to have a secret life."

She stared at him, wondering if he was mad. What sane man would say such a strange thing?

"I am sick of you looking at me in that way, eyes full of martyred innocence," he snapped. "Why are you not with child by now? God knows I have tupped you enough- not that it is any great pleasure. It is like fucking a marble statue. You want to deny me a son. You want to force me to buy myself an heir just like Bartholomew bought me."

She made no attempt to reply, letting his words wash over her. She closed her eyes to shut him out. The pain in her side now reached up into her chest. She felt faint and realised how weak she had become over the last few months, aware that she was not eating enough to sustain her. When she opened her eyes again, Anthony was beside the bed unlacing his breeches, muttering about producing his own heir, not acquiring a stray.

"No, not now Anthony please." Lizzie sat up, wincing with pain. "I hurt myself when I fell against the bed. I think I have broken a rib bone. The pain is very sharp. I need to rest."

She expected him to ignore her plea but to her surprise he snarled, "Oh to hell with you. I shall be going back up to London tomorrow and as I am not welcome in my own bedchamber, I will spend the night in town with more amusing company."

He was eager to get back to London. Uta was still on his mind. He needed to find her, make sure she was not spreading rumours about him- more than that, he wanted her back. His wife he could deal with at any time. He re-laced his breeches and snatching up his coat and sword left the room, banging the door behind him.

He met Sir Bartholomew in the hall. His uncle's face was suffused with pleasure. "Ah, Anthony, Agnes said you had returned. I have just heard the most interesting bit of news about the Bishop of Salisbury."

"What do I care about the Bishop of Salisbury?" Anthony interrupted. "No time to listen to idle gossip. I'm going to town- off to London tomorrow."

"But my boy," Bartholomew was flustered by his nephew's abruptness. "You have only just come home. Supper is almost ready. We hoped to hear all about your business venture."

Anthony made a noise that could best be described as a growl and pushed past his uncle, who with a puzzled frown watched him walk out of the house.

Agnes threw some light on the situation for him when she explained that Anthony and Elizabeth had an argument earlier which had also upset James because he had misunderstood the circumstances. Somehow the boy had got in the way and been struck accidently by Anthony.

Supper was a quiet affair. Both Agnes and Bartholomew were disappointed that their nephew had left so suddenly. Elizabeth did not come down to supper, saying that she felt unwell and would prefer to sleep. James sat there sullenly picking at his food, his swollen lip throbbing. Bartholomew tried to engage him in conversation but James limited his contribution to yes and no. He was furious with them both for their blindness to Anthony's faults. He listened to Lady Agnes twittering on about how handsome Anthony looked in his latest fashionable suit of clothes and thought how foolish she sounded. He wanted to bang his fist down on the table and yell at them, to release his frustration. Instead he expressed a desire to go to bed and excusing himself, left the dining room and ran upstairs. He knocked on the door of Lizzie's bedchamber.

"It's only me Lizzie. Can I come in?"

He peered around the door before entering, afraid of what he might find. She was laying on the bed, propped up with pillows, no trace of colour in her face.

"I am so sorry I could not stop him." James burst out, "Has he hurt you badly?"

"No, not at all, but when I fell against the bed I struck my side hard and it is causing me some discomfort." She pressed her hand to her side to support it. "I may have cracked a rib, but hopefully it is only bruised."

The room was dimly lit. She had snuffed out most of the candles, intending to sleep and only a single candle burned on the table by the bed. She encouraged James to sit on the side of the bed and as he came closer she saw his swollen lip.

"You show more evidence of being in the wars than I do," she murmured, reaching out and running her finger lightly over his mouth.

"Oh, it does not hurt much," he said with bravado.

She smiled because she could see that it did hurt.

"Thank you for trying to protect me. It was very brave of you. What would I do without you?"

"We must get away from here Lizzie," he urged. "Go somewhere safe where you can rest and get your appetite back, grow healthy again. If we don't, I fear he will kill you one day. Perhaps he will not mean to, but he will go too far and you will not be strong enough to resist. I will not let him kill you. It is my duty to look after you."

"But it is impossible James. Wherever could we go to be safe from him? If we went home to Norrington Hall, he would come and claim me back. I am his wife; it is his right and I doubt if Father would attempt to stop him. Aunt Jennet would be scandalized if we turned up there and would send a message to Anthony within an hour of our arrival."

"What about Mother's family?" James was clutching at straws.

"She has some cousins in Suffolk, but Father never kept in touch with them, so I do not know where they live."

James refused to be defeated. "Sir Thomas Mountfield- he will help us. No one will imagine we have gone there and the house is so difficult to find. You could rest there for a while and he could advise us what to do. We can trust him I know."

Elizabeth was well aware that her brother had changed his mind about Tom Mountfield's character. He had told her with great eagerness about their conversation at Frome Fair, how he had talked about Zutphen and his love for Philip Sidney. For James now, Thomas was bathed in some of Sidney's glory and had become a hero himself, despite his singular way of living.

Lizzie shook her head, protesting, "It would be wrong to involve him in this. It could bring trouble down on him. You know that many people view him unfairly already because he chooses to go his own way."

She spent so much time with Tom in her secret life, the one Anthony forbade her. Her husband knew no details of that life or who was the centre of it. The idea of seeking his help in reality was exciting but also dangerous. She feared the possible consequences.

"Sir Bartholomew knows we stayed overnight there last year, though I don't believe he ever told Anthony. Surely it would come to his mind that we may have gone there."

"Why should it? They will go to Norrington Hall first and then to our other kin. While they are searching it will give us time to think." He looked earnestly into his sister's eyes. "We must do it now. Anthony is staying in Frome tonight and going on to London in the morning from there. This is our chance. We can slip out of the house just before first light. Bartholomew and Agnes never rise before ten o'clock, unless there is some special occasion in the offing. We could leave a note saying we had gone out for an early morning ride. That would give us even more time."

"Oh James, I don't think we should. We will be discovered."

"Lizzie, do you want Anthony Hanham to lay his vile hands on you again?"

She was silent for a moment and then replied with decision, "No, I do not think I could bear him to touch me again."

"Then what choice have we? Do you think you can ride that far with your injury? We could bind it up to lessen the pain and you could sit astride rather than side-saddle. It would be easier."

She felt her pulse quicken as she realized she was going to do this impulsive thing and allow herself to be led by James. They spent an hour planning the details of their escape and what they would say if they were seen by servants up early. James helped his sister bind her waist with a wide sash. She dressed in warm clothes and laid her thick cloak on the bed in readiness. Her brother said he would call for her at five in the morning and she must try to sleep until then.

She could not sleep. So many thoughts coursed through her head in unending succession. The possibility of freedom from Anthony was something she longed for yet she also feared it was wrong to run away from her husband. Most people would condemn her actions. She also asked herself if she would have agreed to James' plan if their destination was anywhere else but Tom Mountfield's house. It would be much safer for them both if she kept him in her secret life, but her desire to see him, hear his voice again over-rode that knowledge. She awaited James' early morning knock with both dread and a thrill of anticipation.

Chapter Five

THE INSISTENT SCRATCHING OF the quill sounded out a rhythm in the quiet room. Tom's ideas were flowing freely and the only pause in the sound came when he stopped to dip his pen in the inkwell. The early morning light was now penetrating the room and he had extinguished the candles on his desk. He had spent a restless night, confused, disjointed dreams stalking his sleep. The walls of Flushing fused themselves with the wooden fortress at Roanoke, but it was surrounded by his own woodland. All his friends drifted through the dreams; Philip, Harry, Matthew, Simon, Joshua, John White and Thomas Harriot, the naturalist who had spent much time training Tom and his fellow adventurers in navigational skills before setting out in 1585. Even baby Virginia Dare, White's American born grand-daughter was there, her features distinct, although Thomas had never set eyes on her. The air was full of impending danger. There was fear, but also excitement and a sense of the warmth of fellowship.

Thomas woke before dawn with a powerful feeling of loss and loneliness. Looking at Waaseyaaban sleeping peacefully beside him, her head on his shoulder, he knew he had no right to feel lonely, but he could not shake the melancholy off. He kissed the top of her head and eased himself out of bed, careful not to wake her. He had a strong urge to write and slipping on his shirt and breeches went downstairs in his bare feet and lit the candles in the library.

He had been working for almost two hours now and had described in detail the day the Secotans had attacked the fort and the ensuing effect on the morale of the colonists. He was with a party of six others, including Matthew Collier, coming back to the fort from a hunting foray when the natives attacked. They were all carrying muskets, but after the first volley had no time to reload for the natives were upon them, driving them back towards the walls of the fort. They had to fight fiercely to keep the Secotans at bay while part of the gate was opened to let them back into the fort. At the corner of his vision Tom saw Matthew engaged with one opponent unaware that another was about to lunge at him from the side with a spear. He stepped across and drove his sword into the Secotan's midriff. As he withdrew his weapon, the Secotan falling towards him without a sound, blood foaming at the corners of his mouth, Thomas felt a sharp pain in his back, near his shoulder-blade. Two of their party lay dead, but the remaining four scrambled back into the fort, helping to push the gate closed. Matthew then saw that there was a short-shafted arrow lodged in Tom's back. It had struck at an angle, entering the flesh sideways, restricting the depth of the penetration. The wound was shallow but jagged, made more so when Matthew and another man extracted it. There was no time to deal with the bleeding for the attackers were screaming war cries and attempting to scale the walls of the fort. Arrows and spears were flying into the compound. Thomas recharged his musket and joined the others up on the platform that ran along the top of the walls, to fire down on the enemy.

It was not until the natives had retreated that his wound could be attended to properly. Within a day it was showing signs of infection and three days later he was in the grip of a burning fever.

The Croatans from the village had not interfered in the fight between the settlers and the Secotans from the mainland for fear they would suffer reprisals, but when they saw the Secotan canoes leaving the island many of the villagers ventured to the fort to investigate the damage.

When Waaseyaaban came with her brothers to bring food to the settlers she found Thomas delirious with a raging temperature and when her brothers went back to the village she refused to leave him. Tom was convinced that he would have died without her ministrations and he made that clear in the text.

 He did not stop writing until he heard the sound of activity in the kitchen; Joan talking to Sarah and chivvying the wolfhounds outside so she could brush the floor. He was pleased with his burst of creativity and as he read through what he had written he was aware that he had captured the urgency, the atmosphere that was present in his dreams. It was vivid and compelling, just what he had been searching for. He leaned back in his chair, closing his eyes. The dreams had disturbed him, but if they had inspired this, he was grateful. He could still see the face of that Secotan warrior, the first man he had ever killed. He was a handsome man with broad cheeks and a high forehead. Tom recalled how his eyes widened in astonishment as the sword pierced him and froze in that expression as he fell forward. The young Spanish pike man he had cut down during the second charge at Zutphen had just the same expression in his eyes. A very different face, sensitive, delicate even; he could not have been more than seventeen, but his eyes held an identical expression of surprise, as if even in the midst of battle the hand of death was unexpected.

"When did you get up?"

Dawn Light was standing in the doorway. He had not heard her come in; her tread was always so soft. He opened his eyes and gazed at her. She was dressed only in her sleeveless white smock, the contours of her body visible through the thin cotton. Her hair, flowing over her shoulders gleamed black.

"You are so beautiful," he said quietly. "I should tell you that more often."

Her expression was enigmatic as she came over to him, putting her arm around his shoulder and leaning down to look at the sheets of paper on his desk.

"You write all this since you get up?"

He nodded. "Yes, I rose just before dawn. I could not sleep anymore and I was in the mood for writing."

She traced her fingers over the words on the last page he had written. The ink was still wet in places and one line smudged, leaving ink on the tip of her finger. Although her grasp of spoken English was excellent, she had never learned to read it, despite Tom's offer to teach her. The reason why she hesitated lay in the fact that she so loved Thomas to read to her, she feared he would no longer do so if she learned the skill herself. Yet there were times when she wished she could decipher these mysterious patterns. She could pick out some words and on this page her own name jumped out at her.

"This speaks of me?"

He pulled her on to his lap and she sat with one arm around his neck, but still tracing the writing with her free hand.

"Of course, how can I write about Roanoke without speaking of you?"

"What does it say?"

"I am describing how all you brave Croatans came creeping out of your houses when the Secotans had paddled away after attacking the fort."

She looked indignant for a moment until he smiled and said, "I am only teasing you. The villagers did the right thing not to get involved. It would have been very foolish to incite hostility from the Secotans. What I have written is how grateful we were when your people came to see us afterwards, bringing food. This paragraph here tells how you and your brothers found me lying on a bed talking like a madman to myself in a strange delirium- not that I remember aught about it. I have described it from what you told me when I was in my right mind again."

"Read it to me, all you write this morning."

He did as she bid him and she listened intently, nodding now and then in approval. When he had finished he asked, "Well, does it pass muster?"

"It is good, just as it happen. We see Secotans come up from the shore. I want to run to fort to warn you but my brothers say no, too much danger. I was afraid they kill you. When I find you so sick, I fear then too, but my Makwa does not die. He is too strong for death."

"Oh Waaseyaaban, no mortal man is stronger than death, at least not his physical body, though we have the hope that his soul triumphs over it. I did not die because you cared for me so well and it was not my time."

Sometimes she could feel the heaviness in his heart as if it was her own. He had not been sleeping well for weeks. She was certain that Simon Bailey's troubles and wherever her husband had journeyed in December had stirred up these dreams and unsettled him. Despite her sorrow for her lost children, Dawn Light was content with her life. She did not desire more than to move with the rhythm of the seasons, share her life with the creatures of the forest and the domestic animals. She loved to watch things grow, to gather the fruits of her husbandry. But Thomas was the centre of her world. She could not imagine a life without him. She hated him to be away from her for more than two days.

When she lay in bed at night in his absence, it was as if part of her own body was missing. She had no doubt that his heart was hers, but she wished he could be as content with their life as she felt. She could sense longings in him that she did not understand, but knew they were important to him. He carried an emotional wound inside him that leaked blood and she did not know how to reach it to complete the healing.

Hector and Ajax padded into the room, pushing the door open wide, letting in the smells of breakfast preparations from the kitchen.

"You want breakfast?" Dawn Light inquired rising from her husband's lap.

"Yes, I'm starving. All this brain activity has made me hungry. Looks as if the dogs have had their fill already. It smells as if Joan has been making pancakes."

Taking hold of his wife's hand Tom made for the kitchen to find both sweet and savoury pancakes on the griddle.

He was unaware of course that at that moment Elizabeth Hanham and James Norrington were weaving their way along the forest paths towards his house. It had taken them longer than James anticipated to ride the thirty miles from Hanham House to the path that led off the main road into the forest. His sister was much weaker than he realized. The effort of controlling the horse, the vibration in her body as its hooves struck tracks hardened by frosts, caused her to fight for breath. Her whole body ached as if every bruise and scar Anthony had given her were freshly done. Any sudden movement brought a stabbing pain in her side like the bite of a knife blade. Despite her fur-lined cloak, she felt cold, the kind of chill that emanated from the inside outwards rather than the reverse. The morning was not particularly sharp for March. James rode close to her, aware that she was shivering. They stopped several times to enable her to catch her breath and rest from the jarring motion of the ride.

He hoped that the note he had pushed under Sir Bartholomew's chamber door would buy them some time. He had written that as the sunset had promised a fine day on the morrow, he and Elizabeth had a fancy to see the sun rise on the downs and had gone for an early morning ride. He did not indicate when they would return. Lizzie was dubious about the note, sure that Hanham would think their behaviour strange, but James argued that the grooms would soon find their horses missing and Bartholomew would find it even stranger if they had saddled their horses and ridden off without any explanation.

They had crept out of one of the three back doors of Hanham House while it was still dark. They just avoided bumping into the two servant girls whose job it was to light all the fires at the crack of dawn, starting with the kitchen. The girls wandered sleepily down from their rooms high up on the third floor of the house, each carrying a candle in a tin glaze holder. James and Lizzie stood back against the panelling beneath the staircase until they had gone and then escaped by the back door.

The accommodation for the grooms and stable lads was a long, barn-shaped building adjoining the stables. As they passed it, they heard someone coughing and spitting and guessed the grooms would be about their work soon. James did not light his lantern until he was right inside the stables and led the saddled horses out of the exit farthest from the adjacent building, out on to a grassy area, avoiding the gravel path so the horses' hooves would not echo in the quiet of the early morning.

He was proud of the way he had executed his plan so far, his only concern being Elizabeth's frail condition. It was a relief when he spotted what he had been looking for, a heap of stones like a cairn beside the road. He remembered Jacob commenting on it when Sir Thomas had led them out on to the main road the previous May. The pathway they needed to take was just beyond it.

"Here we are Lizzie," he encouraged. "This is the path. It will be much easier than before because most of the trees are not in leaf yet so it will not be so dark and confusing."

He took hold of the reins of her mount and drew it alongside him so that the two horses walked in step. There was just enough room on the path for them to walk side by side.

"It will not be long now."

In his memory, the path they had taken out from the house in May was a direct one without any twists and turns, but he was non-plussed when they came upon a place where the path divided into two and he had no idea which one led to the house. He closed his eyes tight, trying to create a picture in his mind of the most likely direction and wished he had viewed his surroundings more sympathetically on his previous visit. It might have given him better instincts now. He turned to Lizzie.

"Which way would you choose?"

"The one to the right."

She was so positive it gave him confidence and they took that path.

It was nearing eight o'clock when James heard the barking of dogs, a deep throated sound that reverberated through the trees. A shaggy, grey shape appeared in front of them, quickly followed by a similar one.

"Hector and Ajax," Elizabeth murmured. These wolfhounds were an essential part of her secret world and were so familiar to her.

"Sir Thomas' dogs?" James asked, surprised that his sister had remembered their names for he had not. They loped beside the horses until a whistle ahead attracted their attentions and they ran on. Their speed was impressive for such heavy-boned creatures, long legs stretching out to their full capacity. They were running to their master who was standing in the pathway whistling for them. Beyond him was the front approach to the house. Thomas looked hard at the riders coming towards him to confirm his first impression. It was indeed young James Norrington urging his horse forward with his sister following.

"James, Mistress Elizabeth, this is an unexpected visit." His surprise showed in his face.

"We need your help," James blurted out. "We are looking for a sanctuary and we did not know where else to come."

Tom's mind flashed back to December and another unexpected visitor. At least he knew these two young people had not been espousing radical protestant views in public. He could guess their problem however and a close look at the girl confirmed it. She was ashen white and trembling beneath her thick cloak. He was shocked by the change in her appearance.

"We should not have come," she murmured. "It is wrong to impose on you, but we were at a loss to know what to do."

"My sister is not well," James said.

"I can see that." Thomas had also noticed the boy's cut and swollen lip.

Elizabeth made an effort to dismount but it took up her last reserve of strength. She felt a tightness in her throat, coupled with a strange light-headedness and fell into Tom's arms. As he held her he could feel how her body was chilled.

"Lizzie!" James' face was full of concern.

"She has fainted with cold and anxiety. No explanations yet James. We must take her into the house and get her warm. Bring the horses."

Tom ran towards the house with the girl in his arms. It took no effort for she weighed so little. He calculated that the kitchen would be the warmest place and startled Sarah Bushy when he burst through the door.

He laid Elizabeth gently in a chair by the open range as Joan came out of her own parlour carrying a bundle of washing. Between them they tried to revive Elizabeth by chafing her hands and feet, but she did not respond. Joan ordered Sarah to run upstairs and light the fire in the guest bedchamber.

"There are bruises all over this child's arms," Joan declared. "Whatever has happened to her? Why has she come here?"

"I have a shrewd idea," was Tom's grim reply. "No doubt James will explain it all later."

"Her brother is here too?"

Thomas opened the small door that faced the barn and looked out to see James Norrington being escorted across the yard by Dawn Light. Ned Carter was leading the horses into the barn. James may have revised his opinion of Thomas Mountfield but he was still uneasy about his wife. He was wary of her walking behind him and thought how odd she looked wearing a man's jerkin over a smock. He was sure those liquid eyes were penetrating his thoughts even though she was behind him and could not see his face.

He was distressed to find that Lizzie showed no signs of stirring. Dawn Light looked at the girl, then at Tom's face trying to gauge his reaction. She could see that he was angry but guessed that it was not directed at the Norringtons.

"Girl is sick," she stated in her flat, practical tone. "Put her to bed. I help Joan look after her."

Thomas lifted Lizzie out of the chair and carried her upstairs to the end bedchamber, laying her down on the bed. That morning she had left Hanham

House without observing the married woman's propriety of plaiting up her hair and putting on a hood. When Joan took off her cloak, Lizzie's hair fell in profusion across her breast. Tom recalled that he had likened it to the colour of ripened corn when he had seen strands of it escaping from beneath her hood. Now he could see it in all its glory, warm, burnished gold and its beauty stirred him.

James stood in the doorway biting his finger nails and Tom put an arm around his shoulder to reassure him.

"Come, we must leave the ladies to tend your sister and prepare her for bed. Let us go into the parlour and you can explain everything to me."

It was a relief for James to tell Thomas the whole story of their misery at Hanham House. He concealed nothing, eager to justify his coming to Tom for help.

"I thought at first it was only his tongue that was cruel. I did not realise he was hurting her in other ways. I believe he has done shameful things to her that she will not mention. If I had known I would have tried to persuade her to get away earlier than this. How I hate that man."

Thomas listened to his story without interruption. He felt the anger rising inside him and also some intrepidation that he was now involved in this. Ever since his suspicions at Frome Fair, he had tried to put the Norrington's out of his mind; now he was being drawn into a complicated situation. It was dangerous legal territory, interfering in the relationship between man and wife. This was something that should be handled by Sir Neville Norrington. It was his duty to protect his children.

"Why did you not take her straight home to Norrington Hall?" he asked.

"Lizzie feared that Father would insist she go back to her husband. Anthony is always smooth and two-faced in front of my father and Sir Bartholomew is a very old friend of his. She thought Father might believe she was the one who was in the wrong."

Thomas nodded, knowing that was possible. "All the same, it is the only course you can take. You can't hide here for ever. There must be a proper resolution to the situation. If she is here for any length of time, it may be suggested that I abducted her."

"But I can prove that isn't true because I brought her here."

"Yes I know, but I am an outsider James, a man who does not conform to all of society's demands and people are always ready to believe the worst of men like me. You were ready to do so yourself at one time remember."

"Oh, have I done the wrong thing Sir? Have I made it all worse?"

James' distress was so genuine Thomas felt obliged to offer some comfort.

"No, you did the right thing. You had to get her away from him before he did her irreparable harm. We will find a solution to this. In a few days, when she is feeling stronger, we will put her in a carriage and take her to your father. Then you can both tell him the truth and I will support your actions. Whether my involvement will be a help or a hindrance I cannot say because I doubt if my reputation stands very high with your father. Besides Sir Bartholomew, he is also a longstanding acquaintance of my father's and no doubt sees me as a very ungrateful, errant son. Never mind- we can always play the Philip Sidney card. His name still has a magical influence. Philip would be highly amused to think that my friendship with him was about the only thing that keeps me from being considered a complete reprobate."

He smiled at James, a warm, reassuring smile. The boy was certain now that he was right to come there. Thomas inspired confidence.

Later Tom went upstairs to check on Elizabeth. Joan reported that the girl had regained her senses for a short while, but was confused and exhausted. They had given her a few sips of wine to help warm her and now she was sleeping soundly.

"I will get some nourishing broth into her as soon as I can. The girl is skin and bone. Such a change in her since we saw her last year."

She lowered her voice as if the shame of it all must not be spoken too loudly.

"Her body is a mass of bruises and small wounds. Some look like burns."

"The vicious bastard," Tom muttered through clenched teeth.

"Her husband do this?" Dawn Light queried.

Thomas nodded, asking Joan if Elizabeth's ribs were badly damaged.

"I bound her up more fully. It did not feel as if any bones were snapped, nothing projecting, but they may be cracked."

"If man do that to me, I kill him. I put my knife across his throat."

There was no vehemence in Dawn Light's voice, but no one looking at her then would have considered it an empty threat.

"I believe you would Waaseyaaban."

Tom looked at his wife thinking that her fierceness was part of her fascination. She could be gentle, loving, full of sympathy for the natural world, but there was a fiery independence in her that matched any man. She would fight like a tigress to defend herself and those she loved. So different from the girl sleeping in the bed, yet Elizabeth too had struggled to maintain her essential self in her own way. He could not resist stroking her hair back from her face, savouring the texture of it.

"Poor child, she did nothing to deserve such treatment."

"I tell you before, she is not child. She not see you as father."

She smiled at him provocatively. When he did not rise to it she demanded, "Where is her father? Why does he not help his children?"

Thomas explained what James had said about Elizabeth's reluctance to go to Sir Neville.

"I believe she is unwilling to put the burden of guilt on him for giving her to such an unsuitable man and is afraid that he will be too ashamed of the scandal to admit it."

Dawn Light snorted in scorn. "Then she is foolish. Father must stand by his children. You and your father bad friends because of me, but if one of his daughters is beaten and shamed by her husband, would he call her liar and not protect her?"

"Never, he would be outraged." Tom was certain about that, no matter how much he disagreed with his father on other matters.

"Then she must go to her father and trust him. She cannot stay here. Bring you trouble."

"I am well aware of that. I have already told James that in a few days when Elizabeth is rested, we will take her home in the carriage and argue her case to her father. There is physical evidence enough of Hanham's excesses."

She was pleased to hear him say this. She did not need to ask why the Norrington's had come to Thomas for help. Elizabeth's desire for Tom was obvious to her and she saw more than just an avuncular sympathy for the girl in his concern, even if he was not fully aware of it himself. She had less sympathy for Lizzie because she could not understand why a woman would allow herself to be so victimized. She was not jealous; in fact she anticipated with amusement how Elizabeth would be making those big, innocent, melting eyes at her Makwa, all helpless and adoring. Yet she did not want her presence in the house to bring trouble down on them, causing strangers to intrude on their lives. The men who asked questions were bad enough; she did not welcome the prospect of others. She relished the fact that James Norrington was still nervous in her presence and had a wicked desire to frighten him in small ways.

Thomas was also thinking about James. The boy had shown courage in making a decision to escape and persuading his sister that it was the right course. The previous year James had talked so proudly of Elizabeth's coming union with Anthony Hanham, filled with pleasure to think his family would be linked to one that had aristocratic forebears. His father had schooled him so thoroughly in the importance of maintaining status and making sure that status was made visible to the rest of society. Now he was confused and on uncertain ground. Tom had picked up hints of his growing disillusionment last September when they talked under the tree and sensed he was struggling to adjust his values.

He found the boy sitting in the kitchen, toasting his toes by the fire and feeding the wolfhounds with scraps of meat that Joan had set aside for them. He looked up anxiously when Thomas came in.

"Can I see Lizzie now?"

"If you wish, but she is sleeping comfortably. Perhaps it would be best if you waited until later. She is in good hands. She will soon recover. Your love and concern for your sister does you honour. I admire you for it."

He could see that his words pleased James, who smiled at him.

"Elizabeth said your dogs are called Hector and Ajax. Which one is which?"

"Ajax is the bigger fellow with the brass studs in his collar. They are brothers from the same litter, four years old now. Their mother is a valued member of my parents' household in Salisbury. My sister Cecily had them sent to me when they were almost a year old, knowing I would be looking for some dogs to share my new house. I cannot imagine a life without dogs. Various breeds have been my companions since I took my first steps."

James gave Ajax the last piece of meat and showed them the empty dish, which Hector began to lick.

"I like their warrior names. My father keeps dogs too, but they are not allowed in the house. They live in the kennels and are looked after by one of the grooms. I never had a particular dog of my own." He hesitated, then added, "Sir Bartholomew gave me two fine greyhounds for hare coursing. I named them for their speed, Swift and Lightning. Yesterday morning I bought them new collars decorated with silver."

He regretted leaving those dogs. They had walked around so proudly after he had fitted their new collars on them. A sudden thought filled him with dismay.

"Oh, I do so hope Anthony will not take his spite out on them when he finds out we have gone. I should have brought them with us. He knows how fond of them I am and he may be cruel to them to get his revenge. I have seen him whip and kick his own dogs for no reason at all."

He was screwing his hands into fists as he spoke. Sarah Bushy had been going about her work in the kitchen, but when he talked of beating dogs she put down the carrots she was preparing and stared at him.

"I am so angry with Sir Bartholomew and Lady Agnes," James said vehemently. "They were kind to me always but why did they ignore all the vile things Anthony did? They are not cruel. They are convivial, civilized people. I cannot understand how they could bear it all in silence."

Thomas shook his head. "I cannot give you an answer to that, but I do know that we all close our eyes at times to things we prefer not to see. They have lavished so much care and attention on Anthony. He is their hope for the future and it would be hard for them to acknowledge that hope had turned sour or contemplate the possibility that they might be partly to blame for his behaviour. The motives of others are difficult to unravel James. I don't always understand my own. Perhaps that is why dogs are always such a comfort to us; their motives are blessedly transparent."

He looked at Hector and Ajax licking their lips in satisfaction before they wandered off, convinced that all the meat had gone now.

Sarah was still gazing at James with a disturbed look in her eyes. Tom regretted that they had spoken so freely about the Hanhams in front of her.

"I think we should go into the library. Joan will be back in here soon and we shall be under her feet. You must beware of getting under Joan Bushy's feet. Is that not so Sarah?" He gave the girl a conspiratorial smile, distracting her from the images that troubled her mind. "We might get swept out with the rubbish."

Sarah began to giggle, imagining her mother brushing them out with her extra-large broom and Thomas escorted James into the library saying,

"If I am not mistaken, there is something in here that you are very eager to see, although I vow, I wish you had chosen a less dramatic plan to get to see it."

James knew at once what he meant. He recalled how he had expressed his disappointment at the Frome Fair that he would not get the chance to see Philip Sidney's sword. Thomas' face was serious and the boy feared for a moment that Mountfield might believe he chose this house as a sanctuary only for selfish reasons. He was about to protest when he detected the curl of amusement at the corner of the man's mouth and told himself he must become accustomed to Tom's dry wit. He honoured his father and could enumerate his qualities readily, but a sense of humour was not one of them. Sir Neville was an austere man whose conversation was economical and practical. James had not been brought up enjoying the interplay of witty badinage, not trained in the nuances of irony. When first exposed to Tom's remarks last spring he had reacted with indignation, feeling them to be mockery. Now having spent almost a year under the lash of Anthony Hanham's tongue, he realised there was warmth and purpose in Sir Thomas' humour.

Mountfield was taking down a sword from the wall beside the fireplace. He pushed aside the pile of papers and drawing the weapon from its scabbard lay it across the top of his desk. It was a fine example of a spada da lato, a side sword designed for military engagements. The rapier was fast becoming the weapon of choice for young gallants to wear at their sides. Its thin elegance complemented their clothes and many of them took lessons from Italian fencing masters in the use of the rapier. The spada however was more useful in battle because it could cut as well as thrust and stab, having a wider blade than the rapier and sharpened on both edges. It was a featherweight compared to the broadsword of previous centuries, easy to handle and manoeuvrable, enabling fast changes in direction.

This particular weapon had a blade just under three feet long and a width of two inches, tapering to a point of half an inch. The grip was bound with leather. An openwork cage of curving pieces of steel, sweeping up from the blade to connect with the cross piece formed a guard to protect the hand and a single curve ran from the cross piece up to the pommel.

James stared at it in wonder. It was not an elaborate weapon; the lines were very clean and the only decoration was a pattern incised on the round pommel, inlaid with silver, but for James it was imbued with an aura like the Holy Grail because Philip Sidney had carried it into his last battle. He ran his finger along the flat of the blade with great reverence.

"Pick it up," Tom encouraged. "Feel the balance of it in your hand."

James grasped it carefully and was surprised by how it felt.

"It is so light. I expected it to be much heavier."

"Yes, that's the beauty of a spada. It allows you to attack or defend fast on either side and deliver an effective slashing blow as well as a thrust. Try it."

James was hesitant at first, thinking he would look foolish, but after he had lunged forward, then switched the action to a sideways slash, the ease of it excited him and he began to swing the sword from side to side to simulate a battle situation. Thomas smiled.

"Sits well in the hand does it not? My father has a great broadsword, a family treasure from the days of Edward III. It is magnificent to look at and the damage it can do is fiercesome, but Jesu, the weight of it. I used to try to wield it when I was a small lad and caused my father great amusement because I would fall over under the weight of it. Fighting men then must have been bone weary after a battle, muscles aching so sorely they could scarce drag themselves along. I would rather have something like this in my hand any day, which gives me freedom to move fast and does not make my arm feel as if it is about to drop off."

He thought about his father's laughter as he struggled with that broadsword; how he would help his son to his feet and assure him that in a few years' time he would be strong enough to handle it. Robert Mountfield was a disciplinarian, who expected obedience from his children, but he loved them and was always willing to listen to them, share their interests. Despite his rebellious nature which often caused friction with his father, Thomas remembered many happy hours in Sir Robert's company. Those memories made his father's present attitude towards him all the more painful.

"When did Sir Philip give you this sword?" James asked as he put the weapon back down on the desk. Tom slipped it back into its scabbard.

"I took charge of it when we carried him to Arnhem in the litter. He asked where it was the next day and I laid it beside him, but he insisted I keep it. Even then, before the fever came on him, I think he knew he was going to die. He said he was sure I would never shed blood with it except in a noble cause. To tell you true James, I hope never to shed any more blood with any sword. I killed a native at Roanoke and four men at Zutphen, that is blood enough on my conscience. I cannot help but sing the praises of a good weapon, but I do not advocate over much zeal in the use of one."

"But you cannot be held to account for killing men in battle," James protested, "For they would kill you if you did not defend yourself."

"I know, but that knowledge does not prevent their deaths weighing on your soul. I chose to fight in that conflict, no one forced me to do so. I was dazzled by Philip's vision."

"Do you think now that he was wrong?" the puzzlement was evident in James' voice.

"No, not wrong for Philip, but perhaps wrong for me. But don't trouble yourself with my confusions. What is important is that this sword is precious to me because of my love for Philip and the memory of our friendship and it pleases me that it is important to you also."

As he hung the sword back on its hook on the wall, he scattered some of the papers from the desk. James retrieved them asking, "Is this your description of the campaign?"

"No, I haven't got as far as that yet. I am still in the fort at Roanoke, just recovered from fever and we are all anxious in case the Secotans attack us again. I fear that I do not progress very fast. I have bursts of activity when I write easily, then long periods when all I do is chew the end of my pen and curse my dull brain, although I was writing very fluently early this morning."

James hung his head. "And now we have come to distract and worry you."

"Who knows- it may have the opposite effect and inspire me to write more."

"Can I read it? Lizzie said the few pages she read when we were here before were most interesting."

"You are welcome to read it, if you can decipher my writing. I cross out frequently and don't take enough care with the shape of my lettering when my thoughts are flowing freely. I blot the page too, like a careless schoolboy. My old tutor would smack my knuckles for that."

"Oh mine did that too when he thought I wasn't paying sufficient attention. I found Latin very hard. I am not very proficient in it even now."

"Well, all this is written in plain English. As grateful as I am to have been taught the skill to read the classic writers in their own tongues, I feel very strongly that now men should write in their native language and that as many folk as possible should be given the chance to learn to read."

"Even servants and labourers?"

James felt that was going a little too far.

"Most certainly. Their lives are hard enough as it is; should we suppress their imaginations too? To be able to read a well written tale or a chronicle of the past can open out whole new worlds in the mind. If it were possible for Hector and Ajax to learn to read, I would teach even them."

Tom's face was animated with enthusiasm for his theme and James wished he had been given a tutor like this man. Perhaps learning would have become a pleasure for him.

"I think I will sit here if I may and read some of your account of

Roanoke."

"Good, I shall be interested in your opinion, whether it is lively enough to hold your attention and I promise that I will not come in and rap your knuckles if your thoughts appear to be straying. If you want to start at the beginning the first few chapters are in the drawer on the left – I think."

He pulled the drawer out to check, not sure if he had moved them. "Ah yes, they are still here. Please give up on it if you are bored."

He left James Norrington sitting at the desk, starting from the beginning.

Elizabeth sat up in bed resting against a bank of pillows. Her body was tingling with a pleasant sensation. Joan and Waaseyaaban had bathed her and salved all her bruises with arnica although she had not been aware of it. She had slept all that day, all through the night and well into this morning. When she woke to find herself in the room that was so familiar in her secret world, she was not sure if it was real. Then Joan Bushy came in and finding her awake hurried back to the kitchen to fetch a bowl of porridge. She sat beside the bed and encouraged Lizzie to eat every morsel. It was creamy, easy to digest and warming. This was reality. She was in the bedchamber again that looked out over the back gardens.

When she discovered how long she had slept, she realised that a messenger would be well on his way to London by now, to tell Anthony they had not returned from their morning ride. A shiver of fear went through her thinking about his reaction. She pushed it away, not wanting to think of Anthony, but wishing to enjoy the atmosphere of safety that enveloped her now, even if it was to last for a short while only. Joan left her to rest, but she wished to get up. She was eager to test her strength. Her weakness during the ride frustrated her; she had always been an excellent horsewoman. She recalled how hard it had been to get her breath, how her chest was tight and sore, her throat so restricted it felt as if fingers were pressing on her windpipe. She took several deep breaths to make sure her breathing had returned to normal. She found to her relief that there were no wheezing noises and she could breathe easily, so she took the decision to get out of bed. She dressed slowly and walked around the room with care because her legs did not feel very strong. The effort of dressing tired her and she sat on the edge of the bed for a while. The pain in her side was now a dull ache and did not stab so sharply as long as she did not make a sudden movement.

She went over to the window. It was a bright morning, the sky a pale, washed blue, lit by silver-gilt sunlight. Down in the gardens she could see Thomas Mountfield and Dawn Light. She was kneeling beside a patch of ground, pressing plants into the freshly turned, dark brown soil. Tom was playing the lute. They both appeared to be singing. What on earth are they doing she thought, longing to be out there with them. She could recall the moment when she tried to dismount and fell into his arms, the feeling of him holding her close and running with her, but after that all was blackness until she woke this morning. Had he sat by her bed, anxious for her? She hoped so and was angry with herself for hoping.

She opened the casement a fraction and could just catch the strains of the lute, but it was too far away for her to make out what they were singing. She saw James walking out of the long arbour adjusting his clothing and assumed he had visited the privy. On their previous visit he had insisted on using the close stools in his room, nervous of venturing into the unknown territory beyond the arbour. The thought made her smile and reminded her again of how much he had grown up. His determination to rescue her from Anthony and the way he had encouraged her on that difficult ride; his confidence that he could find the right path through the forest, all these things had surprised her. James could not remember his mother and Lizzie had always tried to compensate for that empty place in his life by mothering him herself. As he grew older she did so as discreetly as possible not to wound his pride, but there were times when he seemed so young in judgement, so much in need of her support. Now he had shown her that he was capable of decisive action and also how much he loved her. Her heart filled with affection for him and she had a desire to hurry downstairs and hug him.

Hurrying was something that was beyond her as yet however, so she walked into the gallery at a sedate pace. The stairs looked daunting and she gripped the rail as she descended to find James standing at the bottom about to come up.

"Lizzie, I was just coming to see you. Should you be out of bed?"

He took her arm to help her negotiate the few remaining stairs and was taken by surprise when she embraced him warmly.

"Oh James, I am so proud of you. You have been so brave and clear thinking. I could not wish for a better brother."

"I only did what a good brother should do," he replied both pleased and embarrassed by her praise. "And it was for me as well as you. I could not stand his cruel scorn any longer."

She told him she had seen him walking out of the arbour and he admitted that he had braved the privy.

"It is a proper room with a door that locks and quite clean, no crawly things inside," he said seriously. "If you wish to use it, I will escort you to the arbour"

She was sure that she could walk that far and was keen to go out in the garden.

"Did you see Sir Thomas and his wife out there? I heard the lute from my window."

James nodded. "Yes, I think she is putting a spell on the plants to make them grow. The words of the song are in a strange language- hers I suppose. I kept well out of the way so they did not see me. I want nothing to do with magic spells. Sir Thomas does these things only to please her I'm sure."

He added this as if he needed to excuse someone he now admired for singing mysterious words over a row of vegetable plants.

"The minister at Norrington blesses the spring and winter sowing from the pulpit," his sister reminded him.

"That's different Lizzie."

"No it isn't. He is saying prayers, asking God to grant the people a good harvest and that is what Dawn Light is doing."

James grudgingly assented to some similarity between the two ceremonies, although he was worried about equating heathen chanting with the services of the Church of England and wished that Thomas was not taking part in it. He made sure that he steered his sister along the covered walk way and into the arbour without attracting the attention of their hosts.

He waited a discreet distance from the privy door, intending to take her straight back into the house, but when she joined him, Lizzie had other ideas. She wandered up the garden path obliging James to follow her.

Dawn Light had just finished planting. She was standing beside her husband surveying her work with satisfaction. They had stopped singing, but Tom was still playing the lute, a jaunty, rhythmical tune to which Waaseyaaban clapped her hands, marking the beat. When Thomas saw the Norringtons approaching he stopped playing and Waaseyaaban turned her head, her hands poised in mid-clap.

"Mistress Elizabeth," Tom said. "It is good to see you on your feet. How do you feel?"

"Much better thank you, but please do not stop on our account. I assume you are blessing the planting."

"We finish now." Dawn Light's voice was brusque. They had not quite finished the final piece of music and she was annoyed at the interruption; she did not want to complete the ceremony in front of them. They were strangers and this was very personal to her.

"Not blessing." She looked pointedly at James. "Music magic. Make plants grow."

Thomas sensed her irritation and said, "Well, it is a kind of blessing I suppose."

"Not blessing," came the staccato reply. There was a stubborn set to her mouth. Tom shrugged.

"Very well, not blessing. Dawn Light's people believe that music encourages plants to grow. The song we were singing is a traditional Croatan song that compliments the plants, flatters them by telling them how beautiful they will look when they are grown- the assumption being that they will be in a hurry to grow so everyone can praise them for their beauty."

"This corn plant." Dawn Light waved her hand at the large area they had just planted. "Corn plant very vain because of golden colour."

She looked at Elizabeth's hair as she spoke. The girl had not bothered to plait her hair and the sunlight emphasized its golden sheen. She felt self-conscious under Waaseyaaban's penetrating gaze and looked down at her feet.

As unwilling as he was to incur Waaseyaaban's displeasure James could not prevent himself from declaring, "But plants can't have vanity. They cannot think like humans. Sir Thomas, you don't really believe that music helps them to grow do you?"

Tom smiled. "I have an open mind about it. Music has the power to stir even the hardest heart, reach down to your very soul. The vegetative world may be on a plain below mankind, but plants are living entities, touched by the hand of the creator. I don't find it impossible that they can respond to music. There is plenty of music in nature; the wind in the leaves and the grass, running water, bird song, the rhythm of horses hooves drumming on the ground, all those strange little noises in the forest at night. The natural world appears to me to be full of music."

"Do you believe in the music of the spheres?" Elizabeth asked, looking up at him with that wrapt expression that so amused Dawn Light.

"Who knows what music there is in the universe? The idea that when all the planets are in perfect unison, a heavenly harmony is heard up there is very attractive. I would like it to be true although I fear it would be too beautiful for the human ear to bear."

"You play the lute exceeding well." Elizabeth told him.

"Passably. I should play more often, then I would improve."

"He play well as you say." Dawn Light tossed her head at him. "He always deny, he and all his friends- always look away as if it is bad to boast when they do good things. Croatan men always boast of their deeds, bring them respect in the tribe. It is good to boast, but not for English gentlemen. His friend Philip write long story, many, many words. You tell them what he call it."

Thomas had begun to laugh. "She means his great heroic romance 'Arcadia'. Such a complicated, carefully plotted story. He had been working on it for ages and he called it "a trifle and that triflingly handled." It is only around 180,000 words. Some trifle. But that was typical of him, that air of nonchalance he always adopted."

"You laugh," his wife accused, "But you are just as bad."

She turned to the Norringtons. "I boast for him, my Makwa."

"I am sure you have every reason to do so," Lizzie said with sincerity.

It was Waaseyaaban's turn to laugh, that harsh, throaty sound, so sudden that it made James start back. She reached out and taking hold of a long strand of Lizzie's hair ran it through her fingers appraisingly. Then just as abruptly she ran over to the chain of copper discs on the pole at the edge of the newly planted crops and set it swinging so that it played a metallic tune.

"This music too," she announced. She laughed again and darted down the path to disappear into the house. Elizabeth fancied that Thomas was embarrassed by his wife's mercurial behaviour, but he covered it well.

He suggested they should all go inside because it was unwise for Elizabeth to be out in the fresh wind.

"You need to be cossetted a while yet."

He took them into the parlour and talked to them about the best course of action to take regarding their situation, proposing that if Elizabeth was sufficiently rested, he would escort them to Norrington Hall the next day.

"No doubt Sir Bartholomew has sent men out to look for you by now and sent word to Anthony that you are missing. You must not be found here after days of searching. It will be injurious to Elizabeth's reputation. Hanham's supporters will twist the circumstances and may suggest not only that I abducted you, but that you both connived in the abduction. The sooner you appeal to your father the better. I am sorry to speak of something you may not wish me to, but your father needs to see the evidence of Hanham's brutality while it is fresh and at its worst. You do both understand this don't you? I am not turning you away. I will do my utmost to support you, but I must put you in the best position to resist his claim on you."

They both nodded their assent, knowing that he was right, no matter how much they might wish to stay cocooned in the forest. Elizabeth was grateful for the delicacy with which he had referred to her physical ordeal. She was ashamed of her bruised body. She knew it made no sense, for she was not to blame, yet the shame remained. It comforted her that Tom was sensitive enough to see that.

Thomas went into the village that afternoon and the Norrington's spent several hours in the library reading the story of Roanoke and browsing through other books on the shelves. Once, Dawn Light looked in on them. She did not speak, just stood in the doorway watching them. They were unaware of her presence until James happened to glance up from his reading. They had no idea how long she had been there. Her face was impassive, unreadable as she observed them. Elizabeth was about to say how fascinated they were by Tom's tale of Roanoke, but before she could speak Dawn Light walked away, shutting the door behind her.

James shivered. "She still troubles me Lizzie. She is so strange. Witness her behaviour in the garden this morning; how she touched your hair and ran away laughing."

"Her ways are very different from ours I agree. She does not observe the rules of behaviour that we have been brought up to consider polite because they seem foolish to her. She is spontaneous in what she says and does. Just now she wished to see what we were doing, so she came to look and as she had no desire for any conversation she did not try to make any."

"I don't think she likes us very much. I am sure she will be glad when we leave."

"That is because she fears we will put Sir Thomas in danger," Elizabeth said.

"And she is right to fear it."

Lizzie had a deeper understanding than her brother of Waaseyaaban's behaviour in the garden that morning. She saw that the Croatan woman with her sharp observation had penetrated her thoughts, her desire for Thomas and was mocking her for it. She was throwing out a challenge, saying 'Make sheep's eyes at him all you like, he will never be yours, always mine. He may show you kindness and courtesy, his smiles may make your heart beat faster but I am his true and abiding passion.'

Elizabeth was right about this, but she only partially understood Dawn Light's feelings towards her. Waaseyaaban had a fierce pride in her husband's sexual power. She knew Tom was attracted to this soft creature with her creamy skin and sun kissed hair. She was like a fawn crying out for protection and her husband's protective instincts were very strong. His libido was strong also and she was willing for him to bed this girl, let her experience his considerable skill as a lover, learn what power her Makwa possessed. A Croatan woman could boast when others knew for a fact that her husband was a true man. She appreciated the gentler side of his nature but it was his masculinity that had drawn her to him. She did not see Elizabeth as a rival, for she was sure of Tom's heart.

However, her comprehension of Elizabeth's attraction to Thomas was equally partial. She failed to see that it was more than just physical. Lizzie was drawn to the gentle side, his love of the arts, his struggle to grasp the meaning of life, his innate kindness and that air of melancholy that sometimes surrounded him. He had seen so much and she so little. She loved to hear him talk on so many diverse topics.

Waaseyaaban also misjudged the sensitivity of Tom's attitude to Elizabeth. He certainly thought her beautiful but he had no intention of taking her to bed and had no wish to put himself in a position where he was tempted. Her frank admiration, the way she reacted with interest to his every word was flattering and hard to resist. She had an intelligent sympathy, a thirst for knowledge that appealed to him and her eyes told him that despite being shaken by her ordeal, her basic innocence, her belief in goodness remained intact. It was a combination to tempt any man. His desire to take her to her father as soon as possible was for his own sake as well as hers.

That evening after supper when they all moved from the dining room into the parlour, Joan Bushy declared that she and Sarah would clear away the supper things and retire to their own parlour. It was usual for them to sit with Tom and Dawn Light for a while after supper, but Joan fancied the Norringtons might wish to talk of things it would be best Sarah did not hear.

"There are one or two tasks we wish to complete before we go to bed," she said.

As Tom closed the door that led from the dining room into the parlour, he could hear Sarah complaining, "What tasks Mother? What tasks have we still to finish?"

He smiled to himself, appreciating Joan's discretion. In fact the last topic Elizabeth and James wished to discuss was their difficult situation. On the morrow they must face their father and convince him they had done the right thing to leave Hanham House. This evening, as the fire burned up and the wolfhounds lay in front of it, stretching out their long legs towards the warmth it was good to pretend that all was well.

Lizzie admired the tapestry on the wall and Thomas explained that it was almost a hundred years old. It had once belonged to his maternal grandmother. The fact that it still retained its colour attested to the quality of it. The scene depicted was a domestic one; four women wearing the fashions of the previous century, gossiping in a rose garden, while children played around them. There were trees in blossom, daisies in the grass, a frog-inhabited pond full of water lilies and in the distance men on horseback with hunting dogs pursuing a stag. Golden and silver threads were woven into the women's garments and the flower petals.

"When I was a small child, I used to stand and look at it a great deal. I gave all the children names and made up stories in my head about them," Thomas confessed. "Grandmother always said she wished me to have it when I had a house of my own because I was so fond of it. She died when I was at Oxford, but when my uncle sold the house, Mother took charge of the tapestry to keep it safe for me until I had somewhere to hang it."

Waaseyaaban was also fond of that tapestry. She liked it because it told a story and enjoyed the way the gold and silver threads shone in the candlelight.

The James Norrington of the previous May would have regaled them all with descriptions of the wondrous textiles in Hanham House, but this James did not wish to dwell on that place. Instead, to please Lizzie, he asked Sir Thomas if he would play the lute for them. Tom was reluctant at first.

He glanced at Dawn Light, who nodded her assent. He had wondered if she was still resentful that the corn planting ceremony had been interrupted and did not wish the reappearance of the lute to remind her. When she gave her unspoken agreement, he went into the library and returned with his lute and two books bound in stiffened linen. He asked James if he read music. The boy shook his head.

"No, father thought it was unnecessary for a man concerned with business and politics and the running of an estate-which I will be one day- to learn things he considered more suited to a woman."

"So, he thinks all our fine composers and musicians are effeminate does he? My father says much the same thing about actors, although he admires musicians."

"I did not mean to imply that my father would consider you in that way," James replied quickly.

"I doubt if it would bother me much if he did," said Thomas.

He had placed the books on the table and Elizabeth leaned across to open one of them saying, "I read music a little. Father found it suitable for me to learn, though I was never taught to play an instrument."

"Well, these are two books of songs composed by William Byrd, a musician at the Chapel Royal. As you see, they were given the title 'The English Song Book' by the printers. My friend Simon," He hesitated and Waaseyaaban looked into his eyes aware of the pain he felt knowing he might never see Simon Bailey again. "A lawyer in London sent them to me as soon as each edition was printed, one in 1588 and the other the following year. He had ready access to them, the printing house being near his chambers at Lincoln's Inn. He knew they would please me because Byrd has set three of Philip Sidney's sonnets to music. He has also set two elegies to Philip written by others. In truth the elegies themselves are formulaic and dull but the music gives them some lustre."

He sat in the armchair and played some of the melodies while Elizabeth and James followed the words in the book. Dawn Light sat on the floor, resting against Ajax's bony hind-quarters. She always felt more comfortable sitting on the floor than in a chair. She watched the expressions passing across Elizabeth's face as the girl's eyes wandered from the text to Thomas and lingered there. She decided this must be the first time that Elizabeth had fallen in love. She recalled the first time she had laid eyes on Thomas. She had seen twenty two summers pass and had been courted by two men from the village, both of whom were rejected by her brothers as unworthy.

The truth of it was that she was too useful at home with her gift of making plants grow and they had no wish to part with her unless the suitor could make it worth their while. She did not care because she did not fancy either of the suitors. If she had set her heart on a man, she would have had her way. Her will was stronger than both her brothers. She was stringing a bead necklace when her eldest brother, Dasawan, first brought the tall stranger into their house. The Croatan men were stocky and powerfully built, but not tall. Thomas had to duck to pass through their doorway. Straightening up, his eyes met Waaseyaaban's and there was an immediate connection. Her body felt the way it did when there was lightning in the air, a prickly sensation under the skin. It was not long before she knew he felt the same towards her and their relationship progressed rapidly. Her brothers gave it their approval, eager to be on good terms with the white settlers in the fort. They offered her as a gift. She would have been his without their blessing.

They made love all over the island; on the beach, in the corn fields, in a canoe, enjoying the threat of it capsizing and when it eventually did so, continued their union in the shallow water. When he was not with her, her body ached for him. She did not agonize over the decision when he asked her to come back with him to England.

Thomas put down his lute.

"I think you have heard enough of my playing, but you must agree that Byrd's music is beautiful. It has a spiritual quality. I wish he had set my favourite of Philip's sonnets, written as if a woman is speaking. It is Waaseyaaban's favourite too."

"Speak it now," she demanded, sitting forward to give it her full attention, Lizzie seconded the request and the three of them listened to him recite the words that Philip's imagination had placed in the mouth of Penelope Devereux, his beloved Stella.

My true love hath my heart and I have his,
By just exchange one for the other given.
I hold his dear and mine he cannot miss,
There never was a better bargain driven.
His heart in me keeps me and him in one,
My heart in him his thoughts and senses guides,
He loves my heart for once it was his own,
I cherish his because in me it bides.
His heart his wound received from my sight,
My heart was wounded with his heart,
For as from me on him his hurt did light,
So still me thought, in me his hurt did smart.
Both equal hurt, in this change sought our bliss.
My true love hath my heart and I have his.

"That is so beautiful," Lizzie murmured. "It is clever but the invention and skill does not override the genuine feeling in it."

"I find the middle bit confusing," confessed James, "the bit about wounding."

Tom rephrased it in a more conversational way.

"The lover's heart was wounded when he first fell in love at sight of her, so her heart was wounded when she responded to his love, knowing she had caused him his pain. As she now has his heart within her, she can feel the smart of the wound of love that she gave him. Hence they have equal pain, equal bliss. Easy enough when you think it through."

"Oh, I see now." James was relieved to have penetrated the confusion.

Dawn Light snorted. "It is easy to understand. I understand for Thomas has my heart and I have his. So I know it is true poem."

James' cheeks reddened at the implication that he had been slow to comprehend the meaning, particularly as it had given Elizabeth no problem. She was ready to give her heart to Thomas Mountfield without condition, but Dawn Light had just reminded her that his heart was already taken.

When they all retired to their bedchambers that night, Elizabeth sat on her bed for a long time, unwilling to go to sleep. Her body was tired, but she wanted to soak up the atmosphere of this house for as long as possible. In her head she could still hear Tom's voice reciting that sonnet. Tomorrow, once he had taken them to Norrington Hall, he would have to be consigned back into her secret world. The sound of Joan Bushy bolting the doors downstairs and snuffing out the candles in the passage, drifted up to her. There was an owl hooting near the window. She opened the casement, just in time to see a white shape glide noiselessly across the garden into the trees.

She sighed, knowing she must try to sleep. She would need every ounce of strength she could summon up to face her father. She considered saying that she did not feel well enough to travel yet, so she could steal just one more day in Tom's company. It would not be a complete lie; she was still weak. She even contemplated pretending to faint and then chided herself for thinking it. She was not good at dissembling and had often wished she was not so transparent. Besides, Tom was right in his view that they must go to Sir Neville as soon as possible.

She walked across the room to close her door and as she did so looked out on the gallery. Thomas and Waaseyaaban were standing with their backs to her. They were close together with one arm around the other's waist, looking up through the skylight at the stars. Good manners dictated that Lizzie should not interrupt their intimacy, but she had an overwhelming desire to be part of it and went over to them. Picking up the conversation of that morning she asked, "Are you listening for the music of the spheres?"

Tom turned, smiling, but Dawn Light continued to look up at the sky.

"We were just stargazing. It has become a habit with us before we go to bed. In the warm summer months we often sleep outside, but while the weather has a chill in it we look up through the skylight. At my advanced age, I need to take care of my old bones- at least so my little sister Cecily keeps telling me. She is thirteen years my junior and often reminds me of it."

"When I was a child," Elizabeth confided, "I used to stand in the garden and try to count the stars until my neck ached and I felt dizzy. Do you think it is possible to know how many stars are up there?"

Tom shook his head. "No, I believe they are infinite, many lying beyond our capacity to see them. There may be other universes beyond ours that we know nothing of."

He laughed when she asked, "Is that an orthodox view?"

"You should know by now Mistress Elizabeth that I rarely hold an orthodox view. I fear that I am one of those heretics who are dissatisfied with Ptolemy's theories about the universe. I am a heliocentrist."

"Whatever is that?"

Before Tom could reply, Waaseyaaban murmured, "I warm your old bones in bed soon. Maybe first you like to try other bed."

She nibbled his ear and sashayed into their bedchamber. Tom was not sure if Lizzie had heard his wife's suggestion. It did not appear so. Relieved he explained hastily, "Waaseyaaban has no desire to hear me talk about Ptolemy. I think I told you once before that words are not so important to the Croatan. She would rather look at the stars with me than hear me theorize about them."

"But I am eager to listen to your theories."

There was that look again, the one he tried not to countenance for fear of being flattered out of his resolve.

"Too eager Mistress. You encourage me to indulge myself, resulting in too much hot air. You really should go to bed and rest. Tomorrow will not be easy for you."

He took her arm and guided her to her chamber door, but she stopped in the doorway.

"You must explain that term to me first. I refuse to go to bed until you do. Come in and sit down."

She walked into the room and sat on the edge of the bed. Tom hesitated for a moment, leaning against the door frame, before he followed her and taking up a stool, sat down a few feet from the bed.

"You know that the accepted Ptolemaic view of the universe is that the earth is its fixed centre and the stars are embedded in a large outer sphere that rotates rapidly every day, whilst the other planets are within their own, smaller spheres which also rotate."

Lizzie knew some basic astronomy. James' tutor had showed them an elaborate diagram of the heavens once. The pattern and sheer perfection of it fascinated her. She was pleased that Tom did not assume that she was ignorant of the subject.

"Well, when I was at Oxford, we debated this with great ardour, often airing a number of variations. I was never satisfied with Ptolemy's complicated theory of ellipses and epicycles to explain why the other spheres did not appear to have circular orbits around the earth. We were aware that Copernicus, the astronomer had suggested that the earth was not the centre of the universe and that it was not fixed. He believed that all the spheres, including the earth revolve around the sun. It is the earth that rotates daily. This explains some of the inequalities that Ptolemy could not account for with plausibility."

"Then heliocentric means centred on the sun?"

"Yes, from Helios, the Greek word for the sun. I found this theory interesting, but was not fully convinced until I met Thomas Harriot, the naturalist who sailed with us to Roanoke. He introduced me to the work of Thomas Digges, a brilliant young mathematician who had translated Copernicus' treatise on the revolution of the spheres into English. Reading that and talking to Harriot convinced me it was right. Digges was certain that the stars were not limited in number and fixed within spheres, but were endless and scattered all over the universe. That makes much more sense to me and there is so much more we have to discover. We know so little about the universe."

"You said this view is considered heretical. Do you mean that the church condemns it utterly?"

"Orthodoxy takes its stand on Psalm 93- 'the world is firmly established. It cannot be moved"- so to those who believe every single word in the Bible emanates from God himself, we who favour heliocentrism are denying God's word."

Elizabeth was sure that this would be her father's view, although she had never heard him speak of it.

"Does the condemnation of the church not trouble you?"

"No, what does trouble me is their taking the next step and assuming I must be an atheist in consequence. Even St. Augustine taught that every passage in the Bible cannot be taken as truth, particularly the poetry and songs that are included in it. These things have been composed by men who have their own interpretations of God's design. They may contain universal truths and great beauty, but do not come directly from God. Inspired by God perhaps, but that is different. However, the opinions of Augustine and the early fathers don't weigh much with Protestant reformers these days."

He could imagine Simon Bailey giving him an earnest rebuke if he had heard those views on the Bible. He wished he knew how Simon was faring, if he had been welcomed by his Scottish acquaintances and was reunited with Ellen and the children. He lived in constant hope that a message would come from his friend before long, to ease his worry. Thinking of Simon he had fallen into a silence which Lizzie did not break. Looking up from his reverie, he saw such an expression of admiration on the girl's face that he jumped to his feet saying, "There, I warned you about encouraging me- holding forth like some self-important theologian. You see now why my wife made her escape. Goodnight Mistress Elizabeth. I trust you will sleep well."

He bowed and left the room, shutting the door behind him. She sensed his discomfort in the rapid way he departed. For the first time it occurred to Elizabeth that he was attracted to her.

Chapter Six

MARK WHEELER TOOK A furtive look around to make sure no one was watching before he pressed his ear against the door of the guest parlour, hoping to pick up some of the conversation. He had been out in the yard splitting logs to feed the ovens in the kitchen of Norrington Hall when he saw three strangers ride through the arch of the impressive gatehouse. One was a blond-haired, expensively dressed young man with a sulky mouth.

The other two had an unsavoury air about them. Wheeler had grown up in a neighbourhood where that type of hard man with a propensity for violence was commonplace. He could recognise it a mile off. It did not surprise him when he heard their London accents, similar to his own. He had never seen Anthony Hanham for he was not in residence when they had first escorted Elizabeth Norrington to Hanham House, but he had heard descriptions and guessed this might be him. He did not appear to be in a good mood. His complexion was too pale for Mark to say he had a face like thunder; it was more like cream turned sour. He snarled some instructions at his companions and went into the house by the main entrance.

It was still early morning; if they had ridden from Frome they must have left very early. The two men looked frowsy and out of sorts, as if they had slept little. Wheeler dodged into the kitchen with a bundle of firewood and unnoticed by the scullions, filled a leather bottle with small beer and sidled up to the men in the yard. One of them had dismounted and was shaking his cloak, complaining that it was damp from the early mist. They accepted the offer of the beer with eagerness and passed the bottle between them taking long draughts, whilst Mark Wheeler established a form of camaraderie by telling them how good it was to hear his own native accent instead of the country burr of the dullards and lack wits he had to suffer every day. They sympathised and he soon managed to wheedle out of them the reason for their visit.

He left them to finish the beer, an idea forming in his mind. Mark's main hobby, when time allowed was womanizing. Naturally lecherous, he attributed that characteristic to others. He recalled the day when Sir Thomas Mountfield had led them out of the forest on to the main road, how charming he had been to Elizabeth, how she had blushed when Master James suggested that Mountfield was flirting with her. Sir Thomas was a man of the world, brazen enough to display openly in front of them his provocative native whore. What if he and Mistress Elizabeth had a liaison that night at his house and misliking her husband she had gone running to her lover? He knew women who fancied themselves in love would do desperate things. He wondered if Jacob Whyte had ever mentioned the over-night stay to Sir Neville and saw a way to ingratiate himself with his master.

He was listening at the parlour door now to make sure Hanham and Sir Neville were in the room. The sound of voices was just audible through the solid door, but he could not make out any words. He took a deep breath, intending to knock on the door when a deep voice behind him said,

"What are you up to Mark Wheeler?" Jacob Whyte was standing beside him arms folded, looking very dubious about Wheeler's intentions.

"Are you ear-wigging at the master's door? Get back to your work."

"I was just making sure that Sir Neville and Master Hanham were in the parlour," he defended. "I have something important to tell them."

"What on earth could you have to say that would interest them? You are just indulging your insatiable curiosity for things that are none of your business. Be off with you."

Mark stood his ground despite the steward's stern expression.

"I know why he's here don't I. Mistress Elizabeth, aided by Master James has run away from Hanham House. Hanham's servants told me. She's been giving her husband a bad time according to them, putting him in a right foul temper."

"How dare you speak so carelessly about Mistress Elizabeth? You soak up gossip like a sponge."

"Ah, but it's not just gossip; it is true. Hanham is here to see if she came home to her father, but we know she has not, don't we?"

Wheeler's habit of asking rhetorical questions in a know-it-all tone of voice always irritated Jacob. "Of course we do," he replied with undisguised impatience.

"Well I reckon I know where she has gone- run off to Thomas Mountfield's little love nest in the forest. Perhaps he came and rescued her from Hanham House."

Jacob was shocked to hear that Elizabeth and James had gone missing. He remembered how James had urged him to make Sir Neville aware of how unhappy they were at Hanham House, how Anthony did not treat them with respect, but he could not imagine for one moment that Elizabeth would be recalcitrant or unfaithful. He considered himself to be a good judge of character and he had formed a favourable opinion of Sir Thomas. This was not a man who abducted young wives from under their husband's noses.

"Are you suggesting that Mistress Elizabeth and Sir Thomas---?"

"I certainly am. Handsome, dashing sort of fellow. Didn't you notice the eyes she was making at him when he led us out of the forest last year?"

"Stop that at once," Jacob demanded.

"I bet you didn't tell Sir Neville that we stopped overnight at his house."

"As a matter of fact, I did, but he would have no reason whatsoever to think his children would go there. Why would they? They have had no contact with Sir Thomas since that day."

"How do we know that? They could have been sending letters, meeting secretly for all we know. I feel it is my duty to tell the master and her husband where she might be. If I am right and Sir Neville finds out that you didn't mention my request to enlighten him- and I'll make sure he finds out- you will be for it Jacob Whyte, steward or no steward."

Jacob could have wrung the youth's scrawny neck, but he knew it was true and Mark could see that he knew it. He smiled in triumph.

"Right, shall I go in and tell them?"

"No, you will go back to work. I will tell them that you have passed the idea on to me. Sir Neville would not be pleased to have you burst in on his guest in such difficult circumstances."

"But---" Mark was disappointed. He wanted to make it very clear that the information came from him. Jacob was determined to make sure that he did not profit from it.

"Yes, I know you saw this as a chance to curry favour. You have a nasty turn of mind Mark Wheeler and I am sure your suspicions are unfounded. Clear off."

Jacob was standing in front of the door, solid and formidable. There was no way Wheeler could have got past him. He sloped away, muttering to himself. Jacob Whyte straightened his doublet with determination and knocked on the door. A brisk voice bade him enter. Sir Neville Norrington and Anthony Hanham were standing in the centre of the room. The expression of Norrington's face was puzzled and anxious. Anthony was drumming his fingers on the table beside him, with angry impatience. He gave Jacob a hostile glance.

"Ah Jacob," Sir Neville seemed relieved to see him, "I was about to send for you to see if you can throw any light on a most disturbing turn of events. My children have disappeared from Hanham House and we are at a loss to know where they might be."

Sir Neville was a tall, rangy man with a pronounced stoop. Even stooping he was several inches taller than Hanham. He moved stiffly as if his back was painful. His iron grey hair was coarse textured and stood up like the bristles of a brush. The bushy eyebrows were too abundant for his narrow face.

"Do you think they have gone to my sister's in Bath? I want you to send a messenger to Lady Ashbury at once. It is the only place I can imagine they would go."

Jacob was about to put Mark's suggestion to him when Sir Neville continued,

"I find it hard to believe that they would do something as impulsive as this. They have always been obedient children, both of them. I begin to fear they have been captured by ruffians."

"I doubt it, "Anthony drawled. "Told you, Elizabeth was petulant about a disagreement we had and that son of yours has never taken to me. The feeling is mutual."

Norrington raise his eyebrows at such bluntness. He had been surprised by the abruptness of Anthony's manner, quite unlike his courtesy at Hanham House.

"I suspect they have hatched this up between them to spite me. You know how vindictive women can be over the smallest things."

"I have never found my daughter to be resentful or frivolous. What does Sir Bartholomew say about this?"

"Oh he is no use. The old fool just runs around in a lather begging my forgiveness for letting it happen."

Bartholomew Hanham had thought it strange that Lizzie and James had gone out so early, while it was still dark, particularly as she had professed to feel unwell the previous evening. When they had not returned by midday, he sent men out to look for them. The search proving unproductive, he dispatched a messenger to catch up with Anthony on the road to London. He caught the party on the outskirts of Reading and Anthony turned back at once. It was almost dark when he got back to Hanham House, so he set out first thing the next morning, taking Ralph Lawrence and Dick Shaw with him. He had been convinced that he would find them at Norrington Hall and even now was suspicious that Sir Neville might be hiding them from him.

"Do you know anything about this?" he demanded of Jacob Whyte.

The steward shook his head.

"Sir Neville may be right to suggest they have gone to Lady Ashbury Sir. However, one of the servants, who had been talking to your men in the yard, came to me with the notion that they may have called on Sir Thomas Mountfield."

Jacob was not going to give Mark the satisfaction of mentioning his name.

"Why the devil would they go there?" Anthony snapped.

"Well, as Sir Neville knows, last year Sir Thomas gave us hospitality over-night when we lost our way taking a short cut through the forest on our way to Hanham House last spring."

Norrington confirmed his statement, but added, "It is hardly likely they would have gone there. James would have more judgement than that."

"Did Sir Bartholomew know about this overnight stay?"

A look of realization was dawning on Anthony's face.

"Yes Sir. I told him when we arrived, to explain why we were delayed."

"Did you by Christ? Well, he didn't see fit to mention it to me, nor did you it seems." He directed this at Sir Neville.

"I assumed you already knew and did not see any significance in the matter anyway." Norrington replied.

"Maybe not, but I do now. So that is the reason she has been so cold to me. She has been yearning for Mountfield, unfaithful to me from the very first. Damn the fellow, so cool sitting under that tree, being so uncivil as not to stand in my presence."

"What are you talking about Anthony?"

"Frome Fair, last September. Left her for a few minutes to discuss some business. Found her and James all snug with Mountfield, sitting under a tree. Wondered why she jumped up as if she had been scalded. I was surprised to see him venturing into civilized society. Have the answer now. They had arranged to meet. The little bitch, casting those innocent eyes on me and all the while she was playing me false with that adventurer, with James acting as her go-between."

In his anger he had abandoned any pretence of regard for Sir Neville's feelings, although he could see that his father-in-law was affronted. Norrington let out a long exhalation of breath in an effort to control his voice.

"Anthony, I will not have you call my daughter that name in my own house. You cannot seriously believe that she had dallied with young Mountfield. I know Thomas' father as well as I know your uncle. They are a distinguished family. Thomas may have come back from the Americas with some bizarre notions, but he would not seduce Elizabeth and even if he had a mind to, she would not respond. As for suggesting that James would encourage it---"

Anthony's sharp laugh was more like the barking of a dog. It made Jacob Whyte very uneasy. He took an instinctive step back as Anthony hissed,

"Deluded fathers are the worst fools on earth. You are a double fool to trust the honour of a man who defies all convention and decent company to live with a wild heathen whore just because you know his father well; or do you trust him because he trailed in the wake of that sanctimonious, over-weaning aristocrat, Philip Sidney, with his outmoded notions of chivalry, whom everyone seems to worship."

Sir Neville was shaken by this verbal onslaught. This was an Anthony he had never seen before."I understand your anger if you do truly believe this has happened, but I know you are mistaken. The only way to prove it is to visit the house. I find riding difficult at present because I suffered a fall from my horse last week and injured my back. Jacob will guide you there and report back what you find."

The steward gave a slight bow of assent although it was not a mission he relished.

"You still wish me to send a message to your sister Sir Neville?"

"Of course, because I am sure that is where we will find them."

Anthony had already left the room. Norrington lowered himself down into a chair, relieved that his son-in-law had gone. He realised that his hands were shaking. Jacob also noticed.

"Shall I pour you some wine Sir?" There was concern in his voice.

"No, follow after Anthony. Do not try his temper even further by making him wait. The sooner he realizes that he has made a mistake in his assumption, the better."

When Jacob went to the stables for his horse he found Mark Wheeler boasting to the Smith twins how he would be rewarded by Sir Neville for locating his missing children.

"God's Blood," Jacob said irritably, "Are you slacking again Wheeler?"

He did not feel kindly towards Mark for getting him involved in this.

"Did you tell him? Is he going to Mountfield's house?"

"Yes, he is and you will say Sir Thomas Mountfield when you speak of him. You must accord a knight due respect."

Wheeler was more interested in Sir Neville's reaction to the news.

"What did the master say? Do you think he will want to see me?

"No, he will not. I think he would have been happier if the subject had never been mentioned." Mark's face fell and the Smith twins grinned at each other.

"But I have been given the task of guiding Master Hanham to Sir Thomas' house to prove that your fervid imagination is mistaken."

"I could go if you like. Save you the bother."

Mark looked hopeful again.

"I have another task for you. Ride as fast as you can to Lady Ashfield in Bath to discover if Mistress Elizabeth and Master James have arrived there and come straight back with the news."

"What, now? I haven't had my meal break yet."

"Yes, now. Hurry yourself."

As he led his horse out to join Anthony, waiting with mounting fury in the yard, Jacob thought to himself, 'And tomorrow Mark Wheeler I'll make you empty all the garde robes and clean them out."

Tom cupped his hands and dipped them into the water he had just drawn from the well. He let the water drip into his mouth, sliding through his fingers in a thin rivulet. It was so fresh, so pure, coming from an underground spring. Normally, water was so polluted around human habitations that it was unsafe to drink unless boiled. Small beer was a safer substitute. This water however could be consumed without fear. Whenever he drank it Thomas thought of the water of life, that stream that fed the spirit and refreshed it.

He looked up into the sky. The sun had passed the midday position; it must be nearer one o'clock and time they set out for Norrington Hall.

The day had dawned in a gauzy mist, wreathing itself around the trees, more like autumn than early spring. He had decided to wait until that cleared before leaving. Elizabeth and James would have a while to prepare themselves and eat a light meal for sustenance. They had finished that meal now and were ready to depart. Thomas did not feel hungry. He was tense and restless, uncertain how Sir Neville Norrington would react to him. Instead of joining the others at the dining table he had helped Toby and Ned dust down the two-seater carriage and drag it out of the barn. It had not been used for some time but the wheels were turning smoothly enough.

Painted black with a gold trim, it had a maroon seat and a hood that could be raised to shelter the occupants in bad weather. Toby Aycliffe considered it a smart equipage as he backed Hetty, Tom's cob into the shafts. The mare was a docile creature, well used to drawing carts and manoeuvred herself into position with the precision of experience.

"There Hetty my girl, this is a bit more grand than that old wood cart," Toby murmured in her ear as he fixed the harness. "Old Samson couldn't fit his great bum into these shafts, so you have one up on him there."

Thomas brought two buckets of freshly drawn water over to the horse trough and filled it. As he walked back to the well, he saw a movement in the trees of the orchard, flashes of white, the spotted flanks of fast disappearing fallow deer being seen off the premises by the wolfhounds. They no doubt hoped to raid the garden. Tom had encountered them earlier when the mist was at its thickest. They had come leaping out of the swirl at him and as they sprang away, the mist seemed to hold them suspended in the air like mythical creatures in a dream. Thomas was still in his shirt sleeves and as he placed the wooden cover back over the well he told himself he must dress for the occasion. At least he could look respectable in front of Sir Neville even if the man was inclined to believe him otherwise. The sudden noise of barking caused him to turn round. Four riders came out of the trees, but there was no sign of the dogs and Tom realised that the barking was more distant, Hector and Ajax giving voice to their excitement as they pursued the fallow deer deep into the forest. Ned and Toby looked at each other. Toby was convinced for a moment that the Archbishop's commissioner had returned, but Ned recognised Jacob Whyte, the steward from Norrington Hall, who had been so impressed with Joan Bushy's domestic talents the previous spring.

Tom Mountfield's gaze was focused on the man riding in front of the others. He swore under his breath. This was the very last thing he had wished to happen. He cursed himself for not leaving earlier that morning. James Norrington had just emerged from the side door, intending to inspect the carriage. Lizzie was about to follow him but when her brother saw Hanham he turned back and hustled her into the kitchen.

"It's Anthony and Jacob Whyte is with him. They must have come straight from father. I never dreamed they would find us so soon."

Elizabeth's face paled and she began to tremble.

"What shall we do?"

"You stay here. Do not come outside on any account."

So saying, James ran back outside, keen to explain what had happened to Jacob, who surely must believe him now. Joan Bushy put her arm around Elizabeth's shoulder.

"Master James is right. You stay here with us. Sarah and I will protect you."

She cast a significant glance at the cauldron of water heating above the fire.

"If he tries any of his cruel tricks in here he will get that water thrown over him, but I very much doubt he will get past Master Tom."

Dawn Light was in the brew house when she heard the horses approaching. She stood in the doorway for a moment, watching. Her keen senses picked up the smell of danger in the air and she strode over to join her husband by the well. James came to stand beside them.

Anthony's face was twisted with anger, the muscles in his cheeks jerking convulsively.

"I knew I was right," he said to Jacob in a tight voice as if something was constricting his throat. "There is that little rat James. She has come running to her lover, damn her. She will suffer for this, so will Mountfield."

He rode his horse up close to the group by the well, his eyes fixed on James. "You perfidious little whoreson, I will have all the skin off your back for this."

He urged his mount forward to intimidate the boy but Jacob Whyte turned his own horse sideways and blocked him. His first duty was always to Sir Neville's children. Ned Carter picked up a pitchfork and Toby grabbed an axe, ready to support Sir Thomas. Anthony, waving Jacob to move out of his way, dismounted and turned his attention to Tom.

"Where is she? Where is Elizabeth?"

Thomas looked him in the eye with his steadiest stare determined to keep calm. "Mistress Elizabeth is safe."

"Safe!" Anthony repeated with a high pitched laugh. "Safe- with you, a heretic who lives with heathens, an adventurer, a seducer. You are in great trouble Mountfield. The law looks very unkindly on men who abduct married women."

He turned to look at his henchmen. "Did you hear him- Mistress Elizabeth- So formal? But look at him in his shirt as if he has just come from a wench. Who have you been fucking, that grotesque creature next to you or my wife?"

Tom ran his tongue over his lips. They were very dry. He had a feeling that this would not be resolved without violence. He took a quick glance at Hanham's companions who were smirking, but looked ready for confrontation. Jacob Whyte had shifted his horse to one side to separate himself from them and seemed embarrassed.

"Your insults are wasted on me Hanham," Tom said in an even tone.

"Used to them I trust. You deserve them. Elizabeth, Elizabeth come out here at once. I have come to take you home."

Anthony shouted this as loudly as he could with his tired voice that had always lacked power.

In the kitchen Elizabeth almost started to her feet, but sat down again and covered her ears with her hands. She did not want to hear his voice, to contemplate that in law he owned her. Sarah Bushy began to cry, looking at her mother with wide eyes. Joan ushered both of the girls into her parlour so they could see what was happening through the small window. She saw Anthony step forward as if he intended to enter the house, but Thomas put the flat of his hand on the man's shoulder and applied a gentle pressure to stop him.

"I have not invited you into my house. I know you will not believe this because you wish to think the worst of everyone concerned, but I did not abduct your wife, nor have I ever enjoyed carnal relations with her. James and Elizabeth came to me freely for refuge to escape your tyranny.

I advised them that their best course was to appeal to Sir Neville for protection and I was about to accompany them to Norrington Hall when you arrived. The carriage over there is waiting in readiness. Thanks to you, your wife is in no fit state to ride."

"She was fit enough to ride to you though." Hanham was not convinced. "Make that story up just now did you? Well, should it be true, there is no need for you to accompany them to their father because I am here now and you can hand them both over to me."

He gave James an evil look, then tried to step forward again, but Thomas blocked him once more, this time pushing more firmly. He had heard enough of this.

"Oh no, you evil piece of shit, you are not going to lay your hands on that girl again. You must possess a black, twisted mind to subject an innocent young woman to such unspeakable treatment. I have promised to protect both

Elizabeth and James until I deliver them into the care of their father and that I will do."

Hanham drew his rapier. It hissed like a viper as it slid out of its scabbard.

"Ralph, Dick, you are my witnesses. You heard him abuse me, refuse to deliver my wife into my hands. He is breaking the law and I have every right to take Elizabeth back by force."

Lawrence and Shaw dismounted, their hands hovering over their own swords. Growling, Toby Aycliffe raised his axe in a threatening manner, but Tom warned him, "No Toby, Ned, you must not get involved in this. These men are trained assassins. Don't risk it."

He had not finished his sentence when Anthony lunged at him with the rapier. Tom managed to avoid the blade by the narrowest of margins. Joan Bushy, watching through the window, let out a startled cry. She wanted to run outside, but knew her task was to keep Elizabeth in the house. However, her cry at the open casement distracted Hanham for a split second, enough time for Tom to grab hold of the well cover to use as a shield and parry the next thrust.

"You coward," James yelled. "You vile coward, he is unarmed."

He tried to run at Anthony, but Ralph Lawrence stuck out his foot and tripped the boy, causing him to sprawl face forward on the ground. Jacob Whyte had dismounted now. He was appalled at the course of events. He could scarce believe what was happening. He hurried over to help James to his feet, protesting as he did so.

"You shut your mouth old man," Lawrence warned, "or I'll shut it for you."

He saw Toby Aycliffe trying to throw his axe to Mountfield and ran across to prevent it, threatening him with his sword so that he backed off. Ned however was covering Dick Shaw with the pitchfork.

"You take one step towards Sir Thomas and I will skewer you with this you bastard, so help me."

Elizabeth and Sarah had joined Joan at the parlour window. All three watched in horrified silence as Anthony continued his assault. The well cover was thick; Hanham had to take care that the point of his rapier did not become embedded in the wood and neutralised. Tom was quick to anticipate the direction of his thrusts although one of them nicked two of his fingers as he clutched the edge of his makeshift shield. Blood soaked into the wood, diffusing over the surface. No one noticed Waaseyaaban run into the house. The three women in Joan's parlour heard the side door open, soft, swift footsteps, another door open and then saw a blur of speed as Waaseyaaban shot out of the side door, behind the main action. She was carrying a sword which she gave to Tom, at the same time hurling a heavy copper pan at Hanham with deadly accuracy. It smacked him across the side of the face, causing him to stagger back.

"Now you fight fair you beater of women," she hissed savagely, "and my Makwa will kill you."

Thomas realised that he now held in his hand Philip Sidney's sword. His wife had run into the library and snatched it down from the wall. He was the one with the advantage now for although the spada was shorter than the rapier it was more substantial with that dangerous double cutting edge. As much as he despised him, he had no wish to kill Hanham. He had told James that he hoped he need never shed any more blood and he meant that, particularly with this sword. He advanced towards Anthony with the stance of a man experienced in the use of a spada. Hanham recalled that his adversary had fought in the Netherlands. He gave ground, glancing over his shoulder to see if his companions were in a position to give him any support. There was a stand-off between them and the labourers; both of Hanham's men were wary of the prongs of that pitchfork.

"Let us stop this Hanham," Thomas said. "I am sure you have taken lessons from some Italian sword master, but I would not back your chances against my spada. I have battle experience whilst you I fancy pay others to fight your battles for you. Go back home and I will escort Elizabeth and James to Norrington Hall as I originally intended. Then it will be Sir Neville's decision what happens next. I cannot imagine that once he sees the evidence of your handiwork that he will be willing to send her back to you." Tom continued to advance as he spoke and saw a dart of fear in Anthony's eyes. "She is my wife. He will have no choice. I will not surrender her to an arrant knave like you."

At that moment he saw Elizabeth's face at the window, deathly white and the knowledge that all her anxiety was for Mountfield fuelled a final, desperate rage. He let out a strange, half-strangled scream and rushed at Thomas, thrusting with his weapon in a frenzy. Tom parried, then attacked. It was instinct and training combined; the skill that had kept him alive in the Netherlands campaign. In the wildness of his rush Anthony stumbled and fell forward on to the blade of Tom's sword. It pierced his chest and found its way with unerring accuracy into his heart. Thomas stared transfixed by the sight of Hanham pinned on that blade, not sure whether he had struck the blow on purpose or if it was accidental. It seemed an age before he could bring himself to withdraw the weapon and hear that unmistakable sucking noise. Anthony toppled towards him making glottal choking noises in the back of his throat, his body twitching as it fell but he was dead before he hit the ground. Everyone was frozen in a horrified tableau, shocked by the suddenness of it all, everyone except Waaseyaaban, who had a triumphant smile on her face. She was keeping a wary eye on Anthony's hard men who were unsure what to do next until Ralph Lawrence shook himself out of his torpor and knelt down by the body. He half turned Anthony over and whistled through his teeth.

"Right through the heart. Dead as a door nail. You've murdered him Sir Thomas."

Tom shook his head, "No, I had no intention of killing him. I told him to back off. You heard me. When he attacked, I defended myself. I am not sure what happened. He must have tripped."

Lawrence grinned. He did not seem very grieved over his master's demise.

"Them poxy stupid boots, that's what done it. Fashion mad he was – see."

He lifted Anthony's foot to demonstrate his point. "Extra- long toes and built up heels to make him look taller. I reckon he stepped on the toe of his own boot."

Inside the house Elizabeth declared that she was going outside. She longed to go to Thomas although she had no idea what she could say to him. None of this would have happened if she and James had not come to his house. She felt so guilty, even more so because she could find no pity in her heart for Anthony, only remorse that this had happened. Joan advised her not to go out yet.

"Not while those two men are still here. They may snatch you and take you back to Hanham House."

"But what will happen now?" Elizabeth asked.

"Nothing I hope. There are enough witnesses to tell the truth of the matter. Master Tom was only defending himself. Poor boy, he looks so shaken."

Ralph Lawrence's casual disregard for his master had brought Tom to the full reality of the situation. He needed to think clearly.

"We still need to take that girl to Sir Bartholomew," Lawrence said in an amiable tone, leering at Dawn Light. He had a broad face, criss-crossed with old scars. There was one at the side of his neck that was more recent for it was still red and raw. His nose looked as if it had been broken more than once.

"No you don't," Tom contradicted. "That is no longer your concern.

Your duty now is to take Anthony Hanham's body back to his uncle with my sincere regret that this has happened. But first you must call in to see the constable in Devizes, Josiah Parry, show him the body and report the death."

"And what if we disagree with your advice?"

"Well, you can try your hand against the three of us—"

"Four," Jacob Whyte interrupted.

"The four of us," Tom acknowledged his support with a nod, "But I would not advise it. Pitchfork wounds are notorious for turning poisonous and that axe of Toby's could take the top of your head off. I would hazard a guess that you and your friend are not the kind of men who would fancy a fight against the odds."

This was the kind of talk Lawrence understood.

"And what will you be doing if we do as you suggest, making your get-away?"

"I have no reason to do so. I have no idea what you will tell the constable, but I have five witnesses here and three more in the house who can testify to what happened. Josiah Parry knows he will find me here when he wants to talk to me and I will make sure that Elizabeth and James Norrington return to their father."

Ralph Lawrence did not have to consider for long before deciding to do as Thomas asked. Dawn Light fetched some horse blankets from the barn and Anthony's men wrapped his body in them and strapped it across his horse. Toby and Ned still stood alert with their weapons ready just in case Lawrence and Shaw tried any last minute tricks. Before he mounted his horse, Ralph gave Tom a mocking smile.

"I reckon you know that we won't be telling the same story as you Sir Thomas. We have to keep old Bartholomew sweet. He will want to see you swing for this- worshipped Anthony he did. We will tell him the story he wants to hear."

"I don't doubt it. I imagine it will not be the first time you have borne false witness."

Ralph laughed. "You are right there- old hands at it, both of us. I should enjoy your whore while you still can. Good day to you."

No one relaxed until they had ridden out of sight, Tom, his face bleak, watching Hanham's body swaying across his horse's back. He sat down heavily on the edge of the well and looked at the sword in his hand, stained with blood and dust.

"Oh Philip I pray you would consider this a noble enough cause," he murmured aloud.

James caught his words and knew what he meant.

"It was Sir, it was. You saved us both from his revenge."

"But I did not want to kill him James."

"You had no choice. He meant to kill you."

Thomas laid the sword down on the ground at his feet and buried his face in his hands. His fingers were still bleeding and droplets trickled down on to his shirt.

"Shall I take the sword and clean it for you," James asked," Then put it back where it belongs?" He wanted to do something to help and this was the only thing he could think of that might be of use. Tom did not take his hands away from his face when he replied, "Yes, please clean it. I would be grateful."

James picked up the sword with care and reverence and took it into the kitchen just as Joan and Elizabeth came out. Sarah was too scared to venture out of the parlour. Dawn Light stood close to Thomas. She said nothing, but she was puzzled by his despair. He had been attacked by an enemy and had despatched him as a good warrior should. She had worried about trouble coming, but now it had come and been defeated. She was elated and could not imagine further consequences. Elizabeth's mind was full of possible consequences. Tom looked so dejected sitting on the wall of the well, his face in his hands. She wanted to put her arm around him and hold him close to her, but stood back avoiding Waaseyaaban's gaze, as Joan Bushy said, "You're hurt Master Tom. Let me look at those fingers."

She pulled his hand away from his face and began dabbing at the cuts across his fingers with a handkerchief she produced from her apron pocket. He looked up and saw Lizzie standing there, her eyes full of tears.

"I am so sorry Elizabeth. I would to God this had not happened."

"Oh no, you are not to blame. It is my fault. I should have never let James persuade me to come here. I have brought trouble on you and added to the weight on your conscience. I am the one who should say sorry Thomas."

Dawn Light shifted her head to one side, observing the girl closely. This was the first time she had heard either of them address each other by their first names only, without the formal addition of title. The fact interested her.

Thomas stood up determined to appear resolute, even if he did not feel so. He walked over to Jacob Whyte who was talking to Ned and Toby and thanked all three for their support. "I fancy I would be the one wrapped in horse blankets if you had not kept his two henchmen occupied."

"I am sure you are right," Jacob agreed. "You have two loyal servants, who showed great courage."

"Toby and Ned are not servants. They work for me for a wage, but they live their own lives and come and go as they please."

"Yes, I see the difference. Your wife also was remarkable in her reactions, so swift and positive; more like a man."

"Waaseyaaban is unique," Tom replied, smiling, "And certainly brave as any man."

"This is a most unfortunate circumstance Sir Thomas," Jacob continued, shaking his head. "I had no wish to lead those men to your house, but Sir Neville insisted. He was sure his children would not be here and wished to prove so to Anthony. I am not certain how he will take this."

"I did not abduct his daughter. I told Anthony the truth. He subjected her to physical and verbal abuse that is shaming to even mention. James will witness to that; her own body will be witness to it. James was brave enough to try to save her by bringing her here. Sir Neville should be proud of him."

Jacob had always held an affection for Sir Neville's children. He had been a steward at Norrington Hall for ten years and had watched them growing up. The thought that Hanham had treated Lizzie with such cruelty appalled him so much he could not bring himself to speak of it.

"You must take them home now Jacob without delay. I intended to escort them but after what has just happened I think I had best not impose myself on Sir Neville just yet. He will need time to come to terms with it all. Besides I need to be here in case the constable calls. You do believe that I have done nothing improper regarding Mistress Elizabeth?"

"I do Sir Thomas. I believe you to be an honourable man and I am grateful to you for protecting Sir Neville's children. I will do my best to make him see the truth. If you need me to witness before the constable please send word."

It was a great relief to Thomas to know that someone as level headed and fair-minded as Jacob Whyte would put the case for Elizabeth and James to their father. Both the Norringtons were reluctant to leave so soon, worried that the constable might come and need their testimony, but Thomas assured them it could be days before Josiah Parry turned up. It was vital that they go home now to support the truth of his original intention.

When they were ready to go, James held out his hand to Thomas.

"Will you take my hand Sir Thomas and forgive me for bringing you such trouble?" he asked solemnly.

"I told you to call me Tom and there is nothing to forgive."

He was surprised when James on impulse threw his arms around him and embraced him.

"I thought at first how fortunate you were to be a friend of Sir Philip Sidney, but now I think that he was also fortunate to have you as a friend."

Tom patted the boy's back. "A moot point young man."

He gave James a leg-up into his saddle adding, "I hope to see more of you in the future."

Toby Aycliffe was sitting on the driver's seat of the carriage. He had never visited the village of Norrington and was quick to volunteer his services to drive Elizabeth home, curious about Norrington Hall. Elizabeth was speaking to Dawn Light and Thomas wondered what she was saying. His wife was listening intently, but she made no reply. Lizzie had seen James embrace Tom She longed to do the same, but dared not. It would be impossible now though to confine him back into her secret world. She knew she must see him again. She did not know how long she could bear not to hear his voice.

He picked her up and lifted her on to the seat beside Toby. Then he pulled the ends of her cloak around her so that she was snugly wrapped up.

"It is a mild afternoon, but you are still frail. You must take good care of yourself."

He took hold of both her hands in his own and looking into her eyes continued, "You must not worry. I am certain your father will support you when he knows how you have suffered. How can he do otherwise?"

As he spoke he was caressing the backs of her hands with his thumbs in a gentle, affectionate way. She felt the sensation of his touch all over her body.

"I worry most about you- what Sir Bartholomew will charge against you. You must promise me that you will send for us at once if we are needed to speak in your defence."

"I promise. Drive on Toby."

He put his arm around his wife and they stood together in the yard watching as James waved goodbye, riding beside Jacob Whyte behind the carriage, obscuring Elizabeth from view.

"What a morning!" Ned Carter was leaning on the handle of the pitchfork, shaking his head. "My wife will think I have made all this up in my head when I tell her."

"You can go home now if you wish," Tom said. "I think you have done more than your fair share today and it seems unequal that Toby should be enjoying a day out."

Ned laughed. "Yes, he jumped in there fast I warrant. Always ready for a bit of variety is our Toby. I'll get the rest of that hay forked into the horses' feed troughs and I'll be off then, but I'll be back early tomorrow, just in case there is any more trouble."

He ambled off into the barn, whistling. He had enjoyed threatening that city born ruffian with his pitchfork. He was sure his children would be impressed when he told them the story.

"Joan say you must go into kitchen, wash fingers, put salve on them," Dawn Light told her husband.

Tom gave her a wry smile. Now that everyone had gone and he was no longer required to appear resolute, he felt depressed and near to tears.

"Joan Bushy remains consistently herself no matter what happens around her. She helps to keep me sane." He ran his hand through his hair, a gesture that often signified his confusion. "We are very fortunate to have such confident, sturdy people around us as Joan, Toby and Ned. I might have sore need of them soon."

He had a sense of foreboding that he could not shake off, but he squared his shoulders and walked into the kitchen to submit to Joan's doctoring.

They had been planting oak and beech saplings since early morning, replenishing a strip of woodland that they had felled the previous year. Three days had passed since Anthony Hanham's death and work continued as usual but an uneasy atmosphere hung over the Mountfield household. Thomas found physical labour a relief. The effort of digging a hole deep enough to give the young roots the space to spread down into the soil and sustain a healthy tree was satisfying and diverted him from dwelling on the possible consequences of the events of Wednesday. He knew it would take several days to set things in motion. The constable would be obliged to contact the sheriff, who would summon a coroner to view the body at Hanham Hall. What happened next would depend on the testimony of Lawrence and Shaw and Bartholomew Hanham's reaction to it. Thomas wondered what kind of welcome Elizabeth and James had received from their father. At times he wished they had never come into his life, reminding him that a kind of neutral seclusion from the outside world was an impossibility, just as Simon Bailey had reminded him last

December. He knew he should send word of what had happened to his sister
Cecily, now the mistress of her own household in Salisbury, but he hesitated
not wanting to alarm his family too soon. He did not wish to contemplate his
father's reaction.

Toby Aycliffe dug his spade into the earth deep enough for it to stand
unaided and walked over to the cart. He took from the back a ceramic jar filled
to the brim with cider made from the autumn's plentiful apple crop and sitting
down on the shafts of the cart, took a long swig. Samson, tethered to a tree by
a length of rope, grazed contentedly on the undergrowth. Toby smacked his
lips with satisfaction and wiping the neck of the jar with his sleeve, handed it to
Ned who had joined him. When Ned had sampled it he said with appreciation,
"By Jesu that's good stuff."

He called out to Thomas asking him if he wanted a drink but Tom,
treading down the earth all around a freshly planted sapling was so lost in
thought that he did not hear him. Ned looked across at Toby. Thomas had
tried his best these three days to act normally, but they could see it was a
strain. They felt it in themselves. Every time the dogs barked they were on
edge, expecting unwelcome visitors. Even Joan Bushy was out of sorts although
she endeavoured to hide it from Sarah, who had been nervous and tearful ever
since the incident. The only person who appeared to be unaffected was Dawn
Light. She was content. The Norringtons were now where they should be.
The trouble she had feared had come and been defeated. She was sorry that her
Makwa was so distressed by what had happened, that he was restless and could
not sleep, but that would pass. He tried to explain to her that this might not be
the end of it but she was convinced that no one could blame him for defending
himself and dismissed it from her mind.

Ned Carter tapped Thomas on the shoulder to rouse him from his reverie.

"Take a swig of this Master Tom. I reckon this is some of the best cider
you have made yet."

Thomas smiled at him and took a drink from the jar murmuring his
appreciation as he handed it back.

"Yes, I think we can be justly proud of that."

Ajax was lying near Tom's feet gnawing and licking at his paws, intent
on cleaning the dirt from between his claws. Hector had gone off on a mission of
his own. Then Ajax paused in his task and stood up growling, looking beyond
the cart to where Samson was tethered. Two men on foot, leading their horses
by the reins, stepped between the trees.

"It's the constable," Toby said.

Thomas nodded, feeling his pulse quicken.

Josiah Parry was the Borough Constable of Devizes but as the county Bridewell was in the town his responsibilities stretched beyond the borough. Devizes was chosen to house the Bridewell because it was first thought that the castle could be used for that purpose, as it had been in years gone by, but it was soon apparent that the once magnificent edifice was now too dilapidated and insecure for such duties. So they built a Bridewell in 1579, near St. John's Church in the shadow of the castle. It faced towards the narrow street that led into the main thoroughfare past St. John's into New Port which had become the centre of trade in the town. A modest building, it bore no resemblance to the palace near St. Bride's Well in London that had become a house of correction and given its name to other prisons, but Josiah Parry was proud to be in charge of it.

His assistant constable, Andrew Shepherd was aware that Parry was not happy with the duty they were charged to perform that morning. When he first read the arrest warrant delivered to him bearing the seal of the Sheriff of Wiltshire, he clicked his tongue in disapproval. He had viewed the body, noted the accuracy of the wound to the heart, listened to the story of the two men who brought it to him and found it hard to believe their version of the story. He knew Sir Thomas Mountfield well and respected him. He was popular with the local folk for his generosity, fairness and lack of arrogance. They tended to overlook what they considered his eccentricities, puzzled as many of them were by his devotion to that heathen woman he had brought back from the Americas. Parry could not imagine such a man would abduct a young woman and murder her husband. It was completely out of character.

Thomas stepped forward to greet them saying, "Josiah, I have been expecting you. I am sure you have many questions to ask about what happened at my house this week. If you and Andrew come back to the house with me, I will show you where it took place."

"Sir Thomas, I am sorry to have to say this, but I did not come to ask questions."

Parry unrolled the document that had been tucked into his doublet, cleared his throat and read, "The Sheriff of Wiltshire issues this warrant on the 10th day of March 1590 for the arrest of Sir Thomas Mountfield, resident of this county on the charge that on Wednesday last he did wilfully murder one Anthony Hanham of Hanham House, Frome after abducting Hanham's wife Elizabeth and carrying her off to his house."

"But no one has considered my side of the story yet," Thomas protested. He was shaken by the abruptness of this, not expecting a warrant so soon.

"Do you deny that the wound was administered by your hand?" the constable asked in a quiet tone.

"No, I killed him, but I did not murder him. Quite the reverse; he attempted to murder me. I was defending myself."

Toby and Ned were nodding, backing up Tom's statement, but Parry continued, "Were Mistress Elizabeth Hanham and her brother James Norrington at your house on that day?"

"Yes, they were but they came of their own volition without my prior knowledge or conniving. I did not abduct anybody. I have a number of witnesses, including Elizabeth and James who can attest to the fact that Anthony attacked me when I was unarmed and that I did not abduct her- witnesses far more reliable than those two bully boys of Hanham's."

"I am pleased to hear that Sir Thomas," Parry said gravely. "You will be able to prepare a good defence to put before the Quarter Sessions' justices, but I am afraid my instructions are to take you to the Bridewell. The warrant stipulates that because of the seriousness of the alleged crime, you are to be incarcerated until the trial."

"The Bridewell," Thomas turned and looked at Ned and Toby, who could not believe what they were hearing, "But the quarter sessions are six weeks away. I have work to do here. I give you my word that I will not leave the environs of the forest and will present myself to you the day before the Quarter Sessions. You know that you can trust my word Josiah."

Parry looked uncomfortable.

"If it was up to me Sir Thomas I would be more than willing to allow that arrangement, but I must carry out the Sheriff's orders."

"Of course, I understand now why the warrant is so specific on that point. Bartholomew Hanham is a close friend of the Sheriff of Somerset and has persuaded him to put pressure on the Wiltshire Sheriff. I am up against a conspiracy of confederates," Thomas countered.

"I am not in a position to comment on that Sir. I am sure you will be sensible and come willingly."

"I must go home first and explain this to my wife. She will find this hard to understand."

"I would prefer not Sir. I think it best we go now. I find that the calmest of men grow more desperate when faced with the anxiety of their families."

"Damnation Josiah Parry," Ned Carter shouted. "It's a hard case when a man's not allowed to bid farewell to his wife."

Thomas put his hand on Ned's arm. "Peace Ned, there is nothing you can do except go back to the house and tell them what has happened. Tell Joan first, she will know best how to explain it to Dawn Light. One of you can bring them in the carriage to visit me tomorrow." He turned back to Parry. "Well, I have no horse here. Will you tie my hands and make me walk behind you like a felon?"

"God forbid Sir Thomas. I ask you not to turn a bitter tongue on me. I find this a most painful duty. You can ride behind me on my horse. I know a way that comes into town behind St. Mary's Church and round to the Bridewell across the common- a very secluded route not frequented by many folk."

Thomas sighed. He knew he should be grateful for the respect Parry was showing him, but he was not feeling very charitable, Never-the-less he apologised for the sharpness of his tongue.

"I am sorry. Your delicacy does you credit, but you must understand that I am not in control of my emotions as yet. May I put my jerkin on at least?"

He found it hard to keep a touch of sarcasm out of his voice despite his apology. Toby handed him the jerkin which Tom put on, taking the time to lace it up first just to delay the departure a few more minutes.

Parry and Shepherd had mounted and Tom vaulted up on the back of the constable's horse from behind causing the animal to take a few paces forward in surprise. Toby and Ned stood watching helplessly as their master rode away with the constables. Tom turned and called back over his shoulder, "Don't forget- tell Joan first and don't put them into a panic. We can deal with this."

His words faded away from them as the riders disappeared into the trees. Toby shook his head. "This is a bad business. I am afeared of the outcome of it. That Bartholomew Hanham is a justice himself and if he has county sheriffs in his pocket they can appoint juries favourable to his point of view. Master Tom could be sentenced to hang."

"Don't even think of it," Ned replied. "You finish up here and I'll run back to the house."

He set off at a trot followed by Ajax who had started to run behind the constable's horse but had been sent back by a sharp command from Thomas. The constables and their prisoner rode to Devizes in silence, Thomas struggling to control his rising apprehension. He had been pretty certain he would have to answer to the Quarter Sessions but he had not for one moment considered he would be put in the Bridewell. He remembered his own words to Simon Bailey about how the prospect of being shut away for a long time in a damp dark place terrified him. Six weeks he told himself- only six weeks- I am man enough to endure six weeks, but he had always found it hard to be confined in a small space. He would imagine the area was growing smaller all the while, pressing in on him until he was fighting for breath. He was bold as a young boy, but that was one of the few things that frightened him. He recalled playing hide-and-seek with his sisters when he was about eight and climbing into a coffer in the hall, closing the lid. When Grace and Margaret had run past he intended to get out but he could not shift the lid. The catch had clicked shut. He had never known such fear. He could see the sides of the coffer moving in, threatening him until the lid was almost pushing on his face. He screamed and yelled, kicking at the sides. As the lid grew ominously closer it cut off his breath so that he feared he would faint.

Logically he knew there was plenty of air and the sides could not contract but logic could not defeat the power of the illusion. A passing servant heard the kicking noises and opened the coffer to find Tom ashen white and shaking all over. He felt very ashamed of himself for feeling such terror and begged the servant to tell no one. The experience remained with him however and the fear always came back to him when he was confined. He tried not to think of it now, but could not get it out of his mind.

Josiah Parry was right about the quiet route from St. Mary's Church to the Bridewell. They met few people on the way. The prison was a long building fronting the street. A thick oak door studded with iron formed the main entrance. There was a grill in it at eye level so that the gaoler could take a good look at any visitors before deciding to let them in. An alley way at the side led to a walled yard at the back. The wall was forbidding; about eight feet high with a massive double door part way along it. Opposite the wall was an area of open ground with stabling for the constables' horses at the far end.

Parry took Thomas to the front entrance and knocked on the door while Andrew took the horses to the stable. A pair of bright blue eyes peered warily through the grill, then the door creaked open and a man stood back to let them enter. He was a well-built man around Tom's age with a thatch of black hair and dark eyebrows that emphasized the blueness of his eyes. There was a quick intelligence in his face. "Williams, this is Sir Thomas Mountfield, the prisoner I told you of this morning. Is his cell ready?"

"Oh yes, I have emptied the bucket, changed the straw- if I could have found a vase of flowers I would have provided that too. Like a proper little palace it is now constable."

Daffyd Williams' accent instantly revealed his Welsh origins. Parry was not amused by the gaoler's sense of humour.

"Sir Thomas is a gentleman and must be treated with respect. He is accused of a serious crime but there is every chance that the accusation may be proved false. On no account must you put anyone else in his cell. All his visitors are to be allowed access and to bring him extra comforts within reason."

Williams looked Thomas over, noting the gold earring and the turquoise pendant.

"Extra comforts is it? Well that's fine as long as I get my fee for them. Would you care to follow me to your lodgings Sir Thomas?"

Thomas had been studying the room that was the gaoler's office. It was sparsely furnished with a table, a chair and a wall cupboard. An iron brazier stood in the corner filled with firewood ready to be lit in the evening. Several large keys hung from hooks on the wall. Williams took down two of these keys and with one of them opened a door that led into the passage way to the cells. Along the passage were four more doors like the one they had just passed through. Despite it serving the county, the Bridewell was a basic, limited facility. There were only four cells; two intended for individual prisoners, although they sometimes accommodated three unfortunates and two more cells that could house six at a crush. One of the larger cells was occupied for Thomas heard coughing and swearing. The door to the nearest cell stood open and Williams stood aside bidding Tom to enter with a flourish of his hand. The room was around six feet square, empty except for a heap of straw on the floor and a bucket which still stank of urine and excrement even though it had been emptied. High in the wall, well above eye level, was a small, barred window. Confronted with this Tom took an involuntary step back. He felt the sweat break out on his forehead. Josiah Parry was behind him and put a steady hand on his shoulder.

"Have courage Sir Thomas. You are brave man who has faced more fearsome things than this. The days will pass sooner than you imagine."

Though grateful for the encouragement Thomas was too intent on holding himself together to reply. He moved slowly into the room and stood in the centre of it, taking deep breaths. At a nod from Parry the gaoler closed and locked the door. The constable was sensitive enough to realise that Mountfield would need time to compose himself and was relieved that this painful duty was accomplished. He informed Williams that he and Shepherd were going to investigate a complaint by one of the butchers about a fight in the Shambles and would call back later.

When he was gone the Welshman came back to Tom's cell and raised the wooden flap that covered the grill in the door. He was intrigued by this new prisoner accorded so much respect by the constable.

"Bit different from what you're used to I'll warrant," he said. Tom did not look towards the door. "Fine looking boyo you are- a cut above what we usually get in here. Don't worry; it won't seem so bad when you get all those little comforts the constable was talking about. I charge sixpence a week for extra food, a shilling for clothes and two shillings for each piece of furniture."

This time Thomas did turn with a look of disgust on his face, thinking of the plight of those who could not afford the gaoler's rates.

"Oh don't look at me like that now. I see the curl of your lip. A pittance I am paid for this job. I am entitled to a bit extra. It's my right. I am a reasonable man- a talkative man too. I know you are too overwhelmed to talk now, but when you have settled down a bit, I am looking forward to some discussions with an educated man like yourself."

Tom turned away again and Williams shut the flap, murmuring to himself as he walked away down the corridor, "Oh yes and something good to look at besides."

Left alone in the dingy room, the only light source the tiny barred gap that served as a window, Tom sat down on the floor with his back to the wall. He drew his knees up and hugged them to his chest. The wall felt cool and damp. At that moment he was far less confident about his reserves of courage than the constable.

Dawn Light was feeding the chickens. They scurried around her feet squabbling as she scattered the corn and kitchen scraps. It amused her to see how they argued over particular scraps even though there was plenty enough for all of them. She had not noticed Ned Carter run into the house, although she spotted Ajax ambling towards her.

She wondered if her husband had come home for it was unusual for either of the dogs to return without Thomas. She scanned the perimeter of the trees for any sign of him and Hector. Out of the corner of her eye she saw Joan Bushy emerge from the side door. Ned Carter stood in the doorway behind her. She smiled as Joan approached but the smile faded when she perceived the expression on the housekeeper's face.

"My dear," Joan said in a quiet voice, putting her hand on Dawn Light's arm, "Ned has brought us some grave news. Master Tom has been arrested by the constable."

"Where is Thomas?" Dawn Light demanded, not sure of the significance of the word arrested.

"He has been taken to the Bridewell in Devizes."

"Bridewell?" She repeated the unfamiliar word with a question in her voice.

"It is the prison. He has been charged with murder."

"He come home tonight?"

"No my dear, he will have to stay in prison until the Quarter Sessions when there will be a trial. That will be some weeks away."

Waaseyaaban's eyes flashed with anger.

"He does nothing wrong. Why do they shut him in prison when he do nothing wrong? My Makwa hate to be shut in. He is like me. His heart is for the outside, to look at the sky."

Joan Bushy felt sick with worry. She knew Thomas relied on her to be strong and sensible in this situation, but it would have been such a relief to cry. She kept up a positive front however.

"Master Tom said we must try not to worry too much. He will be found innocent at the trial. We can go to see him tomorrow."

"No." Waaseyaaban threw down the bowl causing the chickens to flap away in a panic. "They do not keep him from me. I go to Bridewell now."

She began to run, Joan calling after her to wait, shouting to Ned Carter to stop her, but Ned was not quick enough. She flew past him, leaving him standing flat-footed in the yard. He turned towards Joan, his hands spread out helplessly as Dawn Light disappeared into the trees.

Waaseyaaban had visited both the markets in Devizes many times with Thomas or Joan. She knew how to get to that town with the strange name that locals often called the Vyse. Thomas, interested in the origin of the name, had managed to consult some old documents in which the castle was referred to as "castrum ad devisas"- the castle on the boundaries because it sat on the boundaries of three different manors.

It was his opinion that the area around St. Mary's Church was probably the most ancient part of the town and the newer market area would have been within the castle bailey at one time. He had explained to his wife that the castle was once one of the largest, most impressive in the country, described by writers in glowing terms, but it had been partly demolished by Henry VII, the present queen's grandfather and was now in a sad state of repair. The keep on its high mound and the defensive ditches, one of which came right to the back of the Bear Inn still made an impression on her because of the scale of it. She did not know where the Bridewell was located, but assumed it would be in that crumbling castle building.

Her long, easy stride soon took her out of the forest and on to the road. Labourers working in the fields paused to watch her run past, her bracelets jingling, her hair streaming around her. A man clearing out a ditch shouted a crude comment after her and a woman standing in the doorway of a one-room cottage pulled her child inside and shut the door, fearing there was a mad woman on the loose. Waaseyaaban saw or heard none of this. Her one intent was to reach Thomas. She knew nothing of the ways of constables and feared they may have hurt him. The exertion of running fifteen miles at a good pace had little effect on her. She slowed only when she reached the steep hill that took her on the path to St Mary's.

Near the church was a basket weavers shop. Two women were sitting under an awning attached to the sloping roof of the building twisting canes, their fingers moving with speed and skill. Several children were sprawled on the floor playing a game that involved drawing shapes in the dust with twigs. Waaseyaaban crossed the road to avoid them but she was spotted by their terrier dog, a scruffy brown and white creature with an argumentative turn of mind. It ran at her growling and snapping at her heels. The children were on their feet in an instant shouting, "It's a gypo. Look Ma, a dirty gypo," and gathering handfuls of dirt and pebbles began to throw them in her direction.

She dealt with the dog by addressing it in its own language. She glared at it, bared her teeth and made a snarling noise that was fearsome. The terrier stopped, cocked an ear and then ran back towards the children, who seeing their dog retreat changed their minds about pursuit.

Dawn Light made her way down a narrow alley that came out into the Port Market area. Here she found too many people for her liking; traders, shoppers, folk standing around gossiping. Noise emanated from the closed in shambles and blood trickled into the gutter as it was sluiced away from the floor of the building.

The castle keep loomed over the scene in the background and to reach it she had to cross the open market place. She hesitated. There was an old man sitting on a stool, whittling the top of a walking stick, shaping the wood into a ram's head. He looked at her through rheumy eyes.

"Be you lost maid?" he asked in an amiable voice. He did not seem the least perturbed by her unusual appearance.

"Where is Bridewell?" she demanded. "Is that Bridewell?"

She pointed towards the castle, almost too impatient to wait for an answer. The old man shook his head.

"No, they don't keep prisoners in there now my maid. Tis all falling down. Folks keep taking bits of it away to build their own houses. Shame, twere a wonderful place once so they say, visited by kings and queens."

Dawn Light had no time to listen to stories of the past.

"Then where is Bridewell?" she insisted.

He peered more closely at her. "You one of that tribe of gypsies and tinkers camped up on the downs? What you doing down here on your own? Your man got himself locked up in the Bridewell for fighting has he? Terrible ones for brawling your lot."

"Yes Bridewell, my Thomas in Bridewell."

The man nodded sagely. "I thought as much. See that street that passes by the castle ditch, go on up there, past the Yarn Hall and St. John's Church. You'll see a lane coming in from the left. The Bridewell is in that lane. You can't miss it- big oak door, walled yard at the back—"

She was running away from him before he finished his description. He shook his head, laughing to himself and murmuring, "Wild lot them gypsies."

She passed the barn-like building he had called the Yarn Hall and the cottages clustered behind St. John's Church. Then weaving out of the path of a cart full of bales of cloth and being treated to a volley of obscene oaths from the carter, she saw the lane the old man described. The Bridewell did not look much like a prison to her, but the door was formidable. There was no handle on the outside of it, so she hammered on it with her balled fists. After at least a minute of this hammering, eyes appeared at the grill in the door and a voice said, "We do not entertain strumpets in here. Go away woman."

The eyes disappeared.

Dawn Light stood for a moment, thinking, then walked under the archway at the side of the building to be confronted with a high wall that enclosed the yard at the back. There were double doors in the wall with ring handles. She grabbed hold of them, rattling them fiercely but the doors were locked fast.

She surveyed the territory. A pear tree stood at the far end of the wall, only a few feet away from it. Some of the branches overhung the wall. She climbed up the trunk into the lower branches and taking hold of the sturdiest branch swung herself out into space to drop down on top of the wall, where she balanced precariously until she was steady enough to sit down on it. She then turned around to face the wall and lowered herself down, stretching out her arms to their full extent so that the drop to the ground was only a few feet. The yard was empty except for a water trough beside a pump and a dung heap in one corner that stunk vilely even in this cool spring weather. It must have been unbearable in the heat of the summer. Waaseyaaban could see a door in the Bridewell that was half open. High up along the building were four small barred windows in a line. She ran towards the door.

Daffyd Williams was sitting back comfortably in his chair enjoying a mutton pie that the wife of one of his prisoners had brought him as payment to allow her to see her husband, a clerk who was accused of stealing from his employer, a prosperous cloth merchant. The clerk protested his innocence and wept copiously, much to the amusement of his cell mates, who were regular visitors to the Bridewell for drunkenness and brawling.

The pie was baked to perfection, the pastry golden brown and the mutton spiced with herbs. Daffyd was about to take another bite when someone burst through the side door and the gaoler jumped to his feet astonished by the sight of a woman in a petticoat and a man's jerkin, her flowing hair tangled with leaves and bits of twig.

"What the fuck!" He dropped the mutton pie on to the table, at a loss to work out how she had got there. Her black eyes glittered with animosity.

"Where is Thomas?" she demanded

"It was you banging on the front door just now was it? I don't know how you got in here, but you are going out again, right now. I told you before, we don't have whores in here."

"I want Thomas," Waaseyaaban repeated.

Williams had moved instinctively in front of the door that led into the passage to the cells and she noticed a key hanging at his belt.

"Do you mean Sir Thomas Mountfield? What would a gypsy whore want with a gentleman like that? You shog off my girl before I do you a mischief."

She began to shout at the top of her voice, "Thomas! Thomas!"

Williams was startled to hear a response from the cell of his new prisoner, a strange word, "Waaseyaaban?"

That was enough for Dawn Light; she flew at the gaoler raking her nails down his cheek and kneeing him in the groin with such force that he let out a howl of pain, doubling up and clutching at his privates. She snatched the key from his belt and turned the lock of the door in an instant. Thomas was still calling her name which drew her to the right door. Lifting up the grill flap she was relieved to see Thomas on his feet apparently unharmed in any way.

"Thomas, I get you free." She was struggling to unlock the door and cried out with frustration when she realised that the key did not fit this lock.

"No, you cannot set me free my love. I must stay here for a while."

She shook her head, pushing her fingers through the grill to touch his hand.

"I am sorry that I did not come back to explain to you but the constable thought it best."

He felt such pain seeing her distress that he knew the constable was right. He would have found it hard to go with them faced with the expression in his wife's eyes. Daffyd Williams came into the corridor, still wincing from that well-aimed blow and seized Dawn Light around the waist. He had big, powerful hands which he locked together around her, jerking her away from the door before she could grab hold of the bars of the grill as an anchor. She struggled and twisted, knocking against his shins with her heels but she could not get free. Thomas shouted at Williams to let her go, but the Welshman, who had taken the precaution of opening the front door in preparation, dragged her through the office and hurled her out into the street where she landed in a heap to the great amusement of a group of youths passing by.

"Now clear off you crazy brown bitch or you will get worse than that," he warned, slamming the door with satisfaction. He went back to the cell where the grill flap still stood open.

"By Christ Sir Thomas, do you really know that wildcat whore?"

"She is not a whore. She is my wife."

"Jesu, you're a braver man than I am. You are safer in here. You must like it rough."

"If you have hurt her—"

"Hurt her! It is me who is suffering; my balls will be swollen for a week and she has given me tattoos."

He put his hand to his cheek to feel the ridges where she had scratched him which were dribbling blood. He let the flap fall and hobbled back in to the office, leaving Thomas to rest his head against the door in despair, not knowing what had happened to Waaseyaaban.

Williams took a bowl of water from the wall cupboard and washed the cuts on his face. He sat down very gingerly contemplating whether he fancied the rest of that mutton pie. Then he heard a strange sound coming from the yard. It was a cross between a chant and a wail, changing in pitch and volume. He had never heard anything like it before. It made the hairs stand up on the back of his neck. He peered out of the side door to see the wild woman sitting cross-legged on the floor near the outside wall of Mountfield's cell. She was swaying backwards and forwards making this unearthly sound. Daffyd could see the imprints of her soft boots in the dust and realised how she had got in, not once but twice; she had climbed the wall. The thought of this coupled with that strange wailing unnerved him.

"Shut that noise damn you. You'll have half the town round here thinking we are torturing someone. Shut up woman."

She ignored him and he went back inside, afraid to touch her again, hoping she would soon tire of it. He underestimated Waaseyaaban's determination however and the wailing continued. He blocked his ears, but it still penetrated into his brain and he turned to Sir Thomas for help. Tom had been trying to jump high enough to reach the window in the wall, so he could hang on to the bars and look out, but he could not quite reach. He spun round when the cell door opened.

"Sir Thomas, why is that woman making that noise?" the gaoler asked in a distressed tone.

"She is keening. Croatan women lament the deaths of their menfolk in that way. Because we are separated she is mourning me as lost to her. Surely Welsh women do that too."

"Not a row like that. What did you call her-Croatan? She's not a gypsy then?"

"No, she comes from Roanoke Island in the Americas."

"Fancy that now. But can you make her stop that noise? I shall be in trouble with the constable. She climbed that eight foot wall twice."

Tom knew that little was beyond his wife if she put her mind to it. She was much stronger and more agile than most women. He might have guessed she would do something like this.

"I can, but you must let me go out to her."

Williams was dubious but decided it was worth the risk to get the noise stopped. When Dawn Light saw Thomas she ceased wailing and ran to him, throwing her arms around him and holding on tightly. She repeated his name over and over again as he kissed her.

"I stay with you now; be with my Makwa." He leaned forward and put his forehead on hers so they stood in that close intimate pose, talking softly.

"You cannot stay with me. They will not allow it."

"I stay here in yard, by your window."

"No, they will not let you do that either. Besides, I worry about your safety here in town. You won't get the opportunity to knee every man who accosts you in his private parts."

He smiled and she traced a finger over the contours of his mouth in a gesture so tender that Daffyd Williams could not square it with the whirlwind that had attacked him earlier.

"How long you be in here?"

"Until my trial, six weeks." He held up six fingers.

"Then you come home?"

"God grant it so. If there is any justice I will."

"But six weeks is too long to lie without you."

"It will pass quicker than you imagine. You will have plenty of work to do without my contribution and you can come to see me every day. The constable promised that there would be no restriction on my visitors."

Williams thought he heard knocking at the front door, probably the constable returning from the fracas in the shambles. He hung on, reluctant to let the prisoner out of his sight. Tom could sense his discomfort.

"Go and answer the door. On my honour I will not try to escape."

As Williams hurried through to the front door Thomas said firmly to his wife, "You must go home now. Tomorrow let Joan dress you like a respectable Englishwoman and Ned or Toby will drive you both over here to visit me. I need you to bring me a few things, my warm cloak, a couple of stools- one will serve as a table- and also pen, ink and paper. I must write a letter to Cecily so she can break the news to the rest of the family. Oh and tell Joan to bring some money with her because these little luxuries must be paid for it seems."

Williams returned, explaining in vivid terms to the constable why the new prisoner was out in the yard with his wife in his arms. Andrew Shepherd came behind them grinning at the thought of the indignity the gaoler had suffered. Josiah Parry was trying to look stern, though he too was struggling to supress a smile.

"This will not do Sir Thomas," Parry said. "We cannot have your wife shinning up trees and climbing over our wall. Mind you, it is most unusual for someone to be breaking in rather than endeavouring to break out."

"She will not do so again," Tom promised on her behalf. "She only did so because she was not allowed to see me. It was a misunderstanding. Master Williams did not realise that she was my wife. I know he regrets his mistake. Now she knows she can visit me she will be more decorous."

The look on Williams' face suggested that he did not relish the prospect, although he appreciated Tom not complaining about the rough way he handled the woman.

"Come Mistress." Parry held out his arm to Dawn Light. "Let me escort you to your horse. Your husband must go back to his cell now."

She drew back from him, refusing to take his arm.

"She has no horse," Tom informed him. "She ran here."

"Ran here, all the way from your house?" The constable was astonished. "Then you deserve a ride back. Andrew Shepherd will take you on his horse, at least to the edge of the forest."

Her eyes narrowed. "No, I do not ride with men who lock up my Makwa for no reason."

"Waaseyaaban, these men are not to blame for me being here. They have been ordered by the sheriff to arrest me. If they failed to do so they would be in great trouble themselves. Let Andrew take you home. I will be easier in my mind if you do."

His plea was so earnest she could not deny him. He gave her a lingering kiss and she allowed herself to be escorted to the back gate by a nervous Andrew Shepherd. Thomas preceded the constable back into the Bridewell.

Chapter Seven

THE STRANGER STOOD JUST outside the front door in serious conversation with Jacob Whyte. Neville Norrington watched them from the window of his second floor study. When he heard the sound of hooves he thought James might be going out for a ride and looked out to see a man dismount from a sturdy cob. The fellow was dressed in the simple clothes of a countryman and Norrington had never set eyes on him before. If he had, he would never have remembered someone so insignificant. He carried no letter or parcel, but the steward was very intent on what he was saying.

Sir Neville moved away from the window and lowered himself into a chair, wincing from the pain in his back.

The physician had assured him that he had sustained no lasting damage from the fall from his horse two weeks before and that the discomfort would gradually lessen. It grew worse instead and dealing with it did not help his troubled state of mind. There was a pile of documents on the table in front of him that he knew he should be reading through. Some of them needed his signature. Jacob would be up to collect them later but he could not force himself to concentrate on them. A deep gloom had descended on him that paralysed his will. He had always prided himself on his judgement. His misreading of the suitability of Anthony Hanham for a son-in-law was a profound shock to him. There had never been any scandal attached to his family's reputation and now, if this came to trial, all his colleagues, his fellow JPs, would learn of his mistake and some of them might even doubt his daughter's morals. He had considered both Bartholomew Hanham and Robert Mountfield to be his friends; now he did not know how he stood in relation to either of them.

When Jacob Whyte had brought his children home that Wednesday his relief at seeing them safe soon changed to a stunned dismay. He listened in frozen silence as Jacob, with interruptions from James, told the story. Elizabeth watched her father's face locked in rigid immobility and wished Sir Thomas was beside her. She began to shiver, feeling cold from within once again, as she had on the early morning flight from Hanham House. She wanted her father to put his arms around her and comfort her over what she had endured.

Her mother would have done so she was sure; it was never her father's way to betray his emotions. He just stood there and when she felt dizzy and swayed as if she might fall, it was Jacob who supported her and held her against his shoulder. Sir Neville then insisted she must lie down in her bed chamber to rest and when James attempted to get his approval for their actions all he said was, "You should not have involved Mountfield" and ordered him to escort his sister to her room. He then dismissed Jacob just as curtly.

Ever since he had resisted all his children's efforts to discuss it, shutting himself away in his study, brooding on the best way to cope with the situation. He did not wish to face the details of what Anthony Hanham had done to his daughter. He sat with Elizabeth and James for evening meals, refusing to talk about anything other than what was happening on the estate. He was never a man to indulge in conversation for the sheer joy of it and his children were used to formal meal times, but the atmosphere now was tense and uncomfortable.

He came to the conclusion that if he shut it all out, pretended that nothing had happened and kept his children safely within the world revolving around Norrington Hall for a suitable length of time, it would all go away and be forgotten. On no account must they have any further involvement with Bartholomew Hanham or the Mountfields.

As he sat in his study picking up documents in a desultory way and putting them down again without reading them, his mind worried away at the fact that his children were at Mountfield's house when Anthony got there. He had been so certain they would not. He could not understand why James had turned to a man he had met only twice instead of trusting his own father, a man moreover whose views and manner of living were not respectable. He had always considered that he and his son were in perfect accord, understood each other fully, that he had moulded James to follow in his footsteps. James' admiration for Tom Mountfield hurt him deeply but he could not admit that to the boy. He knew Thomas to be estranged from his own father and wondered what Sir Robert's opinion might be on this unfortunate business, although he rejected the idea of contacting him, fearing it would suggest he wanted to be involved in any consequences.

There was a knock on the door. He did not reply at once and the knock was repeated more firmly. James' voice said, "Can I come in Father? It is important. I must speak with you."

"Not now, I have business matters to attend to."

Sir Neville's reply was sharper than he had intended and he was surprised when James walked into the room anyway. The man talking to Jacob Whyte earlier was Toby Aycliffe who brought the news that Sir Thomas had been locked in Devizes Bridewell on a charge of murder and abduction. Joan Bushy had sent him to warn them they would be needed to speak for him at the trial. James could bear his father's silence no longer and was determined to have it out with him. The news gave him the courage to do so. He stood in front of Norrington, took a deep breath and began, "I am sorry to disobey you Sir, but I must speak and it would be most unfair of you not to listen to me. For days you have shut your ears to me and it can go on no longer."

He had never spoken to his father in that manner before. Even as he said the words he marvelled that they were coming out of his mouth and was excited as well as nervous at his own temerity. Sir Neville frowned but did not interrupt him.

"A messenger has just brought word that Thomas Mountfield has been arrested on a charge of murder and abduction. He has been put in the Bridewell. It is outrageous. Those men of Anthony's have told a pack of lies and Bartholomew Hanham has persuaded the sheriff to issue a warrant."

Norrington shook his head. "That is most unfortunate but not unexpected. However, it is no concern of ours now."

"No concern of ours?" James could hardly keep his voice level. "It is every concern of ours. It is my fault that he is in this position."

"Exactly James, you should have come home and laid your case before me. I fail to understand why you behaved as you did."

"Perhaps I made the wrong choice Sir, but the way you are acting now and what you just said about it being no concern of ours suggests to me that I was right. I think you would have handed her back to that vile man Hanham."

"James be silent."

"No, I will not. I must make you face what he did to Lizzie. He forced her, he beat her, he burned her with candles, he cracked her ribs. He called her terrible filthy names and treated me like the dirt under his shoe."

Sir Neville turned his head away from the righteous anger in his son's face.

"Don't think you can pretend this has not happened. I will not let you. You will be as bad as Sir Bartholomew and Lady Agnes if you do. They knew Anthony was evil, but they shut their eyes to it."

"But why did you go to Mountfield's house?"

"There was no one else I could trust. I knew he would protect us."

"Then you and Elizabeth had been in secret contact with him."

"No, we met him by chance at the September fair in Frome. Lizzie only spoke to him for a few moments before Anthony took her away but I stayed to apologise to him."

"Apologise?"

"I had sorely misjudged him Father when I first visited his house. I was too shocked by the unusual way he led his life and by his strange wife to understand what he is truly like. He is a gentleman of honour and courage. I asked him to tell me about Philip Sidney at Zutphen and although it was painful for him to recall it he did so with courtesy and patience. He spoke with such love and respect for Sir Philip and I knew he was someone who could be trusted always."

Sir Neville sighed. He had encouraged his son to admire Philip Sidney as an example to follow and could understand how someone who had known his hero personally might attract him.

"I had to get Elizabeth away from Anthony," James continued. "He would have killed her in the end Father, I know he would. You have seen how weak she is, how thin. She had no appetite, could not sleep. The ride to Sir Thomas' house so exhausted her she fainted and had to be carried to bed. You always bid me protect my sister and that is what I did in the only way I knew how. I took her to Thomas because I knew he would tell us the right thing to do and he said we must come to you. Jacob explained all this when we first came home. Tom was about to escort us to you when Anthony turned up."

"You call him Tom?" Norrington felt that twinge of jealousy again.

"He said I could because his friends call him Tom. I am proud to be his friend. I will speak on his behalf at the trial, tell the truth and so will Jacob."

Norrington stood up, slapping the flat of his hand on the table.

"You will do no such thing, either of you. I forbid you to have any more to do with this for the sake of your sister's reputation."

"But don't you understand, if he is found guilty Elizabeth's reputation will be even more in question in the eyes of some people. Besides can you be easy in your conscience to let an innocent man suffer for protecting your children? Jacob has promised to stand by him and he will not break that promise even at the risk of losing his post here."

Sir Neville was watching his son grow up before his eyes. Part of him was proud of what he was seeing and it caused great confusion in his mind. James had the bit between his teeth now and could not slow down.

"I do not wish to appear ungrateful or disobedient Sir, but I am not a child any more. I can make my own decisions. I want everyone to know how evil Anthony Hanham was. He attacked Tom with a rapier when he was unarmed. It was so cowardly."

"If Mountfield was unarmed how did he managed to kill Hanham?"

"You did not really listen to anything we told you on Wednesday did you?" James waved his hands around in despair. "He protected himself with the well cover and Dawn Light, Tom's wife, ran into the house and fetched Philip Sidney's sword that he had given into Tom's care as he lay dying. He killed Anthony with that sword although he did not wish to kill him. He had shown me the sword the day before, let me hold it and feel the balance of it in my hand. It was such an honour. He told me that Philip had bidden him to use it only in a noble cause. He also said he hoped never to shed any more blood. I caused him to do that. Would it be gentlemanly to abandon him now?"

"James is right Father."

They had both been so intent on their argument that they did not notice Elizabeth standing in the doorway. She had been there for some time and knew it was the right moment to add her influence. Her father had scarcely looked her full in the face since she came home. James talked about the duty of protecting her but Neville was well aware that the duty was his and he had failed his daughter. He dreaded her accusing him of that. He gazed at her fully now, saw for the first time the extent of her ordeal, how thin and pale she had grown, yet there was no bitterness towards him in her eyes. She knew what he was thinking.

"I know you feel guilty for sending me to the Hanhams but you have no reason to Father. How could you know Anthony's true nature? He dissembled in front of you and Bartholomew deceived you also. He is as much to blame as anyone for he portrayed himself as your friend and then betrayed your trust. I do not blame you in any way. No one could. You have no reason for shame; that must fall on them. Now you must be honest with me. Do you believe that I was unfaithful to my husband? I am willing to swear to my innocence on the Bible if you require it."

Even as she said this she realised that she had been unfaithful to Anthony in her heart but Tom was not complicit in that and she was eager to establish his innocence in her Father's mind. There had been a short period when Sir Neville, dealing with the knowledge that his children had been found at Mountfield's house, feared that Elizabeth had been meeting Thomas in secret. It was Jacob

Whyte's complete conviction that it was not true and James' hot denials that he had acted as a go-between that convinced him otherwise. Now as he looked into his daughter's eyes he wondered how he ever could have accused her of such a thing.

"There is no need for that my child, of course I believe you are innocent."

"And Thomas," she pressed the point, "Do you accept that his intentions were wholly honourable? Like James, I admire him very much but at no time was he ever anything other than kind, courteous and anxious for the welfare of us both."

"I accept that too and I am grateful for the service he has done you."

"Then why do you hesitate to let us support him? It is vital that we speak at his trial. What will make the service he has done seem real to you? Perhaps this will do it."

She turned her back to Sir Neville and unlacing the bodice of her kirtle, slipped her arms out of the garment, letting it fall to her waist, exposing the whole of her back to reveal the full extent of the bruising and burnings.

Her natural instinct was to keep it hidden but desperate measures were needed to move her father. He emitted a half-stifled groan at the sight of her creamy skin blotched with multi-coloured bruises and red blistered patches. His hands instinctively reached out towards her but he took control of them and leaned on the table to steady himself.

"Take a good look Father. Modesty forbids me to show it but my breast and the front of my body are painted in the same colours. Sir Thomas risked his life to protect me from the man who did this. Anthony could have killed him. His own quick reactions and Dawn Light's saved him. His labourers were valiant too. You cannot refuse to help a man who wished to save me from this or criticize James for his courage in taking me there."

Norrington closed his eyes trying to shut out the image that had imprinted itself in his brain.

"Cover yourself Elizabeth," he said gently. "You have made your point. I cannot refuse to honour the debt I owe to Mountfield. James, tomorrow you and Jacob must visit him, take my thanks for his good service to us and assure him that you will speak on his behalf at the trial."

James let out a long sigh of relief and Elizabeth kissed her father's cheek.

"He will be so pleased to hear that all is well between you and us and that he has your support."

"You will not go Elizabeth," Norrington was firm on that point.

"Neither will

you testify in court. I will not have you made a spectacle for gossips. James' testimony, backed by Jacob's will be adequate."

She hoped she had masked her dismay and braced herself for what was coming next.

"You will not see young Mountfield again. It is not a suitable connection for you. If it should become known that you visited him in prison it could add fuel to malicious tongues and could damage his defence. I am sure that the last thing you wish to do is to make things worse for him. He will understand that."

Lizzie dropped her gaze and murmured obediently, "Yes Father."

She made no promise however because she knew that would be a promise she could not keep. Never to see Tom again would seem like being in prison herself. She could bear it for a while if it was the price of her father's support and Tom's safety.

"That's my good girl." Sir Neville patted her shoulder, one of the few physical expressions of affection that he allowed himself. "Your task now is to rest, regain your appetite and your strength, become yourself again."

James and Lizzie left the room together, both in a happier frame of mind, although James was aware of his sister's disappointment with that part of their father's decision that affected her.

"Don't worry Lizzie," he encouraged. "Tom will understand and I will explain to him how much you wanted to come. Why don't you write him a letter that I can take tomorrow? I won't mention it to Father and Jacob won't tell if I ask him not to."

That evening before she went to bed, by the light of two candles she wrote Thomas a long letter describing the events at Norrington Hall since their return; her father's initial reaction and his change of heart. She thanked him in warm terms for his protection and spoke of how she had enjoyed their conversations. She longed to tell him that she loved him beyond description, heard his voice in her head, thought of him constantly, but she must not commit that to paper. Should anyone else read such a letter it could be used to destroy him. Besides, she was not sure what his reaction would be to such an open declaration, so her letter though emotional in places remained within the bounds of propriety. She folded the paper and sealed the ends with wax. Then she wrote his name in bold capitals on the front. It gave her a sensuous pleasure to form the letters of his name, to see it appear gradually before her and when the ink had dried, she kissed each letter of his first name. She had prayed for him every evening since they parted but now that he was in the Bridewell she prayed in greater earnest that he be granted the courage to sustain it and that the physical conditions of his imprisonment were not too severe.

They were certainly more comfortable now than they had been that first night in the Bridewell. Thomas had to struggle hard to overcome his fear of being enclosed. He took deep regular breaths and chanted to himself like a mantra, "This is only my foolish fear. The walls and the ceiling cannot move." His fear lessened when it grew dark. When he could no longer see the frame around him there seemed to be more space, more air. He had slept on the floor on numerous occasions, on the deck of a ship, in a tent on campaign, on the earth under a night sky, but in this cell there was only just enough room for him to stretch full length for his head touched one wall and his feet the opposite one. It reminded him that the frame was still there. The straw too was old and prickly despite the gaoler's avowal that he had changed it.

Tom sat with his back against the wall all night listening to the sounds drifting in from the street and from the other occupied cell farther along the passage, loud snoring, intermittent coughing and a less distinct noise that might have been someone crying. He could not sleep and tried to tune into Waaseyaaban's thoughts as she lay alone in their bed, hoping that unlike him, she could find some relief in sleep.

Just after dawn he heard voices in the outer room and assumed that Daffyd Williams had come back on duty. The night shift had been taken by a sickly looking youth with a chesty cough. Taciturn and abrupt, he was the opposite of the talkative Welshman. Daffyd pulled up the grill flaps and greeted his prisoners with a cheery good morning, letting them out singly for their morning walk to the dung heap to empty their buckets and wash themselves in the water trough. He left Thomas until last, expressing his disappointment on finding that the two slices of bread and piece of hard cheese served for supper was still sitting on the tin plate on the floor.

"It's no good not eating. That's not going to make you feel any better."

"Why would you care?" Tom replied with a weary hostility.

"Didn't get any sleep either by the look of you. Come on out into the yard for a breath of air. You can stick your face in the water trough – brighten yourself up a bit."

The trough was not an enticing prospect to wash in. The scum of previous washings lay on the surface and green algae clung to the sides of the trough. Tiny insects with transparent bodies and attenuated legs skimmed the water. Tom decided to skip the wash. He was not grubby enough yet to risk it. Instead he put his head under the pump and working the handle let a jet of cold water splash over his face. He was pleased to be allowed to walk around the yard several times to get the stiffness out of his back caused by sitting against the wall all night.

Half way through the morning Joan Bushy arrived with Dawn Light, bringing with them the things Tom had requested with the addition of a pillow, his sheepskin lined jerkin and a basket of food. Dawn Light was dressed in a full length kirtle and a hooded cloak. She had pulled the hood over her head and Daffyd did not recognise his adversary of the previous day until he noticed those gleaming black eyes. He took an instinctive step away from her. Ned Carter followed the women in, carrying two stools. Joan was eager to get the business transaction over and Daffyd checked each item.

"That basket of food looks tempting mistress. If you could find it in your heart to bring me something special every time you visit Sir Thomas, I might forget about charging for extra food." Joan pursed her lips and did not reply. The Welshman had no trouble with calculation.

"Right- sixpence for food, two items of clothes at a shilling each= two shillings, two items of furniture at two shillings each= four shillings, sixpence for the pillow. Oh writing materials, that's a real luxury. Very few of the prisoners we get in here can write. Three shillings for that I think. That makes ten shillings altogether."

Joan counted out the money on the table.

"Here you are and you should be ashamed of yourself making money out of other people's misfortunes."

She gave him a disapproving look that so reminded him of his mother that for a few seconds he really did feel ashamed. He let all three of them into the passage way, opened Tom's cell door and announced, "Some welcome visitors for you Sir Thomas." He left the door open and returned to the office locking that door behind him. Tom held his wife in his arms while Joan bustled around tutting at the inadequacy of the cell, arranging the stools, using the oblong one as a table on which to rest the basket of food. She complained about the damp atmosphere and the straw, talking to relieve her feelings.

"It will seem so much better now I have something decent to sit on," Tom declared, attempting to sound cheerful. He sat down on the round stool. Joan stopped fussing, took his face in both her hands and kissed his forehead.

"My poor boy, this is so unfair. You don't deserve this."

"I suspect many prisoners have been held here who did not deserve to be so Joan and who were not fortunate enough to afford these privileges."

"Well at least I can bring you a decent meal every day," Joan said, kicking at the plate of bread and cheese in disgust, "And a cover for that smelly bucket which would put any one off their food."

Tom lifted the linen cover of the basket to reveal some pieces of chicken, a fruit pie, a small rice pudding and a flagon of small beer.

"A feast- I am sure I shall feel in need of that later."

All this while Waaseyaaban had said nothing. She had seated herself on Tom's lap and was combing his hair with her fingers, pausing now and then to kiss him. Her intimate gestures spoke more eloquently than words. She put her hand inside his shirt and stroked his chest murmuring, "In pocket of jerkin-paste for teeth and soap for wash. We do not pay for those. He does not know." She jerked her head in the general direction of the office to indicate the gaoler.

Ned Carter assured Thomas that the forestry would go on as usual. He and Toby would also take good care of the house. He was drafting in his eldest son to help with the work and Tom had visions of the three of them riding from the village on Samson.

"Ten minutes left," the gaoler's voice called from the outer room.

"But they have only just arrived. Surely they can stay longer."

"No, half an hour for each set of visitors. I am good at judging time. You have ten minutes left. You are privileged; the ordinary prisoners only get ten minutes. The constable has granted you longer because you are a gentleman and he has sympathy for you. So don't complain now."

Tom knew he should be grateful for the lenient conditions, but as he considered he should not be the in the Bridewell anyway, it was not much compensation right then. He spent the rest of the time writing a short letter to Cecily asking her to break the news gently to their mother. He did not mention his father, leaving it to Cecily to deal with that problem. It would have been a comfort to be able to turn to his father for support, but that was out of the question. He gave the letter to Ned to take to the stables where Dudley Dent ran a courier service.

"He has fast horses and the letter will reach my sister quickly. His riders have delivered letters to Godfrey's house several times, so they know how to find it." By this time Daffyd had begun to chivvy them out of the passage. "Oh Ned," Tom called after him. "Make sure Hope is exercised. Let him out into the pasture most of the day, but he needs to be ridden regularly also."

"I ride him." Waaseyaaban was holding her husband's hand, unwilling to leave.

"He is very strong my love."

"I know, but he likes me and I talk to him of you. I ride him."

"Yes, I will sit here and imagine the pair of you."

He kissed her and disengaged his hand from hers.

"You too Mistress Wildcat." Daffyd Williams was keeping well back from her as she cast her sharp eyes on him. "You can see him again tomorrow."

As the members of the Mountfield household passed through the front door of the Bridewell into the street, a woman slipped by them into the outer room. She was a small, thin woman with a pointed face. Her skin had the same grey hue as her threadbare kirtle. Daffyd had left the door into the passage open and Thomas caught snatches of the gaoler's conversation with the new visitor. The woman's voice was gravelly as if she had a sore throat. She was begging Williams to let her see her husband.

To relieve his own distress at parting from his loved ones, Thomas called out, "Gaoler, why do you prevent that woman from visiting her husband?"

Daffyd came to the grill and looked through.

"I am not preventing her. She can have her usual ten minutes. She is the wife of Peter Tucker, the clerk you can hear snivelling all the time. Turns out he has been appropriating funds that don't belong to him see. What she wants is for me to give her some extra time. I'm not without a heart. I have been allowing her an extra ten minutes if she brings me a little sweetener- pies, sweetmeats, possets- things like that. But now she is trying to take advantage, asking for extra time as a matter of course without payment."

"Can I buy her that extra ten minutes with something from this?" He held up the basket Joan had brought. "It seems the least I can do seeing I am allowed half an hour and she a meagre ten minutes."

Daffyd was always open to a reasonable proposition. He was still carrying the key to Tom's cell and opened it up. Thomas pulled back the linen cloth to reveal the goods in the basket. It was a hard decision for Daffyd. He fancied the chicken slices and the fruit pie. Seeing his indecision Thomas said," Only one item for ten minutes- two items twenty minutes."

Williams smiled broadly. "Some of your spirit is coming back already Sir Thomas. I'll have the fruit pie. Very partial to pastry I am. And you must promise me to eat the rest of this food today. I can't have you starving yourself while you are in my care. Get me into trouble with the constable."

His tone was friendly. Yesterday Tom had felt that his gaoler's friendliness was mockery, but he was beginning to change his mind. Williams was keen to look after himself certainly, out for all the profit he could get, but he was not vicious or brutal. He was intelligent too, his bright blue eyes full of a lively interest in everything around him.

Locked in again Tom heard the wife of Peter Tucker walking along the passage and inquiring after the name of the kind gentleman who had paid for her precious ten minutes extra.

"You mind your own business Betty Tucker and do try to stop that husband of yours from weeping so much. He will flood the cell out soon."

Now he had pen and paper Thomas decided to keep count of the days so he would not lose track of time and be sure when 7th May, the quarter session date, was close upon him. He did not wish to surrender yet more of his freedom by relying on others for that knowledge. He wrote Saturday 13th March 1590 at the head of a sheet of paper as the first day of his incarceration and added Sunday 14th beneath it.

Sunday- of course- he had heard the church bells earlier. Dawn Light, Joan and Ned had missed church to visit him. He must remind them not to do that again. Every lapse in conformity now could further damage his reputation. He hated having to think in this calculated way.

It was mid-afternoon when the walls showed signs of moving again and he had to shut his eyes, intoning his mantra. That night however, wrapped in his cloak and with the comfort of a pillow, he lay on the floor and managed to snatch a couple of hours' sleep. There were no sounds of coughing and swearing from the other cell because the two labourers had been released by the constable that day and given a week to pay their fines.

During the ensuing days Thomas had no shortage of visitors. Waaseyaaban and Joan came every morning, the housekeeper to chat of small domestic matters to make things seem as normal as possible and his wife for physical contact, to feel his arms around her, to stroke his hair and to rub her head against the side of his face in that feline way. Her desire for him was so palpable that it stirred a burning in his loins to match it and there were days when it was a relief to see her go, his yearning was so strong.

Cecily and Godfrey came the day after they had received his letter. They thought it best to check on his circumstances before telling Sir Robert and Lady Anne in case they should need to prepare them for something shocking. Spartan and cramped as it was his cell was not as bad as they had feared and he was not in irons. None-the-less Godfrey was genuinely distressed. He paced up and down the passage, his brow wrinkled, murmuring variations on, "Oh my dear fellow, how unfortunate this is. How it troubles me to see you here."

Tom had only related the barest outline of what had happened in his letter and Cecily was full of indignation when he told her the full details of the event that put him in the Bridewell. She looked so colourful in her fashionable outfit, a wine red kirtle with the most exquisite lace collar and bodice, contrasted with a flowing outer gown of leaf green. The green gown heightened the colour of her emerald eyes which flashed in anger at the injustice of her brother's situation. She illuminated the cell with her colour and energy. She was full of encouragement and positive ideas. Godfrey offered to attest to the worthiness of Tom's character and hesitantly because he feared it might offend, added, "And if there should be any shortage of money- any hardship, I should be only too happy to contribute."

Thomas thanked him but assured him that would not be necessary. It was Cecily's task now to break the news to their parents.

The cell seemed doubly dark and cheerless once her effervescence had left it. The walls moved early that day.

On Tuesday James Norrington and Jacob Whyte arrived mid-afternoon to confirm their support. He was pleased to know that Sir Neville believed and supported his children. It had been on his mind because if their father had rejected them, his action and its result would have been for nothing; a bitter pill to swallow. He understood why Sir Neville had forbidden Elizabeth to visit him and thought it a wise decision. He read her letter written in a round, careful hand, smiling at the contrasting mixture of formality and emotional frankness. He was grateful that she had not come. In his present frame of mind he did not think he could bear that expression of yearning admiration in her eyes. Even James' eager optimism grated on his nerves, though he did not once show it knowing how much the boy wished to help him. He decided against replying to Elizabeth's letter.

It was his Wednesday afternoon visitors who made the greatest impact. Dawn Light had come alone that morning with his basket of fresh food because Joan and Sarah had gone to Chippenham Market. His wife had ridden in to town on his stallion, Hope, accompanied by both the wolfhounds who bounded into the Bridewell ahead of her, almost knocking Daffyd Williams off his feet. The Welshman loved dogs. His grandfather had bred dogs for herding sheep and cattle. He had grown up surrounded by short-legged dogs that nipped at the heels of cattle to keep them on the move and lightning fast collies that could weave between the flocks of sheep. He could see in an instant that Ajax and Hector meant him no harm. When he spoke to them kindly he fancied it was the first time the wildcat woman had looked at him without hostility. He let the dogs into the passage and when he opened the cell door they climbed all over Tom in their eagerness to greet him. His delighted smile, his pleasure in seeing them was so warm and genuine that it struck a chord in Daffyd. Thomas Mountfield was the most intriguing, the handsomest man he had ever encountered in the Bridewell. He was determined to ask the constable about his background.

Tom was so reluctant to part with Waaseyaaban and his two old friends, Hector and Ajax that morning. He knew Hope was hitched to a tree in the area beyond the wall, the tree that had aided his wife in her assault on the Bridewell when he first arrived there. He longed to caress his horse's glossy coat and swing himself into the saddle. He reminded himself that on Saturday it would be just five weeks until the Quarter Sessions.

He ate some crusty bread and a slice of ham from the basket, washing it down with small beer. Betty Tucker came on alternate days to see her husband; she was due today so he put aside some of Joan's finest marchpane to buy Betty her extra ten minutes. It cheered him that even shut in this place he might do something useful. He had decided to begin his account of the Netherlands campaign to fill his time over the next few weeks and now he sat down at the stool that served as a table, taking up his pen, but he had slept so little the past few nights it began to catch up with him. He found that his eyes kept closing try as he might to keep them open and at one point he almost fell off the stool. Abandoning his literary effort before he had even got started, he spread his cloak over the straw and lay down, soon drifting into a fitful sleep. He was startled awake perhaps an hour later by the sound of his cell door opening and a voice speaking his name. He scrambled to his feet as his mother came swiftly towards him, her eyes full of anxiety. Seeing him lying on the floor, she feared he was ill. She hugged him to her asking, "My dear are you unwell?"

"No I was asleep mother. Weariness overcame me. I am in good health; there is no cause for concern."

She stood back to look at him. Apart from that air of sleepiness that betokens a sudden awakening he did look well enough.

"I am so sorry to give you this anxiety Mother."

"You have no need to be sorry. You are the victim of a grave injustice."

The voice came from a man standing in the doorway of the cell, a voice very familiar to Thomas. He looked up to see his father standing there, upright, imposing with that air of authority that always impressed people when he exercised his duties as a Justice of the Peace. Tom had not expected him to come unless it was to upbraid him. He was taken off guard by that initial statement.

"I am surprised to see you here Father."

"Why? Do you hold me in such low regard that you imagine I would let my only son be accused of murder and abduction and do nothing about it?"

"Ah, the family reputation. Your renegade son has done so much damage to

that already I wonder you think it can be saved."

"Damn it Thomas, why must you always go on the attack? It's you I care about. This is a serious business. Your life could be at stake here."

Robert Mountfield strode right into the cell. Tom then saw that Cecily and Godfrey were in the passage.

"Do you think I don't know that?" he retorted.

"Tom, my dear boy," Lady Anne stroked his cheek soothingly, "Please listen to your father. Stop this foolish feud. We must all work together to make sure your defence is a firm one."

"There is no doubt of that," Robert declared, "I think Bartholomew Hanham has gone addle headed to imagine those two roughs of his will be the kind of witnesses to sway a jury. I know grief can derange a fellow's mind. I went to your house before we came here to talk to Joan Bushy and her daughter and those two labourers of yours. They are good, solid respectable folk. They saw it all."

His father had never been near the house before, always refusing to accompany Anne and Cecily, but now he was adding, "I must say it is a pleasant, well-constructed building. I was surprised by the amount of light that penetrates it- all down to the design of course. You did excellent work there. It appears your forestry venture is paying dividends also."

Thomas was staring at his father, shaking his head.

"So you are astonished that a reprobate like me should be able to design an acceptable house and run a business that makes a profit. I see you felt it necessary to speak to my household to confirm my story before you accepted it. My version as told to Cecily wasn't good enough for you it seems."

"Nonsense, nothing of the sort. I wished to get the whole picture before we discussed it together and it pleases me that your business venture is a success. I am puzzled though why you should wish to live in the middle of that damn forest. When the trees are in full leaf it must be a dark, dismal place. Waste of a pleasant house surrounded by that gloom. I always worry about your mother and sister driving through those trees even though Jack Ross is with them. I know the land was given to you as a bequest and you need to live close by because of the forestry work, but surely it would be better out in the open, nearer the village, where you can breathe the air and see the sky properly."

Thomas laughed at the irony of it. These cell walls were his oppression; the forest was a friend where he could breathe freely. His father saw it as another form of prison.

"I doubt you spoke to my wife about the incident while you were checking the veracity of my story," Thomas challenged, looking his father directly in the eye. That defiant stare was so familiar to Robert. Tom had stood up for himself from an early age.

"The woman was not there when we called. Joan Bushy and her daughter had just returned from market and she was not with them."

"You would not have addressed her if she had been would you?"

"No, if you must insist on it, no I would not."

"Did you close your ears when Joan, Ned and Toby told you, as I am sure they did, that Waaseyaaban saved my life by fetching a sword for me to defend myself against Hanham? You have her to thank that you are not in mourning for me."

"No doubt she would have fought the man herself," Robert replied, a sarcastic edge in his voice."

"Yes she would and may have overcome him too."

"Exactly and what sort of woman is that? A wild creature that behaves like a man with a heathen name that twists the tongue to speak it. How can she be a wife to you?"

"I will tell you what manner of woman she is. She is a brave, loyal, hard-working, loving woman and no other woman could make me as happy as she does. Like it or not Father I love her."

Cecily gave a cry of frustration. It was little wonder that these two men avoided each other for any conversation always came down to this particular cause of dissension.

"Oh, you two are as bad as each other, so stubborn, both refusing to give ground. Tom you know I am with you concerning Dawn Light. I love her too and regard her as my sister-in-law, but we are not trying to resolve that issue now and you must try to be fair to Father. He is as desperate as we are to save you from this situation."

Thomas sat down on the stool, with a long sigh. "I apologise. My nerves are raw and old wounds bleed when your mind is in this state. What course of action do you recommend Father?"

Sir Robert responded with another question.

"What is Neville Norrington's view on this?"

"He is supportive. His son James and Jacob Whyte his steward will be giving evidence on my behalf. He prefers that his daughter be protected from the public gaze after what she has suffered."

"Quite right too. I shall take a trip to Norrington Hall and discuss it with him. I will also have a word with the Sheriff, see if I can persuade him to relent over the imprisonment, modify it to house arrest. I must tackle Hanham too. I have known the man for years. Mayhap I can talk some sense into him. I fail to see how he hopes to prove his case in the face of so many respectable witnesses. It is clear that his nephew was a sadistic brute who made an attempt on your life. I do not see what he has to gain by this."

"He hopes to preserve his own self-delusion," Tom replied, "By making others believe it too. He clings to the story fed him by Anthony's cronies because the truth is irrelevant to him now. He has convinced himself that their version is the truth and everyone else is lying. I am not so confident as you concerning the outcome. No one knows better than you after all your years on the circuit that juries do not make decisions on the facts of the event. What influences them is whether the accused or the accuser appears to have the best character, is the most honourable. I fear I might lose out to Sir Bartholomew on that score. He is a respected Justice and Member of Parliament of many years' service, while I on the other hand am known to be estranged from you for some time, to live with what many people, including you, regard as a heathen whore, hold unconventional views on many subjects, not to attend church every week, to have been visited by the Archbishop's commissioner—"

He stopped, remembering that he had neglected to tell any of his family about Simon and the commissioner. He had thought it best at the time, but now wondered if it was a mistake. His father's brow was furrowed in puzzlement.

"The Archbishop's commissioner- I have heard nothing of this."

He turned to look at Lady Anne as if he suspected she had kept something from him. She was staring at Thomas.

"No- I forgot to mention it to Mother."

"Forgot to mention a visit from Whitgift's commissioner? I hardly think that is something you would forget Thomas."

"Very well then, I chose not to tell her in case she worried about it. You remember my friend Simon Bailey, who studied with me at the Middle Temple?"

Robert nodded. "Yes, the Yorkshire lad - became a lawyer. You used to see much of him at one time."

"We continued to keep in close touch. You may recall that he always had a religious temperament. He has a great desire for reform in the church and his views have moved to the more extreme end of the movement, more towards Presbyterianism and Calvin. He was always outspoken; it is his nature. Last winter he was too outspoken in public and Westminster Palace issued a warrant for his arrest. He fled with his family but Whitgift sent out commissioners to question all his friends."

"I see and when did they call on you?"

"Just after Christmas. We were expecting Simon and his family to join us for Christmas and when they did not arrive or send any message, we were concerned. The commissioner's visit made it all clear."

"You did not mention that you were expecting Simon when Godfrey and I came at Christmas," Cecily commented, searching her brother's face for signs of something he was not divulging. Tom was attempting to relate the story without telling outright lies. He smiled at her.

"We were having such a merry time with you both at Christmas- must have forgotten."

"Another strategic loss of memory?" his father demanded sharply. "What did the commissioner do?"

"He came with an assistant who scribbled down notes and four soldiers from the Westminster Palace guard who searched the house from top to bottom and all the outhouses. He quizzed the whole household and had the courtesy to address my wife as Lady Mountfield." He paused to emphasize this point giving Robert a keen look. His father grunted.

"As they found nothing and were satisfied with our answers they left and I have heard nothing since."

"You have not heard from Bailey since then?"

"No and I worry what has happened to him, but Hanham may hire lawyers to investigate my background who will discover the visit and try to use it against me."

"I see your point. We must get a written confirmation from Westminster Palace that it was part of a general investigation of Bailey's friends and that nothing was found to suggest your involvement."

There was no room for Godfrey's portly frame in the cell, but he put his head around the door to suggest that he knew an excellent lawyer, Ezra Holt. The man had prepared cases on behalf of the Salisbury Corporation and Godfrey often put business his way. He would be just the man to chase up details and write the defence statement to put before the justices.

"I will see him first thing tomorrow Thomas," he promised.

Tom was cheered and reassured by their positive support, their readiness for action. Godfrey was the essence of reliability and his father had always been a force to be reckoned with. His anger with Sir Robert over his refusal to accept Waaseyaaban still burned as hot as ever, yet he had to admit he was relieved to have him on his side. He could see how much it pleased his mother and Cecily that he was willing to welcome help.

When Daffyd's "Time's up" call came his father embraced Tom in a firm hug of encouragement. The last time they had embraced was four years back, that day he had come to his childhood home, newly knighted, hoping for acceptance for his wife. They were so happy to see him home safe from the Netherlands and Robert had held him in his arms with such warmth. An hour later Tom was striding out of the house, vowing never to return. The memory of it caused him to stiffen in his father's embrace and Robert was disappointed by his son's lack of response. He was hoping that this circumstance, unfortunate though it was, might be the means of softening Tom's attitude and bring them closer together, that there might be some way of getting around the obstacle of that Croatan woman. It pained him to consider that Thomas did not appreciate the depths of his love for him and did not return it. He failed to realize that it was because Thomas loved him that he was so sorely wounded by his father's rejection of Waaseyaaban. Despite their past differences Tom had always believed Sir Robert to have a comprehensive understanding, to be above paying strict lip service to social convention. His parents' own marriage was a love match and he expected his father to perceive and respect the extent of his love for this exotic young woman who had captured his heart. Yet Robert rejected her without even meeting her. Robert's failure to look beyond differences in culture and stand firmly on the platform of status and form was a shock to him. He felt betrayed. Betrayals by loved ones take a long time to heal. Sometimes they never do.

Robert and Godfrey returned two days later with Ezra Holt. He was brisk, asked shrewd questions and appeared to be the right man for the job. The task of shaping a defence was taken well in hand.

Thomas continued to mark down the days on his sheet of paper but made little progress on his account of the campaign. He was too restless and could not marshal his thoughts into any sensible order. Always there in the back of his mind was that moment when the walls would start to press in and he could not settle.

His visitors were constant. Daffyd Williams told the constable he had never known a prisoner to have so many visitors, coaxing some details of Tom's background and his case out of Josiah Parry. Drunks and brawlers came and went at various intervals, fined, bound over to appear at the Quarter Sessions or just given a caution. Tom and Peter Tucker were the only longer term residents. He continued to bribe Daffyd with Joan's superb cooking to buy extra visiting time for Betty Tucker although he never saw her or her husband.

He would hear her feet pattering along the passage and Tucker's cell door open, Daffyd making some flippant comment. Prisoners were not allowed to mingle in the yard because there was only one law officer present, so morning excursions to the dung heap and the water trough were lonely affairs, but they were a lifeline to Thomas. He looked forward to that short time in the open air, despite the stench of the dung heap; a chance to look up at the sky and stretch his muscles. He was used to a varied range of regular physical exercise. Sitting around in that small space for most of the day made his body feel stiff and cramped. Now that he had a piece of soap, a wash cloth and a towel he took to bathing in the water trough every morning. It was still chilly in the early morning but he welcomed the stinging sensation of the cold water. He would skim the accretions off the surface with his hands, pump some water into the trough, strip off his clothes and step in. The first time he was self-conscious, stripping naked in the middle of that empty yard. It was completely enclosed and they were not over-looked, yet it seemed a strange thing to do. The only other persons who might be aware of him besides Williams were the constable or his deputy. Perhaps it was Williams who made him uneasy. He had taken off his shirt but as he seemed disinclined to remove his hose Daffyd said, "You can keep them on if you like, but they will never dry off in your cell with no heat. No one can see you except me and I will turn away if you are shy."

Tom had often bathed naked with friends. On Roanoke the settlers would run into the sea or jump into a lake to cool off on a hot day, discarding their clothes with no sense of immodesty. Deciding that it was just the situation that inhibited him, he pulled off his hose and stepped into the trough.

Daffyd did not look away and Tom's morning bath became something to which he looked forward also.

Tom's other ally in his fight with the walls was the passage way to the cells. When visitors came and his door was left open, he could step out into that passage and enjoy the extra space. It gave him almost as much pleasure as the visitors themselves.

The members of the Mountfield household might be free to come and go as they pleased and their daily tasks were completed as normal, but nothing seemed quite real. Their best efforts to repress their fear for Thomas could not prevent an atmosphere of anxiety pervading everything. Ned and Toby with the help of Ned's eldest son Saul worked with a will but they found it hard to whistle or sing in their usual way.

Joan relieved her indignation that her beloved Master Tom was suffering such an injustice by cooking far more food than was necessary, by brushing, dusting and polishing three times over with exaggerated vigour and chivvying poor Sarah for being slow. She refused to let her daughter visit Thomas for she knew the girl would burst into tears and that was the last thing he needed.

Waaseyaaban found her greatest relief in riding Hope around the forest paths as fast as she could, bending to dodge the stinging branches and startling creatures out of the undergrowth. Sometimes she rode up onto the downs where she could let the stallion stretch his powerful muscles in full gallop. Every morning before she visited Thomas she would sit on the ground by the graves of Adjidamo and Wawackechi and talk to them in her own language about their father, why he could not come to see them now, but that he loved them very much and would come soon. Then she would watch the copper discs for a while as they flashed in the light, making their metallic music. During each visit Thomas would show her the days he had marked on his sheet of paper, how many had gone by and demonstrate how many more were left on his fingers. The nights were the worst for her. The stars above the skylight were the same, yet it did not feel the same gazing up at them without Tom's arm around her waist. She hated lying in their big bed alone. The emptiness beside her was like a living entity. She took to staying up very late and some night s did not go to bed at all, but lay down in the kitchen with the wolfhounds. The sensation of their warm bodies against her was comforting. She made sure she was awake

before Joan emerged in the morning. The housekeeper however was well aware
that she often slept in the kitchen. She said nothing, understanding why Dawn
Light avoided the bedchamber. She was a widow. She knew the pain of a lonely
bed.

Elizabeth Norrington, as she walked daily between the geometric
squares that made up the knot garden at Norrington Hall thought constantly
of Thomas Mountfield shut away from his garden and the forest he loved. She
was disappointed that he had not written a reply to her letter, sending only a
verbal greeting through James. She wanted something of his to keep; a few lines
of his handwriting that could be folded away in a pocket or purse and treasured
in secret. He had heard rumours that when Robert Dudley, the Earl of Leicester
died unexpectedly, right in the midst of the joyful celebrations over the defeat of
the Spanish fleet, the Queen had shut herself away in her bedchamber for several
days, reading his last letter to her over and over again.

If she could find no way of ever seeing Thomas again she had no
memento of him that she could hold in her hand. She envied James his freedom
to visit Thomas, which he did every week, reporting back to her how he looked
and what he had said.

Lizzie's favourite spot in the garden since childhood was the small wooden
pavilion on the top of the mound built against the corner of the surrounding
wall. She loved to run up the serpentine path to the top. The pavilion was a
simple structure, four wooden posts supporting a pagoda –shaped roof. Panels
four foot high enclosed the lower half, but the rest was open to the elements.
Sitting up there Lizzie could survey the garden, the modest maze with its low
hedges, and the four square beds, the geometric shapes within them , circles,
diamonds, oblongs, crosses, all formed by clipped hedges. There was a raised
walkway on the opposite side to the mound with a summer house at each end.
What Lizzie liked most was that from the pavilion she could see over the wall
across the surrounding countryside; the cattle in the pasture and the narrow
river beyond.

The walks in the garden were restoring the colour to her face and she
felt herself growing stronger. Her father was kind in his formal way, making
sure she had everything needful for her comfort and respecting her desire to
spend time alone. It was the twelfth of April. She was walking back towards
the house wishing there were more flowers in the knot garden. Only one of
the four squares was planted up with a variety of herbs. The shapes inside the
others were filled with coloured sand in one and broken brick arranged like a

mosaic in the other three. She thought of the lavender borders leading up to Sir Thomas' house and how late snowdrops, early primroses and violets would be brightening the grass under the apple trees. He had told her that in late spring one area of the woods was ablaze with harebells, like a blue sea under foot that you fancied you could sail on. The poetry of that phrase fired her imagination. She could see that shimmering blueness if she shut her eyes.

Going up the staircase to her chamber she met James on the way down. He was about to embark on his weekly visit to the Bridewell and was full of a particular piece of news that his father had told him that morning. Thomas liked to be kept in touch with what was happening, despite his reluctance to engage with the political world. James was hoping that none of his other visitors had told him this already.

"I am going to see Tom now," he told Elizabeth as they stood midway on the staircase. At that moment his sister had a flash of inspiration, a way to get possession of something personal relating to Thomas.

"I have been trying to remember the words of that sonnet of Sir Philip Sidney's that he recited to us. Could you ask him to write it down for me? I would love to learn it."

James pulled a dubious face. "I don't know if I should. He may not wish to do that. Anyway, it is a love sonnet isn't it? If someone- Father for instance-should discover he sent it he might believe Tom was paying court to you after all."

He liked to say Tom. The familiarity of it made him feel important.

"Don't be foolish James. He will not sign it or dedicate it to me. It will be just a poem written on a piece of paper. I will not show it to Father or anyone else for that matter."

"But if you keep it secret, won't that seem even more suspicious?"

"Oh, it won't hurt just to ask him, please."

Her brother agreed although he was already thinking up an excuse for returning without any poems.

When he arrived at the Bridewell he was the third visitor Thomas had received that day.

"Another visitor for you Sir Thomas," Daffyd said, as he opened the cell door. "It has been more like the Port Market than a Bridewell since you came in here. Not that I'm complaining mind, makes my life a deal more interesting."

James was eager for the gaoler to leave so he could impart his news and once he heard the outer door close he burst out, "Have you heard yet? Francis

Walsingham has died."

Walsingham was Philip Sidney's father-in-law, the reason that James was so eager to be the first to bring the news to Thomas.

"No, I had not heard. It does not surprise me. He has been ailing for some time."

"He died on the sixth, six days ago, but Father only got word of it this morning. He is buried already, in Old St. Pauls, next to Sir Philip."

Thomas nodded reflectively. "They shared a common cause, although you could not have two men less alike in temperament. The queen will miss his shrewd mind although I don't think she ever warmed to him. He was too dour, too severe to catch her fancy. He was never given to excessive flattery. She appreciated his dedication to her safety and that of the nation, but not his company."

"Did you ever meet him?"

"Once, at Philip's wedding. I fear the cost of it was giving him a headache."

"But surely he was a rich man."

"Not excessively. He did not get all the monetary rewards that many of the courtiers with more sugary tongues lay their hands on. That house of his at Barn Elms is quite modest by the standards of Privy Council members. I fear much of his fortune was dissipated paying off Philip's debts when he died."

James' eyes opened wide. He had not imagined for one moment that someone as splendid as Philip Sidney would have debts. His face betrayed his disbelief. Thomas smiled at his naivety.

"I am sorry if that shocks you, but Philip was deep in debt. You cannot entertain princes and ambassadors, which he was expected to do, without great expense. Also he loved to patronise scholars and finance projects. He put money into our journey to Roanoke. The more his reputation grew, the bigger the drain on his means. He needed the best clothes, the finest horses. When he was in the Netherlands he borrowed money to buy better equipment for his men. Most aristocrats are in debt. They spend too much of their resources trying to outdo each other in splendour. At least Philip had some nobler goals. Is there any word yet who her Majesty will appoint to replace Walsingham as Secretary of State?"

James shook his head. "No, Father says there are rumours that the Earl of Essex is trying to persuade the Queen to appoint William Davison."

"I doubt she will be of a mind to let Robert Devereux believe he has influence over the offices of state," Tom said in a dry tone.

He was amused by the irony of politics. William Davison was the man who had been officially blamed for the execution of Mary, Queen of Scots. Elizabeth always maintained that although she had been persuaded to sign the death warrant, she never meant to send it. Davison, an inexperienced under-secretary in those turbulent days of 1586/7, realised that he was in danger of being offered up as a scapegoat and took the warrant to the other councillors, who decided to go ahead with it. To salvage her reputation Elizabeth accused Davison of acting improperly by showing it to the councillors and them by acting on it. Davison was tried in Star Chamber, fined and imprisoned in the Tower at Her Majesty's pleasure. After the defeat of the Spanish Armada he was quietly released and his fine remitted. Now Essex was pushing for him to be made First Secretary. What Tom found even more ironical was that those world leaders who were scandalized at the idea of subjecting an anointed ruler to judicial trial and execution would have found murder acceptable. They would not have blinked an eye if Elizabeth had commissioned an assassin to poison Mary or suffocate her in her bed one night, counting it a wise expediency.

He looked at the innocence in James Norrington's eyes and was sorry that the boy would have to become aware of the devious ways of the world.

"The Earl of Essex is soon to marry Philip's widow though," James was saying as if he thought Thomas would be pleased. "She will not have to worry about loss of support because her father has died."

"She will be taking on a man with far greater debts than Philip, but I trust she knows what she is doing. I always fancied Frances could look after herself. I just wish Philip's little daughter might grow up under a wiser influence than Devereux's. I am sorry for her that she never knew her father."

James was puzzled. He had assumed that Tom admired the Earl of Essex. Philip Sidney's brother Robert was a close associate of the earl. He studied Mountfield, who was sitting on the stool, moving his earring around within its piercing with his thumb and first finger in an absent minded way as he thought about Philip's daughter. James found that he was always misjudging Tom's reactions and it frustrated him.

"But did not Sir Philip commend his wife into the care of the Earl when he was dying? He would not have done so if he did not think him an honourable man."

"No indeed," Tom agreed," But part of his affection for Essex lay in the fact that he was once very much in love with Devereux's sister Penelope, now

Lady Rich. Besides, dynastic ambitions always weigh heavily with the great aristocrats, even the noblest ones like Philip. He could only bequeath his wife to a man of equal rank."

"But he gave you his sword."

"How full of buts you are today James Norrington. I am no aristocrat. I come from a long line of country gentlemen, JPs and Members of Parliament for generations- the same pedigree as you. A sword was more fitting to my status. Do not mistake me, Philip was a loyal and loving friend to me, but even if I had been free, he would never have bequeathed his wife to me. Now enough of this before gaoler Williams tells us our half hour is up- does your sister's health continue to improve?"

He was aware that James was deflated by some of the things he had said and thought it best to change the subject. The boy gave an encouraging account of Lizzie's progress, saying that her colour was much improved and she seemed stronger.

"She walks in the garden most days and she says she is sorrowful to think that you are kept from your own beautiful garden."

"Thank her for her kind thoughts."

James was feeling twinges of guilt because he had not mentioned her request for the sonnet. He was always eager to please Lizzie because she cared for him so much. He made up his mind to try, coming out with the request in a rush. Thomas frowned. It was not something he had expected. A clear image came into his mind of the expression in Elizabeth's eyes that night he sat beside her and expanded his theory on the universe, an expression that had caused him to beat a hasty retreat, so aware he was then of her beauty and her desire for him. James, seeing his hesitation, said, "I told her you might not welcome the idea, but she said you need write nothing other than the poem. It would make her very happy because she does so want to learn it by heart."

On reflection Tom decided it could do little harm. It was not his own composition and a poem on a piece of paper could have been copied out by anyone. She had suffered much over the past year and if it gave her some comfort who was he to deny her? In his present circumstances he was very sensitive to the value of comfort. He took a blank sheet of paper, dipped the quill in the ink and wrote swiftly in his bold, looping hand. He blew on the ink to help it dry, folded the paper and handed it to James.

"Tell her that the rhythm of it will help her to commit it to memory. I would prefer her to be discreet about it. It is best that your father does not know it comes from me."

James nodded. "She will. She told me she will not show it to anybody."

That statement confirmed what Thomas had suspected; Elizabeth had an ulterior motive for wanting the sonnet. He could envisage her tucking it away in some pocket near her heart and instantly regretted writing it down, but it was too late then. Visiting time was up and James was leaving.

Daffyd had left Tom's cell door unlocked which was usually a prelude to him wanting to converse with his prisoner for a while. Thomas had come to welcome conversation with his gaoler as a diversion and it also meant the cell door would be open for that little bit longer. The Welshman sauntered into the cell and plonked himself down on the stool, as Thomas positioned himself to get the benefit of the space beyond the open door.

"Well," Williams said, smiling his broad, affable smile, "I think that will be the last of your visitors for the day. Your father has not called for a few days now."

"He is a busy man. He has many public duties to perform in and around Salisbury. It's a long journey across the plain. I am surprised that he manages to come as often as he does."

"How old is he?"

"Sixty four, but he has always enjoyed good health. He has the energy of a much younger man, vigour of body and mind."

"Handsome man too. You take after him."

Thomas made a dismissive noise and did not comment.

"I fancy there is some trouble between you though."

Tom was not inclined to discuss his complicated relationship with his father with the gaoler. His silence did not discourage Daffyd however who continued, "Was he very strict with you when you were a child? Did he beat you?"

"He had very high standards of behaviour and expected obedience- as most fathers do. Unfortunately my nature was never framed for obedience, if it had been perhaps I should not be here now. I remember a couple of canings that made my backside sore, but on the whole he did not favour physical punishment- endless serious lectures though- which I deserved for the most part on reflection."

"My old man used to knock us about something wicked. The drink was his problem see. When he was sober he was a quiet man, hardly spoke a word unless it was necessary."

"You don't take after him then." Tom could not resist making that point.

Daffyd laughed. "No indeed. It's my mother I take after in that regard. Talk the hind leg off a donkey my Mam, bless her. When my Da got drunk he was right bastard, different man altogether, as if some demon had got inside him. He was big too, handy with his fists. Me being the eldest, I got the worst of it.

So, soon as I was old enough to look after myself I hopped it and here I am."

"What part of Wales do you come from?"

"Little village on the south coast, right by the sea. I say village but it is just two straggling rows of houses along a dirt road, most of them falling down."

"So you don't miss it then, not even the sea?"

Tom was reminded that he had intended to visit Matthew Collier around this time and a longing to smell the sea, to watch the tide come in all along that bay, hit him so sharply it was like a physical blow. Daffyd's bright eyes rested intently on Tom's face.

"No, I never had much love for the sea. In truth to stand on the cliffs and see that expanse of water with no sign of land frightened me. The constable tells me though that you have been a sailor, sailed right to the other side of the world. I cannot even imagine how anyone could do that."

Tom leaned back against the wall wondering what else the constable had told him.

"Sometimes I can hardly believe that I did so. It was a rare experience, one I would not have missed."

"Is that where you met the wildcat woman?"

Daffyd never referred to Waaseyaaban by any other name. Thomas nodded.

"Josiah Parry also told me you had been in the household of some great nobleman and fought beside him against the Spaniards. Scholar too he said. No wonder he admires you- sailor, soldier, scholar, fine figure of a man. You truly impress me."

Thomas found he was irritated by the course the conversation had taken. He was not sure why. Perhaps it was the way Daffyd looked him up and down as if appraising every inch of his body.

"Are you heaping all this praise on me to make me forget I am locked up in this hole?" he snapped. "If so it is not successful, so just lock me in will you?"

The gaoler was surprised by his sudden change of tone, but he did not show it. He was used to being rebuffed. He locked the cell door but before he left he looked through the grill and murmured, "Don't worry, not long to the Quarters now. You will be freed then I'm certain of it."

Chapter Eight

MAY SIXTH, THE DAY before the Quarter Sessions, was a day of alternating brightness and heavy showers. Men were busy within the inner area of the castle setting up benches and raising a tent over them to keep out the worst of the fickle weather. No part of the castle was now in a fit state to accommodate the justices, the accused, the accusers and their witnesses, so the arrangements were temporary and inadequate. The idea was often voiced at council meetings that a new building should be erected to house the Quarter and Petty Sessions, but nothing ever came of it. Members baulked at the expense and the justices continued to sit in the shadow of the castle's crumbling remains.

Dawn Light ran down the path and into the house by the back door. She had been telling Adjidamo and Wawackechi that tomorrow their father would be home. Her bare feet were wet from the damp grass. She sat in the kitchen and dried them before pulling on her deerskin boots. It was mild despite the sudden downpours and she wore only a sleeveless smock. Joan Bushy advised her to choose a kirtle for her visit to the Bridewell but she shook her head.

"No, we go in carriage. I do not need more clothes. Tomorrow, for trial I wear kirtle."

The household was full of the hope that this would be the last morning visit to the Bridewell. Tomorrow they would attend the trial and bring Thomas home with them. Joan, as she packed the basket with slices of ham, cheese, some crusty bread and a plum pie was confident that this would be the last time she would need to do this. She could not see how anyone could find Thomas guilty of murder in such circumstances and her confidence had been boosted by Sir Robert's positive attitude. She added a minced beef pie to the basket for Daffyd Williams before she drew the linen cover over it.

They found Thomas in good spirits, a mixture of excitement and apprehension. One minute he was sure he would be freed on the morrow, the next he had doubts. Waaseyaaban had brought him a decent suit of clothes for the trial, a white shirt, russet brown doublet and breeches and fresh nether hose. Joan grumbled because there was nowhere she could lay them out so they would not get creased up or soiled. To please her Tom swept all the paper from his makeshift table on to the floor, put the ink pot and quills beside it and said, "There, spread them over that."

His wife then insisted he sit down while she trimmed his beard with a pair of scissors. She did this with skill and precision, completing her task by taking an inch off the length of his hair. Standing back to admire her handiwork she nodded in satisfaction.

"For tomorrow, so you look- what is the word?"

"Respectable?" he suggested. "As if I ever could."

"I like how you look, always."

"Well that's good enough for me then."

He stood up, smiling at her. He was about to pick up the paper on which he marked off the days, to add this one, for he knew Waaseyaaban liked to watch him do it. He paused however because two men came into the passage and looking up he saw his father and Josiah Parry in the doorway. Sir Robert rarely arrived before midday and his visits had never coincided with one of Dawn Light's. Tom instinctively took hold of her hand. A cold feeling descended on him when he saw the grave expression on the faces of both men.

"You are abroad early Father. Have you come alone?"

"My boy, I have some news that will distress you. You must bear it bravely. I had word from the sheriff yesterday evening that your case is to be held back for the Summer Assizes. It is considered too important for the Quarter Sessions."

"The Assizes," Thomas repeated in a flat voice.

"Yes, in Salisbury. I suppose I should have predicted this. As the Sheriff, William Eyre pointed out, none of the justices of Quarter Sessions wanted to touch it, not with three of their colleagues, myself, Hanham and Norrington, having an interest in the case."

"The Summer Assizes in August- three more months of war with the walls," Tom was talking to himself now. It seemed to him that he was in a strange, echoing vacuum. The sound of his father's voice had faded into the far distance. All he could hear was his own heartbeat; everyone else had disappeared.

Robert was saying, "I had another attempt to persuade Eyre to release you into my custody but he will not budge. He says it will look as if he is showing partiality because he is a near neighbour of the Norringtons. Refused to countenance my counter suggestion that the Sheriff of Somerset, Hugh Portman had initially shown partiality to Bartholomew Hanham. I had another sally at Hanham too. He blustered away like a turkey cock, his face purple with indignation and ordered me out of the house. Been drinking heavily by the look of him."

Waaseyaaban looked at Joan Bushy unsure of the significance of all this. The housekeeper put her arm around her murmuring in a low voice, not to interrupt Sir Robert, "My dear, Thomas is not to go to trial tomorrow. He must wait for the summer assizes in Salisbury in three months' time, twice the time he has been in here already."

"No, they cannot keep him here so long."

She was ready to fling her anger at the constable and Robert but she looked at her husband's face and stopped. Thomas sat down mechanically on the stool, staring ahead of him as if he was in a trance. Robert Mountfield was still talking, under the impression that his son was listening.

"I know it will be hard for you to endure another three months, but there are advantages to the case being heard at the Assizes. The Assize judges will be impartial and will ask searching questions of the witnesses. Also the Sheriff will have to choose a jury from the citizens of Salisbury, most of whom will know and respect Godfrey. When he speaks on behalf of your character they will trust his words." Puzzled by Tom's lack of response he added, "Thomas, are you listening?"

Waaseyaaban had moved across to Tom and sitting on the floor beside him put her head in his lap in a gesture of loving sympathy.

Now she raised her head and looking directly at Robert she demanded,

"Do not speak to him. He cannot hear you now. Tomorrow perhaps he hear you."

Since he entered the cell Mountfield had acted as if she was not there, not giving her one glance, but now he could not avoid those compelling almond eyes.

"Young woman be so good as not to instruct me when I should speak to my own son," he snapped. "I tell him these things for his comfort."

"No words comfort him just now. Leave him in peace."

Josiah Parry touched Robert's arm and said in a respectful voice, "Sir Robert I think perhaps Mistress Mountfield is right. Your son has suffered an unexpected blow. You see how shaken he is. He needs some time to come to himself. He will be ready to face it soon."

Mountfield tried to stare down Dawn Light but she would not avert her gaze. He was angry that everyone thought they knew better than he did how to deal with Thomas. He glared at the constable.

"Parry, I will thank you not to refer to that woman as Thomas' wife in my presence again." So saying he turned on his heels and marched out of the cell, calling for the gaoler to let him into the outer room. Parry made an apologetic gesture to the others with his hands and followed him.

Thomas hardly seemed to notice when Waaseyaaban and Joan left him. He did not respond to his wife's kiss or Joan's murmured encouragements. Daffyd was worried by his frozen stillness. He peered through the grill at regular intervals to find Thomas still sitting on the stool staring into space. When he spoke to him he received no reply.

It was just before dusk when Tom emerged from his catatonic state with little memory of where his mind had been except that he had an impression of a deep vault with sheer glassy sides that could not be scaled. What roused him was the sound he always dreaded, a noise like a heartbeat, deep, reverberating. The walls were beginning to pulse, swell, draw towards him on all sides. The ceiling lowered itself more slowly with an insidious stealth. The words 'three months' ran through his head over and over again until they appeared to be emanating from the walls. His own heartbeat accelerated so fast that he felt dizzy and began to struggle for breath.

"Leave me alone damn you," he shouted in desperation, sinking down to the floor. He drew his knees up to his chest and hugged his legs to him, burying his face in his own lap to shut out his tormenters. His whole body was shaking and he began to sob. Daffyd hearing the shout unlocked the outer door and ambled into the passage way. When he lifted the grill flap and saw Thomas crouched on the floor he ran back for the cell key. Flinging the door wide open the Welshman sat on the floor beside Tom and put his arms around him, holding him in a firm grip.

"There now, what's this all about? Don't distress yourself," he soothed in his lilting voice.

"I never before thought myself to be a coward," Thomas gasped, fighting for breath.

"No, no, you are no coward"

"I am - a coward and a fool. I will not survive another three months. These damn walls will win, moving ever forwards, sucking up the air like some malign spirit, taking the breath from me. See how the very ceiling threatens and mocks me."

His body was shuddering in Daffyd's grasp. The Welshman looked around nervously as if he expected to see something move.

"Look, the cell door is open wide. There's the passage see- plenty of air, the walls do not move."

Tom managed to focus his wavering vision on the open door and the perspective of the passage beyond. He felt the constriction in his throat lessen.

"Not for you perhaps," he said, attempting to exert some control, "But they do for me every day. Oh I am such a fool to believe that I could hide away and shut out the world- that I could cure my pain by writing, by fathoming the universe and the reason for our existence, create a world for Waaseyaaban and I where I could forswear all those things that I, in my moral arrogance, found distasteful- reject all corruption and hypocrisy. Fool to think I could stand against it all, for the world breaks in on me, takes me by the throat and throws me in here to crush me utterly for my defiance."

He was breathing more freely now as the air from the passage reached him, but he was still shaking. Daffyd continued to hold on to him.

"You can withstand it. Your position is far easier than many prisoners. You have your family and friends to help you and you have me. I will do all I can to make it easier. You can stay out in the yard longer. I will leave the cell door open a while after your visitors have left and prop the grill flap open to let in more light. I promise."

Williams had to admit that he was pleased when he first heard that Sir Thomas would be his prisoner for another three months, but he did not wish to see him in such distress. It alarmed him. As he spoke, he ran his hand along Tom's thigh, angling it towards the groin, a light caressing touch for such a large hand. Thomas brought his own hand down on the top of it to arrest its progress.

"No Daffyd no," he said quietly. "I do not need comfort that much. I have never felt the inclination to lie with a man. I have been accused of many things, some rightly, but sodomy is not one of them."

He disengaged himself from the Welshman's arms and stood up, leaving Daffyd sitting on the floor, head bowed.

"You are disgusted by me."

"No, not disgusted, who am I to judge? I thank you for your ready sympathy but I should never have made such a display of myself. Thank God it was not in front of my father."

He felt ashamed that he had lost control, laid bare his fear and disillusionment, but he had rather the gaoler witness it than any of his family. He clenched and unclenched his fists trying to stop the trembling in his hands.

"Your relief will be here for the night shift soon. You can leave me alone now. I shall be safe enough."

A feeling of exhaustion had come over him and he hoped it meant he would sleep. Williams was still concerned.

"I'd leave the cell door open but Andrew Shepherd, the under-constable is on duty tonight and he would not approve."

"There is no need to worry Daffyd. Lock the door and I will endeavour to be more of a man."

When Andrew Shepherd arrived for duty he was in an irritable mood. The youth with the weak chest, who took the night shift, was sick and Andrew had been instructed by the constable to take his place. He was not pleased because he considered the task beneath his dignity. He was assistant constable not a gaoler and he resented being called from his comfortable bed and the arms of his eager young wife. Daffyd was reluctant to leave, still worried about Thomas.

"Keep an eye on Sir Thomas will you? He expected his trial to come tomorrow and now he must wait another three months. It has distressed him."

Shepherd snorted. "I'm sure it has though I fail to see what he has to complain about. Josiah has given him more privileges than any other prisoner we have had in here- visitors allowed at all times of the day, his housekeeper bringing him fine food and fresh clothes, that wife of his sitting on his lap and fussing over him. He's not suffering much.

It is Peter Tucker who has the greater reason for distress. He is going to be found guilty tomorrow without doubt and get his neck stretched."

"You don't understand," Daffyd defended. "Sir Thomas is not one of those gentlemen who cosset themselves in a big mansion, waited on hand, foot and finger by a legion of servants. He leads an outdoor life, physical labour and exercise. He has travelled all over the place, even to the Americas. Confinement in so small a space oppresses him to the point of upsetting the balance of his mind."

"Well he should have been more careful what he got himself into. He has killed a man after all."

Shepherd sat down at the desk and swept on to the floor with his hand the empty plate and the crumbs that were the only remnants left of Daffyd's last meal.

"But it seems that he was the injured party Andrew. He was defending himself."

Shepherd gave him a malicious smile. "You would say that. I am sure you are joyful at the prospect of Sir Thomas staying in here for a few more months. We all know about you Daffyd Williams. There's many a young fellow around here who is uneasy at the thought of you coming up behind him. No doubt you came here from the wilds because you were bored with shagging sheep like the rest of you Welshmen. I've seen you in the early morning watching Mountfield bathe in the trough. Josiah told you to respect him not fall in love with him. You are never going to get your hands inside his hose."

"Shut your mouth you self-satisfied son of a bitch," Daffyd growled, snatching up his lantern to light his way the short distance from the Bridewell to his lodgings in the tavern on the Common. "What do you know about anything? Just keep an eye on him that's all I am asking."

Andrew's words stung him because they underlined Tom's rejection. As he opened the front door and stepped into the dark street, Shepherd called after him, "Never mind Daffyd- at least you can dream about fucking him tonight."

Laughing he bolted the door, poured himself a drink and sat by the fire. Later that night he did take a look through the grill of Mountfield's cell. Thomas was laying full length on the floor wrapped up in his cloak with the hood pulled up. He appeared to be sound asleep and Andrew wondered why Daffyd had been so agitated. He could hear the familiar sound of Peter Tucker weeping and said to himself, "At least he has good cause, poor little bastard."

Thomas remained in a dazed and listless state for several days, afraid to respond too readily to any of his visitors for fear he would lose control of himself again. He submitted to their kindnesses passively and listened to their conversation without saying too much in return. He sensed his father was growing impatient with his apparent lack of spirit. He wished there was some way he could explain to him about the walls but knew Robert would never understand. How could he when Tom could not understand it himself. It was as if some form of madness invaded his brain and he was afraid it would grow worse, driving him insane. Waaseyaaban came closest to understanding. He felt it in her touch and was grateful that he need not search for words to explain it to her.

Two things happened at the end of the week that helped to restore his equilibrium. It was mid- afternoon and he was sketching an outline of the street pattern of Flushing to get it clear in his mind before he attempted to put it into words. He was interrupted by a noise in the gaoler's room, shouting, scuffling and a volley of oaths that scorched the air. He recognised the constable's voice and Daffyd's amidst the furore. The noise grew louder

as the passage door was unlocked and two men were bundled along past his cell with a fair measure of violence. Parry, Shepherd and the gaoler were needed to force them into separate cells where they continued to shout and swear, threatening to kill each other. The vituperation went on after the constables had left and eventually Daffyd yelled at them, "If you two don't shut up I will cudgel you both senseless and don't think I don't mean it."

This had a sobering effect on their tempers and things quietened down. The Welshman opened Tom's cell door and stood in the doorway.

"Sorry about that noise. One of the butchers from the shambles reckoned his neighbour, a carpenter, was bedding his wife- went after him with a meat cleaver, chopped his back door down and smashed up his furniture. They were rolling about on the floor trying to choke one another when the constables got there. Calmed down a bit now though."

It struck Thomas then that he had not been aware of Betty Tucker visiting this week.

"Peter Tucker's case was to come before the justices at the Quarter Sessions was it not? What was the result?"

"Found guilty."

"So he is back here again then?"

"No," Daffyd shook his head. "That was a big sum of money he stole- too much for any mercy. He was hung on the same day. Better really not to let him contemplate his fate for too long."

"Oh God forgive me for whining about my own condition."

Thomas felt ashamed that he had been so self-absorbed that he had not thought about Tucker until this moment. "What will Betty do? Does she have children?"

"Six I think. The two eldest are old enough to shift for themselves. Trouble is Tucker's employer owns the house he rented so the family has been turned out on the street Andrew Shepherd tells me."

"How will she manage?"

Daffyd shrugged. "Go on the parish I suppose, like any other pauper, ask the poor house to take her in if they have room."

"And if they do not have room?"

"Don't fret over it Sir Thomas. There are too many folk in her position to be fretting over them. It's the way life is. Perhaps she has a relative who will take her in."

Tom felt a kinship with this woman he had never seen, but whose life he had been able to touch in a small way. He began to dwell on how he could help her even more and it put him in a more positive frame of mind. The minister of St. John's Church was known to be a charitable man who cared for the welfare of the poor. Tom wrote a letter there and then, describing Betty Tucker's misfortune, asking the minister to inquire into her whereabouts and to support her if necessary, offering to a pay a contribution towards her lodgings. Reading it over, he laughed at himself, sitting in the Bridewell accused of murder, instructing a minister to care for one of his flock. The irony of it did not prevent him from giving it to Ned Carter the next day to take to the minister.

The second event that gave him heart was a letter he received himself. Joan Bushy put it into his hand saying in a quiet voice, as if she did not wish to be overheard, "Someone brought it to Toby Aycliffe's house early this morning. Toby did not recognise him. He wasn't one of Dudley Dent's couriers. He said he was a brother in Christ."

Tom's eyes filled with expectation. Joan and Dawn Light were thinking the same thing. He broke the seal and sighed with pleasure to see that neat writing, so small and precise for so big a man. The message read, "God's work goes on apace here. Your advice was sound as always. I am reunited with those I love. I pray for you daily. Do so for me."

Thomas read it aloud to his wife and Joan who were both delighted to hear that Simon Bailey was safe. They knew how much it meant to Tom, how it would lift his spirits. He read it several times over, conjuring up Simon's broad, affable face. Then he folded the letter and gave it back to Joan. "Take it home and burn it. I know it reveals little but we cannot afford to take any chances."

Later that day he was thinking about Simon and recalled what Bailey had told him about Anthony Hanham visiting the brothel near the docks. His father had been urging him the previous day to think if there was anything that could prove the cruelty of Hanham's nature other than his treatment of Elizabeth. Simon had spoken of a case he had dealt with concerning the owner of the inn where the brothel was located, when Hanham refused to act as a witness. Clearly he did not wish his habit to come to light and it occurred to Tom that he may have treated the whores with the same sadism he practiced on Elizabeth. Evidence of this would weaken Sir Bartholomew's case. When Cecily and Godfrey visited next day he explained this to them and asked his brother-in-law to send Ezra Holt to Simon Bailey's chambers to inquire about the law suit involving the brothel. Simon's clerk or one of his colleagues might remember the details or be able to lay a hand on the documents. Godfrey did so the same day and within a week the efficient Holt had visited the Anchor Tavern and uncovered the whole story of Uta the Dutch girl. He persuaded Gideon Barlow to witness to Hanham's depravity, The visit proved doubly useful because Ralph Lawrence and Dick Shaw were well known in the area for thuggery and intimidation. It was thought they were responsible for several murders though it was not proven. Both of them had spent time in Newgate for violent affray and theft. Barlow could name the constable who had last arrested Lawrence. Holt tracked him down and got a written statement from him detailing Lawrence's criminal career. Robert Mountfield was delighted with this progress, not least because his son had come to life again.

Somehow Thomas got through May and June with the help of his visitors and Daffyd Williams, who kept his promise to let him stay out in the yard beyond the specified half hour, left the cell door open awhile after the visitors had gone and kept the grill flap in the door wedged up. That open grill was a vital ally in Tom's struggle with the malevolent walls. When the pounding began in his brain he would press his face against the open grill and look out into the passage, taking in its length, endeavouring to expand that space beyond his own cell. He would gulp in the air from the passage, repeating his mantra, until his heart rate slowed down to normal and he was calmer again.

His thirty second birthday was marked by a visit from his older sisters, Grace and Margaret who came with his parents.

They had written to him when he was first arrested expressing their regret over his situation but both apologising that their husbands were too busy to escort them on a visit. The tone of both letters, particularly Grace's, suggested that neither of his sisters were surprised that he had landed himself in trouble. They were very uncomfortable throughout the visit, keeping the hems of their skirts up off the floor and exchanging disapproving glances at the words of a bawdy song emanating from the cell at the end of the passage. Their fastidiousness amused Thomas. They were so different from Cecily, who despite her fashionable clothes, would happily sit on the floor to leave the stools free for others. His mother also remained untroubled by any inconvenience created by the cramped conditions. She was her elegant self in any situation. He recalled that Grace and Margaret were ready enough to rough and tumble with him when they were children and was saddened to see how the social mores of their husbands' families had so shaped their behaviour. He hardly recognised them as the sisters with whom he grew up and was convinced they had ceased to feel any love for him. They made sure that his nephews and nieces kept well away from him. He suspected that they would not have visited at all if their parents had not insisted on it.

In mid –July, less than three weeks away from the assizes, Thomas suffered a setback. He was assailed by severe sickness and bowel pain. Violent bouts of vomiting and diarrhoea caused him to spend most of the day and night using the bucket. The stench was so bad he persuaded Daffyd to let him empty it several times during the day. He also requested that none of his visitors be let into the cell for fear that the sickness could be passed on to them and he was ashamed of the sulphurous odour that hung in the atmosphere. This was hard for Dawn Light who so needed to touch him every day, but Joan persuaded her to accede to his wishes.

When his condition had not improved after three days Sir Robert demanded that the constable send for a physician. Tom could not touch food or liquid and was dehydrated. He was beginning to feel weak and dizzy. It was as much as he could do to drag himself out of the bathing trough on the fourth morning. He almost fainted with the effort, but pulled himself together, disguising it as best he could from Daffyd. The physician had several theories as to the cause, one of which was food poisoning which did not go down well with Joan Bushy. He prescribed a medicine, the only effect of which was to make Tom sicker.

It was not until Waaseyaaban and Joan had blended a mixture of agrimony, meadowsweet and coriander, recommending that he took a spoonful three times daily that the symptoms began to lessen and by the end of the week they had disappeared. He found he could drink liquid again and take small quantities of food, but his appetite did not return to normal for some time.

The illness had not left him in the best physical shape to face his trial.

It was just past ten o'clock but the August sun was already hot. The first two weeks in July had been stormy. Heavy rains caused the roads to flood. Ditches filled to overflowing and spilled out into the dirt tracks and lanes. The feet and legs of travellers were mired and smelly long before they reached their destinations. They were lucky if they managed to avoid being sprayed with jets of water thrown up by passing carts and riders. The elderly folk grumbled and swore they had never seen a July like this one, which of course was not the case. They had experienced many wet Julys over the years but the weather had not seemed so troublesome when they were younger and fitter.

It all changed in the middle of the month to clear blue skies and high temperatures. The water soon retreated from the roads. There had been no rain for three weeks and the ruts that had been ploughed up under foot during the storms had baked hard in the sun making progress painful for the feet of folk with worn, inadequate shoes. The wild plants that grew along the edges of the tracks, campion, meadowsweet, valerian, fumitory and startling red poppies had just recovered from the flooding, only to wilt in the fierceness of the sun.

Four parties of travellers were crossing Salisbury Plain that morning, all at different stages in their journey, but all heading to the same location, the Bishop's Guildhall in the centre of Salisbury where the Summer Assizes were due to begin at eleven o'clock. Josiah Parry and Andrew Shepherd, assisted by two men from the Sheriff's staff were escorting their prisoner, Sir Thomas Mountfield to trial. Thomas had been provided with a horse and because he needed his hands free to manipulate the reins, he was not manacled at the wrists. The Sheriff's officers were concerned about this and even though Constable Parry assured them Sir Thomas would make no attempt to escape they insisted on riding with their prisoner boxed in, a man in front, behind and on either side. They had started out very early and were now entering the outskirts of the city.

Perhaps half an hour behind them was a small carriage driven by Toby Aycliffe arrayed in his Sunday clothes. His passengers were Dawn Light and Joan Bushy also dressed for the occasion. Joan had persuaded Dawn Light to wear the mulberry coloured outfit she had worn at Cecily's wedding to make a good impression on the jury. There was no shelter on the open plain and as the sun beat down Dawn Light wished she could dispense with her flowing outer gown. Beads of sweat were standing on the flanks and broad behind of Hetty the cob as she trotted along at a steady pace. Waaseyaaban, as an act of confidence with a touch of sympathetic magic mixed in, had tied Hope to the back of the carriage so that Tom could ride him home once he was freed.

The tapering spire of the Cathedral was already visible in the distance, soaring upwards as if to touch the very gate of heaven itself.

Converging on to this road from different highways were two more groups of travellers. Sir Bartholomew Hanham and his wife Lady Agnes were being conveyed in a luxurious carriage driven by a man in green and gold livery and escorted on horseback by Ralph Lawrence and Dick Shaw. They would hit the main road to Salisbury barely ten minutes before Sir Neville Norrington. He rode in a more Spartan equipage although his coat of arms was on the door on both sides. Jacob Whyte was the driver and James Norrington rode beside the carriage. Sir Neville had a fellow passenger. Elizabeth sat beside her father, wrapped in a hooded cloak of deep midnight blue. He had not intended her to come. Members of the public were allowed into the hall to watch the proceedings. The Assize trials were a big draw, considered prime entertainment. Norrington was sure his daughter would be embarrassed by the staring and whispering that was bound to occur. Lizzie pleaded with him, arguing that her absence might look as if she did not care about the result of the trial. She did not want Sir Thomas or anyone else to think she was unappreciative of what he had done for her. She was so fervent that he gave in on the condition that she cover her head with the hood and sit beside him without speaking to anyone concerned in the trial.

She was disappointed that Thomas had not replied to any of the four letters she had sent him during his imprisonment. The last letter described her distress in very emotional language on hearing that he had been so ill and expressed her great relief that he had recovered. She had come as close as she dare to declaring her love for him and hoped that it might elicit some manner of response, but it did not. Philip Sidney's sonnet on that sheet of paper was still her only treasure. She carried it with her wherever she went, tucked into a pocket in her petticoat.

Thomas could not fail to pick up the implication in that last letter. Waaseyaaban, though she could not read it, could tell by the expression in his eyes what was in it- the equivalent in words of Lizzie's adoring glances. She teased Tom about it, but the letter disturbed him. He did not wish to give Elizabeth more pain. He tore up all four of the letters after he had read them and gave them to Joan to burn.

Godfrey and Cecily Roper had called for her parents around ten o'clock and the four of them left Sir Robert's handsome house at the end of the Cathedral Close twenty minutes later to walk to the Guildhall. It was a strange feeling for Lady Anne, strolling past the west front of the Cathedral, passing beneath the arch of the great North Gate and following the familiar path that led to the Market Place, as they did every Sunday to attend St, Edmund's Church or visit the market during the week. This was not an ordinary morning for in a few short hours her son might be condemned to death. Not one of them would admit to that possibility in words but it was fear they all shared.

The Guildhall was the property of the Bishop of Salisbury, where the ecclesiastical courts were held and was often referred to as the Bishop's Guildhall.

The Borough Council had built a new establishment for themselves in 1584 over the other side of the Market Place. In this Council House they stored all the city records and the treasury, but their most frequent meeting place was in St Edmund's Church. There was often tension between the bishop and the council when their jurisdictions over-lapped. The mayor was subordinate to the bishop but he was always keen to extend his influence and the power of the council.

The Assizes however continued to be held in the Guildhall. It was a building from an earlier century with a venerable dignity, the length much greater than the width and a high, barn-like ceiling of arching beams. Robert Mountfield's party arrived just in time to see Thomas being escorted through the side door. Anne could not prevent a murmur of dismay at the sight of him so closely guarded as if he really was a criminal. Robert patted her hand assuringly and she smiled at him saying, "Well at least he is not in chains. He has been spared that humiliation."

Even as she spoke three men in manacles were shoved clanking through the same door into the prisoners' holding room. Ten people were to appear before the Assize Judges, Richard Colborne and John Chichester, that morning; eight men and two women. Thomas leaned against the wall and surveyed his fellow prisoners and their guards.

He had been allowed to dress respectably in the clothes he had hoped to wear at the Quarter Sessions back in May but the three men in chains were in a pitiful state. They were unwashed, a sour odour emanating from them, their garments torn and filthy. One of them had a weeping sore on his ankle where the leg iron had been chafing. Yellow puss trickled down on to his foot. The remaining male prisoners were in better condition. They were mostly silent, but a balding man in his fifties walked up and down muttering prayers. The two women could not have made a greater contrast. One had thrown her herself down on the floor, refusing to heed her guards demands for her to get up. She would have been comely once. Now her hair was matted beyond combing, her eyes wild and staring. She beat the floor with her fists and moaned.

The other woman was dressed primly with a white coif and collar. She was in her early twenties with a clear, untroubled face and sat with her hands folded in her lap as if she was in her own parlour. Thomas wondered what she could have done to be brought before the Assizes. She showed no sign of fear. He noticed that Josiah Parry was also looking at her and the constable to satisfy his own curiosity wandered over to speak to her guard. He came back shaking his head and said to Tom, "Would you credit it? That innocent looking young woman poisoned her husband with bella donna, put a massive dose in his soup. She admits it and vows she has no remorse."

"We put too much store on appearance," Thomas murmured. "That poor wretch grovelling on the floor is probably innocent of whatever she is accused and has been driven mad by the injustice of it."

He closed his eyes and rested his head against the wall. His head ached. The ride to Salisbury had tired him. He realised that the bout of sickness and his enforced idleness had weakened him far more than he had imagined. It was hot and airless in the holding room. He was familiar with Assize proceedings. The judges had the details of the indictments for each case. The prisoners would be called in turn to stand before the bench while the indictment and defence statements were read aloud by the clerk. The judge would ask the prisoner for a plea of guilty or not guilty, then the witnesses could be called. The judge could ask questions to clarify witness statements and both accuser and accused could interrogate witnesses. When all ten cases had been heard the jury, who were also supplied with written details of each case, were sent out to decide a verdict on each one. They would write the verdict down at the head of the indictment and when all cases were decided, return to the court and hand the papers to the clerk. All the prisoners would then be paraded out together and the verdicts read out by the clerk. Tom's case was the fifth one to be heard. There was nothing in this holding room for the comfort of prisoners or guards, no chairs, nothing to drink. His mouth was bone dry and he craved a cool drink right then; a long draught of cider would have hit the mark. He ran his tongue over his lips trying to create some moisture. He wanted his voice to be clear and strong when he spoke in his own defence. The hearings went much faster than he had imagined. The calm young woman who had poisoned her husband was directly before him and when she returned, she gave him a beatific smile which was more chilling than comforting. He was led out of the room by an officer of the court. The main body of the Guildhall was spacious. A dais was set up in the centre on which the two judges in their scarlet robes sat behind a table with the case papers in front of them. The jury sat on benches facing the judges and the general public in rows behind and at the sides, with those concerned in the various cases seated at the front. Tom was instructed to stand before the judges while the indictment was read out. There was a murmuring from the public benches and Judge Colborne asked, "Thomas Mountfield, how do you plead, guilty or not guilty?"

"Not guilty your honour."

Tom was relieved that he sounded confident and unafraid. He was directed to a bench beside the jury and was grateful to sit down for his legs were not as steady as he would have wished. Looking around him he saw his wife, Joan and Toby sitting quite close; his parents, Godfrey, Cecily and Ezra Holt just behind them. The Hanhams were on the other side of the judges, flanked by Lawrence and Shaw. He could not see the Norringtons for they were behind him, so he was not aware of Elizabeth's eyes fixed on him.

Before the first witnesses were called, Master Jardine the lawyer who had prepared Hanham's case, stood up and addressed the bench.

"I beg your pardon Judge Colborne but I believe the clerk has omitted to read part of the indictment relating to Sir Thomas' character, concerning a visit from the Archbishop's commissioner for aiding the escape of a recusant."

Colborne gave him a cool look.

"That was my doing Master Jardine. I was about to give the jury instructions on that point." Jardine apologised and sat down as Colborne continued, "It is suggested here that Sir Thomas was implicated in helping –one- Simon Bailey evade the law. However I have checked with the office of the Archbishop's commissioner who explained that all Bailey's friends and colleagues were visited during the inquiry as a matter of course and there was no evidence to suggest that Sir Thomas played any part in his escape or was even aware of it until told by the commissioner. Nor is there any suggestion that he holds the same religious views as Bailey, despite his rather patchy attendance at church. Hence I rule that this has no part in the case before us and instruct the jury to disregard it."

Robert Mountfield gave Ezra Holt a satisfied nod and Thomas felt a twinge of conscience that he had not told his father the whole truth.

The case proper now began. Hanham's two false witnesses took the stand, Lawrence first, both swearing on the bible. As they had no faith in anyone but themselves it did not trouble them to commit perjury. Their story was a reversed version of the event. Anthony Hanham demanded reasonably that his wife be returned to him and Mountfield attacked him with a sword before he had a chance to draw his own weapon. Colborne's gaze was shrewd. He was appraising the two men as they spoke. Chichester murmured something in his ear and he nodded.

"Were you wearing a sword when Anthony Hanham rode into your yard Sir Thomas?" he asked.

"No your honour, I never wear a weapon on my own property. I was in my shirt sleeves having just drawn water from the well."

Colborne turned back to Dick Shaw.

"But you say he was wearing a sword."

"No sir, his whore gave it to him."

"I presume you mean Lady Mountfield. Please moderate your language in this court. So, Sir Thomas' wife was wearing the sword?"

Laughter rippled along the public benches.

"No your honour, she ran inside the house and fetched it."

"Why would she do that if Hanham had not drawn his own weapon?"

"Well, she's a wild foreigner your honour."

Colborne raised his eyebrows and dismissed the witness after asking Thomas if he had any questions. The next person to speak was a man called Nahum Allerton. He claimed to be at Christchurch College, Oxford at the same time as Thomas and described how Mountfield was one of a group of students who held dangerous views, denying that the earth was the centre of the universe, following the teachings of Copernicus. Tom had never seen the man before. Granted he would not remember the face of everyone who was at Oxford with him, but this man looked to be around fifty and when you are fourteen, as Tom was when he first went to Christchurch, you tend to remember much older students. It was unusual for men in their thirties to study there.

Allerton went on to say that Thomas had been influenced by Walter Raleigh, who was at Oriel College during the same period and it was well known that Raleigh was a sceptic and consorted with known atheists like Marlowe the poet. He talked about secret meetings at night to make it all sound sinister.

Thomas had not bothered to question Lawrence and Shaw knowing it was pointless, but he was curious about this man.

"I must apologise Master Allerton but I do not remember you at Christchurch," he said courteously. "You must have taken up your studies much later in life than most of us. Tell me if our meetings were so secret, how did you know about them and more to the point, what we discussed in them?"

"I was told by others."

"There was no secrecy about our meetings. They were open debates so everyone knew what was discussed. I was only seventeen when I graduated. We were young men with unformed minds discussing many topics and possibilities. We had no settled views on them. As for Raleigh, yes I did admire him. He was four years older than I and seemed so much more confident, but I have never heard him express atheistic views and I warrant you have never heard me express them. Well, have you? Remember you have sworn an oath."

The man looked away, glancing across at Bartholomew Hanham.

"No, not myself, others I trusted confirmed it."

"One more thing Master Allerton, who was the porter at Christchurch during our years there?"

Allerton cleared his throat with a nervous cough.

"I do not have a memory for names."

"What did he look like then? After all he was unforgettable in that regard."

Ambrose Hollins was an unfortunately favoured man with a bulbous red nose and a multitude of warts on his face. The students made his life a misery playing tricks on him. Allerton insisted that he could not remember.

"I suggest that may be because you never were at Christchurch, at least not at the same time as I was," Tom said sitting down.

Colborne asked Allerton, a sharp edge in his voice, "Were you or were you not at Christchurch College between 1572 and 1575?"

Allerton was flustered. He suggested that his original statement must have been copied down wrongly. He was at Oxford, but at an earlier period than Sir Thomas.

"Then your evidence is second hand Master Allerton and you should have made that clearer. Sit down."Allerton was glad to do so and he avoided Bartholomew Hanham's gaze when he returned to his seat. Hanham's blotchy face was growing redder as the trial proceeded. A vein in his temple pulsed. Agnes gave him anxious looks as if she feared he would explode.

A tall woman in a grey kirtle with a woollen shawl around her shoulders was the next witness. She gave her name as Jane Mundy and after she had taken the oath curtsied to the judges with a simpering smile on her face. Thomas glanced across at the members of his household with a questioning expression, wondering if they knew who she might be. She claimed to live near the Mountfield house and was appalled at the goings on there.

"That woman he calls his wife runs around the forest half naked. He exercises no control over her. She indulges in wicked heathen ceremonies and he helps her- things no Christian should have to witness."

Judge Colborne was about to ask her a question but changed his mind, indicating that Thomas should do so.

"Where exactly do you live Mistress?" Tom queried.

"Wedhampton Common."

"But that is more than twenty miles distant from my house. When was it that you saw these alleged ceremonies?"

"When I was walking through the woods."

"Why would a Wedhampton woman be walking through my woods? You give a colourful description of my wife; you have had a close look at her?"

"Oh yes, I would recognise that creature anywhere."

"Indeed. Is she in this room today?"

Jane Mundy let out a loud laugh.

"Bless you no, their worships would not allow an untamed heathen into this hall."

"Your honour," Tom addressed Judge Colborne, "May I ask my wife to stand up so the jury can see her?"

Colborne nodded. Thomas walked over to Dawn Light and took hold of her hand. She stood gracefully, her eyes taking in the faces of each member of the jury. It was hard to equate this woman in her velvet gown, her hair in sleek plaits laced with ribbons with the picture Jane Mundy had just drawn. She looked exotic and striking, but hardly wild and out of control.

"You've tricked me," Jane Mundy shouted, "Dressing her up like a respectable woman. How was I to know her dressed like that?"

"You had just sworn you would know her anywhere Mistress," Judge Colborne interrupted her. "Now think carefully before you answer this, have you at any time seen with your own eyes Sir Thomas and his wife engage in heathen rituals?"

She hesitated and then admitted grudgingly that she was passing on what others had told her. Colborne clicked his tongue impatiently.

"More hearsay."

He dismissed her with a gesture of his hand and gave Jardine, Hanham's lawyer, a severe look. Turning back to Thomas, who had escorted Dawn Light back to her seat, Colborne asked, "Your wife is from the Americas I believe?"

"Yes your honour, from Roanoke Island."

"Has she been received into the Christian faith?"

"No she has not been baptised if that is what you mean."

Robert Mountfield's intake of breath was heard by Lady Anne. They both feared their son would offend the solid, church-going merchants and tradesmen of the jury by being too outspoken on this point.

"She attends church when I go and has been attending with my housekeeper since my imprisonment, but English is not her first language and she cannot follow all that is spoken by the minister."

"You have made no attempt to convert her?"

"The Croatan people are very religious. They believe in a benevolent, supreme being just as we do. I have told her stories from the Bible and explained God's act of love for mankind through the incarnation. She respects Christian beliefs, accepts many of them as similar to her own."

There was another murmuring around the benches at the back of the room.

"Does she carry out heathen ceremonies?"

"They are not heathen in so far as they are antipathetic to the Christian faith. They are simple customs carried out by her race, just as we have May Day customs, dancing round the Maypole and other things connected with the seasons. They are agricultural customs to aid growth and a good harvest."

"Do you take part in these ceremonies?"

"They often involve singing and I play the lute to accompany her. In truth, I sing too sometimes, but there are also times when I sing hymns to her. I see no contradiction in allowing my wife freedom of worship when it does not interfere with my own faith or anybody else's for that matter."

"Arrogance, arrogance! " Bartholomew Hanham shouted. "He is claiming to know better than the Church of England."

"Far from it Sir," Thomas countered. "I do not claim to know better than anyone. This is why I can tolerate the views of others." Elizabeth and James Norrington exchanged apprehensive glances. They both sensed that their father was uncomfortable with Thomas' statement, but James did not have time to worry about it for the clerk of the court was now announcing that witnesses on behalf of Sir Thomas Mountfield were to be called and James was the first to speak. He was nervous but his zeal to tell the truth overcame his nerves. He drew himself up to his full height when he put his hand on the Bible to swear to tell the truth and gave his evidence in a clear, unfaltering voice. He explained how they first met Sir Thomas and then described the pain and humiliation Elizabeth and he had suffered at Anthony's hands. When he spoke of beatings and burnings Bartholomew called out, "Ungrateful, lying boy! I accepted this boy into my household with nothing but kindness and see how he repays me."

"I do not deny that you were kind to me Sir, so was Lady Agnes, but I could never understand why you closed your eyes to Anthony's cruelty."

James went on to relate the details of their flight and what really happened when Anthony Hanham arrived at Tom's house.

"Pure invention," Hanham contradicted. "They had arranged to go to Mountfield I am sure. The boy must have been taking letters from Elizabeth to him and planning secret trysts."

Colborne asked James if there was any truth in this accusation.

"No your honour, from the day we stayed overnight at his house to the day I took Elizabeth there for refuge we had seen him but once and that was by chance. We met at Frome fair, September last. My sister spoke to him for a few moments only but I lingered a while. You know that Sir Thomas was a valued friend of Sir Philip Sidney and fought beside him at Zutphen. I have always admired Sir Philip and asked Thomas to tell me about Zutphen. He did so most courteously even though the memory of it caused him some pain. I formed a very good opinion of his nobility of character."

James was so ardent; it was evident that some of the jury were impressed. Colborne nodded and then asked, "But if you had met Sir Thomas only twice why did you choose to take your sister to his house on such a slight acquaintance? Why did you not go straight home to your father?"

"A good question indeed," Hanham declared, looking around him as if he was justified.

James had been dreading this question because he would be obliged to admit that he was not confident at the time of their father's support. He did not wish to imply criticism of Sir Neville in front of a roomful of strangers. Yet Norrington's only advice to him that morning was to tell the complete truth. He took a deep breath before answering. "We misjudged our father Sir. He has known Sir Bartholomew for many years and Anthony was always false and deceiving in his presence. We were both afraid that Father would insist we return to Hanham House and resolve the matter. I could not let Anthony take Elizabeth back for fear he would kill her with his cruelty."

"I understand that, but why Mountfield?"

"I admire him your honour and I knew he could be trusted to protect us and give us good advice, which he did because he told us we must go to our father as soon as possible. We could not go straight away because Elizabeth was not well enough. She needed to rest, but as I explained before, we were on the verge of leaving for Norrington Hall when Anthony came to the house. I am truly sorry that I misjudged my father and brought such trouble on Sir Thomas, but I only did what I thought best."

When his testimony was over James went back to sit beside Lizzie who squeezed his hand and murmured, "You did well James. We are so proud of you."

His father said nothing but gave him a terse nod of approval.

Jacob Whyte confirmed James' version of the events. He stressed his discomfort at Anthony's discourteous behaviour to Sir Neville and the demeanour of his two rough companions. He described how Lawrence had tripped James when he tried to go to Mountfield's aid and when he went to help the boy up, how Lawrence had threatened him, calling him old man in a most disrespectful manner. He also admitted that he wished he had passed on to Sir Neville what James had confided in him at Christmas about how unhappy he felt at Hanham House. Jacob had honesty and reliability written all over him. He made an excellent witness, as did Joan, who laid emphasis on the nature of the injuries Elizabeth had suffered, describing how she and Dawn Light had bathed and soothed them with arnica.

"That poor child must have suffered dreadfully. I have never seen anything like it nor wish to again."

She also defended Tom's character, her voice full of indignation that anyone should dare to cast a slur on it.

"Master Tom could no more attack an unarmed man than he could fly to the moon," she stated with a look on her face that would have quelled anyone's desire to say otherwise.

Toby Aycliffe pointed out that Lawrence and Shaw would have helped Anthony kill Sir Thomas if he and Ned had not held them off and added that they had all heard Lawrence admit that he was ready to swear anything Bartholomew Hanham wished."Sir Thomas is a fair-minded man with no malice or aggressive intent toward anyone. All the villagers around the forest respect him for his generosity. My cousin and I think ourselves fortunate to be in his employ. Why, even when Dawn Light had given him a sword and he was on equal terms, he tried to talk Hanham into backing off and letting him take the Norringtons to their father as planned. The last thing he intended was to kill him but Hanham rushed at him like a madman; he had to defend himself."

Godfrey Roper's task was to witness to the honourable nature of Tom's character. He did so with a warmth and naturalness so typical of the man, mentioning Tom's desire to set up a school in the near-by village.

"This is a most worthy act of charity, which I and several of my business associates have agreed to sponsor and is just one example of my brother-in-law's genuine desire to alleviate the lot of those less fortunate than himself."

The task of the last witness for the defence was not to attest to the worthiness of the character of the accused. When his name was called, Gideon Barlow, the owner of the Anchor Inn, strolled casually from the back of the room and swore his oath in a flat, Midland accent. There was nothing striking about his appearance. He was of middle height with muddy brown hair and regular features. He gave the impression of a man who would not be hurried or intimidated. Colborne and Chichester consulted over the papers in front of them before the former said in a frosty tone, "I believe you are brothel keeper Master Barlow."

"You are misinformed your honour. I run the Anchor Tavern, a respectable establishment near the docks in London. At the back of the tavern is a house which also belongs to me which I rent out to a group of ladies who do indeed ply the trade to which you have alluded."

"He's a pimp," Bartholomew Hanham was on his feet again. "Are we to be insulted by evidence from a pimp?"

"Well, we have heard evidence on your behalf from two convicted felons Sir Bartholomew. I fail to see the distinction," Colborne replied dryly.

Agnes tugged at her husband's sleeve eager to restrain him. He pushed her hand away but sat down none-the-less.

"You do not procure clients for these ladies then?" Colborne emphasized the word ladies with a sarcastic smile.

"I do not. They pay me rent for the building and I in turn make sure it is a clean establishment if you understand me- that the condition of the rooms is good, they have facilities for washing and other bodily needs. I also protect them should they need it. Those ladies get a good class of customer. You might be surprised if I furnished you with a list of names. Some of them you would know well."

"I don't doubt it Master Barlow. Anthony Hanham was one of these customers I gather."

"He was your honour, a regular, generous payer but few of the ladies liked to lie with him."

"And why was that?"

"He had perverted tastes."

"Could you describe those to the court without causing offence to the gentlewomen present?"

Judge Colborne was well aware that most of the gentlewomen to whom he referred could not wait to hear the details.

"He liked to cause pain," Barlow explained. "And take a bit of it back himself. I was dubious about him from the start but there was one girl, a Dutch girl who was willing to submit to him for a while. But his violence grew worse so she told him she didn't want his patronage anymore."

"What was his reaction?"

"He tied her to the bed and cut a heart shape on her breast with a knife."

A gasp sounded around the room as if it emanated from one source but in fact came from many different spectators. Hanham tried to speak but he choked on his words in his rage that this fellow dare say such a thing in public.

"He was fearful afterwards that he had gone too far I think because he gave her a whole purse-full of money to keep her mouth shut. She was terrified that he would come back so we sent her to stay with some relatives."

"Did he return?"

"Oh yes your honour, the very next day demanding to see her and when I refused to tell him where she was, he drew his sword and held it at my throat, threatening me. I was also unarmed," he added pointedly," Just come up from the cellar in my apron."

"When was this?"

"Beginning of March your honour. I warned him that his secret would come out if he harmed me and he departed in a foul temper. I fully expected trouble from those guard dogs of his, the felons you mentioned earlier sir."

"They are known to you?"

"Oh yes and to most folk in the area. They are willing to do anyone's dirty work. Hanham used them to frighten and beat up tenants in those pig sties he called tenements when they couldn't pay their rent on time- them and another fellow- a Frenchman with one eye, Gaston Ralleray. Lawrence is the worst, as evil a piece of work as I have come across and I've encountered a few. He's been in Newgate innumerable times but one of his masters always gets him free."

Colborne directed the jury's attention to the signed statement among the trial papers by the retired constable, detailing Lawrence's criminal record.

"You are the evil one," Bartholomew Hanham accused Barlow. "A shameless pimp who has been bribed to besmirch the reputation of my nephew- bribed by Robert Mountfield in a desperate attempt to save his son."

Thomas saw his father sit more upright than he was already, bridling at Hanham's implication. Barlow was unruffled by the accusation.

"I beg your pardon Sir, I have taken no bribes. I have come here all the way from London at my own expense to aid the course of justice. However much it pains you to hear it said, your nephew had a dark and twisted disposition and cared not who he hurt. There are plenty besides me who could testify to it."

Gideon Barlow was a cool customer, confident and precise in giving his evidence. Tom was convinced that he was nowhere near as respectable as he purported to be and was sure that Colborne was thinking the same thing, but the evidence was of inestimable value to his case. As Thomas was escorted back to the holding room he looked at Waaseyaaban who had been sitting so still, so attentive during the proceedings. He dare not smile in case the jury interpreted it as over-confidence. She made a gesture with her hands that indicated how much she wanted to touch him and half rose, but Joan Bushy dissuaded her, so she turned her head to watch him all the way to the holding room door.

This was the worst time for the families and friends of those who had already appeared before the bench. They had to sit through the trials of the four remaining prisoners before the jury left the main hall to deliberate in another room. Everyone was then free to walk around, go home or eat a meal in a near-by tavern but as no one knew how soon the jury would come to their decisions, they were reluctant to move too far from the Guildhall. Bartholomew Hanham's band of witnesses all made themselves scarce, aware that Judge Colborne was not pleased with them. Lady Agnes persuaded her husband to take some fresh air.

The redness of his face was tinging purple and she was worried he would suffer an apoplectic fit. She steered him outside murmuring soothing words. Tom's family and household were too restless to leave the building. Joan with her usual foresight had brought a basket containing jugs of small beer and fruit juice and some cheese flavoured biscuits. She busied herself distributing these. No one was hungry except Godfrey, who could never resist a biscuit of any flavour, but everyone was grateful for a drink. It was hot in the hall despite the lofty ceiling. Dawn Light watched Sir Robert interested by his likeness to Thomas, the shape of his brows, the way his hair grew, his hand gestures. She wished he did not dislike her so much, not for her own sake, but for Makwa. Robert was aware of her appraising eyes and refused to countenance it, avoiding her gaze.

The wait was even worse for the prisoners in that small, airless room. They did not have the relief of small beer. The balding man continued his praying, the dishevelled woman her moaning, while the woman accused of murder still sat composed as if she was listening to a Sunday sermon and seeing some great truth revealed beyond it. Tom sat down on the floor with his back to the wall and closed his eyes hoping that these walls would stay in their place. He tried to empty his mind to prevent it from running over all the pros and cons of his case and trying to calculate how they had been viewed by the jury. He was not successful in this exercise so he focused on something that gave him pleasure. Simon Bailey was safe in Scotland preaching the word, fulfilling what he believed to be God's purpose for him. If this case should go against him at least he had the satisfaction of knowing he was partly responsible for Simon's freedom. Other things drifted through his mind, childhood memories of growing up in Salisbury and he lost all track of time. He was seeing his thirteen year old self walking in the water meadows holding hands with Catherine Marshall, a neighbour's daughter with whom he fancied he was deeply in love. She had corn coloured hair and sky blue eyes just like Lizzie Norrington. The image of Catherine changed into Elizabeth. The meadow was full of daisies and buttercups. She had made a daisy chain and laughing, put it around his neck. Then she stood on tiptoe and kissed him on the lips. He opened his eyes, disturbed by the image and heard Josiah Parry say, "Sir Thomas, the jury has returned. It is time to go back into the hall."

He scrambled to his feet as the prisoners were lined up in order of trial. They were marched out in this formation to stand in front of the bench and ordered to face the judges.

The foreman of the jury handed the papers with the decisions written on them to the clerk of the court, who stood at the side of the bench and solemnly read out the name of the prisoner and the jury's verdict. The first two were found guilty and were led back into the holding room. The third was declared innocent and collapsed onto his knees thanking God. He was told by Colborne that he was free to go and walked to the back of the room where he was hugged by his children. When the young woman accused of murdering her husband was pronounced guilty a cheer went up from one section of the audience, clearly the family and friends of the murdered man. She however showed no sign of distress and thanked the judges as she was led away.

"The Case of Sir Thomas Mountfield." Tom steeled himself. "Not Guilty."

The words echoed in his head. He feared for a moment that his legs would give way and then he felt Dawn Light's arms around him, saw the tears of relief in his mother's eyes, heard Cecily call out "Oh Thomas!"

"It is an outrage," Bartholomew Hanham ran forward to the bench. He banged his fists down on the table in front of Judge Colborne. "A wicked judgement. That man murdered my nephew, my heir. He has soured my life for ever and you will let him go unpunished."

Richard Colborne demanded that he sit down.

"The Assize is still in session. You are interrupting the reading of the verdicts." As Hanham showed no intention of sitting down he added, "I am well aware of your grief Sir Bartholomew, which I warrant will have increased with the realization of your nephew's true nature, if indeed you were not already aware of it. I will give you the benefit of the doubt because we all know of your long service as a Justice of the Peace. I will also assume that your lawyer, Master Jardine did not inform you that two of your witnesses were convicted felons and the other two simply reporters of hearsay. I need not remind you that conniving in false witness is a serious offence. I shall instruct the Sheriff to make sure that Ralph Lawrence and Richard Shaw do not come into this county again. I ask you again Sir Bartholomew to sit down."

Hanham turned to Thomas who was staring at him intensely. He had no reason to feel sorry for Hanham, a man who wanted him hanged, yet he so wished none of this had happened. He tried to say so but Hanham shouted,

"Don't you address me. I wish to hear no words from you. This is not the last of this matter. I will have revenge for Anthony, you may rely on that."

He pushed aside a court officer who had stepped forward to restrain him and hurried out of the room. Lady Agnes stood for a moment looking at Thomas. He moved towards her.

"I swear to you Lady Agnes, what you have heard today is the truth. I did not mean to kill your nephew. Do not think it sits easy on my conscience."

"I know." Her voice was so low he barely heard it before she turned and ran after Bartholomew.

"Sir Thomas, you are free to go. Would you kindly do so and let the business of this court continue?" Colborne's tone was peremptory but he added in a less formal voice with a quick smile at Tom's father, "Robert take your son away and keep him out of trouble in the future. I would advise him to attend church more regularly and to make sure his wife is received into the true faith."

Waaseyaaban took hold of her husband's hand and led him out through the main entrance of the Guildhall into the brightness of the August afternoon. The air around him seemed different to Thomas now he was a free man and he felt a wave of affection flow through him for the familiar streets of Salisbury. As he stood on the Guildhall steps looking up at the sky, Bartholomew Hanham's carriage came around the side of the building at a fast pace and above the rumble of the wheels Tom heard distinctly the word "Murderer."

Dawn Light heard it too. "Do not listen to that false word. Come. "

She tugged at his hand and they walked in the direction from which the carriage had sped. At the side of the hall in the shade of a row of elms, several equipages and horses stood at a hitching rail in front of a drinking trough. Next to his own carriage with Hetty still in the shafts was his stallion.

"Hope- you brought him with you."

"Yes, so you can ride home."

Thomas ran over to the horse and pressed his face into the creature's soft neck. "Oh it is so good to see you. I have missed you so much and I am sure you have not missed me one jot."

All those who had gathered at the Guildhall that day anxious for Tom's safety had followed him out of the building. Godfrey Roper slapped Thomas on the back declaring, "My dear fellow, I am delighted with this outcome, truly delighted." His round face was one huge smile.

"Thank you for all you have done to help me Godfrey."

"Oh the hard work was done by Ezra Holt, not me."

"Where is he? I must thank him too."

"He has an interest in the last case to be heard so he is still inside."

"Well, I must settle up with you about his fee."

"No, no not a bit of it, I shall deal with that, my pleasure. The joyful look in your dear sister's eyes is reward enough for me."

Cecily kissed her husband and then her brother, but one thing troubled her.

"Thomas I am sorry that Grace and Margaret were not here today. I visited them earlier in the week and berated them both for their indifference but it did little to stir their consciences it seems."

"I did not expect them to come Cecily. They gave up on me a long time ago. Besides, I cannot complain of lack of support, look at you all."

He swallowed down a lump in his throat as his mother stroked his cheek and he took her hand and kissed it. Looking over her shoulder he saw Neville Norrington approaching them, flanked by his children. Thomas had not expected to see Elizabeth there. The memory of the water meadows came to him again, how Catherine Marshall had transformed into Elizabeth Norrington. He could taste that kiss on his lips and felt uncomfortable. James congratulated him on gaining his freedom, so relieved that his actions had not resulted in disaster. Sir Neville held out his hand to Thomas and when Tom proffered his own, gave it a brief, firm shake.

"This is the first chance I have had to thank you in person for the service you did my children. I regret that it brought misfortune on you, but at least now justice is upheld."

"James paid me back in full with his courageously spoken testimony this morning. The jury was impressed by your son and by Jacob Whyte." He looked across at the steward who nodded to him. "I have a fancy Sir that you were not in accord with all the praise that was bestowed on me by the witnesses, but I have come to regard James as a friend and I hope you will let him visit me now and then."

James turned anxious eyes on his father, who was indeed reluctant to see Mountfield's influence over his son continue, but all he said was, "This unfortunate affair has shown me that James is man enough to make his own decisions. I am sure he will visit you."

His words did not indicate approval or otherwise. He signalled to Jacob to unhitch the carriage and started to move away when Lizzie, daring his displeasure, spoke to Thomas.

"I am so pleased you are free. If anything bad had happened to you I would never be able to forgive myself."

"Then it is fortunate on both our parts Mistress Elizabeth," Tom replied in a quiet voice. "It is good to see you so well recovered and looking yourself again." She was indeed restored to her full beauty; her skin had regained its glow. The deeper blue of her cloak reflected in her eyes and made them seem a shade darker than he remembered. She looked up into his face thinking that he was the one to give concern. The strain of his struggle with the menacing walls showed on his face and there were dark shadows beneath his eyes.

"You do not look well yourself. You must rest and let Dawn Light and Joan spoil you."

"I am well enough now I am a free man and it is exercise I need, not rest."

It was so hard for Lizzie to submit to her father steering her away from Thomas. As she walked to the carriage, she looked back for another view of him and caught sight of the expression on Dawn Light's face. It was resentment. She had never looked at Elizabeth in that way before. Waaseyaaban had been standing beside her husband enjoying everyone's happiness at his freedom until the Norringtons approached. Then her face hardened. She blamed them for eighteen weeks of lonely nights longing for Thomas, the frustration of parting every day after half an hour only in his company. None of it would have happened if that boy and his sister had not come to their house. She had been in danger of being parted from Tom forever. She could not forgive the Norringtons for creating such a possibility.

Robert Mountfield was standing back from the group around Thomas, allowing the others to express their joy. Now he held out his arms to his son and this time Tom walked willingly into his embrace, hugging his father with feeling.

"You look exhausted my boy. Why don't you come home with your mother and me? Rest awhile, have a meal with us. Cecily and Godfrey will come too."

Thomas shook his head. "I am truly grateful for all you have done on my behalf, all those visits to the Sheriff and Hanham to try to persuade them to release me from the Bridewell into your care, making sure that the judges were aware of the true nature of the commissioners visit to my house. Your energy and commitment to my cause has touched me, but I will not come back to the house because you still do not acknowledge Waaseyaaban as my wife. I will not back down on this. Jesu Father, you heard a high court judge acknowledge her this morning and still you will not do so."

"Thomas I –"

"No please, I don't wish to argue about it now. I want to go home- my home- to be with my wife and my household, walk in the woods with the dogs, feel like a human being once more. I am sure Mother and Cecily will visit me soon. Come with them.

I would welcome the chance to see more of you, although I cannot promise that we will not be at odds. You will have to risk that."

Turning away from his father, he kissed his mother and sister, then much to her surprise he lifted Joan Bushy up in his arms and put her into the carriage.

"Mistress Bushy, the fearsome defender of my character, I was sure the jury would favour me after your evidence. They dare not gainsay you. I liked in particular your phrase about flying to the moon. Let us go home Joan. I know you are dying to feed me."

Toby Aycliffe was already in the driver's seat. He was feeling very pleased with himself because earlier Sir Robert had pressed four gold coins into his hand, two for himself and two for Ned Carter as a reward for their loyalty to Thomas. He had not expected any reward but was not so prosperous that he could afford to refuse and knew Ned would feel the same.

Waaseyaaban jumped up beside Joan with the lithe ease of a cat, while

Tom mounted Hope. As Toby turned Hetty in the right direction Dawn Light
gave Robert a triumphant look, underlining the fact that Thomas had chosen
her over his father. Her regret that her Makwa should sorrow over the breach
with his father was genuine, yet when she was in Sir Robert's company she
could not resist challenging him.

"Damn the woman," Mountfield cursed as he watched the party
disappear down the road. "Did you see how she looked at me- so proud?"

Lady Anne slipped her arm beneath his and squeezed it in a comforting
gesture. "You will not win this one Robert. She knows she is Tom's wife. You
will not shake her confidence by denigrating her and the more you do so, the
farther you push Tom away."

"I have to admit," he conceded, "That she looks almost acceptable when
she dresses with taste. If Thomas would insist she did so all the time it would
help. At least she conducted herself with dignity during the trial."

"Well, what did you expect her to do" Cecily cut in, "Dance around
in circles playing a drum and howling to frighten the jury? Honestly Father,
you are as bad as that malicious woman in the grey shawl with her heathen
ceremonies nonsense. Now I am going home. Godfrey is hungry, I can tell by
the way he wolfed down all Joan's biscuits."

She lifted her skirts and set off Godfrey in close attendance, leaving her
parents little choice but to follow her.

Thomas, as he rode across the plain enjoying the sensation of his stallion's
sure rhythm, had no desire for conversation.

When he had ridden to Salisbury early that morning securely boxed
in by officers of the law, he paid no heed to the landscape around him. Now
he could luxuriate in the openness of the plain with its soft undulations and
patchwork of colours; the green of ancient mossy turf with narrow track-ways
crossing it, interspersed with ploughed land showing the dark brown clay soil
contrasted with patches of corn and barley, red-gold in the sunlight. Here under
this vast vault of sky he was certain that the universe was limitless and thanked
God for his freedom. High above him a gang of crows was harrying a buzzard,
driving it from their territory. The buzzard soared higher to avoid them, the sun
emphasizing the whiteness under its broad wings. The crows were persistent,
eager to be rid of a dangerous predator. He knew the crows were acting on
instinct but they irritated him. He wanted them to leave the buzzard in peace.
His elation at being free was tempered by images of his fellow prisoners in the
holding room; the woman with the matted hair half mad with fear, the three

men in chains, foul smelling and cowed. The thick puss that suppurated from the sore on the leg of one of them suggested that he had been in leg irons for a long time. Tom was disturbed by the fact that he was able to buy preferential treatment, not just with coinage but because of the status of his family. No peasant would keep his animals in the conditions that prevailed in most prisons for those unfortunates with no money or influential friends. He castigated himself yet again for wallowing in his own self-pity while Peter Tucker had been swinging on a gibbet. In an attempt to drive these thoughts from his head he rode close to the carriage and asked Waaseyaaban to join him on the horse. Toby slowed down to enable her to stand up in the carriage and swing her leg over Hope's back to sit behind Tom. He felt better with her arms around his waist and her head resting against his back. The contact soothed him for the remainder of the journey.

Descending from the crest of a steep incline down towards Devizes, Thomas declared his intention to call at the Bridewell.

"Would that be wise Master Tom?" Joan Bushy was dubious. "I think it would be best if we went straight home. The sight of that place will upset you. Toby or Ned can call for the stools and writing implements tomorrow."

Tom had not been thinking about his possessions. It was Daffyd he wished to see and did not feel like making the effort to explain it to them.

"I don't intend to linger there. We can go home past the Bridewell across the Common. It was the way I was first brought there by Josiah Parry, so it will be fitting to return that way in happier circumstances."

Daffyd Williams was trying to read a statement by one of his prisoners that had been written down by Andrew Shepherd. The deputy constable's handwriting was idiosyncratic to say the least and the Welshman was struggling to make sense of it. He had been thinking about Sir Thomas, expecting Josiah Parry to return soon to bring news of the Assizes. When he heard a knock at the door, he assumed it was Parry. Peering through the grill he exclaimed with pleasure to see Tom Mountfield standing outside and hurriedly opened the door.

"Sir Thomas, you are a free man then?"

"I am thank God- well as free as any of us can be in this world."

Daffyd saw the carriage just beyond with Joan Bushy sitting in it. Toby was climbing down from the driver's seat. The wild cat woman with no respect for the handsome velvet gown she was wearing was astride a chestnut horse.

"Come in, come in." he encouraged.

"No Daffyd, I have no wish to step inside this place again. I just came to thank you for the aid you gave me. Your small kindnesses- the open grill, the extra time in the yard- they helped me to hold on to my sanity."

Aycliffe joined them asking Tom if he should collect his possessions. Daffyd told him they were all gathered together in the outer room, standing aside to let Toby pass.

"The level of conversation will not be the same without you," the Welshman said, smiling. "I looked forward to our discussions." Toby barged past them with a stool under each arm and everything else bundled up in Tom's cloak.

"I shall miss you Sir Thomas, as pleased as I am to see you free."

There was genuine regret in Daffyd's voice.

"I cannot say that I will miss you," Tom replied, returning the smile, "But I certainly shall not forget you."

They shook hands and he added, "You will do those kindnesses for others won't you, not just for those who take your fancy or who provide you with tasty pies. You are well aware that many of your prisoners come here because of misfortune, not the evilness of their natures and even the true felons have a right to maintain some dignity."

"It is a cruel world Sir Thomas. You will never be able to change that."

"No, but we can make small inroads. You are in a good position to do that and so am I if I come out of my forest more often."

Daffyd watched him climb into the saddle in front of Dawn Light and head off towards the Common followed by the carriage.

"I shall miss the treats from that basket too," he said to himself as he closed and bolted the door, "By Christ I will and there's a fact now."

Chapter Nine

THOMAS MOUNTFIELD TOOK A while to adjust to his freedom. The day after he came home he walked the whole of his woods accompanied by Waaseyaaban and the wolfhounds, stretching his back and leg muscles to the limit to take the cramped feeling out of them. He appreciated the comfort of his bed after weeks of sleeping on the floor, but he was restless at night. He slept in short snatches waking up feeling confined and anxious. Every night during his first week back home Waaseyaaban woke to find he was no longer beside her. She knew where he would be; either out in the gallery looking up through the skylight or sitting under the covered walk outside the back door.

On Friday night he was in neither of those places. She lit a lantern and went searching for him. She discovered him sitting against the trunk of an apple tree in the orchard, enjoying what coolness he could find on that sticky August night. She asked no questions and hanging the lantern on the tree, curled up beside him. They were woken next morning by Hector pushing his wet nose into their faces.

Tom felt hot and his head was pounding when he stood up. He blamed it on the heat and the closeness of the atmosphere. When he went into the house with his wife to have breakfast, despite the appetising smell, he had no desire to eat. The timber cart needed loading with a consignment of timber for Pocock's yard and he decided to start work on that. Ned and Toby would arrive soon to give him a hand. Joan chided him for skipping breakfast. He was eating far too little in her opinion and she was worried about him. He promised to be very hungry by midday after a hard morning's work and left her with Dawn Light and Sarah bottling the crop of early plumbs to preserve them. The dogs followed him out and meandered around the yard, listless in the heat, while Tom began tossing lengths of timber into the cart outside the barn.

He had been working for less than ten minutes when a wave of dizziness came over him. He grabbed hold of the cart to keep himself upright. Heat was rising up inside him burning his chest and throat. "Not now," he said aloud. "I don't want to deal with this now." He recognised the signs. He had suffered several bouts of fever just after returning from the Netherlands. For two days now he had tried to ignore those signs, blaming his rising temperature on the weather, but he could deny it no longer. He could feel the strength draining out of him.

In desperate need of a drink to ease his throat he took an unsteady walk into the barn where there was a barrel of beer with two tankards standing on the lid. He pushed the lid off the barrel and dipped a tankard into it, then sitting down on a heap of straw, he took a long drink. Hope and Hetty both turned their heads in their stalls, wondering perhaps if they were to be let out in to the pasture. When Tom tried to stand up his legs would not obey and he sat down again. He made two more attempts to stand without success. On the third try the thumping in his head was so severe he could scarcely see and he fell back into the straw, the tankard clattering to the floor and rolling towards the open door of the barn.

Toby and Ned rode into the yard on Samson at the usual time, both of them whistling a tune and drumming their heels in rhythm on the shire's flanks. They were in good spirits. Their wives had been thrilled with the gold pieces and showered praises on them, an unusual event, particularly in Toby's case. His Bella had a sharp tongue and was quick to criticize; to be in her good books was like a holiday. He took Samson over to the pasture and let him loose. When he returned, Ned had already begun to load some more of the timber.

"Looks as if Master Tom has already made a start," Toby said, joining his cousin at his labour. They worked away for a while until Ned stopped and wiping his brow commented, "I wonder where he is. It's not like him to start a job and not come back to it."

Toby agreed, adding," He has not been himself since he came back, very quiet, troubled. Don't look to me as if he is getting much sleep."

Ned grinned. "Well, I wouldn't be if I had been away from my wife for five months, especially one like Dawn Light."

"I did not mean that. Joan says he isn't eating well either. This whole business has shaken him more than he would admit."

He was looking towards the barn as he spoke and the sun striking a reflection from the tankard in the doorway caught his eye.

"What's that?"

"What's what?"

"That shining up by the barn door."

He walked over to take a look, picking up the tankard and turning it around with a puzzled expression on his face.

"It's a beer tankard."

"Perhaps the wind blew it out."

"There is no wind."

Toby went into the barn. It was dark and shadowy after the bright sunlight. He could not see much until he adjusted his vision. Hetty was stamping her feet in her stall and Ajax came out to meet him.

"Hello Ajax old lad, where's your master then?"

He reached forward to pat the dog and saw beyond him a body sprawled in the straw. Hector was lying close to Thomas, licking his hand. Toby ran to him calling, "Master Tom, are you hurt?" He lifted him forward in his arms. Thomas was insensible, his breathing laboured and he was shivering although he was wet with perspiration.

"Ned, Ned, get in here quick."

Carter ran in to find Toby splashing water from a bucket on Tom's face in an effort to revive him. It had no effect.

"He is burning with fever. That poxy Bridewell must be full of evil fumes.

Remember how that griping sickness afflicted him a few weeks back. That dung heap in the yard wafts its vapours everywhere and the walls of the cell were damp when it rained and who knows what other disease ridden folk had been in there before him."

"It looks bad Toby," his cousin said, his face anxious. "We must take him in the house."

Toby lifted him under the arms and Ned took his feet. They hurried across the yard flanked by the wolfhounds. Joan Bushy opened the back door to put a bowl of scraps outside ready to take to the chickens later.

"Whatever has happened?" she called out.

"We found him lying in the barn. He is full of fever," Ned explained.

Joan put her hand on Tom's forehead and drew it back in horror.

"Oh dear Lord, his blood is on fire. I knew he was unwell. He should never have started to load that cart."

She turned to her daughter, who had come out of the kitchen, her eyes wide.

"Where is Dawn Light?"

"Gone to the front porch to get more plumbs Mother."

"Fetch her."

As Sarah ran along the passage, Joan instructed the cousins to carry Tom upstairs. She went ahead of them warning, "Gently now, gently, take care with him."

Between them Dawn Light and Joan removed his sweat-soaked clothes, dried him off and put a clean shirt on him. Within minutes damp patches began to appear on the fresh garment. Dawn Light sat beside the bed bathing his face and neck with a damp cloth in an attempt to cool him down.

Joan went to the kitchen to make an infusion of thyme and liquorice which was excellent for reducing fever. She instructed Ned and Toby to get back to work for there was nothing else they could do to help now. When anything distressing happened Sarah was far too eager seek consolation by following Ned Carter around. While Joan poured hot water on to the herbal mixture and left it to infuse, Dawn Light continued her efforts to cool her husband's burning skin. Tom's eyes flickered open. His vision was blurred and for a moment he thought he was in his cell in the Bridewell. He felt as if his whole body was on fire and he tried to sit up, but Dawn Light prevented him with firm pressure on his shoulders.

"No, you are sick. You lay still and rest."

"Waaseyaaban." He was relieved to realise that he was lying in his own chamber. "I am so hot. I need air."

"You have fever. Toby find you in the barn. That bad place where they shut you up, all the hurt you feel inside, bring this fever on you."

"I am so sorry," he murmured, as his concentration slipped away from him. "You have had worry enough and now this."

She stroked his hair and soothed, "You need not say sorry. They are the ones to be sorry, they who bring trouble on you. We will make you well again Thomas."

He loved the way she spoke his name with an emphasis on the last syllable almost as if they were two separate words.

"No one speaks my name like you."

"No one is like me."

By the time Joan Bushy's medicine was ready to be administered Tom was delirious. He no longer recognised them and had entered a world beyond the real one. This fevered world was full of people from the past as well as the present, some of them long dead. He spoke to them aloud, often in great agitation. At one point he was shouting in a language Joan could not understand as she tried to calm him. Waaseyaaban however, although she did not know what the words meant, recognised the sound of the language. Tom was back in Flushing with Philip, giving instructions to the Flemish population.

"He is that town across the water where we live before the big fight when Philip is hurt bad," she explained to Joan." I hate that place- too small, too many people, much sickness. Soldiers die from sickness. It is in his mind often though he does not speak of it."

Joan nodded. Dawn Light had shared the rigours of life on campaign with her husband with a resilience that filled the housekeeper with admiration when she dwelt on it.

"We must send word to Lady Anne and Sir Robert," she said.

"No, I do not want them here. Father try to take him away while he is too sick to say no."

"My dear, he is their only son. They love him deeply. This fever is severe. Should the worst happen- which pray God it will not- they should be here beside him. I will send Ned or Toby over to Dudley Dent now with a message."

They arrived the next day, Sir Robert, Lady Anne, Cecily and Godfrey to find Tom's condition unchanged, spells of unconsciousness broken by restless delirium, his temperature dangerously high. Waaseyaaban sat close to her husband holding his hand possessively. His mother pulled up a chair on the opposite side of the bed and took hold of his free hand, her eyes full of unshed tears. Robert Mountfield paced about the room firing questions at Joan Bushy adopting his usual tactic of pretending that Dawn Light did not exist. Offended on her behalf Cecily put a comforting arm around her sister-in-law's shoulder.

"I could see he was not himself after the trial," Robert was saying.

"Of course he was not himself," Cecily threw at him, "Would you be your normal self if you had been shut up in a six foot square box for eighteen weeks Father, with the possibility of being found guilty of murder hanging over you like the sword of Damocles? That stomach sickness he suffered weakened him. It is no surprise that he has succumbed to this fever."

Robert was about to reply when he stopped and moved closer to the bed. Thomas was muttering in a low but distinct voice and it was evident to his father that he was addressing Simon Bailey.

"Simon it will be safer by sea- up the west coast- Matthew will help us-the Dorset maid- Scotland."

The sequence was disjointed but the words made clear enough sense to Robert.

"By God, did you hear that Anne? He was involved in Bailey's escape. He lied to me. Jesu, will this son of ours never learn sense? Was anyone else here complicit in this deception?"

Cecily looked at Godfrey.

When she had discovered that Bailey had been due to visit Tom at Christmas and nothing had been said to her about it, she did suspect that her brother was keeping something from them and had shared her suspicions with Godfrey. They thought it best not to mention it to Sir Robert.

Joan Bushy felt obliged to tell Mountfield the truth; how Simon had come to Thomas for advice and Tom had ridden away with him the next day, not revealing any details of his plan.

"They have been friends for many years Sir," she defended. "Master Tom would never betray one of his friends and there is no harm in Simon Bailey. He is a good, honest, God-fearing man and did not deserve to be locked up any more than Master Tom did."

Robert let out an explosive sigh.

"Well I must give you all credit I suppose for managing to deceive a seasoned interrogator like Walter Amor, but if Bailey is captured I will be in a most difficult position."

"Oh what does that matter now," Lady Anne replied, "Thomas' health is all we must consider."

"You are right. We must take him back to Salisbury where he can be cared for properly by Enoch Price."

The physician Enoch Price had attended the Mountfield family for some years. As a young man, just come to Salisbury, he was the physician called to the house when the seven year old Tom fell out of that oak tree. Sir Robert had great faith in his skill.

"Price will advise us how best to reduce this fever."

"No!" Waaseyaaban stood up, her eyes smouldering with anger, "You will not take him away. He is my husband. I look after him. I know what you do; you shut him away in big house and not let me see him. We are parted too long already- no more. You think that if you take him back with you, he stay with you and not return to me. You are wrong, my Makwa always return to me. The hurt is not yours alone; the hurt is in his heart too because you make him choose between us."

Robert Mountfield had never struck a woman but he was hard put to it not to raise a hand to her. There was something masculine about the way she challenged him and her last accusation had touched a nerve. It was Joan Bushy once again who mediated.

"Sir Robert, I don't wish to contradict you but I must say that Master Tom is too sick to be moved. The journey to Salisbury in an open carriage across the plain in this heat could kill him. Bring the physician here by all means but Dawn Light and I can give him as good care as anyone."

"Medicine men bring not so good as medicine I make with Joan."

Waaseyaaban sat back down again and taking up the cloth began to bathe Tom's face in a way that suggested she had no more to say to his father.

"You are fortunate young woman that my self- control is strong." Robert was indignant to be so dismissed. "What Joan says is logical however. I would not put him in more danger. I must return home because I have official duties to perform that cannot be put aside, but I shall be back tomorrow with the physician whether you like it or not."

"I shall stay here Robert and help Dawn Light care for Thomas. I am sure she will not deny me that right." Anne looked across at her and Waaseyaaban gave her a terse nod. Cecily also wished to stay.

"I cannot leave Thomas in this state. I must stay with him," she said to her husband.

Godfrey squeezed her hand. "Of course my sweet, of course you must be with your brother. I will come back with Sir Robert and Enoch Price tomorrow to see how he fares. I will visit St Edmund's Church and ask the minister to say prayers for him."

When the men had left, Anne smiled at Joan.

"Joan Bushy you are worth your weight in gold. I bless the day I took you into my service."

The housekeeper was embarrassed by this unexpected praise and took refuge in explaining the frequency of dosing Thomas with the herbal infusion. The four women took turns to sit with him or rather three of them took turns; Waaseyaaban refused to leave his side. No amount of persuasion could convince her to leave him for more than the few moments it took to carry out bodily functions. She slept on the floor beside the bed, waking at the slightest sound. It was as if she still feared that his father would spirit him away if she dropped her guard.

When Robert and Godfrey returned next day with Enoch Price the physician pulled a grave face and shook his head. He declared that there was nothing to be done. They could only pray that the fever would break soon. If it held its intensity for much longer he was unlikely to survive. He recommended they continue to bathe him with cold water and approved of Joan's remedy for fever reduction. All they could do was wait.

Lizzie Norrington held the embroidery out at a distance to get a better perspective of it and screwed her face up with dissatisfaction. She was edging a linen handkerchief with delicate flowers in red and blue silks, but she fancied that her stitching was too big. It did not create the effect she had envisaged. She began to unpick some of it, then gave up and cast it aside.

Sir Neville had gone to visit his sister, Lady Ashbury, in Bath. Elizabeth could have gone with him but she had no wish to be subjected to Aunt Jennet's eagerness to match her up with another husband. Jennet had no understanding of how her niece's ordeal at the hands of Anthony Hanham had left her unwilling to contemplate re- marriage for some time. She was a hard, practical woman not inclined to spare anyone's feelings. Sir Neville on the other hand showed sensitivity towards Elizabeth. He had made one bad mistake and was in no hurry to press his daughter to marry again.

Neither he nor Lady Ashbury were aware of the added complication in Lizzie's case, her yearning for Thomas Mountfield. She had made up her mind that she could not marry again. It would not be fair to any husband because she could love only one man, a man who was not free to love her. She was certain now that he was attracted to her, that there could be something between them if it were not for Waaseyaaban. His devotion to his wife seemed unshakeable yet Lizzie was not inclined to give up hope. She convinced herself that if she could find a way to spend some time with him she could influence his feelings in her favour.

James had ridden out early that morning to visit Thomas. Neville Norrington may have indicated his belief that his son was mature enough now to make his own decisions but James knew his father would prefer him to sever the connection with Tom. The boy thought it politic to take the opportunity while Norrington was away. This time Elizabeth did not write a letter to Thomas. She did not know what to put in it except those things she must not say and he would not reply anyway.

She picked up the sketch she had been drawing in charcoal earlier that morning of the view across the meadows to the river, visible from the pavilion mound in their garden. Turning the sheet of paper over she began to sketch Tom Mountfield's face, her mind's eye delighting in every detail. While she was a competent artist and achieved a fair likeness, she could not capture the depth of expression in his eyes, nor could she get the shape of his mouth exactly right.

She was attempting to remedy that when her brother burst into the room in the way he always did when he was excited or agitated.

She had not expected him to return so soon and the look on his face frightened her. Even so she had the presence of mind to turn her drawing back over to show the landscape.

"You are back early, is anything wrong?"

"Oh Lizzie, Tom is very sick. He has a terrible fever. The physician fears for his life. They let me into his bed chamber for a short while. He is in a delirium and knows no one."

Elizabeth felt cold all over. She recalled the strain on his face when they spoke after the trial.

"His mother and sister are staying at the house to help care for him," James rattled on releasing his tension in the words that tumbled out. "His father visits most days. I felt myself an intruder with all the family there- well not all the family. Joan Bushy was angry because his older sisters had not come although a message was sent to them. I came away to tell you and also because Dawn Light did not want me there."

"She told you that?"

"No, not in words, but the look she gave me- if eyes could kill I would have died on the spot. She blames us for coming to Tom for help. I'm sure she hates me and I tried so hard to put it right when I gave evidence at the trial."

He was so distressed that Elizabeth put her arm around his shoulder and hugged him.

"Of course you did. You spoke nobly on behalf of Thomas, he said so himself. James, I must go to see him. If his life is truly in danger I could not bear to think—"

She cut off her sentence not wishing to hear the possibility of his death spoken aloud.

"But Father will be angry with you. He expressly forbade you to see Tom again and Dawn Light will not welcome us."

James was in a quandary, half wishing to return to the house with his sister, yet half afraid to do so. He dreaded arriving there to be told Thomas had died and he imagined the look in Dawn Light's eyes being burned into his brain forever. Elizabeth was hurrying out of the room, calling back over her shoulder, "I will face up to Father when it is needful and I am not afraid of Dawn Light."

She found Jacob Whyte in his work room going over the receipts for the month's household purchases and told him where she was going and why.

"I know Father would expect you to stop me, so I am willing to say I left without your knowledge. Nothing you say will dissuade me from going."

Jacob put the receipts into the drawer of his desk and donned his jerkin in the precise way that he did everything.

"I think your father would chide me more if I did not escort you Mistress Elizabeth."

"James is coming back with me."

"It will be more seemly if I come also. I will not impose myself on Sir Thomas' family of course. It is not my place, although I am most sorry to hear this news."

He called for the under-steward and put him in charge of the house in his absence, then sent instructions out to the Smith twins to saddle two horses. James' horse was still standing in the yard where he had left it in his eagerness to tell his sister about Thomas. Giles and Peter Smith watched them ride out of the main gate and exchanged a puzzled glance.

"Wonder where they are bound?" said Giles, rubbing his chin thoughtfully. "Jacob made no mention of needing a horse earlier and Master James has only just come back."

His brother was equally intrigued. "Little Mistress Innocent hasn't been riding since all that trouble began. Something's in the wind. Wheeler will know, I warrant. He pokes his ferret face in everything."

They would be disappointed because this was something of which Mark Wheeler had no knowledge.

Sarah Bushy was brushing out the front porch when she saw the Norringtons and Jacob Whyte riding towards the house. She ran back along the passage to the kitchen where her mother was cooking.

"Mother, that James Norrington has come back. His sister is with him and Jacob Whyte. I expect Master Whyte has come to see you. He likes you."

"Don't be foolish my girl."

Despite this admonition, Joan took off her apron, straightened her skirts and adjusted her coif before she went to the door. The thought came to mind that Thomas would have teased her if he had seen her do that and her heart ached. James did not fancy facing Dawn Light again that day so he made for the kitchen to be greeted by Hector and Ajax.

"If you would care to sit in my little parlour Master Whyte, I will be back directly and serve you something to drink," Joan said after Jacob explained that he had no desire to intrude on the Mountfield family at such a worrying time. 'Such a proper man' she thought as she conducted Elizabeth upstairs,' So careful of the feelings of others.'

"Mistress Bushy," Lizzie asked her, "Is he as sick as James says? My brother does have a habit of exaggerating. Is his life truly in danger?" Joan stopped halfway up the stairs, replying, "The fever is very severe and we do fear for him, but Master Tom has a strong constitution."

"I would not have imposed on you if his illness was only a slight one. Oh I hope his mother and sister will not find my visit inappropriate. Perhaps I should not have come but I could not bear to-"

Once again she stopped in mid-sentence afraid of exposing her feelings too transparently. Joan smiled at her.

"I know how much you admire him. I am sure Lady Anne and Mistress Cecily will welcome your concern."

Lizzie noticed that she did not mention Dawn Light and wondered if Tom's wife had spoken to the housekeeper about her resentment towards the Norringtons. Joan opened the bed chamber door and announced Elizabeth. Cecily was sitting in the corner of the room reading aloud to Lady Anne from a leather-bound book. Waaseyaaban was in her usual place beside the bed, bathing Tom's face at intervals and talking to him in her own language in a low, rhythmic tone. Both Anne and Cecily rose to greet Elizabeth and she curtseyed to them demurely. If they were surprised to see her, they did not show it. Neither of them had got a clear look at her on the day of the trial for she had worn her hood up over her head throughout to please her father. Cecily was impressed by her natural beauty and grace. It was just the kind of beauty that had attracted Thomas in the past before he sailed to Roanoke and was captivated by Waaseyaaban. She knew of several women who had enjoyed his smiles and compliments, sighing after him even when it became clear that he intended to make no declaration of love. Simon Bailey once told her that her handsome brother had quite a reputation for flirting when they studied together at the Middle Temple. This bothered Simon, who was always of a constant nature and had married as soon as he set up in practice. He knew Thomas was not shallow though and came to realise that behind his dalliance was a genuine desire to find a lasting love. He found it in an unexpected place. Cecily had been so happy for him when she first heard about Waaseyaaban and opposed her father's attitude from the start. Looking at Elizabeth, so different from her brother's exotic Croatan wife, she wondered about Tom's feelings for her. It was clear to her that the girl was besotted with Thomas. Her attempts to hide it were to no avail.

Lady Anne invited Lizzie to take a chair by the bed, but she shook her head.

"No thank you, I will not stay long. I had to come. He has done so much for me." She dared to look directly at Dawn Light adding, "When James told me the news I was so distressed."

Waaseyaaban's eyes were full of scorn. "You have cause to be dis-tress-ed." She broke that last word up into staccato syllables. It was like the sting of a whip to Elizabeth. Cecily was surprised by the venom in her sister-in-law's voice and intervened before more could be said.

"He is quite peaceful at present. He alternates between a restless delirium when he tosses and turns talking to himself constantly and the state he is in now."

Lizzie drew closer to the bed. Tom was lying very still, his face flushed, his shirt wet with perspiration. His breathing sounded ragged and painful as if the heat of the fever had scorched his chest and throat.

"It is as if the very force of the delirium exhausts him and he falls into this insensible state," Cecily continued. "Then the heat of it flares up again and he is restless once more. This morning he was murmuring so earnestly about the order of the universe. I wish I knew who was in his fevered thoughts as he spoke."

Lizzie's heart lurched. Could he have been recalling his conversation with her that night they gazed at the stars through the skylight? She fancied that Dawn Light penetrated her thoughts and was mocking her.

"Is there nothing that can be done for him?" she asked

It was Lady Anne who replied. She had taken the chair that she offered to Elizabeth earlier and was holding her son's hand in both hers.

"We feed him regular doses of a fever remedy and do all we can to cool his body down. The physician is hopeful that the fever my break within the next two days."

"And if it does not?"

"Then his system may not be able to sustain it and prayer may be our only helper."

Lizzie wondered at his mother's calm demeanour, how she could look so elegant and self-possessed when she must be struggling with such emotion. She wished then that she had not come. She was an outsider, unable to do anything, not even touch him. He was encompassed around by such love and care that excluded her. She longed to hold his hand, relieve his discomfort, stroke his hair, but she was irrelevant. Should he die, she must conceal the full extent of her grief and all she would have left was his writing on that piece of paper and the memory of the gentle way he had stroked her hands with his thumbs before sending her back to her father. The pain of this realisation was exquisitely sharp. She felt tears prick at the back of her eyes and it was as much as she could do to prevent herself from running out of the room. "I will impose on you no longer now that I have expressed my concern. James and I must return home now. I would be grateful if you could let us know if there is any change in his condition."

Anne could see how uncomfortable the girl felt and made no attempt to dissuade her from leaving. She promised to send word to Norrington Hall without delay, whatever the news. Lizzie dropped her another curtsey and left the room in what she hoped was a dignified manner after one last look at Thomas. Out in the gallery she stopped under the skylight. The sky was a hard, unrelenting blue, so different from the softness of that starry night. She was startled by a light footstep behind her and turning, found Dawn Light standing at her shoulder.

"You do not come here again." She fired her words at Lizzie like pistol shots in a low voice. "I do not want you here. You and that foolish boy bring trouble on Thomas. If he die now, you are to blame."

"No, I would do anything for this not to have happened. We did not realise at the time that our actions would harm him. I could not harm him I –"

"Love him?" Waaseyaaban completed her sentence. "You do not understand love. You make your big eyes at him, act as if it is his words, his mind you want, but you desire him with your body. Many women desire my Makwa."

Elizabeth backed away from her, intimidated by her intensity, not wanting to listen but unable to prevent herself.

"I think at times he desire you here." Dawn Light made a gesture between her legs that needed no interpretation, "But not here."

Her other hand touched an area over her heart. "This does not trouble me. I tell him take girl to bed, show her your power, but he does not do this, so maybe he does not desire you so much after all. You write him letters in Bridewell. You know what he do with them? He burn them."

"Stop it," Elizabeth cried out, turning away from those scornful eyes. "Why are you being so cruel? I know he does not love me but I do love him in a different way from you- I do."

Waaseyaaban laughed and walked back towards the bed chamber. Lizzie fled down the stairs trying to shut out that disturbing laugh echoing in her ears. She was in such haste she trod on the end of her skirt and almost fell headlong. James and Jacob were in conversation with Joan Bushy in the kitchen when Elizabeth hurried through the door. She was so agitated that they all feared the worst had happened. James jumped to his feet.

"Lizzie, he isn't - ?"

"No," she cut across his words, "No, his condition is unchanged. I am distressed to see him so ill that is all. I wish to go home now. Lady Anne has kindly agreed to send word should his condition change."

James looked at Jacob Whyte, who was also surprised by her lack of composure and the urgency of her desire to leave although he readily complied with her wishes. As Joan followed the visitors out into the corridor to see them to the front door, she murmured to her daughter, "I fear Dawn Light has been less than kind."

James also suspected that his sister may have had a confrontation with that strange woman. The theory was proved correct when on their way down the corridor both Joan and James looked up to see Waaseyaaban standing in the gallery staring down at them. She made a swift, chopping motion with her hand, which could only mean good riddance.

Three days after Elizabeth Norrington's painful visit Tom's fever broke. It came to crisis point in the night. Lady Anne and Cecily were resting in the next bed chamber. Waaseyaaban dozed in her chair beside Tom's bed when she was jerked awake by him shouting and trying to get up. His eyes were wide open and staring.

"To the left, the left. They have broken through on the left. Plug the hole in the line. Press forward. Where's Harry? Find Harry."

She found it difficult to hold him down as he struggled to throw her off. His mother and sister woken by the noise ran into the room. Between them they managed to get him back into bed. His heart was beating so fast they could feel it under their hands as if it was trying to leap out of his chest and the veins under his skin throbbed. Joan Bushy appeared in the doorway, her face pale in the light of the candle she carried.

"This is the crucial time Joan," Anne said softly. "His life is in the balance now. Pray hard."

He continued to rally his troops and fight against the restraining hands as if they were Spaniards for more than five minutes until the heat in his brain and the speed of his heart beat proved too great. He went limp in their arms; if it were not for the faint sound of his laboured breathing they might have feared he was dead, so swift was the change. Waaseyaaban made sure he was lying comfortably and pulled the coverlet up around him, kissing him as she did so. These few days had proved to Lady Anne how much Dawn Light loved her son.

Her devoted care and tenderness contrasted with those bolder, more outlandish ways that so often jarred the sensibilities and shocked the propriety of respectable folk. Anne had to admit that she wished her son had chosen a more suitable wife, some charming, demure girl like Elizabeth Norrington. The breech between Tom and Sir Robert caused pain to them both and she felt it on behalf of both sides, but beyond that she worried that Thomas was prevented from living his life to the full, so eager was he to insure his wife's happiness. She could not love Dawn Light unreservedly in the way Cecily did, but she could respect her and accept that nothing would separate her from Thomas, only the spectre that hovered in the room now.

"Robert should be here," she said to Cecily.

"He is coming with Godfrey first thing tomorrow Mother."

"Tomorrow may be too late."

Waaseyaaban looked at the tense faces of the other three women in the room and smiled. Despite their prayers they did not have faith that the All Father whom they called God would save Thomas. She knew already that he was safe.

"He will not die now," she announced with complete confidence. "The worst is past. I see this before. He will grow well now. You see."

Her confidence was not misplaced. Over the next hour Tom's temperature dropped. His body grew cooler to the touch and his heart beat steadied. When Robert and Godfrey came the next morning with Enoch Price, Thomas was in a deep sleep, his breathing normal. The physician felt his pulse, lifted his eyelids to inspect the pupils and nodded his satisfaction.

"I believe all may be well now. His vital organs have suffered much strain from the ferocity of this fever; you must not worry if he does not regain his senses for several days. To sleep so sound is good. It is the body's way of healing itself. It will take him a while to regain his strength and he must not exert himself too soon."

It amused Waaseyaaban to see how Robert thanked this man for his pronouncements as if they were the last words in wisdom, when all he spoke was common sense. She knew how to make her Makwa grow strong again without his advice. She stood in the gallery and watched Robert Mountfield shake hands with the physician at the front door. She heard Price say in a patronizing voice, "It was most fortunate that your wife and daughter were able to stay with him. Jesu knows what that foreign woman would be giving him without someone watching her. They have some strange notions about medicine in these wild countries."

Waaseyaaban thought about the medicine the physician from Devizes had given Thomas in the Bridewell which only made him sicker and this man had given him nothing at all. She simmered with indignation over his words and seeing Joan Bushy ascending the back stairs to the gallery, she asked the housekeeper, "Father pay this man?"

"Yes of course."

"For what? He do nothing but speak of things we know already. He does not heal Thomas. It is our medicine, our care that save him."

"Well yes, with some help from Our Gracious Lord."

Dawn Light frowned.

"Last night you do not trust your lord."

"We have a saying my dear, 'the Lord giveth and the Lord taketh away.' We cannot presume to know what God's plans for us are. If He had chosen to take our lovely Thomas from us to be with Him in glory, we would have had to accept it."

"Then why pray?"

Joan smiled at Dawn Light's incisive logic.

"We poor mortals continue to hope that our prayers can move God to pity and change His plan. If He does not, then the prayers will help the soul of the departed on its journey to eternal life."

"I talk to Thomas about this when he is well."

She recalled that her husband had felt the loss of their children with deep grief and found it hard to explain why God would call such little ones to him before they had the chance to live any life at all. Joan patted her arm.

"You do that. He likes you to ask questions about important things."

Robert Mountfield was now coming up the spiral stair in the passage and both women went into the bed chamber, Waaseyaaban thinking how pleased she would be when all the Mountfield family went home so she could have Thomas to herself again.

She had a while to wait. It was two days before Tom woke from his deep sleep with little memory of anything that had happened after he went out that morning to load the wood cart. Anne and Cecily stayed at the house until he was strong enough to sit up and feed himself without assistance. Tom was frustrated by his weakness. He had been confined all spring and summer and he did not intend to spend the autumn in his bed chamber. He was soon taking short walks in the garden. He liked to sit in the front porch or under the covered walkway at the back of the house.

For several weeks he found that he soon tired and fell asleep unexpectedly, sometimes in the middle of a sentence, which embarrassed him, but he regained his strength in stages. By mid-October he was working beside Ned and Toby again and getting annoyed when they attempted to spare him the heaviest jobs. His mother and sister returned to their previous routine of monthly visits. Sometimes Robert came with them. Anne begged him not to exacerbate the differences between him and his son by antagonising Dawn Light while Thomas was still recovering. He could manage to do this only by not speaking to her at all, which suited her well enough. The revelation about Simon Bailey was also troubling Robert and as soon as Thomas was on his feet he could not resist broaching the subject. He chose a moment when he was alone with his son, knowing that Anne would not approve.

"I must have a serious word with you about Simon Bailey."

They were sitting in the parlour and Tom had been explaining the details of his timber business to his father, the quantities cut, the sale outlets and the profits. He was surprised by this sudden change of direction. He gave his father a questioning look. Had something happened during his illness? Was there news that Simon had been caught?

"Joan did not tell you then?"

"Tell me what?"

"In your delirium you said enough to convince me that you had been involved in his escape, despite that innocent front you showed to me and Joan confessed what she knew."

Tom's sigh was one of relief that Simon was still at large, which mattered far more than his father's indignation.

"Amidst all our differences, you have never been a liar Thomas. It is most hurtful that you lied to me, particularly as I went to so much trouble to obtain that written declaration from the archbishop's commissioner that was read at your trial. Should Bailey be taken and forced to speak it would appear that I was complicit in concealing your involvement."

"Pray God he will never be taken. I tried not to lie to you outright. When I first told you of the commissioner's visit, you asked me if I had heard from Simon since and I answered in all truth that I had not. I have received a brief message since then that indicates he is safe."

"Then you know where he is?"

"No, not exactly and I would not tell you if I did."

Robert stood up and uttered a fierce oath.

"Have you any idea what you have got yourself into?"

When this exchange occurred Thomas was still short on energy and a head on clash with his father was the last thing he desired, but he put up a stout defence.

"Of course I am aware of the dangers," he replied with a wry laugh. "I was hardly likely to discuss it with you, a member of the judiciary. Anyway, until my recent misfortune we scarce spoke at all. Until Cecily's wedding I had not seen you for three years."

"And whose fault was that?" Robert shot back.

"As much yours as mine Father. Tell me, would you be proud of a son who betrayed his friends? I have lost many of my close friends. Simon came to me for advice and help. I was not going to advise him to give himself up to the authorities to be thrown into Newgate or the Tower and left to rot in conditions far, far worse than those I have just experienced. You were quick enough to come to my aid."

"Ah, but you were innocent of the crime of which you were accused. Bailey is not."

"I did kill a man Father. All Simon did was declare in public his zeal for the word of God. I do not consider that a crime- unwise in the present climate I grant you, but Simon must always speak out when he considers something unjust. His nature is honest and courageous."

"But he spoke against the Queen." Robert was not inclined to let go of this easily.

"Simon is a loyal subject. What he said was that her statement that she interfered with no man's conscience did not sit well with the persecution of reformers by the archbishop and that her habit of keeping a silver cross and lighted candles in her private chapel confused him. Naive perhaps, but certainly not treasonous."

"The law thinks otherwise my boy."

"In this circumstance I preferred my own judgement and acted on it."

"Indeed you do that far too often Thomas, consider your judgement superior to others who may be far wiser. You have done so ever since you were a boy."

Thomas closed his eyes and leaned his head back in the chair. He felt very tired and wanted this argument to go away. He feared where it was leading, towards what his father considered his greatest lapse in judgement, Waaseyaaban.

"There were no lies in the statement from the commissioner's office," he said, his eyes still closed, shutting out his father's aggressive energy. "They found no evidence that I had any part in it and I certainly do not share the extremity of Simon's religious views, as much as I love him. Should my involvement ever be revealed - and I will endeavour not to fall into another delirium in the presence of officialdom- I will exonerate you and the household of all blame. Now please Father, let this drop. I am weary."

At this point Lady Anne came into the room and Robert had no choice. He did not mention it again.

Apple picking was upon the Mountfield household before Thomas had the chance to adjust himself to how far the seasons had advanced. The orchard was invaded once again by all Ned and Toby's children swarming up the trees like monkeys and Tom had the pleasure of watching Waaseyaaban, as excited as the children, laughing as showers of apples fell on her head and shoulders.

The night of the first apple picking Thomas and his wife lay in bed, wrapped in a contented silence. Dawn Light's head rested on his chest and his arm was around her. The time in the Bridewell and his fever had caused him to lose weight and his bones were prominent to her touch, especially his big shoulder bones. Tonight she fancied he was regaining some flesh at last due to Joan Bushy feeding him up, insisting he eat every scrap of food she put in front of him. The candles were still lit, throwing shadows around the room. All the young people in the orchard had caused Tom to think about James Norrington. Cecily had described how James and Elizabeth visited during his illness and he was touched by their concern. He was not so pleased when Cecily added, "That girl is head-over-heels in love with you Tom. Don't pretend you haven't noticed."

Although he passed it off with a light-hearted remark the notion troubled him. He preferred not to contemplate it. He had hoped however that

James would have come again by now and that Sir Neville's discomfort over the connection was not preventing him. He said so to his wife as he gazed into the shadows.

"He will not come. I tell him never to come again. I do not want them here, boy and his sister."

Tom's brows drew together in a frown.

"You had no right to say that."

"I have right. They are to blame for Bridewell and you falling sick. They must go to father first, not you. I do not forgive them."

"They were two frightened, bewildered young people not sure where to turn. I should be flattered that they trusted me enough to come to me. Besides I was partly to blame for what happened with Hanham. If I had taken them to their father early that morning instead of waiting until the afternoon, they would have been safely in Norrington Hall by the time he arrived at the house. You are too hard on them."

"You are too soft with them."

"I disagree and I shall send a letter tomorrow thanking them for their concern over my health and remind James that he is welcome in this house whether you like it or not."

"That boy is foolish. He is afraid of me."

"I do not blame him. Your hostility is palpable- like a weapon and he does not deserve it. Oh I know I teased him when we first met him with his pompous pronouncements about status and respectability and that childish witch nonsense, but he was only echoing Sir Neville's opinions, with no knowledge of the world to judge by. He has learned much over the past year and learned it well. I see his mind expanding and I would like to help it do so if I can. The boy is in need of a friend and mine are in short supply. I have so few friends these days I can do without you driving them away."

He was always so careful not to suggest that she was in any way responsible for his isolation. He had never spoken to her in quite that way before and she did not care for it. She sat up, leaning over him, looking into his face, her eyes narrowed.

"That girl, she is not so innocent. She say she love you in different way from me. Ha! I tell her I know she desire your body, that I ask you to take her to bed, so she know what a man you are."

"What!" Thomas sat up also, appalled at what he had just heard.

"But I say you will not do it, so you must not care for her and her letters mean nothing for you burn them."

"Waaseyaaban, you should not have spoken to her like that. What devil gets into you sometimes? I burned those letters for safety's sake to make sure no one had cause to assume that there was any past relationship between us, not because I had no care for them. Elizabeth has suffered so much at the hands of that bastard Hanham. It pains me to think that you would hurt her too."

Waaseyaaban turned her back on him, lying down with her knees drawn up and there was a short silence as Tom wondered what Lizzie's reaction must have been to his wife's verbal assault on her.

Then she said in a fierce whisper without turning around, "So you want to be with her, not me- girl with her soft white skin and eyes like sky. I am too brown for you now. She is like soft fruit, easy to bite. She do everything you want, agree with all you say. That is what you want."

"Waaseyaaban," Tom tried to put his arm around her, but she pushed it away. He was firm however and taking her by the shoulders turned her around to face hm. "Listen to me. I do not want to be with Elizabeth Norrington. How could I be satisfied with gentle pliability after living with you for four years? Daffyd Williams calls you the wildcat woman and he is not far wrong. I was captivated by your fierce spirit from the moment I first set eyes on you and I will be to the day I die, God help me. I am your Makwa- always your Makwa, nobody else's."

She put her arms around his neck and said simply, "I die without you."

"I would not wish that my love." He kissed the side of her throat and rested his head there. "But I want you to promise me to call a truce with the Norringtons. I do not ask you to like them. I know you can be implacable, but for my sake if James comes here, do not try to wither him up with those eyes of yours."

She pulled a sulky face, pouting her lips, but he kissed her breast running his hand along the length of her hair in a slow sensuous movement.

"Promise me wife- no more hurtful words."

"I promise," she murmured reluctantly, wrapping her legs around him as he arched his body over her. It would be some while before the candles were extinguished that night.

Chapter Ten

ON ALL SOULS' DAY, 2nd November 1590 Godfrey Roper was elected Mayor of Salisbury by the City Council. The many duties incumbent upon his new office did not prevent him from involving himself in his brother-in-law's project to open a village school. Thomas Mountfield was worried that Nathan Pocock might have changed his mind about handing over his cottage during the weeks Tom was out of commission and unable to keep up the persuasion. He was partly right. Pocock had not re-let it but he had decided he could not give it for nothing. As soon as he felt strong enough to ride to the village and re-open negotiations, Tom used the consignments of timber as a bargaining tool. Nathan bought three full cart loads of timber from him every year. Thomas suggested that Pocock pay him for two loads only in the year to come and he would accept the cottage as payment for the third load. The timber merchant approved the idea in principle, though he asked for a reduced price on the other loads in addition. Thomas stood firm, pointing out that the cottage was in a poor state of repair and it would cost him a goodly sum to bring it to a useable condition. After arguing the point for a while Pocock gave in, knowing it was a good deal and they shook hands on it.

Tom was eager to press forward with the project. He had vowed to himself after his recent experiences to engage more fully with the world, be less introspective and try to make that small difference to the lives of others he had described to Daffyd Williams. He realised how close he had come to dying during his bout of fever and it filled him with purpose. He had survived Roanoke and the Netherlands campaign. Some of those he loved had not. Writing about them was not enough. He must pay tribute to them in his actions by making his own life count for something and he must do this in a way that would not upset the balance of Waaseyaaban's existence. Setting up the school was a good start.

He and Godfrey inspected every inch of the cottage and the land around it, making a list of all the reconstruction needed. They estimated the cost and agreed to go halves on it. Godfrey's business acumen and experience was a valuable asset. He was a pleasure to work alongside, practical, cheerful and positive. Thomas was grateful for his support and Cecily was delighted to see the friendship between them growing. She hoped to use it as an element in her plan to bring Thomas and his father closer together. She was well aware that at present Sir Robert would rather choke than address Dawn Light as his son's wife and Tom was equally adamant that he should do so. Cecily thought that now Robert was visiting Tom's house there was some hope. She intended to persuade her brother and his wife to visit her house regularly as the next step towards some kind of compromise. She had a wardrobe full of beautiful dresses and she hoped that if she could share her pleasure in them with Dawn Light, she might begin to dress more conventionally of her own volition, so Tom would not feel he had pressurized her to do so.

Thomas had written to James and Elizabeth Norrington thanking them for their visit when he was ill and apologising on his wife's behalf for what he described as 'ill-chosen words.' He asked them to excuse her in part because she was stressed about the precarious state of his health and he assured James that he would be welcome at the house any time. After receiving the letter James plucked up the courage to brave Dawn Light and call on Sir Thomas. She kept her promise not to say anything hurtful although the looks she gave James were anything but friendly. Tom took him into the village to show him the work that had begun on the future school house, knowing the boy would be more comfortable away from Dawn Light.

James showed a polite interest but he was keen to hear stories of Tom's adventures and was more interested in the building of the fort at Roanoke. He listened wide-eyed to descriptions of the animals found on the island that did not live in England and was reluctant to leave for home. He knew that his sister longed to see Thomas and hoped Mountfield would give him some personal message to take back to her. She had not revealed to him what Dawn Light had said to her the day she hurried to Tom's sickbed, but she found it hard to hide her hurt even after they received the good news that Thomas was recovering.

Tom on the other hand was wary of discussing Elizabeth too freely beyond polite inquiries after her welfare and yet a few days before he had done something impulsive that he could not fully explain to himself. Riding through Chippenham he stopped at a silversmith and jewellery maker's shop to buy a gift for his wife. The Croatan did not celebrate birthdays and Waaseyaaban had no idea of the exact day of her birth. She had heard her parents talk of her being born at the beginning of winter, after the harvest months had passed, so Tom decided he would mark her birthday in November. He chose an amethyst pendant, faceted to catch the light, set in an oval frame and hung on a silver chain. Waaseyaaban loved all shades of purple. While he waited for the jeweller to put the necklace in a cloth pouch, his eye fell on another jewel that stirred something in his memory.

It was a silver heart with a red stone at its centre. A picture formed in his mind of Lizzie Norrington sitting with him under the tree at Frome fair showing him a trinket almost identical to this one which she had just bought at a stall. He remembered also that James, when first describing to him all the cruelties they had suffered at the hands of Anthony Hanham, had told him how Anthony sneered at Elizabeth's choice in clothes and jewels, tearing the heart locket from her neck and stamping on it. On an impulse Tom bought the silver locket, having a strong desire to send it to Elizabeth. Nothing could compensate her for what she had suffered but he wished her to know that he understood. He felt guilty that she had received cruel words in his own house. He was sure the words had wounded her for Waaseyaaban's perception was sharp and she told him the girl had run down stairs in tears because he did not love her. She was proud that her arrow had hit the mark. Tom wished he could do something to heal the hurt.

When he got home he thought himself foolish for buying the locket and almost gave it to his wife, then changed his mind again, stowing it away at the back of his desk drawer beneath some papers. He could not make up his mind whether more contact with Lizzie would make her unhappier in the long run or whether it would help her to see him in a less romantic light.

When James was about to leave on the day they visited the school, Tom asked him to wait a moment and going back into the house, emerged again carrying a small leather box which he handed to the boy.

"Give this to your sister," Tom said. "She will understand why I send it I am sure. Tell her that despite what my wife said to her when she was last here, I do not blame either of you for what happened and hold you both in high regard. She must not make too much of it, tis but a gesture. I – we- do understand what she has suffered and trust she will find some happiness in the future."

As he watched James ride away he wondered if he had done the right thing. He did not notice Waaseyaaban come out through the porch to join him until she slipped her arm around his waist.

"You keep boy away from me so I do not frighten him," she commented with a teasing smile.

"Hmm- perhaps I did."

"I keep promise. I say nothing cruel to him."

"True, but you did not smile at him either madam."

Tom was trying not to smile at the wicked look on her face. She began to laugh, repeating the word madam several times, amused by the sound of it.

"I have a gift for you, to mark your birthday month, but I am not sure I shall give it to you now," he told her, feigning disapproval.

"Where, where is gift?"

"Ah that is my secret until I decide you deserve it."

She took hold of both sides of his jerkin and tugged at it demanding, "I want to see gift now."

Without another word he disengaged her hands and strolled back into the house. She ran behind him, still insisting, until he turned quickly, took hold of her and slung her over his shoulder like a sack of corn.

"Behave yourself woman or I will dump you in the horse trough," he threatened as he carried her into the library, dropped her into a chair and proceeded to present her with her amethyst pendant.

She wore it next day when she and Joan went to Devizes market in the carriage. Thomas drove them, intending to look around the market and shops for any items that might be useful in the school room. He realised that children who had never held a quill pen in their hands before would have great difficulty learning to use them with skill and much ink would be wasted. He did not want them to be discouraged because the task seemed too tedious and their scripts were covered in ink blots. He decided to buy a consignment of roof slates from the builder's yard, partly to replace the thatched roof of the cottage, which was rotten and to use the rest as slates for the children to chalk their letters and numbers on. Mistakes could then be erased with a cloth and they could be used over and over again.

The market was noisy and smelly, the appetising smells of cooked pies, fresh fruit and herbs mingling with the less agreeable odour of the shambles, animal droppings and unwashed humanity. Joan had brought a basket full of bottled plums to exchange for some commodities she needed. She found Dawn Light to be a great asset as a bargaining tool. Even the most hardened trader hesitated to over-charge when Waaseyaaban's glittering black eyes were fixed on him.

Thomas left them to do their trading while he walked through the old market area near St Mary's Church to visit the builder's yard. He stopped to talk to a donkey over-loaded with packages, standing by the road side head drooping. It was old and tired, patches of its grey coat worn away to reveal red, sore areas of skin and it was painfully thin. Hard callouses adorned its knees like protective armour.

"You should have been put out to grass long ago old fellow," Tom sympathised, rubbing the animal's head with the flat of his hand. "Your master asks too much of you." He looked around for the owner, but no one seemed to be the right candidate. A passer-by suggested he was in the tavern across the way and Tom had half a mind to seek him out and remind him to take better care of his animals. Then he mocked himself for his self-righteousness. The owner might well be in as bad a state as his donkey, earning just enough as a carrier to feed his family. The donkey would not be a priority and yet if it died the carrier's livelihood might die also.

Tom bought an apple from a man wheeling a cart load of fruit to the market. He was at a loss for a moment on how to cut the apple up because he was not wearing his sword, but he spotted a shard of broken glass in the gutter and used it to slice the fruit into pieces, offering it piece by piece to the donkey. It chewed away with its big, yellow teeth, the juice from the apple running down over its lower lip.

"Worrying about donkeys now is it Sir Thomas- not just impoverished felons?"

Tom looked up to see Daffyd Williams standing beside him, hands on hips, that broad smile splitting his face.

"Daffyd, is the Bridewell empty that they have no need of your services?"

"No, plenty of custom still, though none as distinguished as you- the usual petty thieves, drunks and brawlers and none of them with relatives who can cook as well as your housekeeper. I dream about those pies of hers."

Tom smiled and promised to pass on the compliment.

"Our shift pattern has changed," Daffyd continued. "Young Joseph who did the night shift has left town and the new fellow was not happy to work nights all the time, so we agreed to rotate, two weeks on days, two weeks on nights each. That is fine with me. Allows me to walk around the town in the daylight sometimes instead of always in the dark like a poxy bat."

He studied Thomas with appreciation, pleased to see him looking so well.

"It's good to see you so strong and healthy. I heard you were very sick a bit back."

"Where did you hear that?"

It always surprised Tom how widely gossip spread around the local community.

"Joseph Parry when he was going about his constable's duties in the villages met Ned Carter, who said your life was in the balance."

"Well, it was for a while- very bad bout of fever. It first beset me when I returned from the Low Countries and seems to lie dormant in my blood, rising up now and then to remind me of my mortality. I am fully myself again now."Williams nodded. "I can see that."

Thomas was leaning against the donkey cart, stroking the donkey's ears with a casual elegance that stirred the Welshman. He recalled the pleasure of watching Tom climb into the water trough in the Bridewell yard; the deep curve of his back, the perfection of his buttocks and the long, muscular legs. That short while he had held him in his arms to calm him as they sat together on the floor of his cell was something Daffyd could not forget. When those blue eyes rested on him in that way, Tom always felt uncomfortable, even though he chided himself for his reaction.

"I must be about my business," he said, straightening up with determination. "My wife will wonder why I am taking so long."

"The wildcat woman is nearby then?"

As Daffyd spoke, several groups of men were approaching from different directions to cut through to the Port Market. Half a dozen young fellows came out of the tavern opposite, laughing and jostling each other. Another more staid group were walking up from the direction of the Green. Individuals carrying baskets or pushing hand carts wove amongst them. The groups mingled close to where Tom and Daffyd were standing near the entrance to the alley that led through to the market. Daffyd suddenly shouted, "Look out" and gave Thomas a hefty push so that he staggered back into the donkey cart. He felt a stinging sensation across his arm, just above the bicep and was astonished to see that his doublet sleeve had been slashed across. A trickle of blood was seeping on to it. Daffyd Williams was sprinting across the road and disappeared behind St. Mary's Church. Thomas ran after him trying to figure out exactly what had happened. Passing through the churchyard, he came to a complex of dark alleys behind the row of old houses and was not sure which one to take. He did not have to make a choice however for Daffyd emerged from one of them, out of breath and cursing.

"I lost the bastard. He can run like a hare. I reckon he jumped over one of those walls into someone's back garden. Are you hurt?"

Tom shook his head. "No, just a scratch across the arm, but what the devil happened?"

"He tried to kill you Sir Thomas."

"No, surely not."

"He did, I saw it clearly. He came from the back of those lads that bowled out of the tavern and took a quick stab with a dagger. If I had not pushed you the blade would have entered your heart, not caught your arm."

"I can scarce believe it, but if so I am indebted to you once again Daffyd. Did you recognise him?"

"Never seen him before- a skinny whoreson, swarthy with a hooked nose. He had a leather patch over one eye."

A small bell rang in Tom's head, a memory he could not quite bring to the front of his mind, not until Daffyd added, "I reckon he was a paid assassin, the way he went about it."

Then Thomas could hear Gideon Barlow's flat voice talking about Ralph Lawrence and Dick Shaw- 'they are willing to do anyone's dirty work, them and another fellow, a Frenchman with one eye.'

He ran his hand up through his hair in a frustrated gesture.

"You could be right. At the trial Bartholomew Hanham told me that things were not resolved by the verdict and he would have his revenge. Perhaps he hopes to kill me."

"You must tell Josiah Parry. He will keep a look out for him and lay hands on him."

Thomas sighed. "You can mention it to him when you see him next. I am forewarned now and will be more vigilant. I have been fortunate enough to survive ambush by Secotan natives and Spaniards, so I must trust that my luck will hold."

He sounded cool and unruffled, but he wished he had strapped on his sword that morning.

"Where are you going now?" Williams asked.

"To the builder's yard on the edge of the Green, but on reflection I had best go back to Waaseyaaban and Joan in case he tries an even more cowardly way to hurt me."

He had a sudden fear that the women might be in danger. The slates could wait. Daffyd insisted on walking with him, declaring that two pairs of eyes were safer than one. Tom was relieved when he saw Dawn Light and Joan Bushy stowing what they had purchased in the carriage as Hetty stood waiting with her usual patience.

"No mention of this to them," Tom warned. "I do not wish to alarm them. We may be mistaken. It might have been only a drunk or a man with a disturbed mind striking out at random"

Williams could not agree. "No drunk could have run away like that and his target was selected not random. He was an assassin right enough. I will not show myself before the ladies. Your wife has seen enough of me already. I will speak to Parry and send word if I hear anything."

Thomas shook his hand warmly. "Thank you again Daffyd for your prompt action."

"Take care now." Daffyd wandered off in the opposite direction as Thomas joined his wife and Joan. His housekeeper spotted the torn sleeve as he climbed up onto the driving seat of the carriage and demanded to know how it had happened. Thinking quickly he replied that he had stepped aside to avoid a passing cart and had caught his arm on a nail projecting from another cart parked at the side of the road. Joan clicked her tongue.

"You are out of our sight for a bare few minutes and you do yourself a mischief. You have worn that doublet but twice. Still I suppose I can repair it for you. We must put some salve on that cut as soon as we get home. A wound from a rusty nail can poison the blood. You have had your full share of sickness this year. We mustn't take any risks."

Tom and Dawn Light exchanged amused glances and he admitted that he was justly rebuked for his carelessness.

He spoke little on the drive home, occupied with his thoughts. Bartholomew Hanham had always struck him as pompous and self-important but never malicious or vengeful. He usually gave off an air of self-satisfied affability. He saw a different man at the trial, full of rage, not only for the loss of Anthony, but also the public humiliation. Robert Mountfield had suggested the affair had addled Bartholomew's brain and Tom could well believe that it had affected his mind. It was indeed a grave step for a man who had upheld the law with great pride in his performance as a justice for twenty five years, to turn to paying an assassin. Thomas hoped it was not true, but feared it was.

He had no idea of course that soon after the trial Master Jardine, Hanham's lawyer, had been in Devizes asking questions about Thomas Mountfield. He had picked up the intelligence that Tom was very ill and like to die, which he reported back to Hanham. The news heartened him.

"I pray to God that he does die, so he may go to the devil for the harm he has done me and Robert Mountfield will know what it is like to lose an heir."

Lady Agnes was troubled by the thought of praying for someone's death. She shared her husband's grief for Anthony, but did not blame Thomas. She feared it was Anthony's twisted soul that would fall into the hands of the devil and they should be praying for him. Bartholomew would listen to nothing she said, sweeping her aside. She did not know how to comfort him.

He was devastated to hear that Thomas Mountfield had recovered and vowed to make a surer job of it than the fever. He did not tell Agnes, consulting with Jardine, who agreed to make the arrangements. Lawrence and Shaw had been banned from Wiltshire; Sir Thomas knew them by sight anyway. The third member of Anthony's regular gang was Gaston Ralleray.

He had not turned back with the others when Anthony was first informed that Elizabeth and James were missing and was ordered to continue on to London. He was a familiar sight in the taverns of Frome but he was unknown to Sir Thomas and his household. Jardine promised that Sir Bartholomew would pay him well for his services after the job was done and protect him from the law. He was instructed to take care not to hurt innocent people. It was Mountfield's death only that was sought. Jardine was corrupt but he had a vestige of conscience left.

Thomas stood by his original decision not to alarm the women of the household as yet, although he asked Ned Carter if he or Toby had seen any strangers around the village or in the forest. At first Ned shook his head and then on reflection said, "My wife was talking about a fellow who was in the village a few days past. She said he was hanging around by Pocock's yard and dipping water from the communal well. He wasn't a vagrant because he had a horse. She did not like the look of him though- had a shifty manner she thought. I did not take much notice of it. She is always suspicious of strangers."

"Did she say what he looked like? Had he a leather patch over one eye?"

"Yes, she mentioned that. Had a dark sinister face she said, with an eye patch. Gave her the shivers. Why, do you know who he is?"

Ned had dismissed his wife's tale as anything significant because he knew she liked to embroider the details to make the story more exciting. Now as Thomas described the events of market day to him, he wished he had paid more attention to her.

"You really believe he is an assassin Master Tom?"

"I do not wish to believe it, but it seems likely. However I do not want to worry the women, so please say nothing of this in front of them. I will tell them when I am on surer ground, should I need to do so. I would be grateful though if you and Toby would keep a wary eye out."

Tom felt more at ease having warned Ned and Toby. He trusted their keen eyes and common sense. Hector and Ajax were also reliable allies, always ready to flush strangers out of the woods and warn of their approach. Never-the-less Thomas took to wearing his sword when he went any distance from the house.

Two weeks passed without incident. The hot, dry August had caused the leaves on the trees to turn colour early, enveloping the wood in a russet warmth through September and early October, but storms and rough winds, followed by frosts, had torn most of them from the branches by the end of that month. The few bedraggled remnants hung black and limp, twisted by the chill November wind. Above the pattern of bare branches the sky was leaden and as he rode home from a visit to the school room, Thomas felt the soft, damp kiss of snowflakes on his cheek. He hoped that if the winter was dry and snow free they could start to remove the thatched roof from the building and begin the task of replacing the beams that were rotting through. A heavy snow fall would make that impossible.

The flakes grew larger and fell faster. He pulled up the hood of his cloak, laughing at Hector who was jumping in the air to snap at the floating white powder all around him. Tom was thankful that they had brought the animals into the barn at the beginning of the week. The heavy snow fall in 1588 had come unexpectedly during the night and they had woken up to find drifts blocking the doors. The sheep and goats were still in the pasture and had to be dug out. Last winter they had been spared the snow, but this year did not look so promising. Soon enough had fallen to muffle the sound of Hope's hooves.

The dream –like quiet that filled the atmosphere was suddenly broken by Ajax snarling and bounding between the tree trunks to the side of the path. A zinging sound cut through the air and a missile passed close by Tom's head to bury itself into a tree trunk where it vibrated for some minutes. It was a crossbow bolt. He heard a cry of pain, more snarling and then a yelp as he urged Hope in the direction Ajax had taken. The dog came back towards him limping, with blood tingeing his shoulder. Beyond him Thomas could see the imprint of horse's hooves and caught a glimpse of something moving away in the distance. He was tempted to follow but was worried about Ajax. Dismounting he realised that the dog had something in his mouth. Closer inspection revealed it to be a piece of woollen cloth speckled with blood. The wolfhound had no wounds in his mouth and Thomas speculated that he had bitten the shooter's leg, coming away with a fair sized piece of his hose. Clearly the man had slashed at Ajax with a weapon, catching him on the right shoulder. The cut was long, but not deep. The dog threw himself down in the snow and bending his great head began to lick at the part of the wound he could reach. Hector sat down beside him ready to assist his sibling with the licking if he should need it.

Thomas walked back to the tree, where the crossbow bolt had stopped quivering. He whistled when he saw how far it had penetrated into the tree trunk.

"Ajax my friend," he said as the dogs padded over to join him. "I think I have you to thank that my brains are not splattered all over the snow. I warrant you ran at him just as he was firing and sent his aim askew."

He had to pull with some force to extract the bolt. It was shorter and twice as heavy as an arrow, with a round terminus, suggesting it came from an older variety of crossbow. The bolts designed for the most recent weapons had quarrel shaped endings, a metal version of the feathers of an arrow. Proficiency with a longbow required years of training, but anyone with a steady hand and good judgement of distance could use a crossbow, even someone with one eye. Tom could not deny now that he was a target. He wondered if he was being stalked by more than one assassin or if Ralleray was alone. He decided to show the bolt to Josiah Parry and make an official request for an investigation. He was wary of accusing Bartholomew Hanham as yet because he had no evidence. In theory Ralleray could be acting on his own behalf out of some misplaced loyalty to Anthony.

Thomas took another look at Ajax's wound. It was still bleeding in a thin trickle.

"You must limp home my wounded guardian, so we can wash and anoint that cut and no doubt you will lick the salve straight off again."

He was not far from the house and walked the rest of the way, leading Hope by the rein. He did not feel so exposed on foot and the slower pace was easier on Ajax. He realised that now he must tell his wife and housekeeper. He thought it best not to worry Sarah. She was too ready to imagine horrors.

Sarah was the only one in the kitchen when he returned. She looked up at him, her eyes bright.

"It's snowing Master Tom. I love the snow. I shall throw snowballs at Ned Carter this afternoon – and Toby."

"You be careful they don't throw them back. They have stronger arms than you. Look- poor old Ajax has cut himself in the woods. Will you wash it for him and put some salve on it?"

She took up the task willingly, making sympathetic sounds of encouragement to the dog as she did so. Thomas could hear Joan bustling around in the dining room and called her into the passage.

"Where is Dawn Light?"

"In the brew house I think."

"Come with me a moment will you?"Tom walked with her across to the brew house where Waaseyaaban was drawing off beer and cider from barrels to bring into the house. Thomas bade both women sit down on the settle near the door and explained to them in an even tone what had happened at Devizes market and also the incident that had just occurred. Joan shuddered at the sight of the crossbow bolt.

"Oh Master Tom are you ever to be granted a peaceful life? You deserve some reward for your kindness and courage, not persecution. It beggars belief that a Justice of the Peace would stoop to this."

"Well, I have no proof yet that Hanham is behind it, though I fail to see who else it could be."

"What are you going to do?"

"Daffyd Williams has already told the constable of the attack in the market, but I will take this bolt to him today and ask him to make an official search for the attacker. Ned and Toby are aware of the problem and I am warning you so you will be wary of strangers."

Waaseyaaban was ready for the challenge.

"He does not creep around in the woods and I not see him. I am good stalker. I come behind him with soft steps and kill him."

"No, no I want no more corpses laid to my charge. One spell in the Bridewell is enough for me and I certainly do not wish you to end up there. I doubt if a jury would be so lenient with you as they were with me, prejudice running as deep as it does. What we need to do is capture him or them, for he may not be acting alone, so we can extract the truth and act accordingly. Is that clear?"

She nodded, perceiving that he was right.

"I have not told Sarah," Tom continued. "I think perhaps she does not need to know. I leave you to make up your mind about that Joan."

He had also decided not to tell his parents, sure that his father would insist on confronting Hanham face to face, which Tom intended to do himself once he had enough evidence. The housekeeper was grateful for his discretion regarding her daughter. The slightest scare gave her nightmares.

Thomas declared his intention to ride into Devizes to see Parry right away before the snow grew too thick. Dawn Light wished to go with him. She ran into the house to fetch a fleece-lined cloak and she took the precaution of tucking a hunting knife in a sheath down the side of her boot. It would be her constant companion from that moment. No one would attack her Makwa and find her unprepared to defend him she told herself as Thomas helped her up behind him on to his stallion's back.

Happily her services were not needed before Christmas. The snow continued falling for days making travel arduous, in some cases impossible. It was not the weather to favour assassins. Thomas' family were unable to cross Salisbury Plain and the Mountfield household was obliged to celebrate Christmas without visitors. Even Samson struggled to reach the house from the village. The larder and brew house were well stocked. There was plenty of hay in the barn and the well water did not freeze, so the animals were comfortable enough. The occupants of the house in the forest were well prepared to await the thaw.

The crackling of the fire was a comforting sound. The logs at the centre of the fire basket were glowing a gold vermillion and spurts of flame danced along the surface of the topmost logs. Mark Wheeler had just brought a full wood basket into the dining room. No one spoke to him. He might as well have been invisible he thought as he closed the door behind him. He knew well enough that servants were meant to be invisible but sometimes it irked him. He lingered by the door hoping to pick up some conversation in the dining room. He could hear nothing and went back to his duties.

It was the first Sunday after Christmas. Neville Norrington and his children had attended the morning church service despite the snow. The small church with its square Norman tower was only a few hundred yards away from the main entrance to Norrington Hall. The Smith twins, Mark Wheeler and several more servants were sent out with shovels in the bitter cold of the early morning to clear a path from the front door of the Hall, across the road and through the graveyard to the church porch, so that the Norrington family could walk to church safely and with dignity. The servants came back with red noses and blue lips, cursing at the pain in their fingers once the circulation began to return. There was no time for them to have breakfast before they were obliged to trail after their master to church with thoughts that were less than Christian.

The Norrington's had just enjoyed an excellent supper and Sir Neville was pouring himself a glass of wine. When the glass was three quarters full, he held it up to the candle light and commented on the clarity of the colour. James agreed with him although he was not much of an expert. Most wines tasted the same to him. He preferred small beer, a fact he would never admit to his father for fear it betrayed lack of refinement.

There were four tenant farmers on Norrington estate land. Neville had been telling his son how well the farms were doing and that his bailiff, Noah Lee had recommended a five percent rise in rents for the coming year.

"I think it is high time you spent a day or two with Noah Lee James, getting to know the farms and their possibilities- how far you can trust the tenants to bring their productivity to the maximum. Jacob Whyte can teach you all there is to know about the running of the household, but Noah is the man you need for the estate"

James nodded. He was not so comfortable with Noah as he was with the steward. Although Jacob was always correct and respectful, he was open and honest with his opinions. Noah Lee could flatter to the point of obsequiousness, but James suspected that he was sneering behind their backs. Besides, the boy was not as interested in the business of the estate as he knew he should be. The snow had cut off communications with Bath and London, so no news of what was happening in the wider world had reached them for weeks, nothing to feed James' imagination. He wanted to hear about the fortunes of Henry IV of France aided in his struggle by English money and whether the Earl of Essex would be granted his wish to lead an expedition there. He hungered for tales of how much booty had been taken from Spanish treasure ships during the year. Ninety one ships had been plundered in 1589 and he wished to know if 1590 had proved just as profitable. Earlier in the year they had heard that King Philip of Spain had forbidden the treasure fleet from the West Indies to sail for fear of depredation by English privateers and this had caused much financial hardship in Spain. Life at the Hall seemed rather flat without such news. James looked forward to the thaw when communications would start arriving again and he could discuss them with Tom Mountfield. Thomas would always suggest unusual ways of looking at a situation and consider all the viewpoints, giving James a wider grasp of the subject. It helped him to make his own judgements.

Sir Neville turned his attention to his daughter. He was thinking how much she resembled her mother. She could be Mary when he first saw her, the exact same shade of blue eyes and golden hair. Lizzie was dressed in a simple blue kirtle with lace at the bodice. She always looked her best not over-adorned. He noticed how well the silver heart locket with its central garnet suited her apparel. She seemed very fond of that locket. He had given her a gold and enamel chain for a Christmas gift, which she had worn during the festival days, but she had not removed the locket.

James was thrilled with his Christmas gift, a pair of long dogs to replace the greyhounds he was forced to leave behind at Hanham House. He called them Romulus and Remus and rather wished Sir Neville would let them roam about the house like Hector and Ajax. His father remained adamant that the proper place for a dog was in a kennel.

"Would you like a drop more wine my dear?" Neville asked Elizabeth, who smiled at him.

"No thank you Father. Shall I read to you or sing something to fill the evening before we go to bed?"

He shook his head. He had something he wished to discuss with his daughter that she might find disagreeable.

"I was wondering, once the weather has broken, if you would care to spend a month or two in Bath with your Aunt Jennet. She and Martin would enjoy your company and it would be a change for you."

Lizzie had no desire to be exposed to her Aunt's constant efforts at matchmaking. Lady Ashbury had made it her mission in life to find her niece another husband as quickly as possible. Elizabeth was relieved that the snow had prevented her from visiting over Christmas. There was an expression in her father's eyes that caused her to dread what he was about to say next."

"I believe Jennet would like you to meet a young cousin of Sir Martin's, who stays with them on occasions, John Maundrell. He is a well-educated, sober young man so I hear."

"And Aunt Jennet would like me to consider him for a husband." Lizzie finished the sentence for him.

"Well, yes she does think him very suitable. Oh, I know you must be hesitant in view of what happened. I thought Anthony Hanham was suitable, God forgive me, but Jennet's judgement is very sound and it would do you no harm to meet him. I will not insist that you marry anyone you do not wish to, yet if you refuse to make the acquaintance of suitable young men, how are you to choose?"

"I do not wish to marry again Father."

"I understand your reluctance for- intimacy in the bedroom, "Sir Neville struggled for the right words, not wishing to sound indelicate. "But surely that will pass in time."

"It is not that alone. I have made up my mind not to marry."

She stood up and went over to the fire, staring into the flames. Her hand strayed up to the locket at her throat. That thoughtful gesture of Tom's meant so much to her.

Even amidst her relief at the news that he had recovered from his fever, she had felt a lingering hurt from Dawn Light's fierce, mocking words. The thought that he had burned her letters and was not attracted to her was hard to bear. She knew he did not love her, but had fondly imagined they had a special understanding. Did he really regard her as just a silly girl, due only the courtesy he would give to any woman? His letter apologising for his wife's words was welcome but it was intended for James as well as her and had a formality about it. The gift of the locket changed everything and made her spirits soar. He could not hold her in slight regard if he remembered a locket she had showed him briefly more than a year past. His message was plain; her suffering was still in his mind and he wished to assuage it. They did have a special connection after all, one that Dawn Light did not understand.

Her father was saying, "You cannot make such a dogmatic decision at your age, of course you must marry again. You must be the mistress of your own household, raise children. It is a woman's vocation."

"It will not be long before James marries," Lizzie said, not turning round. "I am sure he will give you the grandchildren you wish for."

James blushed at the thought. He had not considered the probability yet. He was shy and awkward in front of girls his own age, preferring not to contemplate the arduous task of courtship until he was forced to do so.

"I say this for your own happiness Elizabeth," Neville countered, "Not out of any selfish desire for grandchildren. God formed women to bear children. You would surely regret the lack of them and what would you do if you did not marry? You are not considering a religious life I hope?"

Lizzie laughed, turning away from the fire to face him.

"Oh no Father, I have no desire to be shut away in a nunnery. I want to do something useful in the world."

"And what better way to do that than to run your own household and be a good mother."

Neville felt he had won the argument. Elizabeth had another card to play however.

"I believe that if your husband is loving and dutiful, a wife should give her whole heart to him. I cannot do that because my heart belongs to someone already but his own heart is engaged elsewhere."

James sat forward, an anxious look in his eyes, hoping his sister would not name Thomas. Their father had accepted her visit to Tom when he was ill because Jacob had accompanied her and attested that she stayed only a short while to express her concern.

"This is romantic nonsense." Norrington was beginning to lose patience. "You know full well most marriages are not love matches in the first instance."

"You loved mother."

"In truth I did, but I had met her only once before I wed her. Our love and respect grew over time. The world is not some poetical romance Elizabeth. People live by practical considerations, by common sense, not by following the effusions of their hearts. We would be in chaos if we all let our emotions rule our heads. Who is this man who so possesses your heart?"

He knew the answer before he asked the question. The events of the past year made it obvious. She did not need to reply.

"It is Mountfield I presume then? The colour in your cheeks gives me my answer. I pray you have not been lying to me about your connections with that man. Have you had a liaison with him?"

Lizzie was relieved to hear it spoken aloud at last. She would have to pretend no longer.

"No, we have had no physical liaison. The love is all on my side. He has never encouraged me to love him. Quite the reverse. He is kind and caring but always keeping me at a respectful distance. I sent him letters when he was in prison but he did not reply to them."

Sir Neville shot a glance at James knowing he must have been the bearer of those letters and the boy looked down at the table to avoid his father's disapproving frown.

"My life has no meaning unless it is in relation to Thomas- when I can see him next, hear his voice again. If he had died from the fever I would not have wished to go on living myself. He is in my mind and heart all the time. This is why I cannot marry another man. It would not be fair to him. I cannot belong to Thomas but I will not accept anyone else. I do not know how I shall deal with this, what kind of life I can make for myself, but I shall find a way. You have the truth now. I doubt if Aunt Jennet will be so keen to offer me her hospitality when you tell her this. I am sorry Father to disappoint you so."

The look of pained incomprehension on Sir Neville's face distressed her but further argument was pointless and she hurried out of the room before he could speak again.

Norrington drained his wine glass and sat in silence for several minutes. James was afraid to move from the table, expecting a dressing down. Eventually his father looked directly into his eyes and asked quietly, "You knew all about this obsession with Mountfield then?"

"Yes Sir."

"And you have encouraged it, conveying letters to him behind my back."

"I am sorry Sir, but Lizzie was in such a low state after she had suffered so much. It meant much to her to send those letters."

"Is it true that he did not reply?"

"Quite true- to none of them. Lizzie told you the truth when she said he has done nothing to encourage her except be kind and protective. He is very devoted to his wife Sir."

Norrington stroked his beard, shaking his head in a puzzled way.

"That in itself is something I find hard to understand and shows up the flaw in his judgement. Even if he were inclined towards your sister, he is not a man I would approve of her marrying. I can see why she is attracted to him. He is a handsome fellow and has led an adventurous life. He is also a scholar."

"And a true gentleman," James butted in. "Honest and generous."

"I am aware that you admire him also. You say so often enough. I wish to God the pair of you had never become entangled with him. His views are dangerous James. He chooses to flout convention, live by his own rules. That is not an example to follow. You cannot prosper by that road."

"Just because I welcome his friendship does not mean I want to live in the way he does," James defended. "I can think for myself. He encourages me to think for myself. He never tries to indoctrinate me with his ideas."

"Meaning that I do?"

"Well you rarely explore any other point than the one you hold dear."

Norrington took a deep breath. "Take care how you speak to me young man. This is how Thomas Mountfield influences you is it, to treat your father with disrespect? This is how he tells you to speak."

"He never tells me how I should speak. That is the point."

"I see now how far he has corrupted you with his free thinking. As for your sister, I always believed her to be a sensible, decorous, pliable girl, not full of these childish over-wrought emotions. Young Mountfield has much to answer for."

James had not meant to try his father's patience so far. His replies were spontaneous, not intended to wound. He still craved his father's approbation but was finding it more and more easy to hold his own opinion. He wondered if it was indeed Tom's influence or if it was just that he was becoming a man.

"I did not mean to be disrespectful," he said with sincerity. "I apologise if you feel I have over-stepped the mark, but as you are displeased with me already, I will risk saying that forbidding Lizzie to see Sir Thomas will not solve the problem. It will only make her love and desire him more.

Although she is gentle by nature, she can be very determined. I think perhaps Tom is the only person who could persuade her to consider marrying again in due course."

"I have heard enough of your opinions this evening James."

"Very well, then I will go to bed. Goodnight Sir."

James left the room slowly, hoping he looked dignified and self-possessed. When he had gone Neville Norrington buried his head in his hands in despair, with no idea what he should do next for his daughter.

"Oh Mary," he murmured aloud, "I wish you were here to advise me."

Chapter Eleven

THE SCHOOL ROOM ROOF was completed. Once the snow had melted it took the gang of labourers and carpenters only three weeks to pull off the thatch, replace the rotten beams, strengthen the frame and tile the roof with grey slates. The cracks in the walls had been re-plastered. Tom was waiting for some panes of glass to be delivered from Westbury to fill up the empty window frames and make the room easier to heat. They should have arrived yesterday, but he had received a message to say that the glazier was not available for two more days. The other jobs that needed doing he intended to do himself with the help of Ned and Toby. The privy in the garden needed some renovation and the picket fence around the property was beyond repair; a completely new fence was necessary.

He was alone in the building that morning raking out all the accretions of ash from the fireplace, which had not been used for more than a year. The dust made him cough as he scooped the ash into a bucket with a fire shovel. He was eager to get the fire lit to dry out the room now that all the holes that let in the wind and rain had been stopped up. Once the windows were in place he would build up a good fire. His father had donated an iron wood burning stove that Tom remembered from his childhood standing in one of the out houses at the Mountfield home in Salisbury. Placed at the far end of the room from the fireplace, the heat from both would soon warm and dry the room. He hoped it would arrive today with the consignment of pupils' desks that were being transported from Salisbury.

One of Godfrey's connections told him of a school that was closing down on the outskirts of the city and was auctioning off all its furniture. Godfrey attended the auction buying twenty desks and chairs at a cheap price.

Cecily said he was so pleased with his bargain that he did not stop smiling all evening. He had decided to accompany the two waggon loads of furniture and the little convoy was on the outskirts of Devizes as Tom raked out the fire.

The snow had lasted to the end of January then the weather turned much milder and within a week most of the snow had melted except for on the tops of the hills and in the coldest corners of the fields. Now in the first week of March all vestiges of white had disappeared. Thomas found some early violets down by the stream and picked a few to take home to Waaseyaaban. He found a broken cup in the house, filled it with cloudy stream water and stood the violets in it to keep them fresh. He stopped his ash raking for a moment, coughing to clear his throat of the dust. The violets on the window sill stirred in the wind, their colour rich and vibrant. The perfume drifted across to him and Thomas drank it in. This year he would be free to take pleasure in the sights, sounds and smells of the coming spring instead of sitting in a cell in the Bridewell. He found it hard to credit that in a few days' time a whole year had passed since Josiah Parry and Andrew Shepherd had arrested him in the forest.

Hector and Ajax wandered into the room and padded back out again. They had been exploring Pocock's wood yard, but they never strayed too far from Tom. They both lay down just outside the door and began cleaning their paws, gnawing away at the clods of mud between their claws and the pads of their feet. From their vantage point the dogs could watch villagers fetching water from the well and trot over to skirmish with some of the local dogs if the fancy took them. The sound of sawing came from the wood yard and carts rattled past at intervals. Farther down the street the metallic clang of the blacksmith's hammer hit the air.

Tom, his hands and face streaked with ash, carried two full buckets out through the back door. He emptied them in a heap in the garden. Ash was good for the soil and he intended to dig it into a cleared patch to make it fertile. He had plans to encourage the children to grow vegetables as part of their schooling. Walking back into the room with the empty buckets he saw a woman in the front doorway making a fuss of the wolfhounds. Her face was obscured by the hood of her winter gown, but he recognised her voice as she spoke to the dogs. He put the buckets down and she looked up.

"Mistress Elizabeth, I did not expect to see you here."

"I did not expect to come here. I was out riding and came on an impulse. James has told me all about your plans for the school and I was eager to see what progress had been made. I knew all I had to do was follow the main road into the village. I did not know if you would be here but I am so pleased you are."

"Are you alone?"

She nodded.

"Is that wise?"

"I don't claim to be wise. I have a quiet, steady horse and it is so good to be able to come abroad again now the snow has gone."

She had spoken the truth. It was an impulsive action. She did not set out that morning to ride to the village, but when she found herself close to the road she could not resist. She did not care if her father discovered where she had been. It did not matter anymore. As she rode into the village she had a strong feeling that she would see Thomas. However she had not expected to find him streaked with ash and soot and smiled at the state he was in.

"You have been working hard I see."

The only parts of his hands that were clean were his knuckles and he wiped the back of his left hand over his cheeks in an effort to shift some of the grime.

"You have caught me at a disadvantage. Cleaning out an old fire is a dirty task. Two days ago I put a brush up the chimney to unblock the flue. If you had walked in then you would have thought me an Ethiope. If you will excuse me, I will try to make myself more presentable."

He went out of the back door, snatching up a rag lying in the doorway and walked down to the stream where he washed his hands and face using the rag. He was only partially successful but fancied it was an improvement. Elizabeth followed him outside, surprised by the size of the area behind the house. He explained his plans for the garden once the frost had left the earth, how he hoped to improve the children's knowledge of husbandry.

"Dawn Light is eager to be involved in that. She is good with children. They take her for granted, accept her as she is far more readily than older generations. Besides, the children of labourers have no ceremony to stand on."

Elizabeth flinched involuntarily at the sound of Dawn Light's name, feeling the sting of her mocking laughter all over again. Her reaction, slight as it was, did not escape Tom.

"I am so sorry that my wife spoke such harsh, unkind words to you the day you came to inquire after my health. There is a fierceness in her sometimes that will not be tamed. Waaseyaaban is a force of nature. The rules of polite conversation mean nothing to her. In truth there are times when I am in sympathy with her view for much of our conventional behaviour is false and hypocritical, but it grieves me that you should receive any smart in my house.

She puts on a brave front always, yet deep down I think she fears that one day I will give in to pressure from my family and the outside world and abandon her. I could never do that. She is essential to me as breathing."

"I understand why she was angry with me. She was afraid you would die and I was to blame- both James and I. It was such a relief when your letter came to know that you did not feel the same."

"You knew that surely. I did burn your letters but not because I scorned their contents. Your care for my situation was a comfort. I had Joan burn them in case they were discovered by those who wished me harm. I did not reply for the same reason."

Lizzie put her hand up to the locket at her throat.

"Any doubts I had that you cared for me were swept away when you sent me this."

Thomas had guided her back into the house as they were talking. He had caught sight of a man coming along the bank on the opposite side of the stream. Thoughts of Ralleray the assassin had moved to the back of his mind while the snow was thick. Now travel was easier again he was wary of strangers. His sword belt was hanging on a nail inside the school room. Looking back over his shoulder as he stepped aside to let Lizzie precede him into the room, he saw the man trudging on past towards the far end of the village. It was a labourer on his way home for his midday meal.

"The fact that you remembered this jewel in such detail gave me courage," Elizabeth continued, pulling back her hood. He was surprised to see that she had not bound up her hair. It fell in golden profusion about her shoulders.

"Elizabeth, you must not magnify the significance of my gift. I act on impulse too. It was an apology for Waaseyaaban's rudeness."

"No, it was much more than that." She moved closer to him, looking up into his face. He detected a sweet scent as if her garments had been sprinkled with rose water. "It told me that you understood my pain. I will wear it always."

He felt uncomfortable and did not know what to say, wishing he had never sent her the locket. Lizzie put her hand on his arm.

"It freed me from pretence. I had the courage to be open with my father and now I will be so with you. I love you so much Thomas. You fill my thoughts day and night."

"You said this to your father?"

"You need not worry. I made it clear to him that you did not return my love in that way and have never made any improper advances to me."

"And he believed that?" Thomas was dubious. He was well aware that Sir Neville distrusted him.

"Oh yes, you see my Aunt has been pressing me to remarry, suggesting suitable young men. I cannot marry anyone when I love you so much. I have made up my mind never to marry again and it gave me such a feeling of freedom, of release to tell father the reason why."

Thomas walked her over to the window sill, moved the violets into the corner and bade her sit down on the sill. He had to do something to distract himself from the need in her eyes, a need that tempted him to take her in his arms.

"Elizabeth," he said trying to sound as fatherly as possible, "You are not yet nineteen years old. You cannot make such a dogmatic statement at your age. I don't wish to talk to you as if you were a child, or belittle your emotions, but it is so easy to fall in love when you are young. When I was thirteen I thought myself so in love I was like to die of it. Then at fifteen I was in love twice with two very different women and again at seventeen and so on. I was twenty seven before I truly learned what love was." She began to protest but he put a finger on her lips. "No, hear me out. Your circumstances and the part I played in them have caused you to view me in too romantic a light- James also due to my friendship with Philip Sidney. You are a beautiful, intelligent, affectionate woman with so much to give to someone who deserves it. You cannot consign yourself to a single life because of a troubled old reprobate like me. You would add a further burden to my conscience."

He did not expect her reply.

"Was it true what Dawn Light said, did she really tell you to bed me?"

"She should never have said that to you."

"But she did. Is it true?"

He nodded.

"She said you refused because you did not find me pleasing and though it may be vanity that did hurt me for I fondly believed that you were attracted to me."

"Well what did you expect me to do Elizabeth," he said with a frustrated sigh, "Take you as a mistress? That would have confused them all more than ever-unpalatable wife, respectable mistress. I would not so demean you."

"Demean." She repeated the word, smiling at how inappropriate it sounded to her. "I would not feel demeaned. It would be the fulfilment of my desire."

In one swift movement she rose from the window sill and put her arms around him, pressing her face deep into his shoulder.

"Thomas, dearest Thomas don't you understand that what would hurt

me most would be to live the rest of my life without the joy of lying with you-
even if it is but once."

Tom stood with his hands held away from her body, endeavouring not
to be drawn into the web of emotion she was weaving around him, but the way
she stroked his back with the tips of her fingers broke down his resistance. He
returned her embrace, holding her close to him and kissing the top of her head,
just a light brush of his lips across her hair.

"I have kissed you once before," he confessed. "In a strange fantasy I
had while I was waiting to be called at the Assizes. Pent up in that small room
with all those other unhappy, fearful people, I closed my eyes to shut it all out
and you came to me unbidden amidst a field of summer flowers and we kissed.
I have tried hard to put the taste of that kiss out of my mind but it comes back."

"Let me reinforce it now with a real kiss," Lizzie urged.

She put her hands either side of his face and kissed him, a kiss full of all
her repressed longing. He kissed her in return feeling the heat rise in his veins,
the blood pulsing into his member. She stepped back to lean against the wall
drawing him with her, encouraging him to unlace her bodice. He kissed her
neck and down across her breast. Her hands were unbuttoning his breeches
when outside the dogs started barking. The deep throated sound ran through
his body like a lightning strike. Jesu, what was he doing? He pulled away from
her and walked rapidly outside taking deep breaths of the sharp air to cool his
desire. The wolfhounds were loping down the road in the direction of Devizes
with a purpose in view. Elizabeth came out to stand behind him. She did not
speak but laid her head against his back. Tom was angry with himself for his
lack of control and also with her for playing on his susceptibility. He could not
deny he had been stirred.

"We must never put ourselves in that position again," he said brusquely
doing up the top button of his breeches with embarrassed fingers. "If we had
gone farther we would both have cause for regret in time to come."

"Never," she murmured. "I would never regret that."He could see his
dogs coming back down the road trotting either side of Godfrey Roper's horse.
Two waggons followed behind laden with furniture.

"It's my brother-in-law with furniture from Salisbury for the school"

Tom was always pleased to see Godfrey, but never more so than at this
moment. He strode out into the road to meet the convoy and Lizzie moved
back into the room to adjust her clothing. She found that both her kirtle and
outer gown were smudged with soot from Tom's clothes when he held her close.

The thought of it pleased her. She had penetrated his defences and was sure she could do so again. Thomas formally introduced her to Godfrey, who bowed.

"I know you by sight of course Mistress," Roper was not sure whether he should say Hanham or Norrington so he said neither.

"And I you Master Roper, your defence of Sir Thomas' character at the Assizes stays in my memory. It was so heartfelt."

"No more than he deserved. Thomas is a good fellow. We all did what we could."

"My father told me the other day that you have become Mayor of Salisbury," Lizzie continued. "Such an important post- the chance to do many things for the city."

"The council was good enough to honour me with that title and I shall do my best to fulfil my duty."

"No more than he deserved," Tom said. "And he is the far better fellow. Mistress Elizabeth was riding nearby and took a fancy in her head to see what progress we have made on the school."

He was sure that Godfrey must perceive that he was feeling guilty, even though his brother-in-law was the least suspicious of men. The marks on Lizzie's gown must have caught his attention.

"I fear she had suffered from standing too near when I was raking out the fireplace. I hope your gown can be cleaned."

"I am sure it can. But I will not get in your way any longer. I must be going home. Thank you for explaining your plans for the school. I look forward to seeing them completed."

Godfrey was horrified to discover that she was riding alone and suggested Tom escort her back to Norrington Hall.

"The three of us can unload the waggons. You have done your share today, cleaning out that filthy fireplace. You can ride straight back home from Norrington Hall and have a good bath. We will come to the house when we have finished here, looking for a reward from Joan Bushy. I have been telling these fellows about the delights of Joan's pantry."Godfrey rolled up his sleeves and began the task of unloading the desks. Tom could not refuse to escort Elizabeth home; it would look discourteous. He did not like the idea of her riding unaccompanied either, but he did not wish to spend more time alone with her. Supressing a sigh, he buckled on his sword belt and helped Elizabeth onto her saddle. He knew a short cut to Norrington and they were soon in sight of the impressive gateway. They had spoken little on the journey. Now Tom reined in and said," I will not come any further. I am sure your father has no wish to see me. What was his reaction to your statement of intent?"

"Oh he was puzzled and frustrated. I feel pity for him because he is not sure what to do next. He does mean to do the best for me. At least he wrote to Aunt Jennet asking her not to proceed in her matchmaking for a while because it was too soon. I am grateful for that. James may have had some influence on his decision. He told father to forbid me to see you would only make me more determined to do so."

"Yes, you have shown me today just how determined you are."

"I can be happy now because I have hope. I know you are attracted to me. You cannot deny it. I felt it in your body when you held me. I must see you again soon. I will come with James when the school is open to see how it fares. You would like that Thomas? Tell me you would."

"Yes, I would, but only as a friend, no more than that. I told you before I am not in the market for a mistress."

She gave him a radiant smile which did not assure him that she had accepted his statement. He turned his horse and whistling for the wolfhounds to follow, rode away very uneasy in his mind about what had happened. He was fearful now that he could not trust himself. He had not expected to be so vulnerable to her allure, to desire her so much.

Elizabeth's feelings were very different. Her spirits were high as she rode through the open main gate. She did not notice Mark Wheeler standing in the doorway of the dairy where he had been trying to persuade one of the dairy maids to meet him in secret that night. She was not eager, but he was working on it. He saw the man on the chestnut stallion riding away from the Hall and recognised both horse and rider.

"No wonder Mistress Elizabeth looked so pleased with herself," he said, thinking aloud. "Been frolicking with her lusty Knight. It's alright for some."

As soon as Lizzie had left her horse at the stables and gone into the house, he scuttled over to tell the Smith twins what he had seen.

When Joan Bushy brushed a floor it was not a casual matter. It was a serious thrusting exercise. Nothing escaped her broom. The school room was being cleaned as if it was a military campaign. Sarah equipped with a long-handled duster was bringing down cobwebs, chasing the spiders from one corner of the room to another whilst her mother attacked the floor. The iron stove and the rejuvenated fireplace combined had dried the dampness out of the building, although neither was lit just then for the April morning was mild despite the intermittent rain storms.

Tom and Waaseyaaban carried the teacher's table to one end of the room. It was made of oak and furnished with four commodious drawers-plenty enough space for all the equipment a teacher might need. Their next task was to arrange the desks in rows in the centre with an aisle down the middle.

Waaseyaaban put a slate and six pieces of chalk inside each desk as Thomas brought the chairs over. He sat down at one of the desks to judge the quality of the light. There was a window either side of the front door and a bigger one in the centre of the back wall, so light entered the room from both sides, but the roof was low and on dark days it would be murky. Tom wished now that he had thought to put skylights in the roof as in his own house.

His main worry however was that he had not yet engaged a regular school master. He intended to give some lessons himself in history and geography in the form of stories that might fire their imaginations, but he needed a master to take on the daily grind of teaching the basics of the three Rs and be there to open up in the mornings and lock up at the end of the day. The time Thomas could spare for teaching was limited for he had his timber business and smallholding to run. He had put up notices in shops in several local towns and in church porches. Godfrey had done the same in Salisbury, advertising the post of schoolmaster, asking any interested persons to leave their details with the shopkeeper or minister. Tom had visited three applicants so far, none of whom seemed suitable for their level of knowledge was insufficient. Godfrey was interviewing a candidate that morning, who had worked as an assistant master in several Salisbury schools and sounded promising. Nathan Pocock was willing to take on a lodger if the schoolmaster came from outside the immediate area. His was a sizeable dwelling and he had spare rooms, although Thomas made it clear to him that the master's stipend would be a moderate one, so he must charge rent accordingly.

The ministers of three parish churches had offered to give religious instruction to the pupils of the new school. Rather than favour one of them Tom suggested all three do so on a rota basis.

He needed the stamp of orthodoxy on the project or it would be closed down. However, he did intend to encourage the older pupils to think more widely than the orthodox view once the school was well established. There were ways of doing this without undermining the basic teachings of the Church of England.

Tom walked over to the nearest window. The rain had begun again, running down the window pane and through the watery curtain he could see beyond the new fencing into the wood yard, where the workmen were scurrying for cover to avoid the shower. Hector, closely followed by Ajax came inside, shaking the wet from his coat, incurring the wrath of Joan as droplets sprayed all over her apron.

"Thomas," Dawn Light came to stand beside her husband. "Children sit still and be quiet all day?"

She found it hard to believe children would do that of their own volition. Tom laughed and put his arm around her shoulder.

"I doubt that very much. I am sure discipline will be a problem at first. They will not be required to sit still and be quiet all the time anyway. I intend them to ask questions and have some lessons where they can be active not just passive listeners. Some time will be spent outside in the garden with you or learning about nature. There will be a break for an hour after morning lessons so they can go home for a meal, then return for more lessons in the afternoon."

"If they do not like the morning maybe they not come back after meal."

"Some of them will not, but I am relying on their parents to persuade them."

Thomas was aware that attendance might be thin at first. Many of the villagers were supportive, eager for their children to get a free education. There were others however who thought it unnecessary. The children helped with work in the fields or in their various crafts and trades as soon as they were strong enough to do so. Some parents did not intend to spare them to sit around in a school, filling their heads with things they had no need to know. Tom was prepared for a hard campaign struggling to change this attitude. This was why it was essential to appoint the right master, one who was firm but also sympathetic towards the pupils' situation and not forbidding. Thomas would not tolerate corporal punishment. Labourers' children were tough and used to physical pain. Some boys would regard it as a badge of honour, others would feel humiliated. Both reactions could lead to stubbornness and be counter-productive. He was also determined that the girls should be regarded as having the same capacity for learning as the boys and not given the impression they were regarded as inferior.His thoughts were interrupted by a sudden noise, an explosive crack followed by a scream. Spinning around he saw Sarah Bushy just behind him sinking to the floor clutching her upper arm, blood seeping through her fingers. He was very familiar with the sound of a pistol shot. Joan had opened the back window casement to let out some of the dust as she brushed round the room. There was still a wisp of smoke and the smell of gunpowder around the window. Joan and Dawn Light ran to help Sarah as Thomas raced outside, the wolfhounds in close pursuit. The rain had stopped again, leaving pools of water in the depressions in the ground. Tom could see a man running at top speed on the other side of the stream. He must have waded across and was now heading for the place he had left his horse. It was clear now what had happened. The assassin was aiming at Tom's back and just as he fired Sarah moved across unwittingly behind Thomas, taking the shot in her arm.

Tom sent the dogs across the stream, ordering them to run the assassin to ground and continued sprinting along the nearside. There was a plank across the stream a short way down, near a stand of trees on the opposite bank. He figured that the man's horse was in those trees. The dogs were baying in their excitement, attracting the attention of the villagers who came out into the street to see what was happening. Thomas had not run so fast for years. He was beside himself with anger, determined to catch the culprit. As he sped across the plank he saw the man flee into the copse with Ajax close on his heels and Hector not far behind. He burst through the trees to find a swarthy man with a patch over his left eye, already mounted and trying to force his frightened horse to break away from the wolfhounds who were circling him, barking and snarling. He let out a string of oaths in French, digging his heels into the horse's flanks to urge it on. Suddenly the creature reared up and leaped forward, picking up speed. Thomas grabbed hold of Ralleray's leg as the horse passed, yanking him out of the saddle and he fell on top of Tom, both of them sprawling on the floor as the horse galloped on.

They wrestled on the damp grass, the Frenchman desperate to reach the dagger in his belt. His fingers touched the hilt but Tom twisted his hand away from it and managed to turn him over on his front, wrenching his right arm up behind his back with savage force. The man cried out in pain as Thomas held him there in a vice-like grip, not inclined to show any mercy. Several men, including Nathan Pocock had come out of the wood yard and were running across the plank and into the trees.

"A bloody inept assassin you are." Tom snarled at Ralleray. "Three times you have missed your mark, but this time you have caused a hurt you will pay for dearly."

"Pardonnez moi," Ralleray gasped. "Je ne parle Anglais."

"Oh you speak English well enough, but tis no matter because I speak passable French if the need be."

The men from the wood yard arrived, Nathan Pocock puffing from the exertion as Thomas hauled Ralleray to his feet, his arm still twisted behind him.

"What is happening Sir Thomas?" Pocock demanded, surprised by the fierceness of Tom's action.

"This fine fellow has just tried to murder me and not for the first time, but in his ineptitude he wounded Joan Bushy's daughter Sarah instead."

An angry sound came from the group of men assembled round them.

"Non, non, Il ne pas vrai. Je vous prie."

"A poxy foreigner," one of the men sneered. "Hark at him gabble. I'll give you something to gabble about, coming here attacking us, you Spanish shit."

He moved threateningly towards the man but Thomas stopped him.

"He is a Frenchman, not a Spaniard, a paid assassin and I mean to discover who is paying him. First Monsieur Ralleray- yes I do know who you are- you will take a look at what you have done. Will someone fetch me a length of rope?"

A youth hurried back to the wood yard to do his bidding while Thomas forced the Frenchman to walk in front of him, keeping a firm grip on his arm. Ralleray talked incessantly, protesting his innocence in his own language but it had no effect on the tight-lipped Mountfield. They had crossed back over the plank when the youth met them with the rope and Tom tied Ralleray's hands behind his back. Then taking hold of him by the arm half dragged him towards the school house as he hung back.

A small knot of villagers had gathered outside the house, looking through the windows and the open front door. Ned Carter's wife Martha was amongst them. She pushed herself forward as Tom propelled the Frenchman into the room, asking, "Master Tom, who is hurt? It's not my Ned is it?"

"No mistress, Ned and Toby are working in the forest. They are safe enough." Tom called back over his shoulder. Martha was relieved and began to tell the person next to her that she had seen that villain in the village before and was sure he was up to no good then.

Sarah Bushy was propped up against one of the desks. Joan had torn a strip from the bottom of her petticoat and bandaged the wounded arm tightly.

Sarah's face was ashen white and she was crying in that soft, miserable way that young children do when they are frightened. Thomas took Ralleray by the scruff of the neck and pushed him in front of Sarah.

"Look you hapless bastard, this is the result of your work. You have injured a simple, innocent girl who never did harm to anyone in her life."

Waaseyaaban, who was kneeling beside Sarah, jumped to her feet.

"He do this? He is the one who tries to kill you?"

Her hand hovered near the knife in her boot. Thomas gave her a sharp look.

"You stay out of this."

It was a command and for all her high spirit she always obeyed him when she heard that tone in his voice. She could feel the extent of his anger towards Ralleray.

"I did not mean to hurt the girl," Ralleray said in English. His accent was heavy but his grasp of the language excellent as Tom had suspected. "She moved as I fired. The shot was for you."

"Who paid you to kill me?"

"A lawyer."

"What lawyer?"

"I do not know his name."

Tom lifted the man off his feet by the lapels of his doublet and drove him back against the wall.

"Don't you mess around with me Monsieur. I have no patience left. If you try me further I shall wring your scrawny neck and enjoy doing it. What is his name?"

Joan looked up at Dawn Light surprise in her eyes. She could never recall seeing Thomas behave in that way. The Frenchman certainly believed that he meant it.

"Jardine," he croaked, his voice restricted by Tom's hand pressing against his throat. His master Bartholomew Hanham wishes you dead because you kill Anthony Hanham. Jardine say he will pay me well and save me from prosecution. I have to make a living somehow."

Thomas snorted in disgust at his last remark but he relieved the pressure on the man's throat. He had the evidence he needed. The men from Pocock's yard were growing restive. The sight of Sarah lying there tended by her mother stirred them up again. One of them shouted, "Rats bane," another "Let's string him up, murdering foreigner." This idea was taken up by the others and passed back to the villagers outside, who began to chant, "Hang him! Hang him!"

"No," Thomas contradicted them. "You will put yourselves on the wrong side of the law and will suffer for it. He is not worth that. Besides I need him to give evidence against Sir Bartholomew. He is the real culprit."

It took a while before he managed to calm them down and one man stepped forward and spat in the Frenchman's face. Thomas asked Nathan Pocock to lock Ralleray up in one of his sheds and he would fetch the constable. Pocock and his men escorted the assassin, the spit still dribbling down his cheek, through the jostling villagers.

Tom knelt down beside Sarah, asking Joan about the severity of the wound.

"I think she is lucky. The shot passed right through."

"Oh God Joan, I am so sorry. I had rather a thousand times the bullet had hit me as it was intended than hurt Sarah. This is my fault."

"How can that be? Did you ask wicked villains to go about the countryside trying to kill you?" Joan replied reaching out and brushing his hair back from his forehead in a motherly gesture. "It's that Bartholomew Hanham's fault not yours."

"Why did he shoot me Master Tom?" Sarah asked a bewildered tone in her voice.

"He did not mean to shoot you sweetheart. He wished to shoot me and you moved into the line of fire. The shot was intended for my back not your poor arm."

"Then my arm saved you." Sarah's face brightened for a moment. "But it hurts so much, worse than the toothache I had at Christmas."

"I know." Thomas stroked her cheek. "Don't worry, your mother will make it well again soon. We must take you home and put you to bed where you will be warm and comfortable."

Tom picked Sarah up and carried her out to the cart. She rested her head on his shoulder. Although she was shocked and in pain she took pleasure in all the attention she was getting. Master Tom was always kind to her but he had never called her sweetheart before. She imagined how distressed Ned Carter would be when he heard the news and what a fuss he would make of her.

They had needed the cart that morning to transport all the equipment to the school room. Now Tom helped Joan into the back of the empty vehicle, then lifted Sarah in, placing her so she could rest against her mother. Waaseyaaban backed Hetty into the shafts and deftly linked up the harness. When she had finished she jumped up beside her husband on the driver's seat. He looked calm but she sensed a storm of emotions passing through him. She put her arm through his and leaned against him.

"What you do now?"

"When I have seen Sarah put to bed, I will ride to Devizes and tell Josiah Parry to collect Ralleray."

"And then?"

"Then I shall pay a visit to Hanham House. This must stop now. I will have no more innocent folk harmed because of me."

He was true to his word. After he had laid Sarah gently on her bed and praised her for being a brave girl, he saddled Hope and rode to Josiah Parry's house in Long Street. He was fortunate to find the constable in residence having just enjoyed a hearty midday meal. Parry had received reports of a man answering Ralleray's description but had failed to track him down. He promised to deal with the matter at once.

"Will you come with me Sir Thomas?"

"No I have a more urgent task."

Parry could guess where he was going.

"Take care," he warned. "I understand your eagerness to settle this matter but do not contravene the law in doing so."

It was a friendly warning and Thomas accepted it as such.

"Do not worry, I have no intention of risking another spell in the Bridewell."

He urged his stallion towards Frome at a furious pace. When his temper was high or his nerves fraught he found that riding at speed eased his tension. The sting of the wind on his face, the drumming of the horse's hooves, the stretching of muscles and sinews all blended together and held him in a hypnotic embrace. He was hardly aware of the distance they covered and was surprised to find Hanham House in view.

He had seen it only once, just after it was built and had forgotten the vast size of it. It dominated the landscape with all the pretensions of a palace. The architecture was very fine but in the mood he was, Tom found it vulgar, a colossal expenditure for the sake of vanity. He thought of all the schools like the one he was trying to establish that could be supported, all the improvements in agricultural techniques and equipment that might be funded, labourers' wages and housing improved, scientific experiments and voyages of discovery commissioned with the money it cost to build that one house. There it stood with its myriad of gleaming windows proclaiming the importance of the name of Hanham, the huge coat of arms over the gateway reinforcing the effect and the owner was a man who paid assassins. If circumstances had turned out as this man once planned, this edifice would have passed to Anthony, a violent sadist capable of any crime against his fellow human beings. At that moment Thomas truly hated the house; the grandeur turned his stomach. He rode under the arched gateway and along the elm-lined drive. The house was surrounded by parkland. A herd of deer grazed near the drive and they all moved away at the approach of the horseman except one handsome stag who stood his ground with a defiant set of his head.

Nothing obscured the frontage of the house, so when Thomas dismounted there was nowhere to tether Hope. He stood looking up at the curved Dutch gable over the main entrance with its elaborate finial carved with symbols of plenty. Then he led his stallion around the side of the house where he found a stable block and coach house. Most of the back of the building was shut off from view by a high wall, but there was a door that led out into the stable yard. This was the back entrance that James and Elizabeth had used to flee from the house the year before. A lad came running out of the stables eager to help. Thomas declared that he had an appointment with Sir Bartholomew.

"I would be grateful if you would tend my horse until I am ready to leave."

The boy had no idea who Thomas might be although he was clearly a gentleman to own such a fine horse. He was only too pleased to take care of it. Tom walked back to the front entrance and pulled the bell chain. The bronze bell suspended from a bracket clanged- a harsh, unmusical sound. It was several minutes before the door opened to reveal a servant in Hanham's green and gold livery. Elegant and precise, he bowed. Thomas inquired if his master was at home and when answered in the affirmative asked to see him.

"Is he expecting you sir?"

"No, I am sure he will be surprised to see me, but I bring him an important message from his lawyer Master Jardine."

The servant invited him into the hallway. Tom was amused by the size of the flower-shaped rosettes on the garters of the man's nether hose. They were as big as cabbages; overblown like everything else about this house.

"If you would care to wait here Sir, I will ask the Master if he can see you."

Thomas studied the display of armour and weapons high up on the wall. It was the war gear of an earlier century, perhaps from the thirteen hundreds and could only belong to a very rich man. In the centre was a shield with a coat of arms that Tom did not recognise. He remembered that Hanham's mother was the younger daughter of an earl who had married beneath her station. Perhaps the armour came from her family.

The servant returned with the news that his master would receive the visitor. Thomas could imagine that Hanham would be awaiting a message from Jardine with some anticipation. He was conducted to the parlour and announced as Master Jardine's messenger.

Bartholomew Hanham was sitting in a chair with his feet up on a footstool. It was eight months since the trial and he looked more bloated and purple than he did then. A decanter of wine and a half empty glass stood on a round table beside him. His back was to the door.

"Come in man," he called out. "I have been waiting eagerly to hear from Jardine. Shut the door behind you."

Tom did as he was bid, quietly turning the key in the lock as he did so. He did not want any servants barging in before he had said his piece, nor did he intend to get involved in any violence. Lady Agnes was working at a tapestry stretched across a frame. The slight click of the key in the lock caused her to look up. She let out a little cry of dismay when she saw who was walking across the room.

"Lady Agnes," Thomas bowed her an acknowledgement.

"What in God's name!" Hanham's feet came off the stool with a bang on to the floor. He struggled to stand up but was unsuccessful. Tom saw that the man's legs were badly swollen.

"God's blood, how dare you come into my house? Get out at once."

"Not the messenger or the message you were expecting Sir Bartholomew? Alas for you your hired assassin has failed three times to kill me. This time he wounded an innocent young woman, my housekeeper's only child. You had better pray there are no complications from the wound because if she dies you must face the consequences."

"Agnes, call the steward. Tell him to fetch a constable because my life is in danger, hurry."

Hanham was genuinely afraid. Agnes stood there with her hand over her mouth as if she was attempting to stifle a scream. Tom realised that she knew nothing of any hired assassin. She was not afraid of what he might do, but horrified by the knowledge of what her husband had done.

"You have no cause for fear Sir Bartholomew. Contrary to your belief I do not attack unarmed men. You are confusing me with your nephew. I have come to warn you that this foolish vendetta must stop. Ralleray is in custody.

His testimony is enough to convict both you and Jardine. The local constable will hand him over to the sheriff and it will be his choice how to proceed. There has been too much bitterness already and I have no wish to persecute you. I can see that you are a troubled and sick man."

"Don't you pity me sir." Hanham writhed in his chair.

"How can I not pity you- a man who has served the cause of justice for so many years, stooping to such means to extract revenge?"

Lady Agnes put her hand on Tom's arm and then withdrew it in a nervous gesture.

"The girl you spoke of, is she sorely wounded?"

"Fortunately not- as long as no festering of the wound develops."

"I swear to you I had no knowledge of any attempt to kill you."

"I believe you Lady Agnes. Your husband had asked Master Jardine to arrange it all."

"I could not bear it," Hanham burst out in an agonised voice, "That you should be walking around free while my Anthony, my heir, my hope for the future lay in a cold grave, his reputation and mine in ruins. I have been in hell since that trial- the humiliation. It warmed my heart to hear that you were sick and like to die, that it was God's retribution on you. Why he spared you I cannot understand, but for some reason he did, so I was forced to turn to a human agency."

He was shaken by a fierce fit of coughing that wracked his body, his eyes bulging. Agnes poured more wine into his glass and encouraged him to take a sip. When the coughing had subsided Tom said,

"You still cannot face the truth. It is clear that your wife did some time ago. You will never have any peace until you let go of this illusion that Anthony was wronged. Your nephew was possessed of an evil, twisted nature with a distorted view of the world. He was well on the way to ruining the Hanham reputation while he was alive. He was not worthy to be your heir. Elizabeth and James Norrington are the wronged ones and myself too. I was drawn unwittingly into all this and Anthony put me in a position where I was forced to fight him to save my own life. I had no intention of killing him –in fact I had hoped never to shed any more blood. Do not imagine that his death is not on my conscience, vile as he was. Look at your nephew in the true light of day, not through a warped mirror of your own devising."

Hanham's face crumpled up, collapsing into itself, a blotched, quivering canvas. He began to weep.

"I will harangue you no longer," Tom began to dislike the sound of his own voice and wish he was a hundred miles away from this wrecked man. "Only I must stress that if you make any more attempts on my life I will press the sheriff to alert his counterpart in Somerset to take action against you. I pray you will have the sense not to make your wife suffer that."

He bowed to Agnes and turned to leave. She ran after him, plucking at his sleeve, begging him to keep her husband's name out of it.

He shook her off, eager to get away and his hand was on the key of the door when they heard a strange, rasping sound. Hanham had half risen in his chair, clutching his throat, making incoherent noises. He fell sideways on to the floor bringing his chair down with him. Agnes ran to him calling his name. She dropped down on her knees beside him and appealed to Thomas.

"Help him Sir Thomas," she pleaded. "Help him."

Tom stood there for a moment wondering if he would ever break free from this unending nightmare. He wanted to quit this oppressive house and never come near it again, blot the Hanham's from his memory, but the sight of that woman flapping her hands helplessly around her husband's body, her eyes full of fear and misery, prevented him. He pulled the upturned chair clear and knelt beside her. Hanham's eyes were open, staring. His mouth was twisted to one side, the swollen lips moving as if he was trying to speak but he could form no words. A vein at his temple was purple and throbbing. Blood trickled from his nostrils.

Tom loosened the collar of the man's doublet and unlaced the neck of his shirt.

"I fear he has suffered a fit of apoplexy. Is he regularly attended by a physician?"

She nodded looking up into Tom's face searching for some comfort.

"Abraham Fry of Frome."

"I have a fast horse. I will fetch him. Meanwhile ask your servants to carry him to his bed chamber. I will be as quick as I can. Where does this Fry live?"

"In the main street just past the blacksmith's forge."

Tom ran into the hall, calling for some assistance from the servants. The elegant man who had met him at the door appeared.

"Your master is gravely ill. I am going to fetch the physician. Your mistress needs your help."

Without waiting for a reply Thomas dashed out of the front door and around to the stables. He was soon riding full tilt down the main street of Frome, causing heads to turn in disapproval at such haste. Master Fry's wife told him that the physician was visiting a pregnant woman at the White Swan Inn and had other calls to make. Tom caught up with him just as he was leaving the White Swan. The mention of Bartholomew Hanham's name made Abraham Fry forget about his other patients. It was clear that attendance on the Hanham family was lucrative. He was a stocky man in his early forties with an open face and a cheerful manner.

He appeared to be an experienced horseman and his horse was young and fit but they were hard put to keep pace with Tom's stallion. Few horses could match Hope's energy and desire to run fast. In consequence the physician was somewhat out of breath when they reached the main entrance of Hanham House to be greeted by Lady Agnes and her liveried attendant. The servant escorted Fry upstairs but Agnes did not follow them. She caught hold of Tom's arm to delay his departure.

"I am so grateful to you Sir Thomas for your kindness after all that Bartholomew has subjected you to."

Thomas inclined his head. "It was little enough. Any decent man would have done the same. Now I must leave you to minister to your husband."

"Do not leave yet. I am alone now and I feel so helpless. I scarce know what to do. Your presence assures me."

"I cannot help you further. You must seek support from your relations and friends. The physician will advise you."

Tom was struggling with a melee of conflicting emotions. He felt sympathy for her but he was embarrassed by the desperate way she clung on to him, digging her nails into his arm and he was angry also that she should expect support from him after all that had happened. He was frustrated that everyone expected so much from him.

"You ask too much of me Lady Agnes, far too much. I must free myself of all this, clear my mind of it all."

He brised her hand from his arm and hurried away fearing she would pursue him. She closed the door behind him with bowed head.

He knew he should call on Josiah Parry on the way back to ask him to advise the sheriff that no action be taken against Hanham. His nemesis was upon him already. He could not face going through it all just then however and rode straight home instead.

That night as he sat at supper with Waaseyaaban and Joan a dark melancholy descended on him. He brooded in silence on his life over the past few years and saw only discord, pain and death. He picked at his food and pushed it aside, drinking far more burgundy than was his normal habit. Tom took pleasure in a drink, being particularly fond of cider, but he was moderate in his drinking habits. This evening he hardly noticed how often he refilled his glass. Joan Bushy noticed. As she began to clear away the supper plates she gave Dawn Light a look which plainly said, 'he has had quite enough of that burgundy', When she did not take the bait Joan waded in herself.

"I think I shall go and read to Sarah for a short while and then go to bed. It might be a good idea if you retired yourself soon Master Tom. It has been a distressing day for everyone and you must be tired out."

He looked at her his eyes full of remorse.

"Sarah is not in any danger is she? You must tell me the truth."

"No indeed, you should have seen her just now sitting up in bed laying into her supper with a will. The wound is clean. Her arm will feel stiff and painful for a time, but that will soon pass."

He took hold of her hand in both his. "Joan, I do not know how I would be able to look you in the face again if that bastard had killed her, your little Sarah, who you protect so fiercely. To think that I might have been the cause of your losing her."

His eyes filled with tears; he could not prevent it.

"Huh, hush my dear. It did not happen and if it had it would have been no fault of yours. You must curb this habit you have of taking the weight of everything on yourself. You have drunk far too much of that burgundy. It is making you melancholy. You will have a sore head in the morning mark my words. I think perhaps I should put it away."

She took hold of the decanter and made a swift exit with it before he could protest. Tom put his arms on the table and lay his head down on them, the picture of tired despair. Waaseyaaban slipped her arm around his back.

"You hurt much. All the bad things come to you now. You talk to me, let the bad things escape. Then I have one good thing to tell you, one big good thing."

"Oh Waaseyaaban, I do not know how to talk of what I feel. Since we came back from Roanoke nothing has gone right."

He lifted his head and sat up in his chair, giving her the opportunity to sit on his lap, a thing she always loved to do.

"I have alienated my family, got involved in a war that I realised I did not believe in, my friends have died or are in exile like Simon, we lost our precious little ones and now all this, when all I did was try to help those two young people-even that resulted in death and misery. I begin to believe that I am cursed, that I bring misfortune on all around me. I should have stayed on Roanoke with you and your brothers."

"No, you are right to leave. Secotans kill all white settlers I think. We build this house. I love this house, these woods. That is good, not bad. Many people's children die. It is the way of things. You must think of this man Hanham no more or those Norringtons."

"How can I not think of them? Elizabeth believes she is in love with me, so I cause her constant unhappiness."

"She must make her own life. Her problem, not yours. You must listen now to my good news."

She took his hand and placed it on her stomach.

"There is a child inside me. I do not say until I am sure, but now I am sure."

He stroked her stomach gently. Joan was right about the burgundy. He shook his head trying to clear his muddled brain.

"Oh my love, I thought when you suffered so much hurt bearing Wawackechi that you might not conceive again."

"I feared that too, but I heal and he is here."

"He?"

"Yes, it is a boy, I know. He will live and be strong. This I know too."

He kissed her and held her tight, lost for words. This had taken him completely by surprise. He was too tired and just that bit too drunk to take it in fully. Waaseyaaban laughed and jumping to her feet took hold of his hand.

"Tomorrow we will tell Ajidamo and Wawackechi they will have brother. Now we go to bed. Good thing Joan take wine away or I have to carry you upstairs."

It was the first time he had smiled since he returned from Frome.

"No doubt you could accomplish even that, but I think I can just about make it on my own."

When they reached the staircase he misjudged the first step and almost fell on his face. Joan Bushy was just getting into bed when she heard them laughing on the stairs. She was relieved to hear him laugh. She would be even happier when she heard Dawn Light's good news.

Tom Mountfield woke up to find himself in a bright shaft of sunlight angling across his bed from the window. He was an habitual early riser, out of bed by six o'clock, but the sun did not penetrate the chamber so brightly at that time of the morning. He must have overslept. The other side of the bed was empty. Waaseyaaban had risen without waking him. When he swung his legs out of bed he found that his head ached abominably and the light hurt his eyes. He sat on the side of the bed with his face in his hands trying to collect his thoughts. Then he remembered the black mood and all that wine.

"Damn the burgundy," he groaned, massaging his temples with his fingers- but the dark melancholy was not surrounding him now; in fact he felt a vague sense of elation despite the pain over his eyes and wondered why. An image of Waaseyaaban sitting on his lap came into his mind. She said she was with child. Did he dream that or was it real? Despite his desire to run downstairs to find out, he was obliged to dress slowly. He decided to use the back staircase because it was straighter. First he knocked on Sarah Bushy's chamber door. There was no answer so he opened the door and looked in. The room was empty. Puzzled he descended the stairs with care to be met at the bottom by a smiling Joan Bushy.

"So you are up at last," she declared.

"What time is it?"

"Well past ten o'clock judging by the sun."

"Jesu, why did someone not wake me?"

"We thought it would do you good to sleep longer."

He gave her a wry smile, wincing as the sound of the dogs barking just outside the back door intensified the throb in his head.

"You were right of course- as always. I do have a sore head. You should have made off with that burgundy earlier than you did. You have good cause to smile at me."

"I am not smiling at that my dear, but at the wonderful news Dawn Light told me this morning. After all the turbulence you have been through these past two years it is the best news in the world."

She hugged him conveying all her joy in the warmth of that embrace.

"Then it is true. I scarce took it in last night and when I woke this morning I feared I had dreamed it."

"No dream. We calculate she is three months gone, so it will be an autumn baby. I know it will be hard but we must make sure she does not over-exert herself near her time, do everything we can to safeguard both her and the new life inside her, so the birth will be easier than the last one."

Thomas dare not contemplate anything but a successful birth with both mother and child thriving. He was not sure how he could bear another sorrow.

"She is convinced it is a boy child," he murmured.

"Well, she was right about the other two Master Tom."

He nodded. "Indeed, her instincts are remarkable and defy logic. But where is Sarah? I looked in on her just now to find an empty room."

"She is sitting by the fire in the kitchen. She was lonely in her bed chamber, wanting some more attention and it does her no harm to sit in the warmth. She is taking great pleasure in watching me do all the work- such a novelty for her and for the present the excitement of Dawn Light's news has taken her thoughts from the pain in her arm."

Tom did not fancy any breakfast. He was eager to see his wife who was somewhere outside. He paid a visit to the privy, closely followed by the dogs. The wolfhounds resented the fact that this was the only room they could not enter. It was far too small to accommodate them and the door was always closed on them. They would prowl around outside until the occupant re-emerged.

The roof of the arbour was greening over as the foliage of the wisteria and eglantine sprouted in abundance. On his way back Tom paused to listen to the sound of the birds in the greenery; sparrows chattering, the thin, silver pipe of a wren, a chaffinch's rhythmical chunter. Blackbirds scuffled in the grass and a robin followed him all the way along the arbour, perching close by his head, treating him to short bursts of song. He had been denied the pleasure of all this the previous year and was determined to appreciate spring to its full extent.

He saw Waaseyaaban talking to Toby Aycliffe, who was forking manure into a freshly dug patch of garden. He called out to her and she ran to him, the sun catching the glossy black sheen of her hair. How could anyone fail to find her beautiful Tom thought as she put her arms around his neck and he lifted her off the ground, swinging her around in a half-circle. Looking up from his digging, Toby called out his congratulations concerning the baby, waving his fork in salute.

"So everyone knows now?" Tom asked.

"Yes, but not the little ones. I wait for you so we can tell them together."

She put her hand on the crown of his head.

"How does head feel?"

"Sore, but tis no one's fault but my own. My heart is so full now I can ignore an aching head. Wait there, I have a gift for the little ones."

The fact that both Ajidamo and Wawackechi had died before they could form any identity or personality did not prevent Waaseyaaban feeling their presence as individuals and her relationship with them influenced Thomas. Adjidamo was premature and still-born but his daughter had lived for a few days. He had held her, had a clear image of her face in his mind. He could imagine how she would look now. They would always be his children despite their short lives and he loved them. It seemed the most natural thing in the world for Waaseyaaban to talk to them as if they could hear her. Perhaps they could.

There were moments when he was working in the garden, when out of the corner of his eye he would catch a swift movement of something light and diaphanous and could swear that he heard the sound of children's laughter.

He hurried now into the library and searched around in the top drawer of his desk. When he had visited the glazier to bargain a deal for the glass to fill the school windows, he noticed a glass prism hanging from a beam in the man's workshop. It was formed in the shape of a triangle with a small hole in the apex, through which was threaded a wire loop. Thomas was fascinated by the play of light through the glass, creating rainbow hues. He thought how much it would please Waaseyaaban and asked if it was for sale. The glazier had shaped it for his own pleasure, but he was willing to sell it, as he could always make another. His was the only glass works for miles around and he enjoyed creating ornamental objects as well as practical ones. Tom had put the prism in his desk drawer intending to hang it near the copper discs as a surprise for his wife but had not got around to it. He knew now just where to put it.

Joining his wife in the garden, he took her hand and led her up to where the two gravestones stood. She asked no questions, waiting to see what he would do. He chose a lower branch of one of the hawthorns behind the graves and fixed the wire loop of the prism on to it. He had chosen well for the sun hit it at once, causing arcs of coloured light to play over the face of the gravestones. Waaseyaaban was delighted.

"Oh- like rainbow." She put her hand out to let the colour reflect on it. "Beautiful. Make Adjidamo and Wawackechi very happy."

"It is called a prism. The angled surfaces of the glass struck by the light cause this effect. I often ponder over the reason for it. Light itself is regarded as white, so where do the colours come from? Is it some property contained within the glass itself or are the colours part of the white light and are somehow released when it hits the glass? Then again do the colours come from the interaction of our brains with the mechanics of our sight? Do you not wonder about the origins of the colours?"

"No, it does not matter. They are there. That is enough."

He smiled and kissed her hand. He would never surrender his curiosity about the world, his desire to understand the structure of the universe and penetrate God's purposes for humanity, but such a quest was a restless, disturbing journey. He could see the attraction of Waaseyaaban's uncomplicated acceptance of the things she saw around her.

When something pleased her, the joy she felt was unalloyed by any reasoning or doubt. It warmed his soul to feel the completeness of her joy. Her nature kept him in balance, offered him a peaceful haven when he needed it. He often thought it strange how someone who could be so fierce and combative could also be so calming and bring him such peace.

She sat down on the grass, tucking her feet up beneath her and patted the ground inviting him to sit beside her. Once he had done so she spoke to the children in Croatan, telling them that their father had given them the gift of the colours of the rainbow and they soon would have a brother, who would grow up brave and strong like their father. She would tell him about his brother and sister and he would never forget them. When she was finished Tom put his arm around her shoulder and they sat for a while in silence, their heads touching, watching the colours dance over the stones before they returned to their daily tasks.

Chapter Twelve

ROBERT MOUNTFIELD MARCHED INTO his son's house an expression on his face that predicted confrontation. Lady Anne was close behind him but she was unable to keep up with him without breaking into a run and had no intention of doing that. Thomas was coming down the passage to greet them. Before he could open his mouth his father declared, "It is a fine thing when we have to hear from a stranger that our son has been stalked by an assassin for months and has had three attempts made on his life without thinking it worth mentioning to his parents."

Tom sighed. He had intended to tell them on their next visit rather than sending a message. He was not sure when they would come and had not expected them so soon.

"Who told you?"

"The sheriff. I had cause to meet with him yesterday on official business. I felt such a fool that he knew all about it and I did not."

Tom kissed his mother's cheek and apologised to them both.

"I was going to tell you when you visited next. It was too complicated for a letter."

"But it all started back in November did it not?" Robert's voice was full of indignation. "That was when we should have been told."

"Well, I was not sure at first that I was a target. After the second attempt I was certain but the snows came and we were cut off. By the time the thaw came I had put it to the back of my mind and did not wish to alarm you. Come into the parlour and I will tell you the whole story."

He proceeded to do just that, his mother listening in sympathetic silence, his father interjecting frequently with questions.

"So you see I have been very fortunate. The first time Daffyd Williams saved me from serious injury, the second Ajax was my saviour and two days ago if Sarah had not moved across at that very moment I would have taken a shot square in the back."

"Poor Sarah, Joan must be so worried about her. I must go and see how she fares." Lady Anne left the room in search of Joan, saying to her son, "What a relief that man is in custody."

"I wish I had been present to see you catch the rogue my boy," Robert said. "Was it difficult to get him to confess who paid him?"

"No, when I threatened to strangle him he soon came out with it. I must have been convincing."

A smile spread across his father's face.

"Well he had no right to expect easy handling. You are a force to be reckoned with when you are angry."

"I might say the same about you father."

"Thank God you escaped it all unharmed. I must give that gaoler Williams a reward for his quick action in the market. I will ask Josiah Parry to pass it on to him."

"Why not give it to Daffyd yourself?"

"I think it more appropriate to do so through the constable. I do not wish Parry to think his authority is being side-stepped."

Thomas smiled to himself. His father must always follow the correct form and besides he would consider dealing directly with the gaoler beneath him. He could sense that Robert did not approve of him using Daffyd's Christian name in such an easy way.

"Did I not say before the trial that Bartholomew Hanham's brain had been turned by it all? I have known him for thirty years and although a trifle shallow and self-satisfied, he always did his duty as a magistrate with complete fairness. I would never have thought him capable of employing an assassin. Is he like to recover from his apoplectic fit?"

Thomas shook his head. He had tried not to dwell on it since Waaseyaaban had told him her good news but the look of fear and helplessness in Agnes Hanham's eyes came back to him now. "I doubt it very much. He has been a sick man for some time. His legs were swollen up, his eyes protuberant and bloodshot. Seeing me and knowing that his plot had been discovered brought on the fit but it would have happened soon anyway. I must admit to feeling some pity for Lady Agnes who was at a loss what to do."

He wanted nothing more to do with the Hanham's yet he wished to know if Agnes had someone to comfort her. His father solved the problem.

"I will pay Agnes a visit. She was always a scatterbrain, always inclined to believe everything Bartholomew told her. Very comely woman when she was in her prime. It was a great sorrow to them that they had no children. Anthony seemed to be the answer to their prayers. I will assure her that Anne and I hold no resentment against her for her husband's actions. I can see that you have no desire to go there again."

Thomas was grateful. "Thank you Father, that will be a courteous thing to do and you are right, I do not want to see Hanham House ever again."

His mother came back into the room at that moment followed by Joan Bushy carrying a tray of refreshments. Robert asked after Sarah's progress, was pleased to hear she was doing well and promised he would come to see her before they left. He remarked how fortunate it was that she moved when she did or Thomas might have been killed. Although it was not meant as such, it sounded dismissive of Sarah and Tom thought it tactless in front of Joan.

"It was hardly fortunate for Sarah," he cut in sharply. "The poor girl was frightened and has been in some pain. I had far rather the shot hit me."

"Nonsense," his father retorted. "Don't you think that is taking chivalry too far, preferring to risk a fatal wound to save that girl a week or two's pain?"

"And what if she had been killed Father, how do you think I would have felt then?"

This was how it always happened. One minute he would feel that he and Robert were understanding each other and the next they were at odds again. He looked at Joan, his eyes full of apologies, but she seemed unruffled.

"Sir Robert, Master Tom has been very distressed by this whole business. He feels responsible for what happened to Sarah and that unpleasantness regarding Sir Bartholomew's apoplexy. His nerves have been stretched to their limit. I am sure you did not mean to be dismissive of my daughter's hurt."

"Indeed I did not, but I find Tom's reactions so extreme at times. His expectations of himself are impossibly high. He has a rare talent for getting himself into trouble but in no way is he responsible for what has happened to him of late."

"Oh," Thomas countered, "Then you do not put my misfortunes down to my stubborn refusal to follow the dictates of society after all. You have always given me the impression that you did."

Lady Anne sighed. She had been shocked by the news that her son was the target of an assassin. She had almost lost him to that fever and what she wished to do today was to hold him in her arms and cherish him. She was irritated that Robert made such intimacy difficult, particularly as she knew how much he loved his son. On reflection she had to admit that the fault was not all on her husband's side. Tom was too quick to take offence. They were too much alike in some aspects to have an easy relationship.

"Joan says you have some good news to tell us Tom dear," she said in her most calming voice. "We would welcome some good news."

"I am not sure you will regard this as good news," he replied.

He had intended to tell his parents about the baby in a confident, cheerful manner so that they could not help but be happy for him. This skirmish with his father had dented his confidence, made him doubt a favourable reception. Joan gave him an encouraging nod before she discreetly withdrew. He wished she had stayed; she was such a doughty ally. He had been standing by the fireplace but now he sat down close to his mother.

"Dawn Light is with child again."

It was important to him to stress the word 'again' to remind his parents that he had suffered the sorrow of lost children. Waaseyaaban was seven months pregnant when they returned from the Netherlands. Tom had left her with friends at Oxford, went to London to receive his knighthood and then to Salisbury to see his family. He had left the house so hurt and angry at his father's attitude, not staying long enough to mention that his wife was only two months from giving birth. He had no idea where they were going to live, but was determined not to enter the family home again. His friend Abel Chandler had a smallholding on the outskirts of Oxford. He was struggling to make ends meet and Thomas did not want to impose on him for much longer. Then the news reached him of the bequest of land in Wiltshire, left him by Harry Carthew. He was eager to see it, so was Waaseyaaban. They bought a donkey cart from Abel to transport their few possessions and acquired Hetty the cob from a farmer who was selling up. Reaching Devizes Thomas took a room in the Bear Inn so his wife would have a comfortable place to give birth and avail herself of the services of a midwife. He would never forget the pleasure on her face when they took their first trip to the forest and he described to her the house he intended to build in the clearing.

The baby came early and never took a breath. Waaseyaaban wished to bury his tiny casket in the forest where they were to live and to stay close by, so Thomas put up a temporary shelter while the house took shape.

His family knew nothing of all this and the death of Ajidamo passed them by.

Anne eventually discovered where her son had gone by contacting Abel Chandler. She was horrified to find him living in what was little more than a windbreak, clearly feverish and with no one to care for him but this strange woman with her tanned skin and coal-black eyes. Cecily on the other hand was excited by what Thomas was planning. His exotic wife appealed to her imagination. They became friends in no time and Cecily shared the pleasure of Waaseyaaban's second pregnancy. Tom recalled the genuine depths of his sister's grief when she and Anne arrived to see the new baby only to find that she had died that very morning. Cecily stayed on for several days to keep Dawn Light company. His mother had expressed her regret and he knew she felt it for him, but was not sure how deep her sympathy was for his wife. He had no idea what his father thought about it and did not ask. Their alienation at that point seemed so complete it was irrelevant to him what Robert thought- or so he told himself.

Now Lady Anne took hold of Tom's hand.

"I am so pleased for you Tom. We must pray that this child is born strong and healthy."

"You will say so to Dawn Light with the same warmth you show to me won't you Mother?"

"Of course I shall, you must take me to see her in a moment."

Thomas looked across at his father.

"Well, have you nothing to say?"

When his wife had brought him the news of the death of Tom's daughter Robert had distanced himself from it. He had been certain at first that his son would climb down quickly after that fierce quarrel and ask his pardon, come back to the house willing to listen to reason, but more than a year had passed and Tom was still defiant. The whole situation seemed unreal, his boy preferring the company of a heathen native woman to that of his own parents; choosing to live in the wilds of a forest rather than the comfort of his childhood home. He needed to cope with his own hurt, not consider Tom's. Now that some of the emotional barriers had been crossed and he was visiting the house, he avoided the gravestones at the top of the garden. There was a moment when he discovered them first that he was struck by the realisation that these were his grandchildren.

It pricked his heart with sharp regret until those names carved on the stones in a strange language to which he could not relate reinforced his resistance and drove out the pity. He was not sure now how he felt, how to respond to Tom's challenge. Thomas was quick to interpret his hesitation as unfavourable and with an expression on his face that blended acceptance of the inevitable with disappointment, he got to his feet and walked back to the fireplace, leaning on the surround, looking down into the empty grate with his back to his parents.

"I might have guessed as much," he murmured, a weary bitterness in his voice.

Robert rose also and joining him by the fireplace, put his hands on his son's shoulders. "You mistake me my boy. Do not imagine I have no understanding of how recent events have affected your spirits. The prospect of a child is just what you need to lift your spirits again and I rejoice with you."

When Thomas did not reply he added," How can I make you believe that?"

Tom turned to face him. "You could start by acknowledging Dawn Light's existence instead of pretending she is not there. You may refuse to call her my wife but you cannot ignore the fact that she is the mother of this child."

"I do not know how to communicate with her. That woman's behaviour is beyond my understanding, my experience."

"It might help if you used her name instead of calling her 'that woman'.

"Her name sits awkwardly on my tongue."

"Why? It is merely a rough translation from Croatan of her name. Respectable English gentlemen call their daughters Aurora and the translation of that from the Latin is Dawn. If you find it easier, drop the second part of the name and call her Dawn."

Robert made an uncomfortable coughing noise at the back of his throat, then said, "Well, fetch her and we will express our pleasure at this news."

"No, I will take you both to her."

Before his father could reply Thomas took his mother's arm and led her out of the room, leaving Robert no choice but to follow.

Waaseyaaban was in the yard feeding the chickens when she saw Thomas and his parents heading towards her. She would run out to meet the visitors if Cecily was in the party, but she would avoid Sir Robert as long as possible. She put down the bowl of scraps and looked up into Tom's face trying to gauge if he had been arguing with his father. He smiled at her and she knew he had told them about the child. She was surprised when Lady Anne came forward and kissed her on both cheeks.

"Robert and I are delighted to hear you are with child my dear."

Thomas gave his father a look so keen it was the equivalent of a nudge in the ribs.

"Yes indeed," Robert confirmed. "Just what Thomas needs after his recent misfortunes- during which I must acknowledge that you have been very loyal to him."

He did not find the compliment easy to make and half expected she would show some sign of gratitude for his condescension. She said nothing however, watching him with a wary detachment.

"My father would like to call you Aurora," Tom said out of the blue, a mischievous smile playing at the corners of his mouth.

"I- I never said that," Robert protested, taken off guard and Anne began to laugh.

Waaseyaaban was puzzled. "What is Aurora?"

"Just as Dawn Light is the English version of your name my love, Aurora is your name in Latin."

"What is Latin?"

"A classical language, much admired by respectable people," Tom emphasized the word respectable. "It is a tongue spoken by a powerful race of long ago called the Romans. Many books have been written in Latin and I was taught to speak it at school. It is the language the minister uses in parts of the church service."

"Oh, that tongue." Waaseyaaban knew what he meant now. "Though I do not understand words he speak, I like the sound of them. Aurora-" she repeated the name, breaking it into syllables in her usual way. "It is the same as Waaseyaaban?"

"Almost."

"Then father can call me Aurora if he wish," she conceded with some grace.

Robert was lost for words and Tom could imagine what amusement the recounting of this would give Cecily.

Before they left that day Robert and Anne Mountfield agreed to return on Sunday afternoon and stay overnight so they could attend the opening of the village school the following morning. Cecily and Godfrey would come with them. As Robert embraced his son in farewell he murmured in his ear, "I will pay you back for that Aurora ambush young man," and they smiled at each other. He did not bid goodbye to Dawn Light in words but he did give her a nod of acknowledgement which marked a small step forward.

The group of villagers who had assembled to watch the opening of the new school was gratified that it was such a fine day. It seemed to be a good omen that the sun shone so brightly on the venture and the April sky was cloudless.

The group consisted mainly of women, who found it easier to leave their work than the menfolk although several venerable grey beards past heavy work, leaning on gnarled walking sticks, were satisfying their curiosity also.

Nathan Pocock had allowed his workmen to stop their labour for a short while to watch. They were lined up against the wood yard fence. Pocock felt that as the house had once belonged to him and the schoolmaster and his wife were now lodging with his family, he should mark the occasion by granting his men this favour.

Very little happened to disturb the daily routine of the village, yet only last week the foreigner had wounded Sarah Bushy, was captured by Sir Thomas and locked up in the wood yard until the constable took him away. That was a rare excitement and was still being discussed that morning, given impetus by the fact that Sarah had come with her mother to attend the opening ceremony. It was also entertaining to see so many well-to-do people gathered in the village and speculation on their identity kept the chatter going. Toby and Ned found themselves in great demand because they could answer the questions of the curious.

Besides Sir Thomas' parents, his sister and her husband Godfrey Roper, several merchant friends of Godfrey's who had sponsored the project were in attendance. The three ministers who were to share the duty of religious instruction were present. The wife of the Reverend Walters, a bustling, rosy-faced woman would be undertaking the task of teaching the youngest children. The school master and his wife had arrived only two days since, so for most of the assembled villagers this was their first sight of them.

Godfrey had sent word to Tom that he found Sebastian Braddon a promising candidate. When Thomas interviewed him he had to beware of liking him instantly because the man reminded him of Simon Bailey. He was not as big as Simon, but he had a similar broad, open face and wore spectacles. His earnest manner too was reminiscent of Bailey. After spending an hour with him, asking some very searching questions, Tom was convinced he was the man for the job. His grandfather was a saddle maker. His father had prospered and come to own a small tannery business which enabled him to send Sebastian to the best school in Salisbury. The masters there soon recognised the boy's ability and trained him as a pupil teacher.

He taught at that school for five years and then spent several years as senior master at a village school before returning to Salisbury to teach at the school that had recently closed down. He was grateful to get another job so soon. In his early forties, he had a confident, authoritative manner and he was open to new ideas. Tom sensed a true enthusiasm for learning in him and his previous experience at a village school should make him sensitive to the problems of teaching labourers' children.

Tom was not so sure how easy Braddon's wife Ruth would find it to fit in to village life. She was twenty years younger than her husband, a thin pale-skinned woman with nervous grey eyes. She spoke little and when she was addressed she did not look into the face of the person who spoke to her but lowered her gaze in a timid way; some would call it sulky. Braddon treated her with courtesy and kindness, yet Tom had the feeling that there was not much true affection between them. The village women were not impressed by their first viewing of her. She looked drab and mousey standing behind her husband, her head bowed as if she was studying the floor boards. The contrast with the elegant Lady Anne, Cecily Roper in her fashionable clothes and the cheerful minister's wife did Ruth Braddon no favours in their eyes. They had found Waaseyaaban very strange at first, wondering why on earth Sir Thomas Mountfield would marry such a woman. They were used to her now and had even come to appreciate her exotic beauty. She brought some colour into the village and she never acted as if she thought herself better than they were, even though she had married a gentleman. They were not sure about the new teacher's wife. Her offhand manner could be attributed to shyness but they suspected that a discontent bred by the prospect of living amongst labouring folk was at the root of it.

Tom's main worry that morning was that no children would turn up. Numbers were thin at first but they gradually trickled in. Around thirty children of mixed ages were now running around the garden pleased to be free from the drudgery of working in the fields or minding their younger siblings. Some of them had come only to watch, while others were eager to attend the school. It was enough to get started.

He had sent a message to James and Elizabeth inviting them to the opening. They had not arrived yet and he wondered if Sir Neville had prevented them.

Just as he made up his mind not to wait any longer and to start the proceedings, he saw three figures on horseback approaching. It was indeed the Norringtons accompanied by Jacob Whyte.

Tom was right in his assumption that Sir Neville had opposed his children attending the opening but he had not put up a fight. He declared that as his opinion had no influence over them anymore, they must do as they wished, although he did stipulate that Jacob Whyte must go with them. The affectionate kiss Elizabeth gave him was only a small consolation for the indignity of having his wishes ignored.

When Thomas had told Waaseyaaban that he was inviting the Norringtons his tone of voice had suggested there was no room for debate and she had said nothing. She was watching them now as they dismounted and stood at the back of the crowd while Jacob held the horses. Her face was impassive but a hint of the old resentment lurked in her eyes. Elizabeth had eyes only for Tom. He looked so distinctive dressed all in black except for his white shirt and garters. She had not seen him since their encounter in the empty school room. The memory of those moments of intense contact, the warmth of his kisses, the desire she felt in his whole body filled her with an exhilaration that kept her spirits high. The hope it engendered in her gave her the courage to face Dawn Light's scorn if the need arose. Now however as she caught sight of Tom's wife wearing the apple green bead embroidered garment that Lizzie remembered so well from their first meeting, she was not so confident. Dawn Light was also wearing a velvet cloak of darker green with matching ribbons woven through her hair plaits. Standing beside Joan Bushy and her daughter, her dark beauty stood out. Lady Anne had grace and elegance, Cecily was pretty and vivacious but there was a power in Waaseyaaban's beauty that went far beyond the simple fact of her being different. Elizabeth was not aware of course that Tom's wife was with child. The inner joy of that radiated from her. Lizzie looked away fearing that the woman with her uncanny instinct would know what she was thinking and turned her attention back to Thomas.

He made a short speech of welcome explaining how much he believed in the liberating power of education and how this school was the realisation of a dream that had taken shape in his mind a long time past. He thanked all those who had contributed in various ways to make it possible because he could not have achieved his goal alone. Robert Mountfield looked at Anne and smiled. He was very proud of his son at that moment and wanted Anne to know it. That speech had hit just the right note, full of sincerity yet humble, completely free of pomposity or self-satisfaction.

The previous week Cecily had visited Grace and Margaret to tell them about Tom's fortunate escape from the assassin and encourage them to come to the opening of the school. They refused with lame excuses. She had expected it but was angry none-the-less and waxed hot condemning their failure to support him at the trial and their refusal now to share in his success. Robert had defended his elder daughters, understanding that their husband's families had no wish to be associated with a loose cannon whose so-called wife was not socially acceptable. Now he regretted their absence and wished he had put some pressure on them himself.

As those children who were willing were rounded up and arranged in a straight line to file into the school room, Robert patted his son on the back.

"Well done my boy, an excellent speech. This is an achievement to be proud of. I know Cecily has made her opinions clear enough already and I must say that both your mother and I condemn Margaret and Grace for failing to support you. They should have made more effort to visit you in prison, attended the trial and they should be here now with their children so your nephews and nieces could see what a fine thing you have done here."

Tom had not expected to hear his father say that. He had been surprised and relieved by how smoothly his parents' overnight stay at the house had gone. Though Robert was still uncomfortable in Dawn Light's company, he had said nothing to try Tom's temper and accorded her the courtesy of bidding her goodnight. Thomas was pleased also that Robert had kept his promise to visit Agnes Hanham. He reported back that Bartholomew Hanham was in desperate straits, paralysed down one side and bereft of coherent speech. However Agnes' sister had come to stay with her. Kate was a practical woman without airs and graces, just what Agnes needed.

"I remember them both when they were girls," Robert said. "You could not find two siblings more opposed in their outlooks. Agnes was for ever fluttering about like a butterfly concerned with gossip and finery intent on capturing a rich husband, whereas Kate was a quiet, serious girl much concerned with religion. Neither of them has changed much. Kate has stiffened Agnes' resolve and organised Bartholomew's care in great detail. She has convinced Agnes that what has befallen them is God's punishment on them for closing their eyes to Anthony's wickedness and then attempting to take vengeance on an innocent man, so she must accept the situation with remorse and humility. Strangely that hard doctrine seems to give Agnes comfort. "

While Tom could see how people's actions could draw down disaster on themselves with a chilling inevitability, he struggled with the notion that God punished individuals in such a precise, particular way. It was good to know that Agnes had found someone to support her. His mother was beside him now, watching the children file into school, some of them more reluctant than others. Dawn Light was helping Seb Braddon and the minister's wife to persuade them. Her staccato directions-"You next, now you"- were very efficacious.

"Most of them are going in," Lady Anne remarked. "I think they dare not defy Dawn Light."

Thomas smiled. "She is good with children. They like her because she has no pretentions, no hidden purposes. Getting the school open was the easiest part of this plan. Keeping the children interested enough to attend regularly and convincing the parents of the value of education will be far harder."

"This venture will be so good for you," Anne said, linking her arm through his.

"The purpose is to benefit the children Mother, not me."

"Ah, but you must grant me the right to worry about your wellbeing my dear Thomas. That is what mothers are for."

Cecily joined them to announce that Godfrey was organizing the guests to make their way to Tom's house. Joan was treating them all to a celebratory meal before they departed. She and Sarah had already left to complete the preparations. Tom told his parents to accompany the guests.

"I wish to see the children registered first, then I will come. Joan will have everything in hand."

As Robert and Anne strolled away Cecily murmured, "You know the Norringtons are here?"

"Yes I saw them arrive."

"Shall I invite them to the meal?"

"You should ask them certainly but I doubt if they will accept the invitation."

Cecily did not need to ask why.

"And what about her?" She jerked her head in the direction of Mistress Braddon who was standing by the school door, her eyes cast down as usual.

"Of course she is invited."

They walked over to her and Thomas said, "Mistress Braddon, are you not going to join the other guests to visit my house?"

She looked up but her eyes slid past his face, fixing on the space behind his shoulder.

"I have no transport Sir Thomas. Besides I should be out of place in such company."

"I hope no one would feel out of place in my house Mistress. You will soon discover that we do not live in the grand style or set store by fancy manners. I intend to entertain both you and your husband on many occasions in the future."

"And transport is no problem," Cecily added. "Godfrey drove me in the carriage this morning. There is plenty of room for you and we can convey you back here on our way home."

"You are both too kind I am sure but I would rather travel with your servants, more befitting my station," Ruth replied with a thin simper that had a sour edge to it.

"There are no servants with whom you can travel." There was a touch of impatience in Cecily's voice. "You will suit us well enough. Now go and tell my husband I wish you to ride with us."

Ruth Braddon bobbed in a half curtsey and crept away like a kitchen maid who had been chastised. Cecily pulled a face behind her back.

"I don't like that woman Tom. She is one of those folk who enjoys being a martyr and frowns on the happiness of others."

Thomas nodded. "I suppose we should not rush to judgement but I must confess I have not taken to Mistress Braddon myself."

Cecily was disinclined to believe that the woman would improve on acquaintance, but she changed the subject her green eyes sparkling with humour, as she asked, "Where is Aurora then?"

Tom had divined rightly that his sister's fancy would be tickled by that particular exchange with their father.

"Last night at supper," she continued, "When he asked her to pass the vegetable dish, I swear he almost called her Aurora but stopped just in time."

"Well he almost called her something," Thomas agreed, laughing," But I think it was the letter d that was on his tongue before he let it die away unspoken."

"She should be at the house Tom to welcome the guests. It will be to her advantage. Joan and Sarah have already left but she can come with us in the carriage, sit with Mistress Self-Abasement."

Tom knew Waaseyaaban had no desire to play hostess although he took his sister's point. It would be a chance for his wife to demonstrate that she was mistress of the house.

"Wait there, I will ask her."

Inside the school room Sally Walters, the minister's wife had singled out all the children she believed to be under seven years old, their own testimony being unreliable and led them to the back corner of the room to sit on rush matting behind two folding screens so they would not be distracted by the activities of the older pupils. After some dissension over who would sit where, most of the other children had claimed their desks. The front row was noticeably unoccupied and Seb Braddon was in the process of persuading some of the shorter pupils to sit there so they could see well. Waaseyaaban was watching it all unfold with great interest. Tom slipped his arm around her waist.

"You have been very helpful herding the children."

She looked up at him, smiling. "Yes they are like sheep."

"But now Cecily wants you to go back with her to the house and preside over the meal."

The smile faded from her face. "No, I stay with you."

"I shall return to the house myself soon. I just want to see the pupils registered first."

"I want to see that too. I like them better than guests."

"You should be there my love. It is your house as much as mine and I want everyone to grow used to that notion. You must take possession of your territory."

"No, I come back with you."

He could see she would not be persuaded and stepped back outside to tell Cecily to go ahead without her.

His sister turned her attention to the Norringtons who were standing with Jacob Whyte beside their horses in conversation with Toby Aycliffe. Toby was regaling them with the story of Sir Thomas' fortunate escapes from the assassin and how Master Tom had caught the villain after he had shot Sarah Bushy by mistake and dragged him down the street. The fact that Toby was not there at the time, so none of it was first hand did not diminish the colour of his narrative. James was truly disappointed that he had missed all that excitement and danger. He wished he had seen Tom drive the assassin back against the wall and threaten to strangle him if he did not reveal the truth. The men from Pocock's wood yard had described this in such detail to Toby that he felt qualified to re-tell it with vigour and he certainly captured James' imagination. The boy was eager to discuss it with Tom and when Cecily approached them, inviting them back to the house, he hoped Elizabeth would agree. Lizzie however said she thought their presence would be inappropriate and they must return home soon. "We would like to wait a few more moments though to give Sir Thomas our good wishes for the success of the school."

"I am sure you would," Cecily replied with an amused expression in her eyes.

"He is supervising the pupil registration at the present. He will be out directly but I must warn you Dawn Light is with him."

She skipped away to join Godfrey pleased with her light-hearted teasing. Elizabeth's infatuation with her brother was so evident, Cecily could not resist drawing attention to it for her own amusement. Lizzie could not mistake the implication and did not resent it. She was sure she would like Cecily very much if she came to know her well. Beneath Cecily's bright vivacity there was sympathy and understanding. There was no malice in her humour. Her deep affection for her brother was clear and that alone drew Elizabeth to her. James plucked at her sleeve.

"They are coming out now Lizzie. Let's go over to them."

Thomas and his wife had emerged from the school room holding hands. Their closeness, the pleasure they took in each other, pricked Lizzie's heart. Waaseyaaban took a quick look in their direction, murmuring in a low voice, "Norringtons come to see you."

"You need not worry. It seems they do not intend to come to the house."

"Good. I fetch horse."

She did not want to risk displeasing Tom by letting her resentment show too much. James was relieved to see her walk away. He launched into a barrage of excited questions about the assassination attempts while Elizabeth stood beside him her eyes fixed on Tom's face. She was appalled to think that while she was still walking on air because of their encounter in the school room he might have been murdered and she know nothing of it.

"We thank God that you escaped unharmed," she said when she could get a word in. Thomas looked directly into her eyes. She was wearing the dark blue cloak she had worn at his trial. The colour suited her so well. Though he had not admitted it to his wife, he was pleased also that these two were not coming back to the house. He wanted to immerse himself in the joy of Waaseyaaban's pregnancy without the complication of any feelings for Elizabeth Norrington. It was too easy to experience once again how much he had desired her that morning.

"Well some good angel was watching over me it seems, undeserving as I am of such a favour. I can only assume that I have been spared to do something of worth in this world. I hope this school is a small beginning. Perhaps it could be that both paradise and the other place considered I would be too disruptive an influence to enter them as yet." Elizabeth responded to his wry self-mocking by taking hold of his hand and assuring him how much he was needed and cherished. James was embarrassed by his sister's forwardness. He understood why she loved Thomas but wished she would not reveal it so openly. He still struggled to balance his own independence with the fear of hurting his father's feelings too deeply and worried about gossip reaching Sir Neville's ears. Gossip twisted and exaggerated the facts. James did not wish his father to believe Lizzie and Tom were acting improperly, breaking the bounds of propriety. He was prejudiced enough against Thomas already.

"Toby Aycliffe tells me you will be taking some of the lessons yourself," he said to prevent Elizabeth from pursuing the drift of her thoughts.

"I intend to take an hour every Wednesday and Friday morning to talk to them about History and Geography. I would like them to have some idea of where other countries lie in relation to England, describe the people, customs, language of some of the countries I have visited myself. I want to convey just a little of the excitement I feel about how voyages of discovery are opening up the wonders of creation to us. It would be good also for them to learn the basic outline of England's history. Later, depending on their progress, I might discuss some philosophy and astronomy with the abler pupils. Nothing too profound, but enough to awaken their curiosity. What do you think? Does this sound like a good plan to you?"

James was full of enthusiasm.

"An excellent plan. Would you permit me to attend some of your lessons? I thirst to hear more about other countries. I was a poor scholar when I was younger. I paid little attention to my tutor because I thought him tedious and he was impatient with me. When you explain a concept it all becomes so clear to me. I can form a picture of it in my head. I will sit right at the back of the room and be no trouble to anyone."

"I am flattered by your request," Tom replied, thinking that the James Norrington of two years ago would have been outraged at the prospect of sharing a school room with labourers' children. "Of course you can come, but your father will not be overjoyed by the notion."

"He has granted us the freedom to do as we wish."

"Yes, but that is not quite the same as approving of it."

James felt obliged to confess. "Well no, he does not approve of our connection with you. He considers your views dangerous. He is very conventional in his outlook. He thinks too much speculation about the nature of things is corrupting."

Thomas sighed. "I guessed as much. I wish you would convey to him that I have no desire to steal your allegiance away from him. It is clear to me that both of you respect and love him and I would not wish it otherwise."

"I have told him that you never try to persuade me to hold your opinions, that what you do is encourage me to think for myself."

Elizabeth could see Dawn Light leading Tom's chestnut stallion towards them and interrupted James by saying, "It is time we left now. We are keeping Jacob from his duties. I will join James at one of your lessons if I may. I have a proposal to make to you."

"A proposal?" There was a question in Tom's eyes, a hint of uneasiness.

"Concerning the teaching. I will explain when next we meet."

She liked the idea that he would be anticipating their next meeting with some curiosity.

Waaseyaaban had given the Norringtons what she considered a reasonable amount of time and now intended to cut it short. She had taken off her cloak and thrown it across the horse's back in front of the saddle, always glad to be free of the encumbrance of long garments. Handing Hope's reins to her husband she said, "We go home now Makwa," not deigning to give either Lizzie or James one look. Tom bid them good morning and mounted his horse, holding out his hand to help Waaseyaaban up behind him. She swung herself up with a feline agility displaying the full length of her smooth brown legs. Now she did look at Elizabeth, her expression conveying clearly without the need for words, "How you wish you could do this with such freedom and you never will." Her aim was so accurate. Lizzie longed to be free from restraint, to sit behind Tom on that handsome horse, put her arms Mountfield's waist and press her face into his broad back. She imagined what it would feel like riding at breakneck speed, clinging on to him. Her imaginings were so strong she felt giddy with exhilaration just standing there. James on the other hand felt guilty because the sight of Dawn Light's legs conjured up a picture of her standing naked in the bed chamber that night he was foolish enough to investigate his witch theory. The memory of it stirred his blood and he was ashamed to be thinking such carnal thoughts. He was sure he must be blushing and walked away to join Jacob Whyte. Elizabeth watched Thomas until he was out of sight before she followed her brother.

The next day Thomas rode to Salisbury in search of a map of the world.

He could have sketched one on paper himself but he wanted something more elaborate and colourful, a visual delight to capture the children's attention straight away, to fill them with wonder. He remembered a shop near the North Gate that might provide what he wanted. Should he fail to find anything suitable he would be forced to send to London for it which could take weeks. He wished to use it with his first class the next day.

The shop was just as he recalled it, an old, low building with tiny windows. Tom had to duck his head to pass under the door arch and then descend two steps into a dingy room filled to capacity with stock. The musty smell of paper and parchment hit his nostrils. It was a smell that was congenial to him because it reminded him of hours of fascinating study at Oxford when he lost himself in obscure manuscripts. Despite the poor light he spotted a copy of "The History of Travel," the collected works of Richard Eden that was published just after Tom had entered Philip Sidney's service. He had always meant to acquire a copy and never got round to it. Standing next to it was Richard Hakluyt's "The Principal Navigations, Voyages and Discoveries of the English Nation." Thomas picked it up with excitement. He was familiar with Hakluyt's pioneering work in cosmography. In the early eighties he gave lectures in Geography at Oxford and recommended the use of maps, globes and spheres in schools. He was an enthusiastic supporter of the notion of expanding England's sovereignty by colonising new-found areas of the world.

He became a publicist for maritime enterprises, drawing attention to the need for finding the North East and North West passages to the orient, supporting Humphrey Gilbert and Martin Frobisher in their attempts. He had backed Raleigh's Virginia project by writing a secret report, "The Discourse on the Western Planting" which he presented to the Queen, setting out the political and economic benefits and emphasising the need for state support.

Elizabeth thanked him for his trouble by awarding him a prebend at Bristol Cathedral, but she did not provide any money to help Raleigh's venture. Thomas knew about the report because of his close involvement in the planning of the expedition. As far as he knew it had never been printed.

He was a great admirer of Hakluyt, but was not familiar with the book he was browsing through now. It must have been published within the last few years because it covered some of the period Tom was endeavouring to write about himself.

"Marvellously comprehensive narrative Sir." The bookseller was hovering near Tom's elbow. "A true epic depiction of our national spirit and confirmation of our right to sovereignty over the oceans."

"I am sure you meant to say Her Majesty Queen Elizabeth's right," Tom corrected, amused by the man's florid vocabulary. "We must choose our words very carefully these days."

The bookseller inclined his head in assent. He was not sure if he was being teased or tested, which was Tom's intention, but he resisted the urge to agitate him further saying, "I am familiar with Hakluyt's earlier work but this must be more recent."

"Yes indeed, printed at the end of 1589 I believe."

The man had noticed Tom's interest in the Richard Eden book also and keen for some business proposed, "If you wished to buy both these volumes Sir I could offer you a good bargain price for the two."

"I am greatly tempted, but what I really search for is a large map of the world."

"Then you are in luck Sir."

The bookseller trotted off to an alcove at the back of the shop and returned with a folded parchment. He removed a pile of pamphlets from a table and unfolded the parchment, spreading it flat. What Tom saw made him exclaim with pleasure. It was a map of the world drawn as a flattened out globe on a parchment roughly three feet square. Hand-copied with great skill in pure colours, it was just what he had envisaged. He fancied it was a copy of an earlier map by one of the German cartographers, Sebastian Munster perhaps, with recent editions made by the copyist. There was no attribution on the map.

"Where did you get this?" he asked, astonished by the quality of it.

"About three weeks ago a fellow came in here wanting to sell it. He was a seafaring man, who had acquired it as booty, but now he had fallen on hard times and was selling all he had of value. I snapped it up. I rarely get my hands on anything so fine."

Thomas hoped the unfortunate sailor had not been done down by the dealer. He asked the price and the answer caused him to draw a sharp intake of breath. He would be one timber payment short this year because of the school house and he had spent a goodly sum on the repairs. At least the money to fulfil his promise to provide new pairs of boots for all the pupils was put by thanks to the contributions from Godfrey's merchant colleagues. He considered his options. He dealt with two other timber merchants beside Pocock, one in Westbury, the other in Chippenham, both of whom took two consignments from him each year. Perhaps he could persuade one of them to take a third load. It would mean much extra work to cut enough timber to make up another consignment, but it could be done.Seeing his hesitation the bookseller said, "It would be a shame to lose such a magnificent work of beauty and science. I am willing to negotiate a price for all three items together."

The map was exactly what he needed; Tom knew he would be a fool not to buy it. He could live without the books, but he had a strong desire for them too, particularly the Hakluyt and if they were being offered as part of a deal it was an excuse to indulge himself. He could give up something else for the rest of this year to recoup some of the money. His stock of good wine was running low and he had intended to visit the vintner in Devizes to replenish it. Yet there was abundant cider, small beer and some ale stored in the brew house. He enjoyed a glass of burgundy at supper but cider would do just as well. It was no great sacrifice to surrender such a luxury. The children who might benefit from this map came from families who could not afford fine wines. Most of them would live their whole lives tasting nothing but small beer and the more potent ale on feast days and holidays. This thought decided him and after five minutes of haggling, a price was settled on that suited both parties. When he left the shop, his precious purchases wrapped in a linen cloth, his purse was empty except for one gold coin and a few silver pennies, but he did not regret it.

Godfrey Roper's house was only a few streets away. He wanted to share his good fortune at finding the map with his sister and her husband. Taking a shortcut he wound his way along several narrow passage ways, leading Hope by the reins. A muscular mongrel dog ran out of the yard of a row of shabby houses that leaned together drunkenly as if holding each other up. The dog bared yellow teeth, snarling and snapping at Hope's fetlocks. Tom was forced to shout at it and make a threatening gesture to persuade it to back off. A stream of invective in heavy local dialect issued from one of the houses. Tom was not sure if it was directed at him or the dog, but the animal slunk back into the yard still growling. Hope was unconcerned by the assault, treating the dog with distain, though Tom felt more at ease when they stepped out into a wider street. He had thought himself unaffected by the assassination attempts; now he wondered if they had left a subconscious impression on him, making him wary of unfamiliar, shadowy alleys.

This street was a mixture of shop fronts, stalls and residential houses, well-populated with folk going about their daily business. Godfrey's house was at the far end of this long street, a two-storey, timber-framed building facing on to the street. It was the house of a man of substance but not pretentious. The timber frame was in-filled with brick.

The bricks were irregular in size and arranged so that the long outward face of one brick was bonded beside the short end of the next brick. They were narrow, so thick layers of mortar filled up the gaps. The house had been in the

Roper family for several generations and Tom surmised that the original infill was wattle and daub. The frame had a curious twisted appearance caused by unseasoned oak taking many years to dry out, leaving it susceptible to warping. A timber jetty projected out over the ground floor windows. The house had a friendly, solid look about it very much like its owner. Godfrey's cloth mill and warehouse were situated two miles away on the banks of the river.

Thomas was disappointed to find that neither his sister nor her husband were at home. A smiling servant girl informed him that the master was in a meeting at the Council House and the mistress was visiting her parents. The servant's cheerful politeness reflected the atmosphere in the Roper household. Tom was sure it would be impossible to be discontented working for Cecily and Godfrey. At that moment he wished there was no barrier preventing him from going to his family home. He could see himself riding through the archway that led to the coach house and stables, then dashing up the flight of steps at the back door. He had a yearning to see the view from his old chamber across the garden to the stream at the bottom but he stifled it. Relations with his father had not thawed enough on the key issue to persuade Thomas to compromise his pride. He rode straight home instead.

Waaseyaaban was fascinated by the bright colours and graphic details on the map. Tom had spread it out over the parlour table and his wife called Joan and Sarah to take a look at it. They both expressed their wonder at such a fine article, although Joan was not so astonished that she forgot to ask Tom if he had eaten a meal while he was in Salisbury.

"No, but I will grab a slice of pie from the kitchen. I want to make a frame for this map."

Joan called after him, "You should sit down and eat, not rush around with your food. You will suffer from indigestion."

There was no reply and she shook her head as she heard the back door close. He returned later with the bottom of a wooden chest he had found in the barn. He had knocked the sides off it and was pleased to find that it was just big enough to accommodate the map. After tacking the corners of the parchment to this wooden panel, he disappeared again taking the map with him.

Sometime later after several miscalculations and numerous oaths he emerged from the barn having attached a simple wooden frame around the panel wide enough to hold down the edges of the parchment all the way round. The map was now rigid and could be propped up on a desk in front of the children or if he attached a cord, hung on the wall.

He was eager and nervous in equal measure when he arrived at the school house the next day, the map wrapped in a blanket. He tied Hope to the fence and let the wolfhounds into the garden, closing the gate behind them. They were not allowed in the school room because they distracted the children and Mistress Walters was afraid of them. He could hear her precise voice talking to the younger children behind the screens as he entered the room.

There were eighteen pupils sitting at the desks, twice as many boys as girls. Tom knew it would be hard to persuade the villagers that their daughters needed education as well as their sons. The children's ages ranged from eight to twelve although one strapping lad Ralph, the ploughman's youngest son was almost as tall as Thomas and looked sixteen despite swearing that he was only twelve. He dwarfed the others but he was an easy-going, pliable lad willing to do as he was bid. After two days of observation Seb Braddon had already marked in his mind the potential troublemakers. An experienced teacher, he recognised the signs and was already working on strategies to prevent it.

Thomas greeted the children as they stared at him.

"Well return Sir Thomas' good morning class," Braddon instructed. "You all know it is ill-mannered not to do so."

There was a chorus of responses, some surly and one small girl lagged behind the others so that her high-pitched salutation was heard on its own, causing all the other children to laugh. Thomas smiled at her. "That was a good clear one Maggie Noakes. Now before we start if Master Braddon does not mind me disrupting your seating plan, I would like you all to bring your chairs to the front and sit in a semi-circle."

This manoeuvre was achieved eventually after some shoving and knocking of ankles with chair legs, not always accidental. Thomas placed his chair in the gap between the ends of the half circle and asked them if they knew what shape the world took. He received some interesting answers. Ralph was convinced it was square like a plough field, though several boys were aware of the notion that it was round like a ball. "God is good and stops us from falling off the end," one of them added helpfully.

Their reaction when Tom uncovered the map, standing the frame on his knees so they could all see it, was everything he had hoped it would be. They were drawn in immediately by the richness of the colours. So intrigued were they in fact that they failed to notice James Norrington slip into the room and bring a chair to the back of the semi-circle. The hour flew by and from then on Tom used the map as a focus for both his history and geography lessons. He could not risk leaving it in the school room for fear it would tempt someone to steal and sell it, so he commissioned a leather worker in Devizes to make a leather satchel with a shoulder strap, just the right size for the map to fit snugly inside. Then he could carry it back and forth without fear of damage.

James tried to come every week to one of Tom's lessons. However if his father suggested an alternative pursuit on lesson day the boy bowed to his Sir Neville's wishes. He also spent more time with Noah Lee, the bailiff on his regular visits to the tenant farmers on the estate, knowing this would please his father. He soon found that Lee adopted a different tone with the tenants from the unctuous, humble manner he displayed to Sir Neville. He was sharp-tongued to the point of rudeness, dismissive of any complaints, enjoying the power he possessed to threaten and bully them. He assured James it was the only way to treat them or they would take advantage of any sign of weakness. What James saw were four hardworking yeomen, too busy with the task of providing for their families to take advantage of anyone. His father had always been haughty and distant when addressing his tenants, but he was fair to them and James wondered just how much Lee passed on to his master. He had the example of Thomas Mountfield's sympathetic attitude towards working folk, how it inspired loyalty and respect. Intimidation might produce obedience but it also caused resentment that simmered under the surface. James did not want to be feared and disliked. On his visits he showed a willingness to listen to any complaints or problems and soon found that they appealed directly to him rather than the bailiff. He enjoyed the sense of importance it gave him but was sincere in his desire to solve the problems in discussion with his father. He had never liked Noah Lee and had no regrets about putting his nose out of joint.

Elizabeth had not come with her brother to hear Tom's inaugural lesson. She was not there on Friday either and Thomas suspected her of holding back on purpose hoping to heighten his curiosity concerning her proposal. The thought irritated him because he did not wish to consider her at all devious. There was beauty in her openness, the way those large eyes spoke the emotions she could not hide.

He could not fail to be flattered by her devotion and did not wish her to think him indifferent, yet how was he to make this clear without raising her hopes? He was wrestling with this in his mind as he stepped out of the school house that Friday morning, the map satchel slung over his shoulder, to find Lizzie Norrington standing by the gate as if his thoughts had conjured her up. It took him by surprise. She observed that her presence had thrown him off guard and interpreted it as a good sign. He could see two horses hitched to the fence beside his own stallion but Lizzie appeared to be alone.

"Elizabeth. I did not think you had come today. How long have you been here?"

"Awhile. I was too late for the start of your lesson and did not wish to interrupt by coming in half way through."

He wondered if this was part of a strategy to spend time alone with him.

"Is James with you?"

"No, Jacob Whyte. Father insists that I go nowhere alone."

"Very wise, there are plenty of vagabonds about who would see a woman riding alone as easy prey."

"You let Dawn Light ride without escort."

"I prefer not to but it is hard to prevent her. Besides, I fancy she is more capable of defending herself than you. Where is Jacob?"

"He is in the wood yard talking to Nathan Pocock."

She made a gesture towards the yard and looking in that direction Thomas could just see the Jacob's iron grey hair beyond the fencing.

"I hoped to have some time to talk with you," Lizzie continued and seeing the hesitation in his eyes she added," It will not take long. Shall we walk by the stream as we talk?"

He nodded without speaking and they walked together through the back garden to the stream, disturbing a pair of ducks who flapped away in noisy protest. As he watched them fly up Tom spotted a formation of swallows come darting across the sky, dipping down to skim the surface of the stream and then away again, twisting and curving in their acrobatic display. Tom smiled. "Look at them. They always seem to take such joy in flight, mocking us earthbound creatures. Several pairs nest in our barn every year. We always know spring has truly come when the swallows return."

"James and I are not the only ones to come to you for a refuge then. Even the animals and birds feel safe with you it seems. You draw things to you like a lodestone and here I am unable to free myself even if I wanted to."

"Elizabeth, you gave me to understand that you had an idea about teaching. I would be grateful if you would explain it to me. I have a deal of work to catch up on at home."

So formal, so careful, afraid of losing control again Lizzie thought. He had smiled at the swallows but not yet at her. His expression was serious, troubled.

"I would like to come every Friday and instruct the girls in needlework."

Tom had not expected that. He raised his eyebrows in query, "Really?"

"Yes, my old nurse Kate taught me to cut patterns from paper to serve as guides when cutting cloth for garments. I have a fair skill in embroidery and lacework also. I thought if the girls could be taught to make clothes and learn fancy stitch work, some of them might get the chance to become seamstresses and improve their lot in life."

Thomas could see another advantage." It might persuade some of the families who see no point in sending girls to school to reconsider if they saw a practical outcome to it. Even if some girls came for that one day only we might be able to get something else in their heads while they are on the premises. But these children can be rough and outspoken. Do not expect dainty manners and fine feelings. Would you be able to deal with that?"

"It will be far preferable to false courtesy that only masks distain. The Hanhams have taught me that lesson. I would like to try. If I am not successful I will soon admit it."

"Have you spoken to your father about this?"

"I have. He is dubious as you would expect. He would never allow me to take a post as a paid teacher. He would consider that below our station, demeaning, but as an act of charity he will accept it and needlework is a fitting subject for a woman in his opinion. Please say yes Thomas."

She was stroking the cuff of his doublet with the tips of her fingers and he moved his arm back saying, "Why do you choose Friday?"

"It is the best day for Jacob to accompany me if James cannot come."

"Well, I must speak to Seb Braddon about it, but I see no harm in trying it out. Jacob could ride over to my house while he is waiting for you and enjoy Joan's hospitality. She has a soft spot for Master Whyte and I think the admiration is returned."

"Oh thank you Thomas." She threw her arms around his neck and kissed him so swiftly he had no time to prevent it. He disengaged her arms, his suspicion of her motives reinforced.

"Are you sure you have not suggested this simply to create an opportunity to see me more often?" he demanded sharply. "That is part of it," she confessed," But I truly wish to do something useful for the children. I have no desire to be an ornament, cossetted by a rich husband, which is my father's vision for me. I want to do some good in this world if I can- like you."

"I would not recommend any one to use me as an example. You kissed me openly then hoping someone would see us. You must stop behaving like this Elizabeth."

He turned away from her and began to walk in the direction of the school house. She ran after him, catching hold of his arm.

"You need not pretend you are indifferent to me because I know it is not true. When you held me in your arms that wonderful morning I could feel the desire in you. It matched my own."

Thomas glanced across to the village well. Two women were drawing water and although they were too far away to hear the conversation, they were casting curious looks in the direction of the two figures in the school house garden. Tom took hold of Lizzie's wrist in a firm grip and led her behind the building out of sight of the street, to a bench under a willow tree on the edge of the stream. There he sat down and pulled her down beside him. Taking both her hands in his, he looked directly into her eyes.

"Now, you listen to me Elizabeth Norrington. When you lay emotional siege to me with that expression in your blue eyes and I feel your heart beating in your breast for certain I desire you. You are very beautiful and the flesh is weak. I had never been a man to resist temptation where women were concerned, not until I met Waaseyaaban. She satisfies me in so many ways. I cannot express in mere words what she is to me. I will never make love to you, never bed you, never fall in love with you. You must get that clear in your head and let go of the hope that I will."

He had never spoken to her so harshly. She was not sure whether he was angry with her or with himself. Tom had come to the conclusion that bluntness was the only course now. She was staring at him, her face pale and he chose to play a powerful card.

"My wife is with child. We are all praying that this one will be born healthy and live. I plan to put my energies into being a good father and a faithful husband. The chance for another child after losing the others means so much to us both. It draws us even closer together. I cannot, I will not be involved with you now."

She was stunned. It was the last thing she had expected to hear. The words echoed in her head. My wife is with child. How could she compete with that?

"Oh- I am pleased for you. I know how much you felt the loss of your children," she murmured, tears starting in her eyes and Tom felt a stab of guilt because she was sincere. That sincerity and warm-heartedness was as appealing as her beauty.

"It is kind of you to say so after the way I have just spoken to you," he said in a gentler tone.

There was an awkward silence as they sat listening to the wind stirring the willow branches above them, both feeling uncomfortable, until Lizzie said in a bleak, lost voice, "But I love you so much. What am I to do?"

"You must learn to live with it. I am sorry if that sounds brutal but it is all I can offer. As I see it there are two options. You can cut yourself off from me, have nothing more to do with me and try to forget me altogether or we can live as neighbours in regular contact and enjoy each other's company in friendship. I will be an affectionate, caring friend to you Elizabeth, always mindful of your welfare, but never more than a friend. If you can accept that, though it may be painful for a time, eventually you may become accustomed to it and grow comfortable with the notion. You must choose which way you think best."

"I could not bear never to see you again. I would wither away. I must choose friendship."

"You still wish to teach needlework?"

"Yes."

"I am pleased. I would be sorry to lose contact with you completely. I want very much to be a good friend to you and James. It will be hard for both of us at first but I pray you will come in time to see that I am right."

He wondered if his words sounded glib and self-satisfied to her, as if he was dismissing her pain as insignificant. He did not know how to put it any other way, but was disgusted with himself even so. He was relieved to see Jacob Whyte walking down the garden.

"Look, Jacob Whyte is coming to find us. Dry those tears."

He wiped the dampness from her cheeks with his finger. She was at a loss to know how she could ever stop loving him when his every gesture, every movement heightened her feelings for him.

Watching them ride away, seeing Lizzie's dejection in the way she sat in her saddle, Tom slapped the flat of his hand into the gate post and swore. When Elizabeth had first entered the garden she left the gate open and the wolfhounds had been out scouting around the village. Now they followed the retreating horses a short distance until Thomas whistled them back. As they pushed around his legs he stroked their heads to comfort himself. "Ajax, Hector, my lads, what else could I do?"

They cocked their heads on one side in query but had no answer for him.

Jacob and Elizabeth had travelled a mile or so when the steward, realising that she had dropped behind him, turned in the saddle to discover that she was weeping.

"Mistress Elizabeth, whatever ails you?"

He stopped the horse and dismounted, holding out his hands to help Elizabeth down. Jacob Whyte had never married. He was always determined to become head steward in a good household and wanted no ties to hold him back. He had come to care for Sir Neville's children as if they were his own. He judged this to be a moment to disregard his usual respectful attitude and put his arms around Lizzie, hugging her tight to comfort her.

"He does not love me Jacob and I can love no one else."

He could feel her tears dampening his shoulder.

"There now my child," he soothed, not needing to ask who she meant. "You are fortunate that he is an honourable man who has not taken advantage of you. That would be far worse. The hurt will fade I promise you."

That evening Thomas Mountfield told his wife about his meeting with Elizabeth. Waaseyaaban smiled but he shook his head.

"It is not a smiling matter my love. It pains me to make that girl unhappy. The night of the first apple-picking last year I asked you to speak more kindly to her and you agreed."

"I do not speak bad things to her since."

"No, but when you look at her and James your eyes shoot arrows at them. I would have you be more generous, more welcoming towards them. Do not triumph over Elizabeth because of this."

He stroked her belly with his open hand.

"What you ask is important to you?"

"Yes, the world is in sore need of more kindness and we must not take the blessing of this child for granted. You do understand my fear?"

She nodded. "I understand, but there is nothing to fear this time. All will be well."

The pupils at the village school looked forward to Thomas Mountfield's lessons. They did not seem like lessons, more like stories although the facts were true. They enjoyed the opportunity to leave the formality of their desks to sit in a semi-circle and listen to descriptions of places they never knew existed. He encouraged them to interrupt with questions and never made them feel their questions were ignorant or foolish. Two of the older boys talked tough as if they did not value any form of education and were only there on sufferance, threatened with a beating from their fathers if they did not attend. They were not going to be ordered about by any poxy school master and Seb Braddon was finding their attitude a challenge. Yet even these two were drawn in by Tom's stories. This man had travelled to these places, fought with wild natives and the hated Spaniards. They could respect this.

When Braddon told Tom how popular were his visits Mountfield took a realistic view. "Ah well Seb, I have the easier task. I stroll in here twice a week and tell them colourful stories that fire their imaginations, whilst you have the day to day slog of getting the basics of learning into their heads. You have the important task of giving them the framework they need to progress. It is bound to seem duller to them and I doubt if I would have the patience or skill to do that. You are the true hero."

After that first lesson when he gave the children some idea of where continents and countries were placed in relation to their own island, Tom had talked to them about how various lands had been discovered because he hoped they would find that exciting. He planned to look in more detail at the geography of Britain and the Continent later when their skills in reading and writing had improved and they could copy names down on their slates without too much difficulty. All he asked of them at present was to draw the shape of the countries that he pointed out on the map.

He had begun with the tales of the Northmen in their longships, sailing around the world in search of plunder, trade and settlement. Next came the Venetian adventurer Marco Polo and his twenty four year travels with his father and uncle through Central Asia to far distant Cathay. Due weight was then given to Christopher Columbus' voyages across the Atlantic ocean to the Americas on behalf of Spain and Vasco da Gama, the first European to reach India by sea, opening up the wealth of the spice trade to the Portuguese nation.

This Wednesday morning in late May Thomas spoke of John Cabot, the Italian who took a commission from the Queen's grandfather, Henry VII to discover new territories and extend English influence. He landed on the northern shores of the American continent at a place since called Newfoundland, where the waters were teeming with fish, but it was to be eighty six years before the land and the fishing rights were claimed for the English crown by Sir Humphrey Gilbert.

The tall, florid Gilbert with his disturbing visionary eyes was a protégé of Philip Sidney's father and had served under him when Sir Henry was Lord

Deputy of Ireland. He was Walter Raleigh's half- brother by their mother's first husband and fifteen years older than Walter. As early as 1566 he had written a pamphlet urging the necessity for a north- west sea passage to Cathay. He had a powerful, original mind but his navigational skills were questionable and throughout the 1570s he embarked on a series of failed maritime expeditions which drained away the family fortune.

Thomas met him several times in the company of Philip, Walter and Thomas Harriot when they were in the early stages of planning new expeditions to the Americas. He was compelling; a passionate, impulsive man convinced his opinions were right. His belief in his mission was almost mystic. Tom found himself drawn to the man yet repulsed at the same time. Tales of a sadistic side to his nature had come out of Ireland when he was involved in suppressing rebellion there and his intensity could be frightening. He inspired men to follow him, but when they did, they were not sure they could put their trust in him. There were rumours that he had a liking for young boys, although Philip would not countenance any such scurrilous accusation against him. Walter on the other hand was more equivocal. He did not confirm it, neither did he deny it.

Philip confided to Tom that Humphrey told him of his strange and marvellous dreams when King Solomon and Job appeared to him promising to grant him secret, mystical knowledge, hidden from all other mortal men. It intrigued Philip, who wondered if it might have some true significance. Thomas was more inclined to regard it as the self-delusion of an imaginative, visionary mind.

When Humphrey and Walter set off on a voyage in 1583 Tom was not tempted to go with them, preferring to stay close to Philip, not convinced that the expedition was properly prepared.

The ships were crewed by a mixture of misfits and hard-men who spent much of their time in prison, because money was short and Humphrey could not afford to pay experienced sailors. Walter's ship was so poorly provisioned that he was forced to abandon the voyage and turn back. The rest of the ships reached Newfoundland and Humphrey claimed it in the name of Her Sovereign Majesty, Queen Elizabeth.

Tom told the children that he had met Humphrey Gilbert but he did not go into any details about his character. Instead he described to them the dangerous return voyage from Newfoundland when Gilbert disregarded the advice of the few experienced mariners in the company and changed course, trusting to his vision. Their largest vessel, The Delight ran aground in consequence but Humphrey pressed on regardless. He preferred to sail in his favourite ship, The Squirrel, an old vessel in need of some repair. When the fleet hit rough weather he was advised by his captains to transfer to another ship, considering that The Squirrel was weighed down with too many guns and would be unsafe in a fierce storm. He was devoted to The Squirrel and refused. When they did indeed sail into one of those howling Atlantic storms, Humphrey was last seen sitting on deck reading a book with calm disregard for the elements. He shouted across to the nearest ship urging the crew not to fear saying, "We are as near heaven by sea as by land."

Then The Squirrel was overwhelmed by a massive wave and swallowed up never to be seen again. The children's eyes were wide, not expecting such a catastrophe.

"What book were he reading Sir Thomas, the Bible?" Ralph Hedge asked.

"Well we cannot be sure. It might have been the Bible although the captain of another ship said it was Thomas More's Utopia. I will tell you about that book some other time- in History lessons perhaps. What might interest you more is that the crews of those ships that managed to limp home swore they saw a great sea monster, the shape of a lion with big glowing eyes."

"What was it? What was it?" came the eager chorus.

"Who knows, but when you are fighting to stay afloat in a terrible storm with the rain and salt spray stinging your face, the wind howling in your ears like fifty demons and you are sore afraid, your vision is so distorted and your imagination so inflamed you see monsters in the shape of the very waves themselves. Yet there are many strange creatures in the depths of the ocean that we know nothing of."

"Did you see any fearful monsters when you were at sea?" Ralph asked.

"I saw a whale when we were sailing back from Roanoke five years ago, but it was nothing to fear, only to be wondered at. It surfaced near us, such a mighty creature, longer than the ship, with smooth grey skin encrusted with barnacles like the of the bottom of our ship and small eyes that seemed strangely wise and gentle. Every now and then it spouted forth a great fountain of water into the air from its blow-hole, making an explosive sound. It swam beside us for some while and I was sorry when it dived back down into the depths for I could have watched it all day. I felt a strong fellowship with it and privileged to share its company for that short while."

"I wish I could see a whale," murmured a frail-looking lad with pimply skin and grubby clothes.

"So you may one day Samuel. Never discount the possibility," Tom replied, ruffling the boy's hair.

He handed the class back to Seb Braddon wondering if he would ever see a whale again himself. James Norrington had not attended the class that morning but there was another visitor leaning against the back wall, arms folded, a wide grin on his face. Tom had noticed him come in just after the lesson started. He had not acknowledged him not wishing to distract the children. Daffyd Williams sauntered up to him and they both stepped outside into the soft May air.

"What are you doing here?" Tom queried

"Listening to a good tale. Imagine that fellow Humphrey Gilbert sitting reading in the midst of a storm. There's courage for you or madness depending how you look at it."

"Yes, he was a strange man." Thomas agreed. "He did not know what fear was. It wasn't as if he was calm all the time; in fact he was choleric, had a quick temper, but he was never afraid."

"Another friend of yours was he?"

"No, I did not really like him too well, but I admired the breadth of his vision. Thomas recalled that although Gilbert's company was stimulating, he was always pleased when he left.

"I am on nights this fortnight and as I heard you were taking some of the lessons at your new school, I thought I would wander up and have a listen. I really do miss my conversations with you," Daffyd explained.

"It is not my school; it is their school. Did you walk all the way up here?"

The Welshman laughed. "No to goodness, you know me better than that. I hired a horse from Dudley Dent." He jerked a thumb towards a bony mare tied to the fence. "Bit broken winded, but she got me here."

A discreet coughing noise caused them both to turn to find Sally Walters hovering behind them.

"Sir Thomas may I speak with you?"

"Certainly, you look concerned. What is it?"

She hesitated, casting an anxious glance at Daffyd who took the hint and bowing walked away, yet not so far that he was unable to hear the conversation.

"It is a matter my husband wishes me to raise with you, a delicate matter concerning your wife."

"Indeed?"

"Her desire to improve the children's knowledge of horticulture is admirable but my husband is troubled by her mode of dress, the length of her skirts. He feels that the older boys attend the gardening for the express purpose of- well- staring at her legs and does not wish them to be tempted by lewd thoughts."

"But you must concede Mistress Walters that my wife's legs are well worth staring at."

Tom could not resist a gentle prod at her primness.

"Sir Thomas, please, that was not a seemly remark to make to me," she replied with offended dignity, avoiding his amused gaze.

"You are right Mistress. I apologise."

Thomas was struggling to keep a straight face as he recalled several occasions when he had noticed the Reverend Walters taking more than a passing interest in Waaseyaaban's legs.

"You may tell your reverend husband I will speak to my wife about the length of her skirts on gardening days."

"Thank you Sir Thomas. I hope you are not offended by my husband's frankness."

"Not in the least. His concern for the boys' spiritual health is all I would have expected from him."

She did not pick up the hint of irony in his remark and hurried away, pleased with discharging her duty on her husband's behalf. Daffyd came back to join Thomas, grinning broadly.

"Did you hear that?" Tom asked, laughing.

"I did. Trust the wildcat woman to be causing trouble."

"Well I think it is a shame to deprive the boys of such a pleasure. When I was their age I was always hopeful of a quick view above a woman's ankle. Waaseyaaban is well aware that they gawp at her legs. She enjoys the admiration but if one of them was to over step the mark he would soon wish he had not."

Remembering the pain of her knee in his privates, Daffyd knew just what Thomas meant. The wildcat woman was capable of looking after herself.

"I hope the good Reverend and his wife don't find out much about me or they won't want me up here again."

"You are right and some might say with good reason."

"I do not prey on children Sir Thomas."

The smile had faded from Daffyd's face and his tone was earnest.

"I did not assume that you did." Thomas was never sure about

Humphrey Gilbert but he was confident that Daffyd was telling him the truth.
"It is just that others who do not know you so well may judge you harshly for
your inclinations."

"I am used to that. I don't care what they say, but I do value your good
opinion."

They had begun to walk towards the horses, Williams anxious because
Thomas had not reacted to his last remark.

"Did you know your father was kind enough to reward me handsomely
for spotting that assassin's knife?"

"Yes, he told me he wished to express his gratitude. He does not know
the half of it, how you helped me to survive the Bridewell, the importance of
the open grill and cell door. How could I not have a good opinion of you after
such a service?"

The Welshman felt the warmth of relief on hearing Tom say that.

"Have you not spoken to him about how confinement in small spaces
troubles your mind?"

"No, he would never understand."

"Mayhap you underestimate his sympathy. If you described the terrors
you suffered from it I am sure he would try to understand. How are relations
between you?"

"Better than they were, although they will never be easy, as much as I
love him."

"He loves you for sure, any fool can see that."

"Well we will see what happens when the baby comes."

"Baby?"

"Dawn Light is with child, due in the autumn."

"That is good news indeed." Daffyd's pleasure was very genuine.
"Nothing like a baby to bring families together."

"Perhaps- as I said- we shall see." Thomas did not sound convinced.

Daffyd asked if it would not appear too conspicuous if he came again on
Friday.

"You can tell them that I am just an ignorant Welshman endeavouring
to improve his education, which is no more than the truth."

"Not so ignorant as he claims to be." Thomas commented before they
went their separate ways.

On Friday James Norrington was not delighted to be sharing a space
along the back wall of the schoolroom with the hefty gaoler from Devizes

Bridewell, who seemed to regard him with a thinly disguised under-current of amusement and was glad to discover that the fellow could not come every week.

There was a grinding noise and the carriage lurched sideways causing Neville Norrington to let go of the reins. Disturbed by the strange sound the horse speeded up and it was as much as Norrington could do to stay in the vehicle.

Wincing at the pain in his back he managed to recover the reins and pull the horse to a halt. He clambered out of the lopsided conveyance and had the presence of mind to pat and soothe the horse for the animal was still scared, making snorting noises and showing the whites of its eyes.

His carriage had lost a wheel. He could see it lying in the road a hundred yards behind him. Since his back injury he had found riding increasingly painful and had taken to using the carriage, often with one of the Smith twins as a driver, but when he had need of privacy he drove himself. Now he was on an unfamiliar stretch of open road with no dwellings in sight and no labourers working in the fields. He walked back to collect the wheel, cursing Giles Smith whose duty it was to maintain the vehicle in good condition. His effort to remain upright and retrieve the reins had tested his back to the limit. He found that carrying the wheel sent stabbing pains all through his body and he clenched his teeth to prevent himself from crying out. His only option was to unhitch the horse and ride home, but when he lifted his arms to unbuckle the harness the pain was so bad his head reeled and flashes of coloured light swam before his eyes. He leaned back against the side of the carriage taking deep breaths. Perhaps the pain would ease in a while and although the road was empty now, some traveller might come along to aid him. The horse had calmed down and was grazing the tufted grass at the side of the road. Norrington slid down into a sitting position resting against the side of the carriage and closed his eyes. He had never been a man to act on impulse and this is what happens, he told himself, when I break a habit of a lifetime. His daughter had been teaching needlework at Mountfield's village school for a month now. He could see that she was filled with a sense of purpose but was not sure if it was the work or the chance to see Sir Thomas that engaged her. When she set off with her brother that Friday morning he had a desire to follow her to see for himself what was happening at that school. He trusted Jacob Whyte's reports, though he feared that James was likely to encourage her relationship with Mountfield.

His sister Jennet had been nagging him again to put his foot down concerning Elizabeth. She was disgusted that he allowed Lizzie to teach labourers' children and declared that her husband Sir Martin was appalled when he heard of it. She urged Neville to insist that Elizabeth meet some of the candidates she was lining up as a potential husband for her niece.

"The longer she is permitted to pine over that man and weave foolish dreams around him, the worse it will be. He had quite a reputation as a lover when he was in Philip Sidney's household you know- left a string of broken hearts in his wake. If people think Elizabeth is still consorting with him no one will want to marry her. We must get him out of her head and the surest way to do that is to give her a husband to think about." Neville had fallen out with Jennet because he had promised Elizabeth he would not put pressure on her to marry, yet his sister's words preyed on his mind, prompting him to doubt if he was doing the right thing. Perhaps if he found the school unsuitable he would have an excuse to forbid her to go there again. He had acted on his impulse and after giving his children a ten minute start, he followed them in the carriage. Now as he twisted his position to try to ease the pain in his back, he bitterly regretted his decision.

It seemed an age before he heard the sound of horse's hooves approaching. Turning his head to look in the direction he had been heading, he saw a rider on a fine chestnut stallion galloping towards him. He struggled to his feet with great difficulty and the rider dismounted.

"Sir Neville, what has happened?"

Tom Mountfield never imagined he would find Neville Norrington on this road. Relieved as he was to see another human being, Norrington could not help wishing it was someone other than this man. He supposed he should not be surprised to see him as it was his territory.

"I have had an accident. The wheel came off my carriage."

"Are you hurt?"

"I have exacerbated an old injury in my back which has incapacitated me somewhat. I was resting in the hope a passer-by might assist me, but this is such a lonely, deserted road."

When he attempted to straighten up a dizziness came over him and he swayed. Fearing he would collapse Thomas put an arm around his shoulder to support him. Neville was embarrassed by his weakness but was grateful for someone to lean against.

"What are you doing on this road?" Tom asked.

"On business," came the brusque reply. Norrington had no desire to reveal his motives. Tom gave him a keen look, but did not question it. Instead he replied, "Me too, I was on my way to the wood yard in Sandridge."

"Ah then perhaps you would be so good as to ask the fellow there to send some men out to repair this carriage."

Sir Neville's face was grey and the extent of his pain evident.

"No sir, I would not leave you disabled and without a weapon on this road. There are those who might take a fancy to that handsome ruby ring you are wearing. There have been several robberies along this stretch of road in the past few months."

"Then what am I to do? I fear I am not capable of riding home."

Tom inspected the wheel and extracted a small piece of metal from it.

"Well the wheel itself is undamaged, but I see what has happened. The pin that holds the wheel on the axle has snapped. Here is the remnant of it."

He held it up to show Neville. "I think I may be able to affect a temporary repair, sufficient to get it to my house at least which is not too far distant. I am sure there is a genuine carriage pin in my barn that will fit this. It will take a while. Perhaps you would care to sit down again."

Norrington allowed Thomas to help him to the other side of the road where there was a mile stone and lowered him down so that his back rested against the stone. Then he watched as Tom unhitched the carriage horse and tethered it to a bush beside his own mount. Thomas put his shoulder against the side of the carriage that was missing the wheel and heaved it over on to the undamaged side. He then strolled a few yards down the road to a tree and lopped off a sturdy branch with his sword. Taking a knife from his saddle bag he cut a length off the branch, peeled off the bark and whittled down the piece of wood until it was the right size to fit the holes in the wheel and axle.

He found a heavy stone on the edge of a field and used it as a hammer to knock the wooden pin into place before he pushed the carriage back to stand on four wheels once more. Neville had to admire his competence and skill. Here was a man used to working with his own hands, not one to rely on servants.

"There," Tom stood back to view the wheel. "That should hold until we get home if we drive with care."

He hitched up the horse, assisted Norrington into the carriage, tied Hope to the back of the vehicle and took the reins. The two men spoke little to each other on the way to Tom's house. Sir Neville felt the irony of being rescued by Mountfield and finding himself on the way to the house whence his children had fled. Thomas was thinking similar thoughts. He could not believe that

Norrington's presence on that road had nothing to do with Elizabeth or James.

Lizzie's needlework classes had gone well so far. Only three girls attended the first one. Now there were seven and Elizabeth's friendliness had won them over. She would listen to Tom's history lesson first and they would exchange a word or two before he left. He could not deny there was still tension between them when they looked into each other's eyes, but he fancied it was lessening and hoped they could be at ease with each other eventually. That morning he had left James helping out with a mathematics lesson while he waited for his sister, pleased to find that he knew considerably more than the children.

Like many others who had only imagined what it was like, Norrington was pleasantly surprised by Tom Mountfield's house. It was modest but well-proportioned and the land around it kept in good order. After the darkness of the forest the bright purple lavender, the red roses and creamy honeysuckle lifted the spirits. Sir Neville was escorted into the parlour and given a comfortable chair.

"You rest here. I will ask my housekeeper to mix you one of her herbal restoratives. They are excellent for dulling pain. If you will excuse me I will see what I can do about that wheel pin."

Thomas bowed and left Norrington contemplating his feelings towards this courteous man who was undermining his relationship with his children.

When Tom returned with the news that the pin had been found and Toby Aycliffe was working on the repair, Neville had consumed a full glass of Joan's restorative. He found the taste unusual but it was warming and did seem to ease the tension in his back.

"Now Sir Neville," Tom said, throwing himself down into a chair in a casual way, "What was the real reason you were on that road this morning? There is no business to be done in the direction you were heading, but it would lead you to the village school."

"You are very direct young man."

"It is often the best way I find."

"Well then if you must know I was indeed on my way to that school to make certain that it is a fit place for my children to spend their time. I am beginning to doubt the wisdom of allowing them so much freedom of action."

"I am well aware that you disapprove of me Sir. I wish I could allay your fears."

"How can I do otherwise but disapprove of you when you win the affection of my children away from me and fill their heads with outlandish ideas so that I am losing all influence over them."

Norrington could hold back his frustration no longer. Thomas sat forward in his chair replying, "You are mistaken. I have never tried to win their affection from you and neither have I done so. Both James and Elizabeth love and respect you greatly, which is just as I would wish it to be."

"That surprises me," Neville shot back at him, "Seeing you have shown your father scant respect these last few years."

Tom stiffened. "I beg your pardon Sir but I do not consider you competent to pass judgement on my relations with my father. We have had a serious difference of opinion over certain matters and have both perhaps been too stubborn in holding our ground, but I have never ceased to respect my father and you offend me to suggest otherwise."

The heat of his indignation was heightened by his memory of the number of times he had thought his father a hypocrite and now felt a twinge of guilt.

Norrington was pleased to see Mountfield ruffled by his remark, feeling he had scored a telling point and hit the target and had no intention of apologising. Thomas, sensing that his reaction was too hot, continued,

"You have nothing to fear concerning James. Your son is not made of the stuff for rebellion. It is not in his nature. He will make an excellent country gentleman- that is what he truly wants, to uphold the family tradition. Have you not noticed how interested he is becoming in the estate lately? But he has come to see there is more to being a gentleman than wearing fine clothes and ordering servants around."

"Do you imagine that is all I believe is involved?"

"No, but I think that was the impression James got when he was younger. He is eager now to expand his mind, learn more about the world and all the fascinating currents of thought."

Norrington snorted. "Yes, notions that will lead him astray into unorthodoxy and trouble."

"Sir Neville, the world, society, changes constantly. Surely your father was horrified at some of your ideas when you were young."

"It does not always change for the better."

"I agree some changes are backward steps, but others are progressive. We live in exciting times. So many things are being discovered in all branches of knowledge. It is mistaken to think that interest in them is sacrilegious, a challenge to God. They may sometimes challenge some of the cherished tenants of the Church, but to me they add to the glory of God because they reveal more of his creation to us. You may have been led to believe I am an atheist Sir. That is far from the truth. I am beset by doubt often times but I trust in God's redeeming power. James needs to know what is happening in the world not to be left behind. It will stand him in good stead in the future when he has the responsibility of running the estate. You can have interest in many opinions without holding them yourself. James admires me because of my friendship with Philip Sidney and the adventurous things I have done in past. I hope also that some of my true beliefs have influenced him for the good- but he will never wish to live like me you can be assured."

Sir Neville had listened to this with a grim smile on his face. Now he said,

"I can understand why young people are drawn to you. You speak fluently and persuasively with a reasonable voice, not the rantings of a fanatic. In my view that makes you more dangerous."

Thomas laughed.

"You are amused Sir Thomas?"

"I find it hard to see me as dangerous- to myself perhaps- but not to others."

"Some years ago- you were not much older than James is now- you came with your father to visit us. I doubt if you even remember it."

"Oh I do Sir. I had occasion to speak to Elizabeth about that visit to tell her how much she resembled her mother."

"You recall my dear Mary?"

"Very clearly, she was a beautiful and gracious lady, who made us very welcome."

Norrington had not expected such a sincere tribute to his wife. It stirred up emotions that he always tried to supress. He was forced to swallow down a lump in his throat before he said, "After you had left my wife complimented you to me speaking of your charm and intelligence. That boy has an original mind she said, he will make a mark in the world."

Thomas gave him a wry smile. "Well that just goes to show that predictions do not always come true."

"You are not arrogant I will grant you that, but you underestimate the power you have to influence others. My daughter is wholly under your spell. She vows that because she cannot marry you, she will have no one else. Tell me, what am I to do about that?"

"I am truly sorry about that situation. I have never knowingly encouraged her love- whether I have done so unwittingly I cannot swear to- but I wish it were otherwise."

"So you say, but how can I be sure that when she tells me she is teaching girls to sew she is not in reality dallying with you."

"You can be sure because I tell you she is not."

Thomas had risen from his chair and was standing by the fireplace his whole body expressing integrity and honour. Norrington could not doubt his sincerity.

"I swear to you on my honour I have never taken your daughter to bed nor do I have any intention to do so and I have made that clear to her. I cannot deny that her beauty and sweetness have tempted me, but I honour her far too much to give in to that, nor would I betray my wife."

There was silence for a moment as both men stared at each other, weighing up their reactions and then Neville said, "I believe you. I may suspect your beliefs but I do not doubt your honour."

"Thank you Sir. Elizabeth has been influenced by the circumstances of our meeting and what happened with Hanham to see me in a romantic light. She truly believes she is in love with me but I am sure that will fade."

"You think it is the right course for her to keep contact with you?"

"I do. I have given it much thought. You are not the only one to be troubled by it. I have hopes that if she meets with me in the course of everyday life and in a spirit of friendship she will come to accept it as the natural way of things. It will not help to press her to marry. She is enjoying her new role as teacher. She has a natural sympathy with those girls. They are growing to respect her and want to copy her manners. Her influence is very beneficial and it is giving Elizabeth more confidence in herself. In due course, if you wish it, I will try to persuade her to start meeting some of those young men your sister deems suitable future husbands. We need to proceed gently though. Her experience with Hanham is bound to make her wary of commitment to someone unknown to her."

Norrington did not need to be reminded of that.

"You would do that, encourage her to meet others?"

"Willingly, I do not want Elizabeth to waste her life yearning after me."

"I confess I am in two minds about you young man. Perhaps I have misjudged you somewhat. Even so, contact with you will not enhance my children's standing in society, but I will not hinder them from attending the school at present. Do not assume that means I shall ever approve of your free thinking."

"I think you have made that quite clear Sir."

Sir Neville was about to reply when the parlour door opened and Dawn Light stood there. She gave Norrington a curious, appraising look and then said to her husband, "Carriage is mended." Another glance at the visitor with those black eyes and she was gone again. Neville had seen her only once before at Tom's trial in Salisbury. She was dressed then in a handsome gown befitting the wife of a knight. This hot June day she wore only a sleeveless linen petticoat, her tanned limbs contrasting with the garment's whiteness. Norrington was startled by the sight of her and it confirmed his feeling that he was right to remain dubious about the suitability of his children's contact with Mountfield. He wondered how Thomas could ever prefer such a strange creature to his beautiful Elizabeth. He could perceive some good qualities in Tom but surely the young man's judgement was impaired. James had informed his father that Dawn Light was with child and as she stood briefly in the doorway, the swelling of her belly was evident beneath the flimsy shift she wore. Elizabeth had not spoken to him of this, perhaps he thought because it was too painful and she wished she was carrying Mountfield's child.

He declared himself rested enough to drive home alone. Thomas would not hear of it.

"You must not risk worsening that back injury. I will tie my horse to the back of the carriage again and drive you home myself. On my way back I could call on your physician if he lives nearby and direct him to visit you if you wish."

"I fear I have much delayed your visit to the Sandridge wood yard."

"Oh that can wait until another day."

Sir Neville could not fault Tom's easy courtesy. It sprang out of a generous nature. He could understand why Philip Sidney had been drawn to him.

Out in the yard Toby Aycliffe was adjusting the harness of the carriage horse. When Tom went to fetch his own mount, Toby said amiably to Norrington,

"Fine little carriage this. Good as new now. Do you want a hand up?"

"I thank you, but I am quite capable."

Neville was not used to being addressed in such a cheery, familiar manner by labouring men.

The tone of his reply was frosty and Toby ambled away, smiling to himself. Turning to look over his shoulder Norrington saw Thomas in the door way of the barn kissing his wife. It was not a farewell peck on the cheek, but a lingering, sensuous kiss full of desire and tenderness, their bodies pressed close together. He turned away embarrassed. He had never kissed Mary like that in the presence of others outside the privacy of a room. It struck him then that he had never ever kissed Mary in that way and deep down within himself he wished he had.

Waaseyaaban was in the brew house reaching up to take a bowl down off the shelf when her waters broke. The fluid that dampened the inside of her thighs was clear and colourless which was a healthy sign. She had suffered contracting pains the day before but they were of brief duration, irregular and far apart, so she spoke little of them, knowing such pains were often a false indicator. The birth could be a week away or more. Now the waters had broken she knew her time was soon approaching and the pains would increase in regularity and intensity.

She walked slowly back to the house thinking how good it would feel to have her proper balance back again, not to have to make allowances for the weight of the child, the pressure relieved from her aching back and bladder. She missed the ability to swing herself up on the back of Tom's horse or to run through the forest with the wolfhounds. She had remained active but as her time drew nearer Thomas had given the household strict instructions to keep an eye on her when he was not there, to make sure she did not over-exert herself.

She felt calm as she walked into the kitchen even though she was shivering. She was not cold on this balmy September day, nor was there any weakness in her legs. The shivering was her body's involuntary reaction to the changes taking place inside her. The kitchen was full of women, Godfrey Roper having dropped off his wife and mother-in-law at the Mountfield house on his way to meet a cloth dealer in Warminster. Lady Anne, Cecily and Sarah were all gathered around Joan Bushy watching the exact measures of ingredients that she was adding to her fruit cake. Their attention was soon diverted however when Dawn Light said in a matter-of-fact voice, "Waters have come- baby follow soon now."

"Then we must prepare the chamber and you must go upstairs." Joan was already washing her hands. "Shall I send Sarah in the cart for a midwife?"

"No, I want no old woman with dirty hands- give me sickness. I trust your hands. They are good hands."

Joan was moved by Dawn Light's faith in her. She had helped deliver three of Lady Anne's four children and knew that with Sarah's assistance she could do this also. She could only pray that Dawn Light would not bleed so heavily as she did when Wawackechi was born.

"Very well, if that is what you wish. Now off upstairs with you. Mistress Cecily will keep you company."

This was more than Cecily could have hoped for, to be present when Tom's child was born. Waaseyaaban as she sat on the edge of the bed thought about what Tom had once told her, how gentlemen's wives often had a lying –in period when they were with child, retiring to their bed chambers as much as a month before the birth and not coming out until the baby was born. They just lay around in bed their every need attended to by servants. She considered this timid and foolish, believing exercise while the baby was in the womb would make the child grow strong and brave.

Two hours later, her pains became regular and acute. She refused to lie down, sure that movement helped the baby on its downward progression, pausing every so often to face the wall and lean into it in a half crouching position. It was while she was in one such position that she called out,

"I want Thomas."

"He is in the forest working with Ned and Toby," Joan replied, "Perhaps it is best not to trouble him yet."

"He must come."

"My dear, you know that a birthing room is no place for a man. It is unseemly. I know Master Tom pays scant regard to convention but even he would wish to respect this one. Childbirth is a woman's preserve."

Lady Anne smiled her agreement, which did not deter Waaseyaaban.

"Not in room perhaps, but he must be in house to hear baby's first cry. Fetch him- now!"

This was not a request, it was a command. Cecily could see how important it was to her sister-in-law and knew it would mean much to Tom also.

"I will fetch him," she volunteered. "Where in the wood is he to be found?"

Waaseyaaban gave her precise, clear directions and Cecily with a quick glance at her mother, set off on her mission. She ran along the paths in the sharp September sunlight, full of excitement. She had to admit that she was enjoying this year as wife of the mayor of Salisbury.

It was pleasurable to sit at the top table in a place of honour at functions and see how all the merchants' wives were eager to be introduced to her. They told her all the gossip and copied her fashionable clothes. She hoped Godfrey would be re-elected at the mayoral election in November. He was very popular so there was a good chance he might be asked to continue in the post for another year. Running alone through these woods was so different from civic duties in Salisbury and brought out the adventurous side of Cecily's nature. The girl who had longed to sail to America with her beloved brother Thomas was still there. Tom had brought a flavour of the Americas back with him, allowing his wife to live in the ways of her own culture as far as possible in her new environment. A part of that culture would be preserved in the child that was about to be born. She wondered how much the child would favour Dawn Light in looks and temperament and whether he would embrace or reject her distinctive behaviour. Cecily laughed at herself for assuming it would be a boy. Dawn Light was so convinced that her sister-in-law believed it too.

Lifting up her skirts to avoid the brambles along the path she hurried on, disturbing a green woodpecker that darted away ahead of her in a blur of iridescence. Then a large shape emerged on the path some distance in front of her, a shaggy, long-legged shape and as it trotted towards her she recognised it as Hector. For a moment in the shadows cast by the thick foliage overhead she had feared it might be a wild boar. The big males could be aggressive and their tusks were lethal, so she was relieved to be greeted by the wolfhound. As usual, Ajax was not far behind, breaking through the undergrowth with a noisy enthusiasm.

"Where's Tom?" Cecily asked. "Take me to Thomas."

They seemed to understand her and loped on ahead, veering off the main path down a narrow track where she found it impossible to protect her skirts from snagging thorns. Following as fast as she could she detected the sound of sawing and soon came upon the place where the three men were working. Tom was sawing branches off a fallen tree and his back was turned to Cecily. It was Ned Carter who saw her first.

"Tis your sister Master Tom- looks to be in a hurry."

Thomas turned his head to see Cecily running towards them calling out,

"The baby is coming Thomas. Dawn Light wants you to be in the house to hear the first cry."

Tom felt his heartbeat accelerate. He glanced at Ned, who patted his arm.

"You go. Toby and I will finish up here. Hurry now and we will pray for an easy delivery."Taking hold of his sister's hand Tom set off at a run flanked by the dogs. Cecily found it hard to keep up with his long stride and by the time they entered the house through the front door her cheeks were flushed and she was short of breath. Thomas stood at the bottom of the staircase and shouted, "I am here now. Is all well?"

Joan Bushy's voice came back down to him from behind a closed chamber door. "Yes, there is no need to fret. All is going well. It will not be too long now."

He hesitated at the foot of the stairs and Cecily could see that he longed to go up to his wife.

"I think Dawn Light would wish you there," she said, "But Joan is adamant that it is not seemly for a man to be present at a birth and of course Mother agrees with her."

Tom smiled. "Joan would never forgive me if I dared to violate the sanctity of such a treasured female ritual. It would seem like blasphemy to her and Sarah would be so horrified she would never stop talking about it. Strange how we men can assist a foal to be born or litters of puppies or piglets, yet we are banished from the birth of our own children by this mystical, protective circle that women draw around them."

"I will stay with you my poor, rejected brother."

Cecily's tone was teasing but she could sympathise with his feelings.

"No, it is clear that you are eager to be there at the birth. You go on up. I can think of no one better to witness the birth of my child than my little sister Cecily."

She squeezed his hand and ran up the stairs, not needing to be told twice.

"Come on lads," Thomas said to the wolfhounds. "We useless men must spend our banishment in the kitchen."

After feeding Hector and Ajax some scraps of meat Joan had left out for them, Tom decided reading might distract him and fetched from the library the book by Richard Hakluyt he had bought in Salisbury. He found that he could not concentrate on it for long however and gave up. Pouring himself a cup of cider he walked around with cup in hand, taking sips now and then.

He went into the passage and stood beneath the gallery listening for sounds from the room above him. Waaseyaaban was always stoical with pain. She never cried out or made a drama of any physical hurt. He could hear voices, movements, footsteps, but nothing that indicated the progress of the birth.

He was pleased when Godfrey returned from Warminster and he could relieve his anxiety by asking questions about his visit and cutting him slices of bread and cheese. Tom was too anxious to eat but Godfrey found the simple repast very welcome. He was willing to admit that few things affected his appetite.

It was almost three hours after he had rushed into the house that Thomas Mountfield heard his baby's first cry, that angry, baffled wail of a new born creature snatched from the warmth and security of the womb into the harsh brightness of daylight.

"Good loud noise Tom." Godfrey said. "Betokens healthy lungs."

Tom's fear had always been as much for Waaseyaaban as for the child. He could not forget how much she had suffered with Wawackechi's birth. He climbed the stairs two at a time, not waiting to be summoned, to be met at the door by his mother.

"My dear Tom you have a healthy son. Just wait for a moment until Joan has finished washing him."

"Is Dawn Light in good health too, no severe bleeding this time?"

"All seems to be well. The afterbirth has come away easily and there is no more bleeding than is normally the case."

Tom let out a long sigh and murmured, "Thank God."

Over his mother's shoulder he could see Joan handing a bundle of linen to Waaseyaaban who was lying on the bed with pillows at her back. There was blood on the sheet that half covered her but no great quantity. He walked over and sat on the edge of the bed. Her smile was full of pride.

"I tell you it is a boy."

"You did and you were right as always. I begin to wonder if James Norrington was correct when he suspected you were a witch. Perhaps you are.

He reached out and wiped the perspiration from her forehead with his finger.

"Are you sure you feel well?"

"I see the worry in your eyes. There is no need. This boy he comes more easy, gives me no bad hurt."

"I confess I was anxious. To lose another child would be a great sorrow, but I could bear it. To lose you would be something I fear I could not bear."

"Hush," she soothed, "Look at your son, my little Makwa, my bear cub."

She held out the bundle of linen to him and he took it in his arms. A face peered out of the folds of cloth, a squashed up, pugnacious face, blotchy pink with the dark blue eyes common to all new born babies. His head was covered in a wispy black fuzz of hair. He stared fixedly at Thomas from under puffy eyelids. "I think he wonders what strange creature he sees before him," Tom said, laughing. "But he is no great beauty himself."

"What a thing to say!" Cecily scolded. "Poor little mite, just because his father thinks himself so handsome."

"His father is handsome," Lady Anne corrected. "And so will this little one be when all the creases come out of his face and his cheeks plump up. In two or three days' time you will think him the handsomest baby in England."

"He is certainly a strong little fellow," Godfrey observed. "See how he wriggles to be free of his swaddling cloth."

He put his arm around Cecily's shoulder, thinking how proud he would feel to be a father. He was sanguine about the possibility.

"We must allow Dawn Light to rest now," Joan advised, ever practical.

Tom handed his son back into Waaseyaaban's arms and embraced Joan with affection.

"Thank you Joan for helping to bring our baby into the world. No midwife could have done better. Mother did a wise thing when she first took you into her service. What is it the Bible says? A good woman is more precious than rubies. You are beyond price and never think that I am not thankful for it every day."

Joan could only say, "Bless you my dear."

Thomas did not forget to thank Sarah, saying he was sure she was a great help to her mother. He wondered if she was reminded of the child she had carried herself for a short while. She had suffered a miscarriage very early in her pregnancy, so perhaps it had never seemed very real to her. She appeared to be happy and excited by the events of the morning and flustered by Tom's praise began to giggle and blush until her mother dispatched her on an errand to fetch clean sheets.

Thomas went downstairs to fetch the cradle. He had commissioned a local carpenter to make it for Wawackechi, but when she died the sight of the cradle distressed the whole household and he stored it away in the cupboard under the stairs. Now he took it out, dusted off the cobwebs and admired the smooth lines of it. The body of the cradle stood on two curved rockers patterned with the grain of the oak. Joan fitted a pillow inside it to make a soft bed and the baby was soon snugly ensconced within it.

Waaseyaaban did not want Thomas to leave her, so when all the others had gone he got on the bed beside her, sitting up so she could rest against his shoulder and she slept for a while as he stroked her hair, watching the strange grimaces passing across the face of his baby son in the cradle.

Later that day he sat beside his wife as she gave their baby his first feed. The infant needed a little help finding the nipple but once he had locked on, he sucked greedily much to his mother's approval.

"You tell me once Thomas that rich women do not feed their own babies, that they pay some other woman who has milk in her breast to feed them. I do not understand this. Your milk is meant for your own child. Why do they not want to feed them?"

"Strange as it may seem to you it has become a custom amongst the wealthy – almost a sign of status that you can afford a wet nurse. It also means that their own milk will dry up more quickly and they can get on with their social lives again, playing the hostess for their husband's important friends. They can have the baby brought in to show visitors and then taken away again so it does not interrupt their lives."

"That is not how a mother must act."

"No, I agree but it does not mean that they have no love for their children. My mother used a wet nurse but has always been a loving, caring mother, showing interest in everything we did as we grew up. Sometimes things are not quite what they seem on the surface."

Waaseyaaban knew she would not surrender that pull on her breast by her baby's gums for anything.

"When will father come to see baby?"

"He has been away for two weeks on the western assize circuit. I believe he should be in Taunton today if they are on schedule. That is the last town on the circuit so he should be home later this week. I am sure he will come as soon as he is free to do so."

Thomas was not sure if he was eager for Robert to see his grandson. He still had some doubt about his father's reaction, fearing he would not accept the child with his whole heart because of his mixed blood. He fervently hoped his doubts were unfounded yet he could not banish them from his mind.

"You must give son name before he comes," Waaseyaaban told Tom as she took her nipple from the baby's mouth and rubbed his back as he began to hiccup. He was eager for more milk so she restored him to his former position.

"Well I have been thinking about it. If you approve I would like to call him Henry. Both my paternal and maternal grandfathers were called Henry, both known as Harry, so it would please both my parents to honour their fathers. Also we have Harry Carthew's generosity to thank for this land which enabled us to build the house in which our son has been born. It would be a tribute to that Harry too. Harry Mountfield- I think it has a good sound to it."She repeated it and nodded. "I like Harry- Harry-my little Makwa."

"Well Harry it is then."

The newly named Harry had drunk his fill and was already growing sleepy, his eyelids drooping.

"We have more children," Waaseyaaban announced. "Two, maybe three."

Thomas laughed. "You are predicting again and I dare not gainsay you. Just give me time to get used to this one. If we have another boy I will name him Philip and if a girl the choice will be yours."

Harry Mountfield was born on a Thursday so when Tom went to the school the next day to give his history lesson he imparted the good news to Seb Braddon and Sally Walters, who announced it to the children. James and Elizabeth Norrington came into the back of the room just as the schoolmaster was making the announcement. Thomas began the lesson not allowing any thoughts concerning Lizzie's feelings to divert him from his task, but when the lesson was over James approached him with congratulations. Elizabeth hung back as Tom and James stepped outside. She hesitated because the girls from her sewing class were bringing their chairs to sit around a table in the back corner on which the garments they were working on had been spread.

Once they had settled she told them to begin work and she would join them in a moment, then she followed her brother, who was standing with Thomas just outside the door.

"I am so pleased that all went well with the birth. Are mother and child both healthy?" she asked, looking up into Thomas' face. She hoped that all he would detect was her genuine relief to know that he was spared the pain of another loss and not that part of her that ached with her own loss. Her eyes betrayed her though for Tom could read her conflicting emotions and he had a strong desire to comfort her. He was grateful that they were not alone.

"Dawn Light was sitting in the kitchen eating a hearty breakfast when I left this morning, acting as if nothing of import had happened. Hector and Ajax are greatly interested in the strange mewling noises that come from the cradle. I think I will train them to push the cradle with their heads to make it rock and soothe Harry when he grows fractious."

"You have called him Henry?" James exclaimed.

Tom detected a trace of disappointment in his voice and knew why.

"Yes, it is a family name. You hoped perhaps we would call him Philip?"

James never ceased to be surprised by the ease with which Tom penetrated his thoughts. "It did cross my mind," he confessed, embarrassed by his transparency.

"As it did mine, but there were several reasons for deciding on Henry. Waaseyaaban informs me that we will have more children, so there may be a Philip Mountfield yet."

"Have you written down any more of your adventures?"

The mention of Philip's name reminded James of how long it was since he had read Tom's memories of the Americas and hoped he had progressed on to the Netherlands campaign.

"Far less than I would wish, but as you are aware I have been distracted somewhat this last year and a half."

"You won't give up on it will you Sir?"

"No, I intend to complete it, though it may take some while yet. Next Friday when Elizabeth has finished her sewing class perhaps you would both come back to the house and take a midday meal with us and meet Harry. Then James, you can make a judgement on my latest literary efforts."

James was keen although one thing still troubled him.

"Will your wife welcome us? She says little when our paths cross but it is clear that she takes no pleasure in our company."

"I think you will find my wife more generous to you now than in the past. Do not expect too much. She will still be distant but I fancy her glances will be less lethal."

James expressed his desire to come. Elizabeth had said nothing and looking at her Thomas wondered if it would be too much for her to bear as yet.

"Of course if you would rather not-" he said to her, his eyes full of sympathy.

"Oh yes," she touched his sleeve for a brief moment. Every physical contact with him, no matter how small, was as vital to her existence as food and drink. "It is kind of you to ask. We will both come."

"Good, I will invite my sister and her husband too. Cecily is eager to get to know you better Elizabeth. She has been a good friend to Waaseyaaban and she will prove so to you also."

He glanced into the school room where the girls of the sewing class were craning their necks to see what Mistress Elizabeth was doing and chattering quietly amongst themselves.

"I must keep you from your class no longer. Your pupils are missing you. I fancy some of their hearts are fluttering over James by the way they look at him."

James flushed as Thomas bowed to Lizzie and she turned away to re-join her pupils.

As he bid farewell to James Tom could not resist adding, "Bessie Weller, the tall girl with the auburn hair, the handsomest girl among them- I am sure she is besotted with you."

He flashed James a teasing smile as he rode away leaving the boy to contemplate in some confusion whether it might be true.

It was three days before Robert Mountfield was free to visit his grandson. He came back from his travels on the western circuit in the early evening, tired but satisfied that he had fulfilled his duty, to discover that he had another grandchild. He was not lacking in grandchildren for Grace had a son and two daughters whilst Margaret was mother to three boys and two girls, but this one was special to him. It was Tom's son, who would carry the Mountfield name through the male line. He was surprised at the strength of his desire to see the child. The next day Anne was committed to visit a sick friend on the outskirts of the city and was in need of the carriage. Robert watched her leave, the groom Jack Ross on the driver's seat, clicking his tongue at the horses to encourage them and then decided saddle sore as he was from his recent journey, to ride over and visit his son.

He arrived in the early afternoon to find Thomas turning over a patch of ground in the back garden ready for autumn planting. Tom had not expected his father to turn up alone. He escorted him into the parlour, wiping the soil from his hands down the sides of his breeches and bade him sit down while he fetched Henry. He returned with Dawn Light carrying the baby in her arms. Before Robert could rise or say a word she had placed Henry firmly on his grandfather's lap, exchanging a conspiratorial smile with Thomas.

"Don't fear Father," Tom said. "He is quite fragrant at present; his clout has just been changed."

Anne had been right about the improvement in Henry's appearance. His face had filled out to its proper proportions and the puffiness had disappeared from his eyelids. He no longer looked like a miniature prize-fighter after a hard bout. He was dressed in a white lawn robe, gathered at the shoulders and wrists with smocking stitch. When Robert tickled him under the chin he took hold of his grandfather's finger and held on.

"He is sturdy," Robert approved. He has a good grip already. Your mother and I are pleased you chose to call him Henry. It's good to have another Harry Mountfield in the family. Your grandfather would be delighted if he was here to see it."

Thomas smiled to himself. Trust his father to emphasize the tribute to the Mountfields.

"I was mindful that Mother's father was also called Henry," he pointed out. "And we would not have had the opportunity to build this house if it was not for Harry Carthew. So there are two more Henrys involved."

"Of course my boy, an appropriate name for several reasons," Robert agreed, then frowning added, "You know do you not that despite our difference of opinion at the time, I would have supported you if you found yourself in need. Carthew's legacy was fortunately timed. You might have been in straightened circumstances without it."

"We would have managed. I would not have accepted your help then even if you had offered it. I was too hurt by your intransigence."

"My intransigence," Robert would have enlarged on his complaint but checked himself. He did not want to quarrel with Thomas at this moment. He turned his attention back to Harry, relieved to notice that the boy's skin was a light shade not the russet brown hue of his mother's complexion. He was wise enough not to voice his thoughts however. Harry was growing restive and began to cry.

"He is hungry," Dawn Light announced. "I feed him now."

She took her son out of Robert's arms and left the room without another word. Robert was always disturbed by the abruptness of her actions, her lack of what he considered good manners and wondered if he would ever become accustomed to it.

"She is feeding the child herself?" he asked.

"You must know by now we have no grand pretensions here," came the quiet reply. "Besides, both Dawn Light and I agree there is nothing better for a child than its own mother's milk."

Robert sighed. "I meant no criticism Thomas."

"Nor did I. Come, tell me how you fared on the circuit. Did you hear any news of import?"

They spent almost two hours talking easily together, Robert passing on what he had gathered concerning the latest indiscretions of the Earl of Essex. Henry IV of France had begged Elizabeth for troops to help him combat the Spanish army in Normandy, suggesting that Essex should lead the expedition. The queen had already sent a small force to support him in Brittany, which Henry had failed to back up with French troops despite his promise to do so.

"I was told," Robert said, "That she was most reluctant to send any more troops, particularly under Essex."

"I can believe that Father."

"However he continued to beg her to let him go, on one occasion throwing himself down on his knees in front of her with his supplications."

"I can believe that too," Tom murmured with a wry smile. "Very fond of the dramatic gesture is Robert Devereux."

"Lord Burghley interceded on his behalf and eventually she was persuaded to let him go last month to assist Henry in the siege of Rouen, but it seems that the shifty king of France was not at Rouen when they arrived, but in Compiegne."

"That's a hundred miles distant."

"Indeed my boy, so Essex quite without responsibility left his troops and galloped with his immediate entourage through hostile territory to meet with Henry in Compiegne. The story goes that he entered the town like a king himself, preceded by six pages in orange velvet garments trimmed with gold, he and his horse being apparelled in the same materials, strewn with precious stones. Trumpeters blew fanfares before him and he was attended by twelve esquires and sixty English gentlemen. What think you of that?"

"It does not surprise me. He has courage but vainglory often mars the honour of it. Foolish too because once the enemy was aware that he was in Compiegne how in God's name did he think he was going to get back?"

"He called on a section of his infantry at Rouen to come and escort him back to their base camp."

"Damn the man!" Thomas felt a surge of anger at such pointless bravado. "Endangering the lives of his men for no cause but his own vanity."

Robert nodded his agreement. "On his return it appears that he decided a show of force outside the walls of Rouen would intimidate the defenders. He paid dearly for it though because his brother was ambushed and killed by a party of men issuing out from the town. Two gentlemen valiantly risked their lives and retrieved the body."

"I met young Walter Devereux several times when I was in Philip's service. He was only twelve or thirteen when I saw him last. He cannot be much above twenty now - another wasted life."

Robert Mountfield was only just becoming aware of the profound effect the Netherlands Campaign had wrought on his son. They had no face-to-face contact after their argument over Dawn Light until the day of Cecily's wedding and he had not been in a position to judge Tom's true state of mind. Since their partial reconciliation he had picked up hints from Tom's conversation that his experience of war was a bitter one.

"I fear you are right because there is no sign yet that Rouen is about to surrender and I am loathe to trust Henry of France to keep his word. What troubles me is that despite the futility of his show of force, the earl knighted above twenty of his men for no good reason. In my view this cheapens honour for it should flow only from the throne. He may be one of the principal nobles of England but only the Queen has the right to bestow knighthoods. To hand out rewards for bravery in such a frivolous and prodigal manner is an insult to Her Majesty's prerogative."

Thomas was pleased to hear his father express such a rational view of Devereux's actions. So many men were dazzled by the earl's heroics, but not Sir Robert. Tom felt more in harmony with his father at that moment than he had for a very long time.

"Well, his purpose is clear. He is attempting to draw men to him, build up a loyal clientele and persuade them that he is a more fitting leader than an ageing, crabby woman, as he considers the Queen to be. He flatters her with his tongue and in his letters but his every action challenges her authority. He would be wise not to underestimate her. If he goes so far that he threatens the balance of the state, he will put himself in a position where she will not be able to forgive him."

"I believe he is on his way home now to try to talk his way out of his indiscretions," Robert said. "The other matter causing great interest is a rumour circulating that one of the Queen's ladies-in-waiting, Bess Throckmorton, a very comely young woman, is with child and the likely father Sir Walter Raleigh. I know it is not always wise to take rumours for truth, but there is often some truth behind court gossip. It seems Raleigh has been paying the girl much attention of late."

"If it is true," Tom replied, "And it comes to the Queen's notice Walter will be in serious trouble. He and Devereux will both feel her ire, though I fear

Walter will come off the worst because he is not of high-born lineage. The Queen may have raised him up but she has not forgotten his origins. Essex is always sneering at him because he is not of noble birth."

Robert was wondering if his son had a latent desire to be back in the company of the great men close to the throne, while Tom was thinking how lucky he was to be free of it all. His life was opening out again, but not in that direction.

When Robert was ready to leave that afternoon he was encouraged by the easy way he and Tom had conversed together with few awkward moments.

Ned Carter had brought his horse around to the back door and as Tom stood holding the reins ready for his father to mount Robert laid a hand on his arm saying in an earnest tone, "Thomas, Anne and I so much desire you to bring Harry to see us in Salisbury. This foolish determination not to enter the house must stop. After all it will be your house one day and Harry's too, God willing."

Tom looked keenly into his father's eyes.

"Are you asking my wife and I to bring Harry to visit you?"

Robert hesitated before replying, "She is the mother of your child of course she must come too."

"You are evading the issue again Father. You know what I want you to say, 'Both you and your wife are welcome in my house.' Can it be so hard to speak those simple words? We were married by due ceremony, not a Christian one I grant you, but a proper ceremony. We exchanged these," he touched the turquoise pendent at his throat, "As a sign of how we are bound to each other. Neither of us has taken them off since nor do we ever intend to."

Robert slapped the flat of his hand on his saddle. "Damnation Thomas, must I be the only one to compromise? I will not stand here and argue with you. Please consider my invitation. It is well meant."

He swung himself into the saddle and rode away without another word disappointed by Tom's reaction.

Thomas was not aware of Joan Bushy standing by the kitchen staircase. She had heard every word of the conversation outside the back door and she was certain that in his heart Tom wished to visit his childhood home again. She was determined to find a way to persuade him. Her first step was to seek out Dawn Light and tell her what she had overheard.

That evening after supper Tom sat in the parlour re-reading by the light of the four branch candelabra, a letter from Matthew Collier that Toby had brought to him the day before. The very paper it was written on had a whiff of the sea about it, conjuring up in Tom's mind a vivid picture of Simon Bailey's face as they said their goodbyes on the deck of The Dorset Maid. He wished he could tell Simon about Harry. Matthew had written to say that his elder son Caleb had married a Weymouth girl in August. The family business was thriving and he hoped Tom would visit them soon. He had heard on the old sailors' network that John White had finally managed to gain a passage on a privateering expedition the previous autumn, whose captain agreed to stop off at Roanoke to visit the abandoned colonists.

He landed there on what was his grand-daughter's third birthday but there was no sign of Virginia Dare or anyone else. All the houses and fortifications had been dismantled but there were no indications of burning or of a battle. They found one word carved into the gate post of the fort that was still standing, one enigmatic word, Croatoan. The first three letters CRO were also carved on a nearby tree. White had agreed with the colonists before he left them in 1587 that should they be forced to leave because of danger, they would carve the shape of a Maltese cross in a prominent place. Search as they might, they could find no cross. White assumed this meant the colonists had moved willingly to Croatoan Island for some reason. He was eager to search for them but a big storm was brewing and the captain of the privateer was not willing to prolong their stay, so White was obliged to sail away ignorant of the fate of the colonists. Tom, as he read Matthew's account, looked at Harry sleeping in his cradle and could imagine John White's despair at being prevented from searching for his daughter and grand-daughter. He could see himself jumping overboard and attempting to swim to Croatoan Island if he was in a similar position.

Waaseyaaban had been watching the expressions pass across his face as he read the letter and now she sat down on his lap, slipping one arm around his neck.

"I am not so heavy now," she said. "I fit better here again. You read Matthew's letter?"

Tom smiled at her, folding up the letter and tucking it into the pocket of his jerkin.

"I was musing on what could have happened to all those settlers on Roanoke, some of whom we both knew from my time there. At least twenty people who went with John White in eighty seven were on the original expedition. I can only pray that they did decide to move to Croatoan for some reason and are settled there safely. Perhaps another voyager will bring news of them."

"Why does he not go to my village and speak to my brothers? If the settlers move to another place my brothers will know of it."

"I doubt if he was granted the time. The captain of the ship was eager to sail on and John had no choice but to leave with him."

Waaseyaaban rarely spoke of her brothers and gave no indication that she felt deep regret at the likelihood she would never see them again.

"At least Esther Collier will be happy that one of her sons has married at last." Tom said.

"She has been nagging at them for years to find wives for themselves. Matthew is eager for us to visit, which I fully intended to do in the spring of 1590. I did not expect to be sitting in Devizes Bridewell instead. This year we have been too busy with the school. I am determined to go next spring. We will take Harry and introduce him to the sea. I would wish him to grow to love the sea. We can stand on the cliffs overlooking the bay and I will tell him that way, way beyond the horizon, countless miles across the seas is the land where his beautiful mother was born."

"That is good story, but before we take Harry to see Matthew there is another place he must go, much more near."

"Where is that my love?" Tom asked, fancying he already knew the answer.

"To house of father in Salisbury. Joan tell me what father say."

"Ah but he did not say the most important words of all. He still backed away from calling you my wife. I gave him the perfect opportunity and he did not take it. I swore I would not enter that house again until he did."

"Makwa, the words do not matter. He knows I am your wife and cannot part us. It does not hurt me now. You do not betray me by going there. I will put on long gown and plait hair with ribbons when we go there. Maybe you buy me pretty clothes to wear. Here I dress as I please- there I will look like lady but I am still Waaseyaaban."

Thomas looked at her in astonishment. He had not expected such a speech.

"But I never wanted you to have to submit to his terms."

"I know how you care for me, but I care for your hurt too. Look me in the eyes and tell me true that you do not in your heart wish to go to father's house."

"You know me too well. I cannot do that because of late I have had a strong desire to go back there. I almost did the day I went to Salisbury to search for the map of the world. I need to heal this rift somehow. It is like a wound within me."

"Then we heal it, slow perhaps, salve first then healing. I want to see house, see where you play as boy, see that tree Joan says you fall out of and break your head. Harry must see these things also. They are part of you just as my village is part of me."

"You truly want us to go?"

"Yes."

He kissed her and held her close murmuring, "Then I will eschew my pride and we shall take Harry to visit his grandparents."

Thomas tugged on the rein to encourage Hetty to turn right under the high archway that gave access to the back of Sir Robert Mountfield's house in the Cathedral Close. The mare turned smoothly and the carriage rumbled over the gravel path into the stable yard. Henry had been wide awake when they started out; now he was sleeping soundly, lulled by the rhythm of the carriage. Although it was a mild day he was well wrapped up in warm blankets, only his face visible in an oval space. The wind could whip across that open plain and his parents were taking no chances with their precious son's health. Waaseyaaban cradled him securely in her arms but her eyes were on her husband's face as they drove into the yard. She was attempting to judge the emotions he was feeling. Cecily Roper sat in the carriage with them. Tom had called at the Roper house on the way, hoping to enlist his sister for some moral support, which she was more than willing to give. She too watched her brother's reactions. Delighted as she was that this was happening at last, she knew how difficult this was for Tom and could see the tenseness in him.

He was experiencing an odd sensation in the pit of his stomach, a nervous excitement, as he pulled up beside the stable block and mocked himself for the strength of his feelings. He had not expected that the familiar sight of the back of the house and the brick wall that enclosed the garden would stir him so. The big ring handle on the door in the wall caught his eye. The iron ring was fitted into the mouth of a lion, the creature's head carved with realistic detail. As a boy Tom had loved that door handle, speaking to the lion every time he turned the ring. He was pleased to see it was still there, guarding the entrance to the garden.

Jack Ross came hurrying out of the stables followed by a rough coated brown and white terrier, as Thomas jumped down from the driver's seat of the carriage.

"Master Thomas, it is good to see ye back home again," Ross exclaimed in his strong Scottish burr. "The whole household rejoices at it."

"Thank you Jack. Nothing seems to have changed in five years, least of all old Snapper."

The terrier was jumping up at Tom's leg, scrabbling for attention with his front paws.

"Why he must be at least sixteen years old now."

"That he is and still a champion rat catcher for all the stiffening of his back legs. He has not forgotten ye Sir."

Tom could remember the summer Snapper was born. He had just graduated from Oxford and was spending time at home before going up to London for his first term at the Middle Temple. Cecily was four and he had not been home an hour before she was urging him to come out to the stables to see a litter of puppies born to one of the coachmen's dogs. One puppy proved to be more lively and bolder than the rest. He was soon snapping at flies and spiders and chasing behind anything that ran away from him, so he was christened Snapper. Cecily was thinking about that day too. Although she was so young she had a misty memory of holding on to her brother's hand and leading him across the yard to where the puppies lay in the straw suckling from their mother. They smiled at each other now, both aware that they were recalling the same memory.

Thomas took Harry from his mother's arms to enable Waaseyaaban to dismount freely from the carriage and then handed him back to her with tender care. He was struck by how beautiful she looked in a blue kirtle, a vibrant summer blue trimmed with silver. He had always thought blue to be Lizzie Norrington's colour, but now he saw how well it suited his wife.

"Do ye wish to go in the back way?" Ross asked.

"No, I rather think we will go in the front door."

"Well, off ye go then. I will look to the horse."

Cecily decided to use the back entrance to announce to her parents that Thomas had arrived. She did not want share their entrance; it was something Tom and Dawn Light must do together. Her place was in the house. Before she left them she squeezed her brother's arm saying, "Courage Tom, you are doing the right thing."

He watched her step lightly across the yard to the low back door with its rounded arch and then taking hold of Waaseyaaban's free hand walked out into the street. Six steps led up to the front door with a stone balustrade on either side of them. Thomas hesitated at the bottom of the steps.

"This will not be a comfortable day my love. Are you sure you want to do this?"

"I am sure," she replied, increasing the pressure of her grip on his hand and pulling Harry closer into her shoulder.

Tom took a deep breath. "Then we shall do it."

They were on the third step when the front door swung open and both his parents stood there to welcome them.

The End